CH01072535

. . . to dwell
in safety

A novel by

Mary Bolster

Pymmes Publications

. . . to dwell in safety
First published in the United Kingdom in 2008 by
Pymmes Publications.

ISBN 978 0 955 1136-1-1

Written by Mary Bolster

A catalogue record of this book is available from the
British Library.

Cover photos by Mary Bolster and Nina Tweddle

Design and printing by The Alpha Xperience,
148 Kings Road, Newbury, Berkshire RG14 5RG.

Pymmes Publications, 2, Windmill Road, Edmonton,
London N18 1PA

Note

During the Second World War the Karen people fought with Britain and the Allies against the Japanese. At the beginning of the war many Burmese sided with the Japanese in the hope of gaining freedom from Britain. The fact that people from within the country of Burma fought on different sides has left scars, which have still not healed.

Burma gained independence from Britain in 1948 and the Karen people, in common with many of the ethnic minorities, have been engaged in conflict with the majority Burman army almost since that time.

The ethnic minorities have tended to hold onto their own territories. This is largely because the terrain is so mountainous and the 'city' Burmese find it is too difficult to sustain a military campaign in the monsoon-sodden forests of the hill tracts that are home to the minorities. It was only in the 1990s, with the acquisition of superior weaponry, that the Burmese began to make substantial territorial gains with the result that large numbers of refugees began to cross the borders into Thailand, Bangladesh and India.

The early part of 'to dwell in safety' describes well-documented events as they took place in 1995, while the characters and the rest of the story are all entirely fictitious.

'Dearest homeland, my thoughts fly towards thee;
Wings of gold bear them on to journey's ending,
Where the sweet scented breezes are blending
In the green hills and vales of our land.'

The Chorus of the Hebrew Slaves
from the opera 'Nabucco'
Guiseppi Verdi

1

December 1995

"Good bye [1]*tharamu*"

"Good bye Eh Htoo. Now go straight home." The child often seemed to linger in the classroom at the end of the day but Htee K'Paw wanted to get home quickly today. She turned to glance round the simple wooden room one last time and bent down to pick up a stray pencil that she saw had rolled onto the floor.

"Ready?" The voice came from the open doorway and Htee K'Paw looked up to be greeted by the broad smile of her closest friend, Hser Mu, who also taught in the school.

"Yes," she declared as the two of them emerged into the bright sunshine and walked quickly along the side of the buildings. The school occupied almost the highest point of the village so once they left the playground they had to pick their way down a very steep path. It was easy at this time of year, but during the monsoon it was often slippery with mud.

"How was your class today?" Hser Mu asked.

"As always. The boys would rather be playing football most of the time. It's hard to get them to stay still. What about yours?"

"The same! Sometimes I think that the way we teach them is very dull. All that chanting may sound good to the headmaster but I hate it. It makes my head

---

[1] *Tharamu* Karen for 'teacher'

5

ache. I'm glad we're going out this evening. Have you remembered the volley ball matches?"

"How could I forget?" Htee K'Paw felt her body fill with warmth and delicious anticipation as she thought about the evening ahead.

"Oh yes, of course, he'll be there. Now I know why you're in such a hurry to get home."

Both girls had come to Ba Lwe six years ago from different villages in Burma. Unlike her sister K'Paw Meh, who had been too young at the time, Htee K'Paw had never forgotten the village where she had grown up and she often recalled how unhappy she had been at leaving it. At that point in her life it had been all she had ever known. Her mother and father had built their wooden house together and each year they had tried to make it a little more comfortable. Her father liked to make things out of wood and so sometimes he added a bench where they could sit in the evening, or perhaps another room or shelves for the kitchen at the back of the house. She remembered going out to the forest with him to find the leaves for the new thatch. Every year part of the roof would need replacing and it was hard work collecting leaves and then threading them onto the bamboo horizontals before hoisting them up and fixing them onto the roof timbers. At first Htee K'Paw had been unsure about the home-made thatch. She had wondered how rows of leaves could possibly keep out the heavy rain that always fell during the monsoon in Karen State, but they did, and the family were always snug and dry inside the house.

Then the whole village had been abandoned and she had never seen it again. The villagers had retreated eastwards, away from the relentless advance of the

[2]Tatmadaw. At first Htee K'Paw hadn't understood why they had had to get away so quickly, but now she knew what fear was; she had seen it so many times in the faces of the refugees who regularly poured into the villages by the river whenever fighting broke out again. And that was what she had seen on her parents' faces as they hurried to gather all their possessions together and walk away from the home that they had taken such care over for so many years.

In the innocence of childhood she had thought that this was a short visit that they were making to another place and that they would soon return to their home, but of course that hadn't been the case. They had taken only the things they could carry with them and she remembered how hard that journey had been; the long days of walking, sometimes through thick forest, sometimes across rivers, had seemed interminable. Their shoes had worn out and there had been none to replace them; some of the villagers had fallen prey to malaria on the way and had had to be carried when they lost the strength to keep up with the rest.

Eventually they had reached Ba Lwe, which was a beautiful place close to the River Salween. Now when they needed to travel anywhere they could go by boat. There was also a school and Htee K'Paw had been able to enrol. She had now done so well that the headmaster had asked her to teach one of the younger classes. She had been teaching since April and was half way through her first year of a job that she had come to love.

---

[2] Tatmadaw The Army of the Burmese Military Dictatorship

The two girls hesitated for a moment outside the house that Htee K'Paw shared with her parents, sister and two younger brothers.

"Will you come in?" Htee K'Paw asked.

Hser Mu visited them most days. She was the youngest by far of the children in her family. Her mother had died and her brothers and sister were all married, so the household consisted only of her father and grandmother and Hser Mu herself. Htee K'Paw had observed how morose Hser Mu's father was. His mood seemed to pervade the whole of the house so she could understand why Hser Mu liked to spend time with other families.

A little barefoot meteorite shot past them as they stood outside the house. That was Ma Nay, Htee K'Paw's brother, who had been born so soon after the family had fled from the village of her birth. Ma Nay had not let the problem of a shaky start to life affect him adversely. He never stood still for a moment and his parents thanked God for him every day. He had survived, unlike little Ko Kyaw who had followed him two years later but had never been strong enough to resist the violent strain of malaria that had ended his little life before he was six months old.

The girls laughed as they watched Ma Nay for a moment.

"Yes, I'll come in, but I mustn't be late."

Once again Htee K'Paw became aware of the broad smile on her face at the thought of the evening ahead. Whenever she wasn't busy with her work, her thoughts were always full of Hsa Mya, who was a soldier in the nearby brigade. But her face quickly fell again as, walking through to the back of the house, she became aware of the sound of loud voices coming from the backyard. As they reached the kitchen lean-to, Htee K'Paw reached out to take her youngest baby brother, who spent his days in cosy innocence strapped to his mother's back.

There was a sharpness and lack of ease about her mother, which Htee K'Paw noticed immediately. As she took hold of Mon Kyaw she caught sight of a thin anxious-looking man squatting to the side of the kitchen. She was unsure who the visitor was and indeed an unsettled air hung over the whole group, which was in sharp contrast to the usual atmosphere of the family gatherings.

"Mother? What's wrong?"

"Uncle here has some news that's worrying him. Let him tell you."

Now she knew who the stranger was; he was her father's brother. They had not seen him since their flight nearly six years ago. Now Htee K'Paw joined the rest of the family who were all watching him.

There was no sound from the man squatting on the ground so her father spoke for him. "Uncle here has come to tell us about something that is worrying him, something that has happened in his village. It seems that some men and young boys have been shot by the [3]KNLA."

Htee K'Paw winced at the sound of those words. Hsa Mya was a member of the KNLA. She herself, along with other students and teachers, had helped them when fighting was fierce. Everyone had had to help to try to ensure their own survival. Surely they wouldn't shoot anybody without good reason?

---

[3] Karen National Liberation Army, the military branch of the Karen National Union

"They were shot because it was thought that they had given information to the Burmese. My brother here tells us that there are many Karen villages where this has been happening," said Htee K'Paw's father.

"If the men are traitors or disloyal then they must be punished," her mother suggested.

"But there must be proof before men are to be punished in such a way. I have heard a rumour that some of our soldiers are mutinying. This sort of harsh treatment will only make things worse," her father said with compassion in his voice.

Uncle spoke up for the first time. "One of the men who was shot was my neighbour. He never seemed to have much money and then suddenly he was spending more than anyone else. His sons were buying beer, new clothes, a motorbike and he would never say where the money came from."

"How did it all come to light?"

"It was always very peaceful in our village, everyone lived in harmony, and then someone noticed that there was a lot of activity going on in the Pagoda. Suddenly there were lots of men visiting - even at night; they would set the dogs barking. I think that's how it was first discovered. The KNLA became suspicious, so a platoon visited the pagoda and found guns there, many guns, hidden under the floor. Then they began to suspect the men who had been behaving differently in any way, spending money or going out a lot at night; so they took them in for questioning and found that lots of the village men had been involved. But we didn't know, many of us hadn't realised what was happening."

Htee K'Paw felt a shiver run through her body; her arms tingled. She was suddenly cold in spite of the bright afternoon sunshine. "But why have you come here?" She asked her uncle.

"I have left my village because I have many friends among the Buddhists. We play music together you see, we live in peace. But now I am afraid that the KNLA will think that I am a traitor because of that. I am afraid that they will suspect me too."

"And you think this is happening in other places."

"Oh yes. My friends tell me that many people don't like the KNLA and that there is a lot of unhappiness in some of the villages. I am afraid for the future. And I don't know who can be trusted now. They were my friends but . . ." His voice tailed off.

Htee K'Paw glanced at her father's face; she was unsettled by what she saw there. He had always been strong, someone on whom they could rely. As a young man he had lived in the plains but had run away to the safety of the hills where the Tatmadaw had rarely ventured in those days. Then, he and many others like him had had to adjust their way of life to that of the hill people. It had been hard work. He had learnt how to wrest a meagre crop of rice from the thin soil of the hills after being used to the fertile plains. Each year he had undertaken the back breaking task of clearing the ground of trees and burning them before planting. Gone were the days of comfort and plenty but he had married there and raised his daughters.

"What does this mean?" Htee K'Paw knew her father would give a considered, careful response; he was trusted and respected for his integrity by all who knew him.

Glancing round at the family group she saw that all eyes were on Saw Ker Reh, hoping he would say that her uncle was worrying unnecessarily. Only

11

Mon Kyaw was laughing, patting the side of her neck in a game of his own.

He looked down at the earth floor of the kitchen. "The Tatmadaw have always thought of our people as a nuisance. It seems they don't want us; that is why they have been attacking our villages. They want to weaken our morale, to beat us into the ground and kill us if they have to, but they never succeed because they never know where our soldiers are. We are too clever for them, and we know the jungle and the mountains too well. But if there are men who are unhappy enough to mutiny, they may be persuaded to go over to them. Then we are in danger. Those men will have the information that the Tatmadaw needs and will pay money, and guns to get it."

"But what about our KNLA, they are all good and true?"

"Not everyone thinks so, *poquamu*[4], not everyone thinks so."

Htee K'Paw was silent. The chill in her arms intensified, so, motioning to Hser Mu standing quietly beside her she turned to go back inside the house. "I don't believe it," her voice had fallen to a whisper, "our people will always stay together; we have to."

"Don't think about it Htee K'Paw," said her friend when they were once more alone together. "Think about our volleyball game or something else that will keep your mind occupied."

Although Htee K'Paw tried, it wasn't easy. Her uncle was worried, that was patently obvious. So was her father, and she had never known him to be wrong before.

---

[4] *Poquamu* Karen word meaning daughter.

2

There was always a lot to do in the house and it fell to Htee K'Paw and her sister K'Paw Meh to help their mother whenever they could. Early that morning they had been out collecting wood for the fire and watering the vegetables in the tiny garden to the side of the house. Now, having done what she felt was her fair share of the evening chores, Htee K'Paw left the house and made for the school playground. As soon as she reached the volleyball pitch her eyes were drawn to where Hsa Mya was standing. There was nothing to really mark him out from the other soldiers watching the game in progress, but still she couldn't resist searching him out. There was no mistaking his head with its thick black hair cut close to his head to prevent it becoming unruly; as he turned his head to watch the game his even features could be clearly seen, causing a jolt to Htee K'Paw's already rapidly beating heart. Shyness prevented her going to speak to him, and besides he was with a crowd of soldiers. She quickly looked for the other teachers and joined them, all the time she watched the game she was also enjoying the sight of him. Thoughts of betrayal and danger were quickly banished from her mind.

Three years ago, when she had been fifteen, the comparative peace of Ba Lwe had been shattered by the sound of distant gunfire.

"It always happens at this time of year," her father had told her. "Now our soldiers have to hold on to what they can until the rains come again." Htee K'Paw knew that once the rains started they were safe; the Tatmadaw would never venture into, what was for them, hostile mountain jungle. But at that point in the year the rains were many months away and the sounds were growing louder and ever more frequent; it was as if the shelling were right there in the village.

Some of the older children began to stay away from school.

"They've gone to fight," Hser Mu told her. "Should we volunteer do you think?"

Htee K'Paw looked around to see who was missing. There seemed to be no difference made between girls and boys, and even quite young children seemed to be volunteering. Then the decision was taken out of everyone's hands.

"The Tatmadaw is threatening to take Manerplaw[5]," the headmaster announced one day. "School is to be suspended so that we can all help to support our troops."

"That means we go to the front line," whispered Hser Mu.

Raw fear gripped Htee K'Paw. She didn't want to go anywhere near guns, fighting or bombs. She couldn't think of anything worse than going to the front line.

---

[5] *Manerplaw* A garrison town situated on the border between Burma and Thailand.

14

"We must supply them with food and ammunition so that they don't have to leave their posts," the headmaster continued. "That means that we must prepare and cook and carry food up to them. Everyone must take part, they need everything that we can provide if they are to defend our headquarters.

So that was to be their work for who knows how long? They would have to do whatever it took to defend their country. If they failed then where would they go? Nobody ever spoke about it but each one knew what defeat meant; they would have to cross the river into Thailand and become refugees. They had already run away once before; Htee K'Paw remembered that terrible march across an unknown country with only what they could carry in their hands, always looking back over their shoulders to see if the Tatmadaw were in pursuit. It had been hard at first. They had had to make a shelter with their bare hands and live on what they could find, but her father and mother had gradually built their home up and they were comfortable and settled once again. But for Htee K'Paw the fear that they might have to run away again was a constant background to every other thought.

Htee K'Paw helped to prepare rice and vegetable stew. She had gone through Ba Lwe to find banana leaves, then she had torn the great leaves into sections and used them to wrap the food. She and the other girls had found some good strong baskets and set out to take the food to the soldiers.

A soldier had acted as their guide and took them to where the troops occupied a high point on Sleeping Dog Mountain. It had taken all day to walk the mountain path. At first Htee K'Paw had wanted to stay back at the school. "I'll cook more food for you to take tomorrow," she had said. She couldn't tell them she was afraid. But the other girls persuaded her.

"We all need to go; we have so much to carry and you will be quite safe; Hsa Mya is looking after us."

And sure enough as she looked into Hsa Mya's dark eyes she did feel quite safe and decided she would go after all. She didn't want him to know that she was afraid; she wanted him to think that she would do everything she could to save [6]Kawthoolei, the land of the flowers, their homeland, the only home they had ever known.

They had walked together along the path that climbed steadily towards the mountains; Hsa Mya led the way with another soldier at the back of the column. Htee K'Paw hardly noticed the weight of her basket as she walked along with her friends and the two soldiers towards the front line. She forgot to be afraid as they chatted and laughed together.

"And what do you like to do Paw Si Si?" Hsa Mya was speaking. Htee K'Paw looked round to see who he was talking to but there was nobody else close enough to hear him; the rest of the group had fallen behind and were further down the hill. When she realised he was speaking to her she felt her face grow hot.

"Oh!" she gulped. "I like music. I have a radio and I like to hear the songs. Now I know a little English I try to listen to the words."

"I like music too. Do you sing or play?"

"No, I can't play anything, but I can sing. We have a choir in our village."

---

[6] Kawthoolei The Name for Karen territory in Eastern Burma.

"Well I play the guitar. When I come to your village next I will bring it and play for you when you sing."

Htee K'Paw hastened to put him right. "Our teacher makes us sing without any instruments, she says that we need to learn to keep our note without help. She says that's good practice for us."

She saw the faintest smile play around his lips.

"I'm sure your teacher is right. I mean that I would like to come and play for you when you sing on your own or with your friends, not when you sing in the choir. I don't want to get into trouble with your teacher."

Htee K'Paw felt foolish. She didn't know what to say. She so much wanted to talk to Hsa Mya, but at the same time she felt afraid of what he thought of her; and now he seemed to be laughing at her. She turned round to see if the rest of the group had caught up yet. No! They were still far behind.

He saw her discomfiture and quickly changed the subject. "What about volleyball? Do you play?"

"Oh yes. We always play after school in the playground. We are very good. Our class often wins."

"We have some teams in the barracks too; I think we should come and play your team."

"We play every Wednesday afternoon and on Saturday mornings. If you speak to our headmaster perhaps he will let you come too."

Htee K'Paw found that she was enjoying the company of Hsa Mya; he didn't seem much older than she was and he was so good to talk to. She hoped very much that he would come to the school, when the fighting was over and the villages of Kawthoolei were at peace once again.

But that was not to be for many months. The path that Htee K'Paw and the other girls took became well worn over the weeks that followed. More and more students had to help and the carrying of ammunition and food up to the front lines became a daily necessity for the troops desperately holding onto their positions. Then one dreadful day, after a long and protracted battle, Sleeping Dog Mountain was taken by the Tatmadaw. From there they had the strategic advantage and were able to fire mortars into some of the surrounding villages and even across the border into Thailand. The news of the defeat spread through the villages like a fire burning through the parched trees of summer, quickly followed by groups of homeless people and those injured in the battles. There were so many sick and injured people that Hser Mu and Htee K'Paw were enlisted to help in one of the overcrowded hospitals.

The village hospital was nothing more than a large bamboo house staffed by medics and nurses who had been trained by some visiting doctors from Europe. Htee K'Paw never forgot her first day in the hospital.

"I have a job for one of you," the chief medic said as the two girls presented themselves at his desk.

Anxious to do whatever she could Htee K'Paw volunteered.

"There is a soldier who has been brought in. He has stepped on a landmine and we need to operate on his foot. We need you to talk to him while we suture the skin. Will you do that?"

Htee K'Paw wasn't sure what 'suture' meant but if she could help the soldier she would do so. She nodded

18

intently, wanting to do anything that was required of her.

"Follow me then."

The medic walked out of his office and through to the room behind. Leaving Hser Mu standing beside the desk, Htee K'Paw walked after the medic past rows of soldiers lying on the mats that had been spread out on the floor. The medic had already reached another doorway. She followed him through it and saw a young boy lying on the floor covered with an old blanket, which was heavily stained with dried blood.

"This is Htee K'Paw. She will look after you."

Htee K'Paw guessed that the soldier was about the same age as her; he might even have been younger. His face looked almost grey. His lips were so pale that they were almost indistinguishable from the rest of his face. He stared ahead in silence, ignoring the medic's words. Another medic joined them and they began to gather together their equipment. Htee K'Paw looked wide-eyed at what they were doing. Suddenly she wanted to run back to where she had left Hser Mu but that was now impossible.

"We want you to hold his hand. That will help him. And you can talk to him too so that he won't be so afraid."

Htee K'Paw wished she hadn't volunteered to help the medic. She looked around to see if anyone else could help, but there was nobody. They were all too busy with their own work so she sat down beside the boy.

The medics took the blanket away and she looked aghast at the boy's foot, which was held onto his leg by the merest shred of flesh on one side. Two small bones stuck out at the end where the foot should have been attached and the oozing blood was glistening and congealing on the exposed flesh. A scarf had been tied tightly around the top of the leg and the medic placed a strong strip of rubber next to it on the leg and pulled it tight. The boy didn't move.

Htee K'Paw pulled her eyes away and reached out for the boy's hand; it was cold and damp. His fingers gripped her tightly. One of the nurses appeared and put a tight band of cloth around his upper arm. She tucked the end of the cloth in and then attached a small pipe, which she inflated using a small bulb. After listening to his pulse with a stethoscope she removed the band and carefully placed it in its case again. She felt the boy's wrist, counting his heartbeat and then wrote some numbers on the chart that she carried with her.

As she wrote Htee K'Paw saw her face tighten for a moment.

"His blood pressure is low because of the bleeding. He needs intravenous fluid and we don't have any."

Htee K'Paw didn't know what intravenous fluid was but guessed that it was something important.

Suddenly the boy winced and his grip on her hand tightened. Htee K'Paw looked up and saw one of the medics holding a large syringe and needle. "This will numb the leg so that you won't feel the pain," he told the boy. Htee K'Paw turned back to him and saw small beads of sweat all over his forehead.

The nurse was speaking again as she rearranged the blanket so that he couldn't see what was being done to the leg. "I have to see other patients. You stay with this one and I will be back very soon."

Htee K'Paw kept her eyes on the boy's face trying to think what she could say to him. "What is your name," she asked him.

"Ko Kyaw," she heard him whisper.

For a moment Htee K'Paw was reminded of her baby brother who had died in infancy. That had been his name. "Well, Ko Kyaw, I will stay by you. You hold my hand and if they hurt you you can squeeze it."

The medics seemed to take forever to finish their work but at last they put down their instruments and bandaged Ko Kyaw's leg. They carefully released the scarf and the thick rubber band, which had stopped the bleeding. Ko Kyaw had slept for some of the time and the nurse had been in again to check him, bringing another blanket with her to try to stop him becoming too chilled. And from that day Htee K'Paw always thought of Ko Kyaw as her patient. She felt a special bond with him and watched as he recovered remarkably quickly from his ordeal. He was soon hobbling around the hospital on a home-made crutch.

Sadly there were some who didn't recover; sometimes the bleeding would not stop, some wounds were impossibly difficult to deal with when there were precious few medicines, little in the way of anaesthetics and no intravenous fluids. Sometimes infection took a hold and the patient would be overwhelmed by sepsis.

And all the time the sound of bombing was never far away.

One day she went home after a day in the hospital and found her father digging a hole in the side of the hill. "This is a bunker for us. We can go in here if they ever hit the village."

"Oh, no, Papa," she cried out." We can't do that. It's too small for us."

"But it will be better than being hit by a bomb."

And then when she thought of all she had seen in the hospital she knew that her father was very wise and good to take care of his family like this; but still she went to her room each night and cried with fear of what was going to happen to them all. In her teenage dreams she tried to picture Hsa Mya's face each night as she lay down to sleep; then she would cry, fearing that she would never see him again. She knew he had been on Sleeping Dog Mountain and she prayed that he had been able to get away when his platoon had retreated. She couldn't bear to think of him being injured, taken prisoner or even killed.

Then as their situation seemed to be as bad as it possibly could be, the Tatmadaw announced a ceasefire. Manerplaw, the headquarters of the Karen National Union had been their goal, but in spite of the daily pounding with missiles the Karen soldiers had succeeded in finally beating back their adversaries. They had held on to the 'Land of the Flowers' in the face of almost impossible odds. And one day, when the rain poured down turning the jungle into an impenetrable fortress to all except it's own people, a young man with a guitar slung over his shoulder came to call on a shy village girl who liked to sing.

3

By six o'clock it was too dark to play any more volleyball. The matches all ended and the players went into one of the teachers' houses to eat supper. Hsa Mya came over to see Htee K'Paw and greeted her with the rueful smile that went with his team's defeat.

"Hello Little Flower," he whispered and the look in his dark eyes was of such intensity that it reached right down inside her to set her heart swelling with happiness.

He always used the same term of endearment with which he had addressed her on their very first meeting three years ago when they had toiled up the path to Sleeping Dog Mountain even though she was no longer 'little' in his eyes. The young schoolgirl had disarmed him with her shyness and her sweet smile; now the schoolteacher of almost nineteen pulled at his heart and disturbed his dreams with her gentle beauty and the steady gaze of her eyes. He pulled off his vest and dried the sweat from his face with it as they walked together to the house. "How are things with you?" he asked. "Did you get my letter?"

"Yes I got it. It's here." She patted her shoulder bag to indicate the precious letter, which it contained. It was a popular practice among the young people of the villages to communicate by letter, sometimes delivered by friends, sometimes pushed between the woven bamboo of the school dormitories when shyness and embarrassment prevented a face-to-face encounter. Hsa Mya regularly sent messages in the hands of one of the soldiers who visited the village and Htee K'Paw treasured each one while sending her own reply through the same trusted hands.

"You're quiet today. Is anything the matter?"

"Mmm . . . maybe! Can we go for a walk later? There's something I want to talk to you about." Opportunities for being alone together were always limited in the village.

"Yes, of course! Where shall we go?"

"There's a place down by the new fish farm now. We can go there."

As they reached the house Hsa Mya went to have a quick wash while Htee K'Paw went round to the kitchen at the back in order to help serve the food. The following hours were spent eating the supper that had been provided by the teachers with the help of some of the older students. It was a simple meal, consisting mostly of rice with the addition of green vegetables that had been grown on the small patch of ground behind the houses, eggs fried into an omelette and, best of all, the fish paste that they all relished so much.

After they had eaten and the dishes were cleared away from the floor Hsa Mya leant against the bamboo wall of the house while Htee K'Paw sat beside him feeling the warmth of his body close to her. A guitar played and members of the gathering took turns to sing while the whole party bathed in the close companionship of those who know they have nothing to share but themselves.

They stepped out into the warm evening where the stars shone in their uncountable millions in the unpolluted sky. His hand found hers and their fingers interlaced together; as they walked along the path towards the fish farm they could still hear the guitar playing its soft accompaniment to the sweet song of one of the girls. As they moved further away from the house towards the darkness of the pool, the sound of the cicadas pressed ever louder to their ears. The pigs that were kept in small pens beside many of the houses grunted a gentle accompaniment while the occasional plop of a jumping fish provided an irregular percussion. Hsa Mya snapped on his torch and once he had found a place he spread out his jacket for Htee K'Paw to sit on. She bent down and sat but still she said nothing.

"What is it?" he could see her quiet, anxious face by the pale light of the stars.

After a long pause she turned her face to his. "I'm afraid Hsa Mya."

"Why Htee K'Paw? What are you afraid of?" his voice was tender. He hated to see her unhappy.

"I heard something today that worries me. I don't know if it's true, but I think it must be. My father is afraid, and he only worries when something really bad happens."

"What is it? Tell me."

"My father thinks that there may be a mutiny by some members of the KNLA." She felt Hsa Mya's body stiffen as it rested against hers.

"Why does he think that?"

"It's because of my uncle. He ran away from his village because the KNLA are suspicious about what is happening there. He said that they found lots of guns

25

hidden under the floor of a pagoda and that some men were spending money that they never had before. My father thinks that they gave information to the Tatmadaw. And the Tatmadaw gave them money and guns. Now KNLA commanders have killed some of the men who were involved."

"But why has your uncle run away? What has he got to be afraid of?" Has Mya interrupted.

"They were arresting everyone that they though might be helping the Tamadaw. He has some good friends who are Buddhists, they play music together, and he was afraid that they would arrest him."

Hsa Mya was quiet for a moment. He turned his body around to face her and she saw him regarding her intently in the darkness.

"Htee K'Paw! Something is happening but we are not sure how serious it is yet. You must not talk to anyone about it. We must all keep quiet until we know what it really means."

Htee K'Paw shivered. She had always thought that she understood the history of their people, the Karen. At school she had been taught that although there had been many times of hardship and defeat by their neighbours, they had still remained a strong and proud people. They had kept their mountain strongholds and no one practiced the skills of the forest better than they did. They had defended the land against the Tatmadaw for over forty years. It had always been quite clear to her; the KNLA were the protectors of their own land and people and the Tatmadaw was the enemy. So what had happened to change things?

"You mean that you know what my uncle is talking about?"

"Yes, I think I do, but nobody can be sure just what is happening. There are many Buddhists in the KNLA; and we all fight together, but a new group has been formed. We are not sure what their plans are yet, but your uncle doesn't need to be afraid, it is only the ones who have been given guns by the Tatmadaw that our soldiers are concerned about."

"What does it all mean Hsa Mya? What's going to happen?"

She watched his face crease into a slight frown before he spoke. "I don't know and even if I did I couldn't talk about it."

She leant her head on his shoulder and stared out into the darkness while the never-ending sound of the cicadas filled the air.

"But you mustn't be afraid. Remember they took Sleeping Dog Mountain? But they couldn't take Manerplaw then and they won't now. We are very strong and very determined."

"Yes! I know, but it was very difficult for us. In the hospital many men died. I saw them." The picture of young men with terrible injuries that wouldn't heal flashed through her mind once again. The same one that was always there, catching her when she least expected it and sometimes disturbing her sleep.

"Don't think about it." He took hold of her hand and kissed her fingers one by one. "Think about you and me, together for always. Remember, I want to come to talk to your mother and father. As soon as you say yes, I'll do it."

Htee K'Paw hesitated. She wanted to say yes to him. She wanted to be with him so much and she knew they would be happy together, she just knew it. But always something held her back. She had seen many soldiers die from their wounds when she had worked in the hospital. It was a danger that they lived with every day of their lives. And she had seen young girls like herself, struggling to rear babies and young children with no support, because their men had been taken prisoner or killed in battle. She didn't want her future to be like that. Much as she loved Hsa Mya she knew what could happen.

"What do you say, Little Flower?"

"I love you Hsa Mya. I love you, but I'm not ready yet."

4

Hsa Mya hunched his shoulders forward and rested his head on his arms. He had lost his hat so had turned his collar up as much as he could to stop the draught of cool morning air going down his back. It was barely light and the mist hung heavily around the trees at the side of the river. It was now impossible to know where the [7]DKBA were. They could have men posted anywhere listening for troop movements. The boatman kept the throttle to the minimum, so the boat moved slowly keeping the noise down as much as possible.

There were around twenty soldiers on the low fishtail boat; all of them except the boatman huddled down against the cold, heading north to join the brigade already defending Manerplaw. An unmistakable air of defeat hung over the company, defeat and disappointment that they hadn't been able to protect some of the villages.

"Defending the villages is as important for our people as fighting for the land," the captain had said for the benefit of the recruits that had joined them this year. The Tatmadaw will advance; there is no doubt of

---

[7] DKBA Democratic Karen Buddhist Association. A group that broke away from the Karen National Union in 1995

that. Our intelligence so far tells us that they are moving into villages that are supporters of our KNU. It is doubly important that we protect these people. They will receive no mercy if the Burmese reach them."

Hsa Mya had heard this many times before and there had been several occasions when he had been involved in slowing down the advancing army to allow villagers to retreat to safety.

But this time the KNU positions had been pounded relentlessly with heavy mortars since the middle of December; more seriously, the enemy fire had been accurate and it had been impossible for the soldiers to hold their positions for long under such fire.

"It's the DKBA," said the captain as he addressed his fellow officers in a hastily called council of war. "They know all our positions. That's why they have been able to move in so fast." As he spoke he looked around the group of men, all of them grim faced at what they knew was happening all around them. The mutiny had been highly strategic; the Tatmadaw had warmly welcomed those Karens who had been dissatisfied with the leadership of the KNU. It was as predicted; many of them possessed important military information which quickly exposed the Karen to attack. "And they have bought new rocket launchers. We have no alternative but to retreat as quickly as possible and help the villagers to cross the river into Thailand. Then we must move north and join the central brigade at Manerplaw. They are going to throw everything they have at the garrison so we have to put everything into defending it."

With the exception of his sergeant, Hsa Mya, at the age of twenty-one was the oldest and most experienced soldier in the boat. As he glanced around with half closed eyes he saw all the soldiers showing clear signs of exhaustion; many were asleep, sprawled this way and that, trying to find some comfort as they leant against each other. He was so tired that his bones ached. Next to him Law Win's head was resting on his shoulder while his own eyelids drooped with weariness and his head came to rest on the side of the boat. He felt the vibrations of the engine against his head but was too tired to adjust his position.

"Elephants," said someone at the front of the boat and a few heads lifted up to look.

"No I don't think so . . . too small for elephants." A few more faces turned to look at the sight with a view to joining in with the speculation. The driver cut the throttle completely and steered over to look at what was floating on the water. Several bodies were caught in the reeds at the side of the river. They were so swollen and disfigured that, from a distance, they had hardly been recognisable as human. As soon as he saw what they were the boatman gently opened the throttle once again and moved away, but not before everyone on board had had time to see that the bodies had their hands tied behind their backs.

A horrified silence hung over the dwindling platoon. Hsa Mya watched as the boy in front of him lurched suddenly and vomited over the side and into the water. He felt his own stomach turn but managed to avert disaster by taking some deep gulps of the cool morning air as the boat gathered as much speed as safety permitted.

He dozed fitfully once more until he perceived the engine slowing again. By the time the boat had reached the small wooden dock he was awake and ready to climb out onto land and survey the scene around him. A short walk from the landing stage took them through a band of trees, which then opened out to reveal a tidy and well ordered collection of solid wooden buildings.

'So this is Manerplaw,' he thought to himself. There had been a great deal of talk among the men. "Manerplaw is important for our future; it's where all the politicians come to meet," one had said while the younger boys had looked on, not really understanding what was being said.

"The students from Rangoon have joined us now so together we are strong enough to beat the Tatmadaw."

"But can they be trusted? They are Burmese. How come they're on our side?" One sceptic had argued.

"Now we don't know who we can trust. Look at what's happened with some of our Karens. . .even some of our own men have betrayed us and gone over to the Tatmadaw."

The group nodded its assent.

The optimist persisted. "But if we are ever to have peace, then we have to work with the students. And if they can help us to overthrow this military government then we can start again with an agreement that suits all of us. And the students are all members of the [8]NLD, the party of Aung San Suu Kyi, we all need to work together," he added, looking round him for some sign of agreement from his fellows. But after all

---

[8] NLD National League for Democracy

the long years of fighting nobody else held out that much hope; it seemed such a high ideal and impossible to achieve.

Every company in the district had been brought in and the town was full of soldiers. Some, like those of Manerplaw garrison, were relatively smart with uniforms and boots and guns. Others like Hsa Mya's company had been cruelly decimated by the recent weeks of shelling and presented a poor spectacle with worn and dirty uniforms, old thongs on their feet or even, in some cases, no shoes at all. Still, all were needed and all were welcomed into the wooden barracks of their fellows.

Manerplaw was situated on the west bank of the Moie River. There were three major defensive points, one to the northwest, one to the west and one to the south. It was to the south that Hsa Mya and his platoon were now heading. After a night of rest in the crowded but comfortable barracks of the garrison he had been up early to see to the packing of machine guns and ammunition into the tall baskets. Porters had been requisitioned from the nearby villages, but it was Hsa Mya's job to see that the loads were well distributed and that there was sufficient equipment and food to withstand a siege. Once all that was done and the company was ready he shouldered his AK47 and pack and began the trek up the path to the high point. His father had fought in the KNLA and his grandfather had fought with the Burma Rifles under the British; he thought with pride of his grandfather who always spoke warmly of the men he had fought with, some of whom were famous throughout the district for their bravery and determination to beat the formidable Japanese forces, sometimes against impossible odds. As a small boy he had often sat and listened to the stories that his grandfather had told of his exploits so long before but the old man sometimes went quiet, his mouth would draw itself into a tight line and the tone of his voice would become bitter. "They said they would help us, then they left us and forgot all about us."

At times like that the little Hsa Mya would watch his grandfather's face in dismay.

"And now we are fighting for our lives and nobody cares about us." Then the old man would shake his head and look at Hsa Mya with a smile and the young boy determined that one day he would fight for his people and do everything he could to make his family proud of him.

As he looked at the young soldiers with him he was impressed with the way they conducted themselves. They had been drilled very hard and so in spite of their youth they were well disciplined and he knew he could rely upon them. And everything depended on them now, on them and other troops like them. The generals were putting all their efforts into defending Manerplaw and just like in the days of the Second World War, the fight was unequal. Every night he had fallen into an exhausted sleep but then had regularly woken in the cold early hours.

The women had clustered round in small groups, unwilling to move. He wondered if they really understood the danger that surrounded them as they tried to pile more belongings into baskets and bags. Then one would go back inside to pick up another item that she decided she couldn't live without and that would cause doubt in another one's mind and she would then find her way back to her house. Hsa Mya couldn't blame them for thinking that way and these women wore clean clothes, some of them were the same age as he was, or younger, and the children skipped around them with a lightness that betrayed their ignorance of what lay ahead. The young boys had wanted to look at his gun, so he had knelt down then and showed them how he took it apart and cleaned it, while the women looked on and the little ones hid in the folds of their skirts.

He hadn't wanted them to know what he had seen, the women whose faces had been flat with exhaustion, their clothes dirty and worn into holes. Sometimes they had tried to rearrange them to preserve at least some modesty but others had done nothing to cover up the grey skin that showed through the rags, past caring who saw them. Sometimes he hated himself because he hadn't cared either. But then their faces came to him in the darkness and he couldn't put them out of his mind.

They had been sent to a village with the intention of defending it. The smell of burning and the strange quiet as they approached should have alerted them, but it hadn't. For some reason he hadn't been prepared for what they had found in the first house, enough of which was still standing for them to climb the steps and find the charred remains of a baby by the fire with what he guessed was its mother, or perhaps grandmother, beside it.

The platoon had retreated then, unwilling to risk the possibility of falling into a trap and Hsa Mya was sickened by his first real failure. From that point on, what had supposed to be an orderly retreat had turned into a rout and the panic on the faces of the villagers had haunted him ever since.

One thought comforted him; he knew that Ba Lwe was near to the river and it would be relatively easy for Htee K'Paw and her family to reach the safety of Thailand should they need to. He wanted so much to see her again.

"It's good to see you, Lieutenant," the captain ushered his young junior into his temporary headquarters.

Hsa Mya, out of breath from the steep climb, could only nod in acknowledgement and glance round to make sure that the supplies were being dealt with properly.

"We need everything you've brought and the reinforcements."

"How are things, Captain?"

"We're holding on so far . . . and we know where all their positions are. We are keeping up our bombardment and they haven't moved forward at all for weeks. But it's the men. There's a lot of malaria, some of them serious cases, and . . the captain's voice tailed off suddenly.

"We've brought some Chloraquine with us for you. The hospital said you would need it." Hsa Mya had detected some unease in the captain's tone of voice and wanted to do what he could to help him.

"I'm afraid some of the men need more than that. We can only give them the most rudimentary medicines here. The medics have been testing the men's blood and finding a lot of *plasmodium*

36

falciparum[9]. . . .some of them are very sick with it. We need your porters to take them back down to the hospital for treatment there. That's why we need the reinforcements. You see . . " The captain hesitated again, so Hsa Mya waited for him to finish. "You see some of the men out there with the enemy are also Karens and our soldiers don't want to fight against them. It's as if they're being asked to kill their own brothers." Hsa Mya was not quite sure what to say. "But we have no choice." the senior officer continued. "Now they've formed the DKBA and have gone across to the Tatmadaw they will take everything from us. We have to stop them . . . but morale is low since this mutiny."

Hsa Mya was shocked at the captain's words.. He had never heard a senior officer speak in such a way and he wondered what he could possibly say to make the man feel better about the situation. "Sir! We took a day and a half to get up here. The porters should be able to take the sick and wounded back in a day. And the brigadier is sending more reinforcements." He wanted to help the captain who was obviously distressed about their predicament.

"Well, let them rest for tonight and then they can start out again in the morning. And thank you, Lieutenant"

Hsa Mya accepted the captain's appreciation of him with a glad heart. In spite of the danger, in spite of the bitter inequality of this battle, in spite of the hard conditions that the men found themselves in, he wanted to be up here on the front line. All exhaustion seemed to melt away as he worked with his company and the others like it to increase the bombardment of

---

[9] *Plasmodium falciparum* The most severe form of malaria.

the Tatmadaw positions. At least the Burmese had lost the element of surprise that had put them at such an advantage in the villages to the south. Now the KNU had mustered all their forces around Manerplaw there was more hope. They needed to hold on for a few more weeks. They had done it before at Sleeping Dog Mountain; they could do it again here.

They set up new gun emplacements, re-stocked the old ones, established a more efficient supply line and sent some small patrols to spy out the enemy positions. Meanwhile, exhausted, sick and injured soldiers were helped down the hillside to the hospital situated by the Moie River.

The men became deafened by the noise of the bombardments. Each night a guard was left at all the gun emplacements and the soldiers would rest in the simple wooden shelters that were hidden in the forest. Hsa Mya would join them, his whole body desperate for a few hours of quiet before the shelling began again the next day.

"I've been watching the enemy positions, Sir." he spoke to the Captain one evening.

"Yes, so have I. What do you see?"

"There's been no smoke all day from one of them and we haven't seen anything coming from the points nearest the river. Do you think they might have retreated?"

"Perhaps . . . I have been thinking that myself."

"What about a reconnaissance party Sir?"

"Are you volunteering, Lieutenant?" He had been very impressed by this young officer's clear-headedness and the way he dealt with the men under him.

38

"Yes, Sir!"

"Perhaps we should wait to see if anything happens tomorrow; then if it's still all quiet we can send a small party at night . . . You can be in it and you can pick the men to go with you."

Htee K'Paw dreaded the thought of having to move again; she had got used to living in Ba Lwe; now she was quite at home in the place and she loved teaching in the school. For many weeks now she had pushed her fears for the future to the back of her mind and had concentrated hard on her work, but now the seriousness of the situation had settled in her mind. New refugees were arriving in the village every day now and in greater and greater numbers, all of their faces clearly displaying fear and defeat. The sound of shelling grew closer too, so that every family unconsciously looked through its belongings and began to get together the best baskets and containers so that they were ready for what they now knew to be inevitable.

A strange hush seemed to descend over the class and the children all got to their feet. Htee K'Paw looked up from the work she was checking for one of the children and followed the eyes of the rest of the class to the doorway where the headmaster stood, his face a mask of grim resignation. This was not the first time he had had the responsibility of announcing that school was now closed. "You are to pick up all your books and pencils, put them in your bags and when *thramu* gives the word, you are to go straight home. No playing games, no visiting your friends, just straight to where your homes are." Looking at Htee

K'Paw he added quietly, "as soon as they're ready, send them home."

"Yes Sir," she whispered, the words almost disappearing as her throat tightened. She stood for a few moments fighting to control the shaking; her hands were freezing cold and she was struggling to get air into her lungs. "Children," she said as she fought to calm herself, "we have to leave now. Take all your things, just as *thra* said, and go straight home. Please, go straight home." She felt she had to make this special plea, especially to the boys. She couldn't bear the thought that one of them should get lost and fall into the wrong hands just because he dawdled home today.

She waited until the last child had left the classroom then she sped across the playground and down the path towards home. Everywhere there were signs of a people on the move, some of the houses were already empty and the sight of them was enough to make Htee K'Paw increase her pace for fear that she might get left behind. The path was crowded with families, all laden with their household goods; children were leading squealing pigs, sometimes cajoling, sometimes simply dragging them in their anxiety to be on their way, while chickens squawked and pecked in their baskets. Some parents carried young children, others helped their elderly and sick the best they could while among them moved the soldiers of the KNU, encouraging, supporting but at the same time admitting by their very presence that they were no longer able to hold back the relentless advance of the Tatmadaw. At last she reached home. "Mama, Papa, K'Paw Meh, Ma Nay," she called out as she ran round the outside of the house and out to the back yard.

There she saw K'Paw Meh and Ma Nay catching the last of their chickens ready to put them into their basket.

"What about the new chicks?" She called out.

"Yes," said Ma Nay, "Papa has another basket for them." And he went on with his task. Activities in the yard seemed to be going well so she turned to go back into the house; there she was met by something that was quite unforeseen. Her mother sat on the floor surrounded by bundles of clothes and bedding while her father stood over her holding little Mon Kyaw in his arms, a look of quiet desperation on his face.

"Papa! Everyone's leaving. We have to go. I've seen them all on the path, some have gone already."

"Yes Htee K'Paw. But your mother . . ." and his gaze again returned to his wife sitting mutely with her eyes downcast.

Then Htee K'Paw understood. She had seen this before. Her mother had been through times when she had seemed frozen and almost incapable of action. The two girls and their father coped very well with the situation and quickly compensated for their mother's inactivity, so that the domestic life of the family suffered little interruption. But today. . . now? Htee K'Paw's mind began to race as she wondered what they could do. Father and daughter looked at each other as together they tried to formulate some way of dealing with this situation.

"Mama!" Htee K'Paw tried again. "We can't stay here. If the Tatmadaw soldiers come here we don't know what they will do. Sometimes they burn the houses, sometimes they kill everyone they find. No! We can't, we can't! Papa?" She could hear her voice rising in panic.

Then her father seemed to make up his mind. "Htee K'Paw! You take Mon Kyaw. I will pack as much as I can into my basket, and find those two and see what they have. We will manage as much as we can between us and you and I will take mama's hands and she can walk between us."

Saw Ker Reh loaded the chickens into a basket for Ma Nay to carry. He divided the clothes and mats and blankets between the children and filled his own basket with as much as he could manage, while Htee K'Paw took her baby brother and secured him to her back with an old cotton sarong.

The family made their way out of the house that had been their home for the last six years with Htee K'Paw and her father coaxing her mother along the path as best they might. It was fortunate that although the woman obviously didn't want to go, she offered little in the way of active resistance, rather she quietly accepted their ministrations. Htee K'Paw began to breathe more easily as the family got on their way. The next problem would be the river; would there be enough boats? She couldn't even begin to contemplate the possibility of having to cross the river on foot with her mother like this. 'Oh, Hsa Mya! If only you were here,' she cried silently to herself. She wanted him to come and help them. Somehow she knew that she would be feeling stronger if only he were beside her. As it was she wished she could go to sleep right there and wake up in the home that he always said he wanted to build for her, with her parents close by and all of them living in a land of peace and safety. She had been thinking about what he had said at their last meeting and yes, she was becoming more and more convinced that he was the one for her. Recently she had taken to waking up in the early morning darkness and had found herself wondering why she was still hesitating. Of course she loved him, of course she wanted to marry him; there was no one else in the world that she would rather be with.

As the family struggled along the path towards the river Htee K'Paw made her decision; she would find Hsa Mya and they would be married wherever they were. Then she quickly brushed those thoughts aside and turned her attention back to the task in hand.

Although the path was dry, it was rough, steep in places, and crowded with people, animals and soldiers, all hastening towards the safety of the other side of the river. It was not easy to manoeuvre with their heavy baskets and a woman who was reluctant to walk. Within a short time the crowd had become so thick that they could not move forward at all.

"Oh dear!" Saw Ker Reh said "It looks like it's crowded right down to the river now."

"Papa! What's happening?" asked little Ma Nay, his voice beginning to rise in panic. What in his child's mind had begun as an adventure to a new home had become bewildering and frightening as more and more people pressed from behind and the family were jostled to the side. Some stumbled as they were pushed on the rough path and had to take care to prevent themselves from falling down the steep embankment to the side.

"There . . . there are too many people and . . ." the children's father tried to keep his voice level and calm. "K'Paw Meh, hold onto your brother's hand and don't let go, whatever happens."

"Yes Papa," she called out as she felt herself slowly being separated from her mother, father and elder sister.

Htee K'Paw held grimly onto her mother's hand as the crowd slowly inched forward. Now she could see the river and could also determine what the problem was. There were three small boats ferrying the people across the river. Although the distance was not great, there was a reasonably strong current and the boatmen had to steer across diagonally to avoid being washed downstream with each journey. This made the whole process extremely slow. Some soldiers were attempting to take charge of the crowd, mainly to prevent large numbers climbing onto the boats, which were tiny and so close to the water that they were in constant danger of capsizing. Even the largest boat took a maximum of only eight people. Some of the men were trying to walk across but, although it was not wide, the river was deep in places so they were almost out of their depth. Others watching them from the shore were reluctant to make the attempt when they saw the difficulties they were having and, besides, their household goods became soaked with river water. There was no real alternative, especially for those with women and children; they had to wait for the boats. And all the time the crowd on the bank became larger and more desperate, while children slipped and fell in the mud.

At last Saw Ker Reh had reached the landing point for the boat and he watched with grim determination as an empty boat came alongside. In his anxiety for his wife he had lost sight of two of his children, so as the boat reached him he began to look around for them, but could see them nowhere nearby.

Then an arm reached across and another family had begun to clamber on board the tiny craft before he could stop them.

"My wife is sick, you must let us get on," Saw Ker Reh cried angrily.

But the other family was already filling the boat with their baskets and livestock. Letting go of his wife Saw Ker Reh began to grapple with the other man who was at that moment stepping onto the fragile craft. The boat began to list wildly.

"Let go! Let go! or we'll be in the water." The man shouted, attracting the attention of one of the soldiers.

"Papa! Please!" Called out Htee K'Paw. "We can get the next boat. Please leave him." She could feel her mother beginning to slip into the water now made muddy by all the trampling feet and she needed her father to help her.

"What is it sir?" The soldier had come across to them. Htee K'Paw felt sure she had seen the soldier's face before but she had to concentrate so hard to keep her mother from falling that she thought no more about him.

"My wife is sick, she must go by boat, she cannot cross on foot. Please!" Saw Ker Reh had let go of the man but the boat was now so unstable that it had begun to fill with water. The children began to scream as the boat swayed dangerously from side to side and finally capsized a few yards from the shore. Some who were close by could see the unfairness of the situation and began to shout while others waded in to help the family whose goods were all completely soaked. In the middle of trying to recover his goods the man looked at Saw Ker Reh and made as if to hit him. Htee K'Paw was grateful that her father was now too far from the man and there were now others between them to prevent a real fight breaking out. Meanwhile the soldier tried to restore order while the boatman righted the wooden craft, which fortunately was still useable even if very wet inside.

Then a gasp went up from the crowd as someone shouted. "Smoke! Can you smell it? They must be burning the houses." And another wave of panic swept through the terrified refugees. Those who had been intent on a fight suddenly regained a fresh awareness of their situation and the soldier tried to quieten them once again.

Htee K'Paw glanced around to see if there was anyone who could help her and saw again the soldier that she recognised. Now she remembered him. "Eh Doh, is that your name?" she asked as he put out his arm to support her mother and their eyes met. He was one of the soldiers in Hsa Mya's platoon. They had often played volleyball together in happier times.

"Yes, and its Htee K'Paw, isn't it?"

"Yes," She wanted to thank him until she saw the cloud pass across his face. "Eh Doh," she said again. "What?"

"I'm the only one left. Our platoon . . . I'm the only one. I'm sorry." As he steadied her mother and then led her to a place where she could wait for the next boat Htee K'Paw saw his eyes once more.

And in that moment, among the crying and fear and the mud and dirty water Htee K'Paw knew, for the first time, what true loneliness was.

5

September 1999

The sound of male voices had slowly entered his consciousness, and out of curiosity Jonathan moved towards one of the tables on the balcony and sat down to see what was happening. He looked over the railing and watched the scene unfolding in the river below him. There were several young boys fishing in the water while a small group sat on the shore. One of them had lit a fire, the centre of which now burned hotly, the flame brightening as he attentively fed it with driftwood from the tiny beach. Two others watched languidly as the others studied the fish, harpoons at the ready. Slowly they moved through the shallows, their milky coffee brown skin glistening silkily in the morning sunlight. Then they turned back towards the fire as one of them lifted his arm high to reveal a net sufficiently full to provide each one of them and more with breakfast. Jonathan was transfixed for a few moments. Then he shifted his gaze up towards the mountains that punctured the horizon and began to wonder vaguely where exactly they were. Was he still looking at Thailand or were those mountains actually in Burma? Was that where all the refugees came from, the refugees he was soon going to live with for several months.

"You want to order, sir?"

"Yes. . .Yes. Coffee and toast, please." He hadn't wanted to eat earlier on. The long overnight bus ride from Bangkok had left him feeling just a little queasy so he had taken a walk down to the small town to buy a copy of *The Nation,* which still lay pristine and unopened on the seat beside him. Now as he waited for his own late breakfast he let his eyes drift cursorily over the newspaper pages, sometimes pausing to watch the children in the river and thinking how fishing like that was a part of an imagined perfect childhood. He paused for a moment as his eyes caught sight of an article about the refugees on the border; it made note of a date over four years ago: 27th January 1995. That was when Manerplaw had fallen, that was why there were so many refugees on this border. The writer, who was obviously well informed, was lamenting the fact that there was a total impasse with no possibility of any of them going home for the foreseeable future and every day there seemed to be more crossing the border.

He was thus occupied when he became aware of someone else leaning across the railing watching the entertainment in the river.

"Beautiful, isn't it?"

"What? Oh yes."

"Not a care in the world."

"No," Jonathan replied vaguely, detecting in himself a slight touch of resentment that his quiet read was being interrupted and immediately feeling ashamed that he should think such an unfriendly thought.

"Don't you wish you could go back to a time when you had nothing more on your mind than the day's fishing and the whole of the summer holidays stretched ahead? Oh, I'm sorry, Timothy Buckley," and the stranger extended his hand. "Everyone just calls me Tim. Look do you mind if I join you? Are you a lone traveller too?"

"Yes, I am. I'm Jon. Jonathan McCune,"

"Are you a tourist? Or a traveller? There is a difference isn't there?" The stranger's accent was clearly English, not Australian or American, which were so often heard on the tourist trails of South East Asia.

"Oh yes. But I'm not really either. I'm a research student. I'm here to do some work for my PhD."

"Wow. You've got brains then." Jonathan detected a slight patronising tone in the stranger's voice.

"I don't know about that. I'm just very interested in my subject, I got a good mark for my masters and so I decided to take it further. Some would question the intelligence of an academic career: my father, for example. He would rather I went into business like him, or law, or something else that makes lots of money. But I'm doing what I want, so here I am. What about you?"

"Me? Oh, I'm one of those awful businessmen that, no doubt, your father would admire. Internet business. Doing very well. But I'm taking some time out. Want to give something back."

A pause ensued while the breakfast was set out onto the table.

"How do you mean, 'give something back'?"

Tim shot a quizzical glance across the table and saw that Jonathan was obviously waiting for an explanation.

"Well, as I said, the business is doing fine. I live well on it but it's not completely satisfying, for all that. I've been thinking that I ought to do something for someone else for a while."

"Me too. My aunt Sarah and her husband David come out here every year. His business allows him time out and they run a charity to help the refugees. A lot of the schools on the border have books and teachers because of them."

"Well, I've done the TEFL course and I intend to use it if I can. I've heard about the refugees living nearby and that they are always desperate for someone to come and help them to learn English. I was hoping that if I hung around in this town for long enough I'd come across someone who knows about them and can get into their camps. It's just a matter of waiting. It looks like you might be just the person I'm looking for. Am I right?"

"Yes, you're right," Jonathan conceded with a rueful smile. "I'm here because I came with Sarah several months ago. I was looking into a subject for research and she suggested I come here. I got to know the refugees a bit and then I've been back home doing background reading, getting to know the subject and so on. Now I begin in earnest. I'm going to live in the camps as much as I can so I can really find out what's going on here and try to understand it. Meanwhile, I'm going to teach English. It's the best way of getting to know the people. And that's my way of 'giving something back,' to coin your phrase."

"Why ever didn't you say? It looks like you and I are on the same wavelength. Good to get to know you, Jon," and Tim extended his hand across the table. "Do you want another coffee or anything else?"

"Yes, that would be great: coffee and more toast please."

"When are you going to start this research? Can you help me get to meet the refugees?"

"The research starts straight away and I guess you could come with me. We just have to be a bit careful. You see, the refugees are only allowed to stay here if they don't cause any trouble. They're not really allowed into the towns and villages round about, although of course many of them slip in illegally. And they're not supposed to receive anything more than the basic humanitarian aid. What Sarah does goes a bit beyond what is really allowed since it's more than the basic education, you might say. The authorities don't like too many westerners in the camps, it draws too much attention to them for one thing, and it might mean that the refugees get too comfortable here and not want to cross back into Burma. You do realise where they all come from, don't you?"

"Oh yes. I've read all about them. There is something in today's newspaper too. I see you've got it there."

"Well, you know why I need to be careful then. Sarah has to be too; everything she does is very low key. I have to fit in with that and that includes not talking about it too much. That's why I didn't say where I was going at first."

"That's quite alright, I understand . . . so what happens next?"

"Well, after breakfast some people are going to meet me here. They have to be careful not to be too conspicuous and of course talking to westerners immediately makes them so. I'll introduce you to them and perhaps they'll take you out to the nearest camp. It's not too far, but you have to be taken in by someone who knows what he's doing. They're all very careful. They have to be."

"What today . . . now?"

"Yes, I guess so. Perhaps you could come and see the place with me, and if you like what you see and they like you . . . well I reckon you could start whenever you like. Have you got any plans?"

"No, as I said, I was just waiting for the right break. It looks like I've got it already."

"All right, I'll introduce you to the people when they get here and we'll go from there."

It was mid morning when a small grey truck entered the square, driven by a young man with a middle aged man sitting at his side. The young man got out and walked across to Jonathan extending his right hand as he did so. "Jonathan"

"Tana, it's good to see you again."

"Are you ready Jonathan? I don't want to wait too long."

"I just have to pick up my bags. Look, this is Tim. He wants to come out with us and see the camp. He thinks he could come and do some teaching. What do you think?"

"Today? Do you want to come with us now?"

"Yes. If that's possible." Tim shrugged his shoulders. "I hadn't got anything else planned."

"It looks like they don't want to stay here too long, Tim. I'll get my bags and you get what you want for the day. Tana can bring you back here tonight, can't you?"

"Of course, no problem," the young driver replied.

"I'll wait here until you come back and then we'll get going. Can we go to the supermarket before we go out to the camp?" Jonathan asked as he climbed into the cab after stowing all his goods into the pick up. "I want to buy a few cokes and other drinks for the students, they never have enough and it'll be a treat for them."

During his first trip the previous autumn he had developed a real affection for the students that he had met, which had truly surprised him. Everywhere he went he had received a welcome that had been warmer than he could possibly have predicted and all the students he had talked to had impressed him with their enthusiasm and desire to help him. What had begun as rather a dry academic exercise had become a labour of love and he had come to almost resent the time that he had been compelled to spend back in London reading around his subject.

Now he was happier to be back here than he would ever have imagined possible and the first thing he was going to do was buy something that he knew the students would appreciate.

6

As she approached the house Htee K'Paw saw her youngest brother waiting for her. He ran to greet her with a smile and she stooped to pick him up. Carrying him round to the back of the house she entered the yard to find all was quiet. She crossed to look into the water container and saw with dismay that it was almost empty. Mon Kyaw needed his wash and one glance at the fire told her that the preparation of the supper had not even been started. And Ma Nay, where was that child? No doubt he was engaged in some make believe game or other that he seemed to spend all his seemingly inexhaustible energy on.

Her happiness at reaching home became tinged with a trace of bad temper as she thought of all that had to be done. And she had been looking forward to this evening so much. They were to begin their teacher training at last and today they were going to hold a party to welcome the leaders and the visitors from the other camps who were going to work on the course with them.

"We'll have to go and meet the English teachers, Htee K'Paw," Hser Mu had said as they walked home together, "I've seen one of them already. He's got blond hair and .." Hser Mu had rubbed her hands on her arms. Htee K'paw had immediately known what she meant and both girls had collapsed into giggles. The thing that they always noticed about the white men who occasionally visited the camp was that they nearly always had hairs on their arms. This was something they never saw on their own men and for reasons now unknown to both of them, the two girls found this very funny.

"And," Hser Mu stopped laughing for a brief moment. "he's very handsome." Then she laughed again.

Htee K'Paw had seen some of the visitors who were to teach on the course. She hadn't thought any of them to be particularly handsome but she had joined in the laughter anyway. Hser Mu was inclined to think all [10]*kolah wah's* were good looking and always wanted to go and meet them whoever they were.

"Yes," she said, "I'll be there. I just have to do a few things at home. Call for me later won't you?"

"I will, but you must be ready and don't forget to put some nice clothes on for the *kolah wah,*" and they both giggled again.

Ma Nay tore through the yard and broke into her thoughts. He had tied a rolled up blanket onto his back and carried a stick across his shoulder. He was patrolling the forest and fighting battles for the KNU.

"Ma Nay, Ma Nay!" she called out. "Ma Nay you have to help me."

"But they're after me Htee K'Paw," he cried out. "I must get away."

"You have to leave your game for now, Ma Nay. I need you to help me, and your friends will have to go in soon anyway."

Ma Nay held up his hands to the other children and the game broke up. "Where's Mama?" he asked as he drank the cup of water that his sister handed him.

---

[10] *Kolah wah* Karen word for a white skinned person.

"She's inside resting."

"She's always resting," Ma Nay panted as Htee K'Paw regarded his handsome features and clear bright eyes, still shining with the excitement of battle.

"That's because she isn't well."

"What's wrong with her?"

"It's her heart. The medic says it's her heart and she has to rest sometimes."

"Can't the medics make her better?" Ma Nay asked turning his eyes up to look at his sister.

"Well they do their best . . . but we can't always get the medicines." Htee K'Paw didn't like to tell her brother that medicines were available but the family had no money with which to buy them. "Water, Ma Nay. I need you to get water for us. Hurry up now, I have to give Mon Kyaw his wash then cook the supper. And I want to go out this evening."

Ma Nay took a container and went to the well at the end of the path to collect the water. Once he had made a couple of journeys and the large container began to fill up, Htee K'Paw pulled Mon Kyaw's tee shirt over his head and took off his shorts. "Now, little brother, it's time to wash all that dirt off." Picking up the plastic dipper, she filled it and poured water over him. Then with the small piece of soap she tried her best to clean the wriggling child before splashing the rinsing water over him. The whole procedure was over in not much more than a minute, but it was accompanied by such protests that the kittens who usually prowled around the yard ran away in terror. Htee K'Paw reached for a clean sarong that was hanging on the washing line and wrapped it round Mon Kyaw. She sat down on the bottom step and held him while he calmed down again and gradually dried off. It was as he rested quietly against her for a moment that she thought of Hsa Mya again. It sometimes happened like that, quite unexpectedly, but always there was a small pain that seemed to pierce her chest for a few moments.

She had kept the letter safely folded and tucked under her clothes in the corner of the room that she shared with her sister. The captain's words were kind; he had written that Has Mya had been the best lieutenant he had ever know. He said that he had worked tirelessly to defend his country and its people. But there had been no comfort and no help for the grief that had settled deep inside her that terrible day.

But as she held onto Mon Kyaw he seemed to know that she needed him. And she thought that she would like to stay there always, holding the little brother that she loved, as if in some way, he was her compensation for the loss of Hsa Mya.

There had been other boys, of course. Some had tried to make friends and write letters and talk with her, but in truth there had been nobody who could fill the gap that he had left. They had tried but hadn't succeeded, so had turned away disappointed.

"Htee K'Paw?" Her mother's voice broke into her reverie. "I heard all the noise."

"It's all right, Mama. I was just washing him. You can go back to finish your rest now. I'll cook for us. Ma Nay's collecting the water and K'Paw Meh will be home soon."

"No. I'll get on with something now."

"But your ankles, they look very swollen."

"Don't worry about that. I can't rest for ever," and saying that the older woman took hold of the now clean Mon Kyaw, and after rubbing his wet hair with the sarong began to put his clothes on again. "Go and get me some logs from the pile, will you?" she said to Ma Nay once he had returned from his most recent trip to the well, and her place as mother of the family was restored once more.

Htee K'Paw scooped some rice from the sack and mother and daughter began to prepare the food for their supper. Once the meal was underway, K'Paw Meh came round the corner and into the yard.

"You're late," began Htee K'Paw accusingly.

"We were playing volleyball."

"That was a very long game."

"It wasn't just a game. I went to the dormitory afterwards."

"Just chatting to your friends! When there's so much to do here and you know Mama's ill."

"Well what about you? I hear you're going out later."

"Girls. Stop it. Listening to you makes me feel worse again. Please don't argue."

Their mother's words were unheeded.

"Who told you I was going out?"

"Kler Htoo," and she wandered across to the fire to inspect the cooking pots. "He likes you and he told me he'll be seeing you later at the party for the teachers. No vegetables, no green vegetables," she exclaimed in dismay, abruptly changing the subject. "*Tharamu* tells us that we should eat green vegetables to keep ourselves healthy."

"Well, we haven't got any," retorted Htee K'Paw impatiently, hearing the note of rising anger in her own voice.

"Saw Ker Reh will be back tomorrow," said the girls' mother wearily. "Perhaps he will bring some with him."

"If you helped a bit more, then perhaps we could grow some things ourselves," Htee K'Paw dug further into her sister knowing that the yard was far too small to allow the family to grow anything, let alone vegetables for the family.

"Please," their mother asked once again, "can we be at peace? We will sit down to eat soon, and I want us to be happy together."

And Htee K'Paw stood quietly by the fire while tears of frustration rose painfully into her eyes, then shaking her head as if to clear them away she called out to her brother. "Ma Nay, come on. You help me to set the table," and the two of them went up the steps together to where the low table stood against the bamboo wall of the house. Together they lifted it and placed it on the floor so that the whole family could sit round it. Their mother always made a point of ensuring that, as far as was possible, they all sat down together to eat, however simple their meal was going to be. Today, Htee K'Paw knew, it was precious little; there was only rice and some chilli paste left over from yesterday and she could hear, and smell some eggs frying in the pan. They would help to satisfy the ever-hungry Ma Nay and placate K'Paw Meh with her teenage sensibilities. And then when father came home tomorrow from his week's work in the hotel at the edge of the town he would bring some of the vegetables that they all needed so badly.

"Htee K'Paw," Ma Nay broke into her thoughts of the practicalities of the meal once again. She turned to look at him. "When I'm grown up I'm going to become a doctor . . . so that I can make Mama better, . . . and the other people who are sick." As Htee K'Paw listened to his words she felt tears beginning to fill her eyes. As a teacher herself she knew Ma Nay to be one of the brightest children in the school. He had the drive and the ability and the love to fulfil his childish ambition, but she also knew that the chances of achieving anything more than a very basic education was almost unheard of here in the camp and her heart went out to him. She took his small, determined hand in hers.

"I know you will, Ma Nay. One day you will."

Any enjoyment the family might have gleaned from their simple meal together was spoiled by K'Paw Meh's face, which was set in a disagreeable frown throughout.

"What is it now K'Paw Meh?" asked their mother wearily. She did her best to maintain a veneer of capability when she was with the family, but it was hard to disguise the exhaustion and shortage of breath that regularly afflicted her. She coughed often too, producing a white, almost foamy substance, which she did her best to keep out of sight of her children.

"Nothing."

"Of course it isn't nothing," Htee K'Paw retorted. "It's obvious you're miserable about something."

"I'm sick of this place. There's no money to buy anything nice and it's just like a prison."

Their mother's spirits sank even further. It was true, however cheerful she tried to be, however much she tried to disguise the fact that they, together with all the refugees, were virtual prisoners on this narrow strip

60

of land; that was what they were. Without documents they couldn't travel and while the Tatmadaw still controlled the land on the other side of the river they had nowhere to go. They were forced to subsist on hand outs from relief agencies, which were just adequate but provided nothing in the way of variety that the children craved so much. "We just have to make the best of things K'Paw Meh and remember we're lucky that Saw Ker Reh has a job in the hotel so he can bring things home for us."

"Yes, but only things like vegetables. He never brings anything interesting. Mu Aye's sister works in town and she brought her a lipstick and a new blouse. What do I have to wear?"

"Don't be so selfish," Htee K'Paw got to her feet and almost shouted at her sister. "Just now you wanted vegetables, now you want new clothes. Papa doesn't make enough for those things."

"Sit down Htee K'Paw. And I don't know about Mu Aye's sister but she should be careful. The police are always on the lookout for people outside the camps. Your father has a pass, but even he can't go into the town itself. She could get herself arrested."

"Mu Aye says that the police don't arrest girls, or not so much anyway, so she doesn't have to worry."

"But she's still in danger, K'Paw Meh, and it isn't worth it for a lipstick and a few new clothes."

"Well how else are we to get on in this place? I hate it . . . I hate it so much."

"Stop it, K'Paw Meh, stop it," her sister pleaded. She had seen their mother growing breathless with anxiety, while the two boys stared wide eyed in dismay at the bigger people around then. She could feel her own rising unease at the feeling of disaffection in the family. K'Paw Meh seemed to respond then. One glance at her mother told her that she had gone too far and she returned to pushing the food that she considered to be dull and vastly inferior around her plate. An uncomfortable silence descended over the family broken only by the sound of Hser Mu's voice at the bottom of the steps.

Htee K'Paw realised with dismay that she hadn't even thought about her evening out, she had been so taken up with domestic chores and her concerns about K'Paw Meh and her mother's ill health.

"Aren't you ready yet?" called the ever-cheerful Hser Mu as she climbed the steps in her colourful *sarong* and tee shirt. She seemed to be wearing lipstick too and had completed the effect by fixing a flower into her hair.

"You look very nice," said the girls' mother, silently comparing the relative polish of Hser Mu's appearance with the rather surly expressions on both of her daughter's faces.

"Thank you, but what about you Htee K'Paw? You're still wearing what you had on all day. You must get changed at least," she said as she joined the family at the table, instantly lightening the mood, for which everyone was silently grateful. "What are you going to wear?" she asked Htee K'Paw as the rest of the family left them in peace a few minutes later.

"I thought I would wear my best white dress, the one I wear to church."

"Haven't you got anything else?" Hser Mu was a little despairing of her friend's lack of interest in modern clothes. To put on the woven white dress that was tradtionally worn by unmarried girls was, in her eyes, desperately old fashioned and betrayed a lack of sophistication that Hser Mu would have found embarrassing if she hadn't been so fond of her friend. Clothes were hardly at a premium in the camp but there was a certain fashion sense among many of the girls, especially, and denim clothes, printed tee shirts and other western items always found their way in via the more enterprising members of the community.

"I thought that would look all right. All my *sarongs* are so washed out and everything else gets worn so much for work. I think my white dress is the best thing I've got."

"Look, I'll go home and get you something"

"No, really, I'm quite happy with this."

"All right then, but what about putting some of this on?" and she produced a lipstick from her bag. "And we can put some orchids in your hair. And wash the [11]*tanaka* off your face. I don't think the *kolah wahs* like it. Now lets go and get you ready."

---

[11] *Tanaka* A paste mixed from powdered bark and water that is worn on the face by Burmese women and children.

7

Htee K'Paw sat on the floor to one side of the dormitory that had been built to house the students who had come for the teacher's course. Several of them had come from other refugee camps and they had to be housed somewhere. In her heart she knew that since she worked in the Huay Ko school she should have been taking a more active part in this evening's party. Hospitality was always taken very seriously in the camp and people would save for weeks in order to make sure the visitors were truly welcomed. Later there would be singing and representatives from all of the camps would be expected to perform their party pieces.

Earlier, she had been busy serving rice and spicy vegetable stew to all the visitors from the large iron cauldrons that rested on the glowing embers at the back of the building. Then there had been all the clearing up to do but as soon as it had been decently possible Htee K'Paw had taken refuge in this corner and sunk gratefully to the floor from where she watched the proceedings with some of the other girls. Hser Mu on the other hand was having none of such seemly behaviour. Instead she moved round the building, anxious to meet anyone and everyone

The room was filling with the gentle hum of the students as they began to get to know each other. The *'kolah wahs'*, the white men, were circulating with bottles of *Chang* beer, which most of the boys seemed to be drinking appreciatively, judging by the looks on their faces. Some of them were sharing drinks from a large bottle of liquid, which Htee K'Paw guessed to be whisky.

She knew she was being unsociable. It wasn't that she didn't want to be friendly; the earlier encounters with her sister had left her feeling dispirited and the evening had so far failed to lift her mood. With an effort she turned to one of the new girls. "My name's Htee K'Paw, I live here in Huay Ko . . . I'm a teacher in the primary school," and she finished with a smile as if to invite an answer.

"We're from Mae Klo. There are four of us: two boys and two girls. We came on the bus this morning; You can't believe how terrible it was. We were hours clinging to the back of the old thing, there was no room inside for most of the way."

The others in the group joined in with their tales of journeys. "We were all covered in dust by the time we got here. You should have seen us," the girl, whose name she discovered was Wa Pah, was recounting her story to the accompaniment of laughter from the rest of the group. It was only small talk but for Htee K'Paw it let some light into the gloom.

"What about the Thai police?" she asked curiously,

"Oh, they stopped us, but we had passes," And they all laughed together while each one of them quietly recognised in the others the shared experience of the dispossessed. Htee K'Paw was reminded of her

65

father, knowing that each week he took part in a sort of cat and mouse game with the police. But then he was no different to anyone else. They all did that, how else were they to live?

"Htee K'Paw, Htee K'Paw," Hser Mu was at her side once again.

Htee K'Paw, brightened by the brief conversations with her new acquaintances turned to her with a smile.

"Over there they're talking about something very interesting. Why don't you join us?"

"What is it?"

"Well come over and find out."

Htee K'Paw allowed herself to be led down the long room. With the rest of the girls she attached herself to the periphery of the loosely assembled crowd that now surrounded one of the white men.

The young man was sitting in the centre of a large crowd of the students with an interpreter at his side. As she sat and listened Htee K'Paw found that if she concentrated hard she could understand what was being said and follow some of the English that was being spoken.

"I want to hear your stories," the young man was saying. He looked to be much of an age with most of the assembled group. "I'm a student myself, and I'm trying to understand what has happened in your country. Whatever has happened to you, whatever you think about things, I am interested to know."

She felt Hser Mu lean close in order to whisper in her ear. "His name's Jonathan,"

Htee K'Paw smiled a response and turned her attention back to Jonathan. "Your stories will help me with my research," he was saying. "And for my part I want to help you. I can help you with your English language. We can have conversation classes. So what do you think? English classes in return for your help with my work."

Jonathan's suggestion set off a buzz of appreciative comments while Htee K'Paw looked on, her eyes slowly wandering around the room with no particular purpose.

It was then that she saw the other English man. Immediately she was woken from her slightly dreamy state by the realisation that he was looking straight at her. For a moment she wondered how long he had been watching her, then she quickly turned away. For an instant she had been filled with a strange sort of excitement. Or was it fear? She lowered her eyes, then heard Hser Mu's voice again, this time coming from a long way away. "You could tell him your story."

"What?"

"Are you asleep Htee K'Paw? We could tell Jonathan our stories. I'm sure it's the sort of thing he means."

"There's nothing special about mine. The same things happened to lots of people. I don't think I want to." She was aware that her heart was still beating faster than usual and she dare not look again towards the place where the white stranger was sitting.

"Well why don't we both go together? You could tell him what happened to you and . . ."

"No," Htee K'Paw interrupted, "no."

"What's the matter, are you afraid of him or something?"

"No I'm not afraid." She glanced quickly around the room taking care not to allow her eyes to stray across to where they had found themselves a few minutes earlier. "Look, I think it will be time for our singing soon."

Htee K'Paw sat down on the floor again, this time with the choir from Huay Ko. Several groups had sung to the sound of guitars or electric keyboard but they had decided to sing without any sort of accompaniment. The group were all good singers and so they had chosen to let their voices speak for themselves without any instrumental embellishment. They practised regularly and were pleased with their efforts. They regularly sang in four-part harmony but for this evening they had decided on a song that divided the soprano part into two. Htee K'Paw herself took the high part and her voice rang out through the building. When she sang it was with confidence and there was no mistaking whom the applause was for when the song drew to a close. The temporary disturbance of the earlier part of the evening was banished from her mind and she turned her attention to the enjoyment of the displays of dancing. Like everyone else she was intoxicated by the monotonous sound of the gong and drum, and the sway and dip of the performers.

"Hello,"

Htee K'Paw jumped at the sound of a foreign voice so close to her and before she knew it she was looking into a pair of striking blue eyes. She turned away in embarrassment then almost immediately turned back again to face the stranger, inwardly chiding herself for her childish fears.

"Hello," she replied while Hser Mu joined her as they both gazed at him.

"You have a beautiful voice,"

Htee K'Paw felt her face grow hot.

"Sorry, I'm Tim. I came here with Jonathan."

"Tim?"

"Yes, it's short for Timothy. And I just wanted to say how beautiful your singing was."

Htee K'Paw turned away again.

"I'm sorry, I'm embarrassing you. It's very good singing, everyone is very good, but I liked yours the best, that's all."

"Thank you Tim," Hser Mu butted in, "my name is Hser Mu and this is Htee K'Paw."

"Htee K'Paw, Hser Mu," Tim said slowly

"Our names are hard for you to say?"

"No, they're just different and I have to learn them. Tell me, is this a traditional dance?"

"Tra . . .?"

"I mean old, or one that people always do from the past?'

"Yes," said Hser Mu, "it's a rice dance. It shows how we plant the rice."

"And does the rice grow better if you do the dance?"

"Yes," said Htee K'Paw ingenuously.

"That's what the old people think," added Hser Mu quickly. She had heard the slight mocking tone of Tim's question. "But now it's just a dance," and she shot a glance of warning at Htee K'Paw whose face still bore a look of transparent innocence. But to her slight disappointment Tim turned his attention to her friend once again.

"I'd like to hear about some of these old traditions, I find them very interesting."

Htee K'Paw gave a slight cough as if she was about to speak but Hser Mu spoke again.

"And we want to hear about your country Tim. What's England like?"

"England? Oh, people think it's always cold and wet in England," he replied with a shrug. "But I like it. It's my home. It's beautiful . . and green, just like here."

"And do they do dances to make things grow in England?"

Tim knew he had been beaten, Hser Mu knew she had gone too far and in the embarrassed silence that followed Htee K'Paw glanced at both of them, one after the other.

Tim spoke first. "Touché," He paused for a moment and then in answer to the quizzical looks on both of the girl's faces he explained. "It means 'you win'," and as the girls tried to understand, their embarrassment quickly dispelled. Then the gong quietened and the large crowd stilled.

"It's our national anthem," Htee K'Paw explained. And the whole assembly stilled as they sang as one.

'My people who are best
I love you much
You love the truth
You welcome others
Because of your goodness
I love you much'

As they walked home Htee K'Paw felt the soft touch of Hser Mu's arm against hers. Then it slipped round her waist and she knew their friendship was just as it had always been.

"He likes you. I know he does," Hser Mu whispered into the velvety darkness.

"Who does?"

70

"Who do you think? The *kolah wah*."

"How do you know?" She asked as a slight shiver rippled its way down her spine.

"By the way he looks at you. You can always tell." And Htee K'Paw felt the warmth of her friend's body as it came closer to her own.

"I don't think I want that."

"And why not? He could get you out of here for one thing."

Htee K'Paw was shocked to hear her friend say such a thing. "But I have no reason to want to get away from here. And I don't want to . . ."

"Htee K'Paw, what are you afraid of? Don't you want anything more than what you have always known? Don't you have any ambitions?"

Htee K'Paw felt stung by her friend's words. She knew it was the drink. Hser Mu had more than enough for someone who didn't usually drink anything more than the simple home-brewed rice beer."

"Yes, I do have ambitions. I want to be a good teacher. I want to be a better teacher. That's why I'm here on this course."

"And you want to marry a good Karen boy don't you? And all the better if he is a soldier fighting for *Kaw Htoo Lei*"

Htee K'Paw was lost for words while hot tears rose into her eyes.

"Oh, I'm sorry, I shouldn't have said that," But then she felt the squeeze of Htee K'Paw's hand on hers and knew that she had been forgiven, even before she apologised.

"I worry, that's all. I worry about mother so much, and father is away and K'Paw Meh . . . I can't even think about the things you talk about. That's all. I

71

know it's what you want but, it's not for me, not at the moment."

The girls slowed to a halt in the path between the houses that were built close together in this part of the camp.

"It isn't what I want either, not really. I say I want to get away from here because what is there here for us? But I admire you Htee K'Paw, you're not selfish like me. You're a good person and I wish I could be more like you." And with that she fell silent as they walked on to Htee K'Paw's home.

"Tomorrow then," Hser Mu called out as her friend climbed the steps.

"Tomorrow . . . and the *Kolah Wahs*." Htee K'Paw answered. But as she lay down on her mat and wrapped the blanket around herself she thought again of Hsa Mya. There had been many times when she had refused to believe that he was dead. She still nurtured the hope that one day he would come back to her and tell her that the Captain had been mistaken and that he had been taken prisoner and had miraculously escaped. But in moments of harsh reality she knew that it was not so and there had been no mistake. And the nights when she dreamt of him and imagined she felt the weight of his arm on her shoulder were becoming rare indeed. She loved the feeling of her little brother as she held him close after his bath, and the gentle touch of Hser Mu's arm around her waist but Tim's presence so close to her had awakened the memories in her once again and she knew in herself the need for something stronger and more insistent and for that need she knew no satisfaction.

8

"I want you to tell me what you think about your situation," Jonathan was saying. "I want to know more about you. I want to understand your country and your people . . . and your stories. And what about the future?"

He was easy to listen to. He spoke slowly and quietly as if he chose his words carefully and Htee K'Paw found that she had no difficulty in understanding him. They had just finished their English class in which Jonathan had given them a game to play. He had told them that they had to talk in English for a whole minute without stopping. In her own native language such a game would have been fun and she had made a mental note to try it with her own classes in the future, but in English she had found the game almost impossible. She had been locked into an almost painful paralysis waiting until it was her turn but then she saw that Jonathan handled the whole thing with such a light-heartedness that she had begun to relax and even enjoy herself. Still, she was relieved that that particular lesson was over and Jonathan was asking them to volunteer their comments. That meant, she decided, that she could rest a little.

"What sort of thing do you want to know?" a tall man from one of the other camps was asking.

"Well, first of all, I want to analyse what has happened since independence in 1948? I need to find out as much as I can. I've read a lot of books and articles but I need to know what you all think. And what about the ethnic groups? Are you all from the same group, or are there lots of different groups here?"

"I'm from Karenni[12]," the tall man was saying. Htee K'Paw was surprised at how well he spoke English and then was glad that someone was prepared to be the first to speak up. "And we are fighting to defend our country and our people. We have no choice, we must fight."

"Most of us here are Karens and we are trying to defend our country too." Another student with an intense expression on his face had joined in the conversation now. "It's the same for us. We have no choice now."

"You say that you have no choice now. Does that mean that you once had a choice in the past?"

The student looked sideways at his fellows briefly then answered. "They tried to make a cease fire agreement. They said that we had a choice then, but no, there was no choice because it had no meaning. They still want to take our land. They want to take everything from us and make us fit in with their life."

"Do you all feel this way? Do all Karens and Karennis feel this way do you think?"

There was a thoughtful silence and several of the class seemed to nod their heads as if to agree. Yes, of course they do.

Htee K'Paw didn't want to get involved, she stayed quietly at the side of the classroom.

---

[12] Karenni: A smaller ethnic group in Burma living close to the Thai border and to the north of the Karen.

"No," the first student spoke again, "no they don't."

"What makes you say that?"

"Lots of things. Some people are so far inside Burma that they have no chance to learn about the Karen way of life. The teachers are not allowed to tell the Karen stories or the schools have been closed down completely. The people speak Burmese and they are unable to defend themselves. The government want them to become Burmese and to forget that they are Karen."

"And what about the rest of you? What do you think about what is being said? Is that really true?"

There was a long silence.

"It's impossible for us to know what any of our people really want," the tall serious student was talking once again. "Nobody has ever really asked them."

Htee K'Paw had her own answers to some of the questions, but she wasn't going to say them in front of the rest of the class for fear of what they would think of her. They had clever ideas of what they wanted in the future, many of them wanted to cling to the *koloh wahs* and hoped that way to get the chance to get away from the camp, like birds in a cage desperate to stretch their wings and fly. But all she wanted was to go home, it was as simple as that. She missed the forest. She wanted to be where the teak trees stretched high and strong up into the sky. Even where her father and uncle had cleared the forest, the trees still grew and provided bananas and papayas and the like for the family and she missed them, just like she did the rivers and mountains where she had spent her childhood.

In truth she was sick at heart at having to live in this place. There was no real forest, and except for the cliffs by the river the mountains were nothing more than misty shapes on a distant horizon. To make matters worse, last year's fire had reduced many of the wooden houses to nothing more than a blanket of ash. The houses that had replaced them were small and simple as if waiting for another fire to put them out of their misery. She never told anyone that she felt that way, how could she? She had to be strong for her mother with father away so much, and K'Paw Meh being so difficult. And little Ma Nay and Mon Kyaw needed her so much.

Jonathan dismissed the class, inviting some of the students to linger if they wanted to talk with him. Htee K'Paw and many of the other girls saw this as their opportunity to slip away from the classroom whereupon they hung about outside for a few minutes before making their way to their respective dormitories and homes.

"How's it going?"

She jumped at the sound of the strange voice and then turned and waited as Tim drew level with her and Hser Mu. "The classes are going well thank you," she spoke in her best English. Ever since the evening when they had first met the new students and teachers and had begun the teaching course that she had looked forward to for so long, she had felt a strange disturbance. It had started when Tim, had looked at her across the room with such intensity. Then she had been shocked to discover how much Hser Mu, the friend who had stayed close to her throughout her time at Huay Ko had such different ideas to her own. Now, suddenly Tim's smile seemed to warm her and she found herself smiling back at him.

"Are you going to the dormitory or . . . ?"

"Oh, I live in the camp with my mother and brothers and sister. I'm going home now. You can come and meet them if you like."

"Yes, is that all right? I would like to."

"Of course."

"I'm a long way from home. I miss my family. It would be nice to meet yours," he was saying as Htee K'Paw and Hser Mu turned away from the volleyball pitch between the classrooms towards their homes on the far side of the camp.

"So you're enjoying the training?" Tim said as they walked along.

"Yes but . ."

"But . . .?"

Htee K'Paw heard Tim's questioning tone that invited her to think further about what she meant. "Jonathan asks so many questions."

"Do you find it difficult to answer them?"

"I don't really want to think about them," she said after a long silence.

"What sort of questions are they?"

"He wants to know about our people so he asks about what we think about our country and what we want for the future. Things like that."

"And you don't want to think about that sort of thing?"

Htee K'Paw stopped in the path for a moment and looked at Hser Mu who spoke up. "I think we should think about these things. We don't know enough. We need to learn, and I think Jonathan is trying to make us do that."

"But not many people answer his questions," said Htee K'Paw.

"That's because they are not used to being asked to think. They just listen to what the teacher says. But Jonathan wants us to do more than that," and Hser Mu turned away down the narrow path towards her home. "I will see you tomorrow Htee K'Paw."

Htee K'Paw turned back towards Tim. "I just came to the class so that I could be a better teacher. That's all I want. And if I am a good teacher then I will make things better for the future."

Tim nodded at her and for some reason she suddenly knew that what she had to say did matter. "And I want to go home. This place, look at it," and she swept her eyes around the narrow vista of untidy bamboo houses built close together, causing Tim to do the same. "I want to go back to the forest. That's all I want. I want to see trees and mountains again and," she hesitated. "That's my home, not here." As she glanced back onto the path she saw the unmistakable figure of her youngest brother ahead of her and in an instant she knew something was very wrong.

"Mon Kyaw," she called as she saw him. There was no sweet welcome for his sister, instead Htee K'Paw felt herself quickening her pace towards the little face that was wide-eyed with fear." What is it?" she cried out as she came alongside him and caught his hand in her own.

"It's Mama," he whimpered, "Mama," the sound came again.

Htee K'Paw felt panic rising inside her as she broke into a run, pulling the terrified child with her. "What is it?" she asked again, her own voice seemed to come from far away.

"It's Mama. She won't speak," said the child almost out of breath himself now.

Htee K'Paw threw a glance over her shoulder and saw that Tim was following her. The little party flew along the path to the astonishment of watching children and adults alike. Then they all turned into a side path and Htee K'Paw and Mon Kyaw stumbled up the steps and kicked their shoes off. Brother and sister quickly ran together through the small area at the front of the house and turned into the bedroom at the side, Htee K'Paw all the time full of dread at what she might find there.

As she took in the scene the air that she had been holding in her lungs was suddenly expired, and she felt relief wash through her. Her mother's eyes were open and she was obviously still alive. But then relief was quickly replaced with a fresh stab of anxiety. She was lying on the coloured mat covered with a blanket just as Htee K'Paw found her most afternoons; but today was different. Her breathing was fast and laboured, so much so that she was incapable of getting enough breath to speak. Htee K'Paw could now see what Mon Kyaw meant. And the customary vague anxiety for her mother now crystallised and took on its full shape. Her mother could hardly breathe; each gasp for air was a fight that was leaving her weaker than the one before. Her face had taken on a new puffiness, just like the swelling of her legs that Htee K'Paw had observed over several weeks but had just not wanted to think about.

"Lets try to sit her up more," the voice came clear and firm from the top of the steps and Htee K'Paw realised that she had forgotten about Tim. If her mind hadn't been so full of panic she might have been embarrassed or ashamed that this westerner was seeing into their home, so lacking in comforts. Instead she was full of gratitude to this stranger who spoke such good sense.

"Yes," suddenly she knew what to do.

"Mon Kyaw, go and get some more blankets will you? Get mine and K'Paw Meh's. Quickly." And the small child awoke from his own terror, glad to be given a task to do.

Then Tim had crouched down beside the pitifully frightened woman and he reached out and lifted her from her lying position. "She will breathe better if she sits up." And quietly and efficiently Tim helped Htee K'Paw to fold the blankets and prop the exhausted woman into some sort of sitting position. But the movement set off a bout of coughing, which racked the grossly weakened body and resulted in a mouthful of white frothy phlegm.

Htee K'Paw threw another look of panic across at Tim and then began to wipe her mothers face with the corner of the towel that she had wrapped around her head.

"Is there a doctor or medic who could see her?" he asked as the sick woman sank back exhausted onto the blankets.

"A medic, there is a medic."

"Can we get him here to look at her?"

"Yes. Yes!" Htee K'Paw was hardly in command of her self. She had never seen her mother quite like this before.

"Mon Kyaw go and find Ma Nay or K'Paw Meh, quickly, quickly." And she looked back at Tim with a gratitude that she could never express in words.

9

Htee K'Paw stood outside the little wooden clinic and took in the freshening evening air. The sky shone a deep dusty pink behind the banana trees and the distant coconut palms and seemed to give her renewed hope after a day that had begun with so little of that precious commodity.

News of her mother's extreme condition had soon passed around the close-knit neighbourhood and the medic had eventually reached the sad little home. After listening to her chest with his stethoscope, feeling her pulse and generally tapping her in a way that Htee K'Paw found fascinating but had never understood, he had diagnosed congestive heart failure.

"What can be done for her?" asked Htee K'Paw and the medic had told her that he would take her mother down to the clinic, where she needed to be an in-patient for a few days.

"I will give her an injection which will make her pass water. She has too much fluid in her and it is putting a great strain on her heart." With that the medic had gone about his business of needles, little bottles of medicine and tablets and then had written some details in a small notebook, all of which were a mystery to Htee K'Paw. Then he had arranged for a cart to be found, and with the help of neighbours and friends her mother had been taken to the clinic. Htee K'Paw had hastily arranged for the care of the rest of the family and had then followed closely behind.

"Thank you," she had told Tim, not knowing how else to express her gratitude to him and he had then left her in a sea of emotions. There were fear and anxiety for her mother, of course, but there was also something she couldn't name, a new hope perhaps, or the stirrings of an excitement that seemed to flutter inside her own heart.

Now, under the expert care of the medics and nurses, Daw Nee Meh had begun to recover slightly and for the first time since yesterday Htee K'Paw found she could relax.

"Hello," the voice came quietly out of the dusk, but the foreign tone startled her.

"Hello," she replied as she watched Tim approaching across the tiny stream outside the clinic building and she felt her heartbeat quickening again.

"How is she?" His voice was gentle.

"A little better, thank you," she wanted to say more, to tell this *kolah wah* how much he had done for her, how much he was doing *in* her, but she could find neither the words nor the courage.

"I've been into the town. And I've rented a motorbike so I can come and go whenever I want to. Sometimes I have a little business to see to there."

She looked at the ground between her feet for a moment, only too aware of the fact that the town was somewhere she could never go in safety. For a moment she recognised in herself a painful twinge of envy, and then felt shame that she should think such a thing.

"And I have a present for you," Tim said and to her amazement he passed her a heavy bag with what seemed like a collection of small packages inside it.

"What is it?" For some reason that she couldn't fathom, she was almost afraid to open the bag.

"Open it and see," Tim smiled encouragingly.

Carefully she obeyed him, taking out the small packets one by one. She read the word *Digoxin* on some of them and *Frusemide 10mg* on others. She couldn't bring herself to understand what she was reading.

"They're for your mother. I spoke to the medic. He told me that she will get a little better for now, but she needs these medicines for the rest of her life. But they don't have enough here in the clinic. They will run out very quickly if they give them to her every day. So I went and bought them for you. And at the bottom there are some noodles for your brothers. And there are some oranges too. They're just a little present from me."

"You bought these? Thank you, thank you," she couldn't think what else to say.

"Yes, I went to the pharmacy in town. They were very helpful." And the storm that had raged inside Htee K'Paw for the whole of a night and a day suddenly broke and she felt an uncontrollable rush of hot tears to her eyes. In her blindness a hand reached out to touch hers, and she grasped it and held it tight, as if she had been drowning and a rope had just been thrown across the dark water to her.

Another day passed and Daw Nee Meh was pronounced well enough to go home. The fluid that had compressed her lungs and heart so much that she could not even speak had gradually drained away. Now she was able to walk a little, but mostly she sat on her mat propped up against the bamboo wall of the clinic.

"We have medicines for you now, too," Htee K'Paw was hardly able to suppress the joy that she felt. "The *kolah wah* bought them for you. These will last for a long time. You only have to take one each day."

"What day is it?"

"Friday: and father will be home later."

"And you must go to the orphanage tomorrow. You have already missed some of your classes. I don't want you to miss out on everything you do."

"I hope I can go. Tim, the *kolah wah* who bought the medicines is coming with me. He says he wants to meet them all. He is so kind, Mama." And the sick woman reached across to touch her daughter's hand, suddenly afraid for the child who had known such hurt all those years ago.

"Bring your second finger right across, like this Po Thaw. Then strum across all six strings. There, that's right. Now try that, alternating with the chord of D like this," Kler Htoo waited for the child to place his fingers, "G . . . D . . . G . . . yes that's right. You practise that for a few minutes and I will try to tune Hey Nay Htoo's guitar for him again." And taking the errant guitar the young student-turned-teacher twisted the pegs and plucked the strings until he was happy with the tuning. "Now, did you see that? You try it. Second finger there . . . and first finger there . . . and little finger there. The G chord."

He watched patiently as the young boy struggled with his fingers. Po Thaw and Hey Nay Htoo both seemed to have a natural aptitude for the guitar.

84

Young as they were, once he had shown them what to do they quickly learnt the chords. This had been the housemother's idea. Up until now she had always asked Kler Htoo to accompany the children's singing, but she had soon realised how capable some of them were and had asked him to teach them. This was only their second lesson but they were already learning their third chord and would soon have reached the stage where they could accompany some of the simpler songs.

Htee K'Paw watched closely; she too was keen to learn from Kler Htoo. Soon the rest of the children would be coming in and then they would all sing together. That was her particular skill, teaching the harmonies and melding the various parts together.

She could see Tim watching her and the boys from the side of the room. Sometimes she glanced in his direction just to make sure he was still there. Then she would catch him looking at her and would experience a thrill of pleasure that seemed to fill her whole body with warmth. It had been his blue eyes that had at first frightened her, but now she laughed at the memory of her own fears.

The quiet satisfaction she felt at watching the guitar lesson was now slowly punctuated with the noise of the rest of the children as they gradually filed into the room. Then all thoughts of Tim were banished as her attention was fully taken up with them.

Tim sat down on the floor of the bamboo hut that was the hall of the orphanage and watched Htee K'Paw and the children with growing admiration. They sang a whole variety of songs, some accompanied with the guitar, some in what was clearly recognisable as English but, Tim guessed, probably not fully understood as such by the children themselves. He was glad to sit down. Even though this was supposed to be the beginning of the cool season of the year it still became uncomfortably hot. Time passed by gently and still their enthusiasm for singing didn't seem to flag. The music stopped and Tim assumed that the session was over.

He was about to cross the room to congratulate Htee K'Paw when he heard her call, "Mu Ghay". The child obediently picked up a small wooden box and carried it to the front of the group of children and stepped nimbly onto it. She lifted her lean arms smartly upwards and as she swept them downwards again, the children all sat. Then, with military precision, the child swept her arms upwards and the whole group stood as one. It was as if everything up to this moment had just been a game. Tim heard a note being played on the guitar and then they all began to sing in harmonies that he would not have imagined children capable of. Even the very youngest child at the front looked as if she was part of a well-drilled army that marches as a body. They were singing in their own language now, and it was impressive by any standard. The young girl who could not have been more than twelve, had, it seemed to Tim, the sort of control that a professional conductor would be proud of. Without the aid of any musical score she brought in the different parts in perfect time and with upward sweeps of her arms and skilful gestures with her hands she controlled the volume. It was impressive; there was no other word to describe it.

He hadn't been sure what he would find here in the camp. He wanted to do good here, 'give something back,' he had told Jonathan and had meant it. But he knew himself now, and however hard he tried, he couldn't stop it. It was like an addiction, a desperate craving that cried out to be satisfied. People said they hated his sort but they had no understanding of how beautiful it was. Lover of children, that's what their word meant and it was true, that described it perfectly.

And there was Htee K'Paw with her astonishing beauty. He had never dreamt he would find anyone like her in such a place as this. But she wasn't just a beauty. What had at first appeared to be a sweet fragility had disguised a steely determination to succeed in what she wanted to do. The performance of the children showed that; she knew what she was doing and she worked hard at it. She had a strong belief in God too; he could see that. Hers was a faith of strong principles and high moral standards and she wore it openly, as did many of her people. But in her innocence she had brought him to just the sort of place that he had longed to find but had never dared hope that he would discover. He looked again at the long, lithe, girlish limbs of the child conductor and knew he had found what he wanted. And he had the motorbike, the cameras and Gunter nicely established in a quiet place just outside the town. Everything was falling into place far better than he could have imagined. It would take time, he told himself, time and patience; but it was going to be worth it. And his flesh began to tingle with excitement at what he had found.

10

The tall young man who hung back at the end of the class was unmistakable. He was one of those along with one or two others, who were the most fluent in English and therefore the most willing to speak out during the classes.

"I'm afraid I don't know your name yet," Jonathan found the bewildering array of monosyllabic names and their myriad combinations tested his memory to the limit. He had tried writing them all down as he heard each one, and their meanings, but still he seemed to be no nearer to understanding them.

"It's Thaw Reh," the young man answered. It's a Karenni name. I'm from Karenni, in the north."

"Yes, I remember you told me," and he smiled an apology.

"It's hard for you, I know."

"I guess it takes time. There's a lot to learn: cultural differences. A lot of things are very different. I don't mind spending the time. I'm finding lots of things very hard."

"The students don't always answer your questions."

"No, do you know why that is? Do they find the language too difficult?"

"That could be part of the problem for some of them."

"But it's not the whole problem?"

"No." Jonathan watched as Thaw Reh thought for a few minutes.

"We have been taught to respect our elders." Jonathan nodded his encouragement. "And we don't learn to think for ourselves. So, when you ask us these things you're asking us to question what our elders have always taught us."

"How?" Jonathan was beginning to see why he was having such difficulties.

"Everything we do is done because it's always been done that way. Then in school we just listened to the teacher."

"So you're saying that I'm asking the students to think about something they haven't thought about before?"

"It's not that they haven't thought about it. But because we always think that the elders are right we never ask those questions."

"But what about when you're on your own, among yourselves? Do you ever discuss politics?"

"Yes, sometimes we do. And I think we should discuss it more. That's why I think what you are doing is so important. More important than you know."

And in the young man's steady gaze, Jonathan found the reassurance he needed so much. "So you think I should keep going?"

"Yes, you should."

"Why? Why do you think that? Why are you the only one to come forward?"

"Oh, the others will come forward soon. It just takes time."

"You speak English very well." Jonathan watched as Thaw Reh turned away for a long moment.

"An English girl came to the camp." Jonathan instinctively felt himself beginning to smile. Many a lovesick refuge boy had imagined himself in love with one of the young women who came to work in the camps as doctors or teachers, their blonde hair and white skin so distinctive in a place like this. Jonathan recognised in himself a sort of masculine camaraderie with them. He in turn found it hard to concentrate sometimes in the distracting presence of the clear almond shaped eyes and sweet smiles of many of the girls in the classes.

But Thaw Reh didn't break into the laughter of shared masculinity. "She helped me with my English and," he hesitated.

"And?"

"She wanted to stay with me. We wanted to stay together."

Jonathan waited.

Then Thaw Reh seemed to shake himself free from a dream. "Now I'm married to a Karenni girl. She's from my village in Karenni State."

And Jonathan could hear the unspoken sadness in Thaw Reh's voice.

"You see, my wife and I, we both have a story."

"A story?"

"Yes, you said you want to hear our stories."

"Yes, I do. That's what I need. Stories help me to understand. If you want to tell me."

"Shall we go for a walk?"

"That sounds a good idea. Where can we walk to, here in the camp?"

"We could walk across to the foot of the cliffs. From there you can keep going until you get to the river, but we won't go too far. It could be dangerous."

"But don't people cross the border all the time?"

"Yes, they do, but they know the path. Then it's OK. I don't know it yet. I'm not from round here."

"Of course, I remember. You're from Karenni."

And as the two set off Jonathan waited for Thaw Reh to begin his story.

'It started nearly three years ago, in 1997 in Karenni State. Everything in my life was good. I was working with my father and was going to get married. I had even started to build my own house next to my father's. Then everything went wrong." Thaw Reh's face turned into a mask of anguish for a moment at the memory. "My brother joined the Karenni Army. He's still with them . . . or he was when I last saw him. They recruited more men, they had to, the Tatmadaw were getting closer all the time. Then what we all feared happened. They came into our village. They started to take people to work for them. It wasn't too bad at first, the villagers had to build barracks and roads for them. Then it got worse and the villagers tried to resist them. That's when it happened."

Jonathan watched as Thaw Reh hesitated.

"It was my youngest brother. They wanted to take him to work for them. They wanted porters. They were advancing and they wanted porters for their equipment. My father tried to stop them. That was when they shot him. He died; he bled to death and there was nothing we could do to save him. It was then that they took Suu Meh, too. That day they took people from all over the village."

"You?"

"No, I was out that day. But I joined up after that. I hated them. I hated them so much. I was mad for revenge, so I joined our army, the [13]KNPP. But it didn't do me much good. After a few months I was taken prisoner myself. The only good thing to come out of it was that I met Pee Reh. He became my greatest friend. We escaped together and came to Thailand. It turned out that his uncle runs the refugee camp school. I became a teacher there. That's how I come to be here."

"But what about your wife?"

"Her story is much worse than mine. I was a soldier and a prisoner of war and you could say that becoming a prisoner was a risk I took. But my wife deserved none of the suffering that she endured."

Jonathan waited while Thaw Reh lapsed into silence. It seemed to him that he was stalling and Jonathan had to struggle not to show his impatience.

At last Thaw Reh spoke. "She hasn't told me everything. She finds it very hard to talk about, but I know some of the story. The soldiers in the company kept the women with them all the time. They worked as porters by day and had to cook for them in the evening too. One of the officers kept Suu Meh with him. She had his child." Thaw Reh turned away for a minute and Jonathan waited knowing that he was intruding into what must be a deeply painful issue for Thaw Reh and his wife. Sarah had told him about some of the atrocities committed against civilians by the

---

[13] *KNPP Karenni National Progressive Party* An ethnic resistance army from Karenni to the north of Karen State.

Tatmadaw but he had never thought to be hearing about such things from one of his students.

"It was when she was pregnant that she escaped. One of the men kicked her in the stomach and the baby died. She was very sick after that. It was Katie who saved her life."

"Katie?"

"Yes, Katie, the English girl. It's a long story. Karenni soldiers on patrol in the forest found Suu Meh and brought her into the camp where Katie was working in the clinic. She saved her. She helped to stop the bleeding and then she looked after Suu Meh. She loved Suu Meh too. They became almost like sisters. It was a strange thing but she brought us together again. I would never have seen Suu Meh again if it hadn't been for her."

"Katie? Yes, I remember her. She was in Camp Tewa last year. I met her but I didn't know any of that."

Thaw Reh was quiet then and the two walked along beside the river. "I'm sorry, my story has made you unhappy. I should not talk about it."

"Oh yes, you should. I was just thinking how sad it was."

"Sad, but we keep going. We must."

"And?"

"And you want us to tell you what we think about our future?"

"Yes, I did. I do," Jonathan had forgotten about his own agenda.

"I can tell you. Life has changed for me so much that I think differently now. Once I didn't know anything more than what happened in our village. Then, when my father was killed I wanted to fight with the KNPP. I thought that was the only way to get justice. I hated all the Tatmadaw soldiers and I wanted nothing to do with them. But a young Burmese soldier, Aung Gyi helped us to escape from their barracks. He came all the way to the border with us and joined us in the camp. He became one of our friends. There were many like him, so many of them. We shouldn't be fighting them. That made me realise that there is no future in fighting."

Jonathan's eyes met with Thaw Reh's and for the first time he felt as if he was getting somewhere.

"I remember the catechist in the church talked to me about forgiveness. He told me I had to forgive all those who had done so much harm to my family. I thought that would be impossible. But Katie talked about that, too. And she was right. Once I learnt to forgive I began to see things differently."

"How do you mean?"

"We have to come to some sort of agreement with them. We always used to talk about them as if they are our enemies. Well they are. But then when they join us in the camps they can't all be. And it won't go on forever. There has to be an end to the fighting and we have to learn to live together."

"Do you believe that can happen?"

"It has to happen. What other future is there for us?"

"Are you hopeful?"

"There's always hope, there has to be."

"And do you think many people think the way you do?"

"Some do. And I think more will when they are encouraged to think about it. Remember what I said. They haven't been taught to think about these things."

"So, do you think we should bring this sort of discussion into the curriculum?"

"Yes I do. That's just what we need. It would help us, I think."

It struck Jonathan that in spite of the sadness of his story, Thaw Reh, of all people, seemed to be full of hope and in some strange way, had lifted him out of his own melancholy. For the first time he felt he had found someone with whom he had something in common.

They had now walked some way along the river, further than they had intended in fact. Jonathan stared intently across the water. This was the border. The country whose story had filled him with a growing fascination was just over the river that flowed at his feet. Thaw Reh seemed to read his thoughts. "The river is still high. But later in the dry season people walk across in some places. I guess there may be one of those near here."

Suddenly an idea came to Jonathan's mind. This could be the break that he was looking for.

"Could you take me across?"

"Me? No. I don't know the country. But Ko Maung does. He's a soldier and I think he knows the country around here very well. I can ask him for you if you like."

"Would you do that for me?"

"Yes, I can do that. Medics visit the villages that are not too far from the border every week. They go further in when they can. It's very difficult but I'm sure you could go with them some time."

"That would be just what I need. You see, my supervisor at university said I must meet as many people as possible to get a good picture of what's going on here. It's very interesting to meet all the refugees but they aren't a truly representative sample, if you understand what I mean?"

"Yes, I think I do understand. If you don't meet all the people you can't really know all the facts."

"But the other problem is the language. Can you find someone who can help to interpret for me. Otherwise I am only able to speak to people who know English."

"Yes, I'm sure we can do that. I'll ask around tomorrow."

"Thanks Thaw Reh. That's just what I need."

"And I think you are what we need."

"Hum. Not many people seem to think so."

"I think they will, once they get to know you."

"You think?"

"Yes, I do."

"He's not strong, my husband. He never was. But they broke him . . . they broke him." Jonathan saw the woman's mouth draw itself tight as she bent down to allow the child that had been sitting on her lap to play on the ground in front of her. He judged that she was not many years older than he was, but the suffering, and anger, had already taken their toll on her appearance. "He's a teacher. He was always so kind to us. He would never hurt anybody. He used to teach history. He was just a history teacher; he never talked about politics or anything like that, but still they took him away."

"What happened?"

"It was over ten years ago now. Things got very bad in Rangoon. I can remember my mother never had enough money to buy anything more than just food for us. And she was a teacher herself. Now, I don't know how some of the poorer people managed for money but I didn't think about that then. I was in the top year of High School and all I thought about was passing my exams so that I could get into university. Then one day we heard that the police had taken a student away. Some of them had been protesting about the government and the money. They were in a teashop and the police found the ones they thought were the leaders. They arrested them. And that was when the trouble started." She went quiet for a few moments while her mind ran over the story that had been told so many times. Even he, Jonathan had heard it, read about it, each time with some different emphasis.

"It was a good day at first. We carried flags and some of the classes had made banners. Everyone was laughing and singing. Some of the older ones chanted and we joined in. We didn't know it would end the way it did."

He watched as her face, which had begun to relax, took on a look of fear once again. He knew how the story went, how hundreds of students, many of them little more than children had fled in terror as the police presence had suddenly become menacing. Vast numbers had been chased into the lake and beaten to death with clubs until the water had run red with their blood, some had been raped while the supposed ringleaders had been arrested.

"We ran away. It was panic. I still think about it. It was terrible to be chased like that but I got away. We were the lucky ones. Some people that had been in my class went missing and nobody knew where they went. My mother told me that Kaw San went to the police to ask about the missing boys and they arrested him too. He was imprisoned, that's when it happened. It was only a few times . . . so he said . . ."

"Tortured?"

"Yes, once you're afraid of them they don't have to do much. Even now, just a noise or the sight of . . . " Jonathan saw her face cloud over as she stopped for a moment, "and he looks like an animal, an animal when it's afraid. It was years ago. And he was never even involved. He didn't know anything."

"He's a Karen, isn't he?"

"Yes, but it didn't matter," he heard the indignation in her voice again: it was a kind of desperation. "We lived in Rangoon. Lots of Karens live there. We all lived together in the one place. My mother knew his family and after he came out of prison we met each other and got married. I tried to make him feel better but he was always afraid. We could never stay in Rangoon after he had been in prison. They don't leave you alone after that, and he was so afraid we came out here. Besides, he wanted to help his people, and he knew that he would find a sort of peace here although it's so hard sometimes."

"And what about you?"

"Me? I go wherever he goes now."

Although, from what she had said, Jonathan knew that she was several years younger than her husband he could see from the set of her face that she knew how much he needed her and willingly gave herself for love of him. He had met Kaw San in the school and was beginning to find out just how much people like him had lost.

"And these people. They've been so good to us. The strange thing is that in the city we all believed that the people who lived out here were wild or even savages. The government didn't try to put us right. Now I know that they wanted us to think that way."

She suppressed a short laugh. "They wanted us to think that they were a danger to us, that they would bring all sorts of bad things into the country. They didn't want us to think that they were people just like us."

Jonathan recognised similar misgivings in himself before he had come to this place with his aunt, and, just like the young woman speaking with him now, he had found only warmth and kindness.

"But I worry about him," her face became serious again as she nodded in the direction of the small child that was playing in the dirt at the bottom of the steps. "What's going to happen to him? What's going to happen to all of us? We can't stay here for ever."

Jonathan tried to smile. He wanted to encourage the woman somehow, to see her smile but the friends she had lost in her school days seemed to hang between them and her face stayed closed.

"What do you want to happen?" he asked even while recognising the hollowness of his own question.

"I want us to live in peace. I mean I think we all have to work together in the future. Kaw San talks about a federation. He says that that's the only way for us."

"So he is involved in politics now?"

"He wants to teach students to be prepared for the future. So yes, I suppose he is."

"He's a good teacher, your husband. The students all like him."

"And the children, they need me now." Her face seemed to brighten, while in the silence Jonathan looked around him at the two sparse wooden buildings that constituted the camp orphanage in which Kaw San and Paw Wah lived. For a moment he felt overwhelmed by it's weight of sadness and the sudden realisation that this was what war came down to: homeless and motherless children being cared for by a woman who herself was living a life of quiet desperation, full of the painful memories of her own dead friends.

His eyes lit on a row of neatly folded blankets arranged along one wall. She obviously saw his surprise and hastened to answer his unspoken question.

"They are new. Tim brought them for us; and he brought us some tapes, and a tape recorder. The children have been learning some new songs from him." Suddenly her voice had become animated and the words were flowing freely while Jonathan became aware that he was no longer listening to her. As if from nowhere he found himself filled with a nauseating dislike for Tim but then almost immediately hated himself for it. It couldn't be jealousy; surely he was past that sort of thing? Yet he couldn't mistake the feeling of disquiet he experienced as Paw Wah talked about him.

"So you know Tim?"

"Oh yes. He comes here very often. The children like him."

"Ah, that's good," was his lame response as he tried to smile, hoping that she wouldn't realise that he was far from smiling inside

"Why don't you stay and meet the children? They will all be home from school soon and today they have music practice."

"Yes, perhaps I will. And thank you, thank you for your story." He smiled again, this time more warmly as he fought the sense of unease that had somehow overcome him since hearing about Tim's apparent success with the children.

"Would you like some tea while you wait? They shouldn't be long."

"Yes, yes I would," he replied and as if on cue he heard the clatter of small feet climbing the steps while two small faces appeared at the doorway. Jonathan and Paw Wah had been sitting in what could be called the dining room. There were three longish wooden tables covered with a check-patterned plastic sheeting and here the gathering crowd of children helped themselves to water from the jug that Paw Wah had placed there.

As Jonathan waited he sipped at his tea; he was glad to have the distraction of the sight of the children enjoying some freedom before their music lessons began. After a couple of minutes he put down the mug of the almost undrinkable liquid with its large, black, floating leaves and went outside to join some of the boys in their game with a flat, but nonetheless serviceable, ball. He was thus engaged when Paw Wah called all of them back inside and Jonathan, his spirits considerably lifted, followed them.

As he entered the building once again he saw, to his surprise, two of his English language students that he had left earlier in the day.

"Jonathan," the boy spoke first and extended his hand.

"Hello Kler Htoo, " Jonathan replied, pleased that he had remembered his name. The other student was one of the girls who had sat quietly in most of the classes hardly uttering a word. Now he saw her closely for the first time out of the classroom he realised how attractive she was.

"Hello, Jonathan," she said with a smile.

"Hello, I remember you. You're the one who sang to us on the first night. That was so beautiful."

"She's very good," said Kler Htoo.

"Yes, but I'm afraid I don't know your name, I'm sorry."

"Htee K'Paw," she smiled shyly, "it means 'clear water'. I think that's easier for you."

"Htee . . "he laughed at his own embarrassment at not being able to say the whole name."

"Htee K'Paw," she said again.

"Htee K'Paw," he repeated as he looked for the briefest moment into her dark chestnut eyes before she turned her attention to the children who now clustered noisily around the room.

Jonathan stayed to listen to the children as they sang under Htee K'Paw's tutelage. But it was she who took his attention; he found himself watching her movements, listening to the sound of her voice and admiring her ability to get the very best out of her young charges. And when it was time to go back to his home in the camp he thought no more of Tim.

11

Htee K'Paw?"

Htee K'Paw heard the playful note in her friends questioning tone but chose to ignore it.

"Htee K'Paw," she repeated. "What's happening to you?" It was a spurious question. The beam on Htee K'Paw's face was an all too obvious clue. Htee K'Paw had said nothing to any of her friends. She hadn't had to. And there was no point in trying to fob off the ever-curious Hser Mu with some vague explanation of the recent uplift in her mood.

"What's he like?"

"You know what he's like. He's very kind to us. Mother is better now and,"

Hser Mu saw the slightest shudder on her friend's face as her mind was momentarily invaded by thoughts of what might have happened if Tim hadn't been there. "I know that," she said.

"And the children in the orphanage. He's so good to them. He visits them and buys things for them."

"I know that, too. But what about you?" Hser Mu was beginning to grow a little impatient with her friend's insistence on talking about what was already widely known among the students and those who knew them.

"Me?" Htee K'Paw's face took on its customary shy expression.

"Yes. You. Does he hold your hand? Does he kiss you?" The excited Hser Moo wanted to hear all the details.

"Well, no, but . . . "

"Oh." Hser Mu feigned disappointment. "Well he will. I'm sure he will. If he really likes you he will. Remember when we saw those movies at General Bo Htoo's house?"

Htee K'Paw did remember, but obviously not as clearly as Hser Mu did.

"Remember the American soldier put his arms round the girl and kissed her on the lips? Then he stroked her neck. Then he kissed her, again. Then he whispered in her ear. . ooooo."

Htee K'Paw broke into laughter at Hser Moo's expression of ecstasy.

"Westerners aren't shy like our boys, you know. They kiss you when they want to. Close you eyes, Htee K'Paw, and imagine Tim. Come on," she encouraged, and Htee K'Paw did her friends bidding.

"His arms go round your waist, then his mouth comes close to yours and you can feel the warmth of it. Then your lips touch, soft and gentle, then his hands come stroking and squeezing and. . . "

And the two girls collapsed into giggles. "Oh, I'm so excited." Hser Mu hugged herself.

"Well," Htee K'Paw began, recovering her composure and becoming serious once again.

"What is it Htee K'Paw?"

"I don't know. I'm not quite sure what to expect."

"Are you a little afraid of him?" Hser Mu was ever perceptive of a change of mood.

"No, not exactly, but . . . " she couldn't think what to say.

"But you can't be afraid of him, not when he has been so kind?"

"No, I'm not,"

"Be happy with him." Hser Mu leaned across to her and was serious for the first time. "He's making you so happy. I can see it; everyone can see it. It's written all over your face."

"Yes, I know. I can feel it myself too. Oh I'm so mixed up sometimes."

"You're beautiful, Htee K'Paw. You're beautiful, good and very clever. Everyone loves you. And this Tim, he can see it too. He can see what a good person you are and he loves you, too. I mean it." And the two of them embraced for a moment.

"Thank you, Hser Mu, you're a good friend."

Htee K'Paw began to stir. She lay curled up against the chill of the early morning with her blanket pulled up to her chin, wishing that she could go back to sleep again.

But there was no escaping the fact that she would soon have to get up, however much she wanted to stay in the warm cocoon that she had created for herself. She could already smell the smoke of neighbours' fires reminding her that that would be her first duty. The smell reminded her of her father. When he was at home he was always the first up and would take on the duty of lighting the fire so that everyone in the family had the benefit of some warmth and hot food for their first meal of the day. But now, most of the time the duty fell to her, and she resented the work she had to do to care for her ailing mother, as well as her sister and brothers. She listened to the crack of the flames as they ate the kindling, then at last peered through the gap in the bamboo walls of the house to try to see which of the neighbours was shaming her into reluctant wakefulness. Then the reality of the situation roused her into full consciousness. "Papa," she exclaimed quietly, and rising quickly she tightened her woven *sarong* around her waist and hastened out to join him, "Papa," she said again as she stepped down to the small yard behind the house, beaming with relief that he was home again, and then running into his arms to welcome him. "I didn't expect you home today," she whispered, only too aware that it was not yet dawn and that the rest of the family were still fast asleep.

"Don't you want me home?" he laughed as his face took on a look of mock sadness.

"Yes, of course I do," she replied, "and mother will be so pleased to see you."

"How is she: your mother?" Now his face was full of concern.

"Oh, you should see her. She's much better. She was very ill. One day she was so bad that we had to take her to the clinic. But they gave her medicines and now she's better. It's Tim; you must meet him, Papa. He bought all the medicines that Mama needs, and now she's going to be all right." The words tumbled out of her in her excitement.

"Htee K'Paw, Htee K'Paw, steady there. Don't talk so fast. Tell me what happened while I put some water on to make some coffee. I brought some with me, so we can have it now if you like."

"Yes please," she replied, impossible dreams and thoughts of regret evaporating like the mist that hung in the remembered valleys of home.

Saw Ker Reh brought out the blackened pan that they used for boiling the water while his daughter fed the fire with the wood that was stored at the side of the house. This is what she liked. It reminded her of the times when she had been just a young girl and she and her father had sat by the fire in the early mornings while the rest of the house was still quiet. This had always been her special place, by her fathers side, perhaps more so for her than for the rest of the children born to Saw Ker Reh and Daw Nee Meh.

He opened the precious packet of coffee, measured some into a small metal jug and made a rich brew that awakened her senses. She sniffed appreciatively, and as she did so it occurred to her that her father's appearance was somewhat unexpected at this time and she hadn't even thought to ask him why he was home.

He, in turn seemed to sense her unspoken questions. "They want to dismiss a lot of the people who work in the factories and hotels. They say we are illegal. And they want us to go back."

"Go back where?"

"Across the border, Htee K'Paw. That's where we came from."

"But we can't go back, it isn't safe for us now." Her voice rose in indignation at the impossibility of such a thing.

"Hush, Htee K'Paw. They aren't asking us all to go back, not at the moment. But they are coming round and looking for us. They don't want us to take work from their people, you see. So they want to get rid of us."

Htee K'Paw sat watching her father, her mind trying to take in the situation.

"We were warned that they would visit our place yesterday, so most of us left in the night and came back here."

Htee K'Paw was quiet for a moment while she thought about the consequences of what had happened.

"Don't worry. Mr Chang likes us. We are good workers. And he doesn't have to pay us as much as the local workers. As soon as things quieten down he will have us back, I'm sure of it. We'll just have to manage, that's all." He handed Htee K'Paw her glass of coffee. "Now," he said as he at last settled himself into his customary squatting position beside the now cheerful fire and lit one of the cigarettes that he had brought from town. "I want you to tell me what's been happening here."

"It's mother. I was so afraid for her," she began and then told him the story of her discovery of her mother, and Tim's intervention in the situation. "So now she takes medicines, which will keep her well. The medic says that she has to take them forever. Her heart has been damaged so she can't live without them. But that's all right because Tim says he will buy them for us. He's been so kind to us, and to the children at the orphanage and . . . "

Her father waited for her to continue. "And? well? And what, *po qua mu*?"

Htee K'Paw gave a small laugh and looked into the fire before returning her father's gaze. "I don't know what."

"And you like this man, this . . . Tim?"

"How can you tell, Papa?"

"Because I know my little Htee K'Paw, that's why."

"Oh Papa, I can't believe how good he is. He teaches us. He teaches English. And everyone likes him. He comes to visit us too, specially."

"And he's making you very happy. I can see that.

Htee K'Paw felt the warmth of her father's smile, "but . . . "

"But?"

Htee K'Paw stared into the fire again while she tried to find the words. "I don't know."

"You say that he's very kind and good, but you're not quite sure of him?"

"Yes, because he's a *kolah wah*. He's different and Hser Mu thinks I'm just being silly. She thinks all *kolah wahs* are like gods.

"Hmm" Saw Ker Reh grunted amiably. "But they are very good to us, the ones who come into the camps. They help with the schools and the clinics. And it's not just here. I meet people from other camps and they all say the same thing. If it wasn't for the *kolah wahs* we would be in a sad state now."

"I know that. Look at the teacher training. We would never have thought of any of these new ideas for the children without them."

Saw Ker Reh slipped his arm around his daughter's shoulders. "The world is changing *po qua mu*. We left our home and we left our old ways. We have to learn new ways to live now. Sometimes it makes me sad when I think of it."

"Yes, I know Papa. I just want to go home, but when? When will that ever be?"

"It's hard when we don't know what the future holds for us. And it takes courage to learn new things but we have to go forward. It's the only way now. I can see why you are so uncertain. It's strange and new, but if he's a good man, as you say he is, then you must give him a chance."

"Oh, Papa, do you really think that?"

"Yes, I do Htee K'Paw. I want you to be happy almost more than anything else in the world. Would you bring him to meet me, Htee K'Paw? That is our way when you young people meet each other, isn't it? Then you can be sure that I like him. Perhaps you will be happier then."

Htee K'Paw could feel her spirits lifting by the second. "I'm sure you will like him. Thank you Papa. Thank you."

12

"Hay Nay Htoo told me that he likes to go fishing," Tim said as he sat on the upturned log watching Paw Wah as she prepared supper with one of her helpers. He had been a regular visitor to the orphanage of late.

"Some of them like to fish, yes," and she gave him a coquettish smile. She knew he was watching her and it made her aware of her own movements. She hadn't felt under so much scrutiny by a man before, especially a *kolah wah,* and she felt awkward. But in a strange way she enjoyed the attention. "They are good children, very good. They bring us fish to eat sometimes," she laughed shyly, afraid that her English was not good enough, although he never seemed to laugh at her or tell her she was doing anything wrong.

Htee K'Paw joined them in the kitchen and Paw Wah turned back to her cooking. She took hold of the bag of garlic that Tim had presented her with and began to break the bulbs apart. Then she took a sharp knife and cut and skinned the cloves and flung them whole into the oil in the large cooking pot that was resting on the fire. The pan hissed and smoked for a moment and Paw Wah shook the pan so that all the cloves were softened and their aroma filled the kitchen.

The sight and scent of the food cooking filled her with pleasure and gratitude towards Tim for all he was doing for the children and for her. The gift of meat, vegetables and especially garlic was just one example. There had been footballs, paper and crayons, biscuits and fruit juice and now this special treat of a break from the monotonous diet of rice and chilli. She added the beans to the softened garlic so they would have just a few minutes cooking time, gave the stew a stir then poured it all into one of the serving plates and took it into the adjoining room to add it to the small array of dishes that were already on the table.

Now Tim and Htee K'Paw sat at one of the wooden tables and Paw Wah again saw the light in the girl's eyes. She could have been tempted to be jealous of the happiness that showed itself all too clearly on Htee K'Paw's face, but instead she bathed in the warmth of it. After all, Tim's visits to the orphanage were making her happy too.

"So, can I ask them to take me fishing too?"

"They only go down to the small river, it's nothing special."

"It's special for me, I've never been there,"

"Well, if you really want to."

"Of course. It would be a pleasure," insisted Tim. "Perhaps on a day when they don't have school?"

"Yes, that would be Saturday."

"Saturday then. I'll come here in the morning and meet them."

"You're very kind," Htee K'Paw whispered to him as they sat together in the darkness on her parent's veranda.

"Well, you're very kind to me."

"But what have I done for you?"

He laughed gently and reached for her hand. "You've welcomed me to your home, what could be better than that?"

"But this isn't a real home. Look at it. It's just a bamboo hut. My real home is back there on the other side. How can I call this a home?" and Tim heard for the first time, a hint of bitterness in her voice.

"But you made me welcome in it, and that's enough for me. My home is thousands of miles away and I was very sad until I met you. Now I'm happy. I have you, and that's enough for me."

Htee K'Paw looked down in embarrassment and then felt the warmth of his body as he leaned towards her. She stayed very still, wanting more than anything to feel the touch of his mouth against hers, but at the same time afraid that one of her brothers or her sister would be sent out to chaperone her and the moment would be ruined. She glanced up and saw his face close to hers, his eyes fixed on her. Then he laughed softly and picking up her hand he kissed it. Then she laughed with him.

Htee K'Paw could hardly contain her excitement as she listened out for the rumble of Tim's motorbike. He stopped the engine in the lane at the end of the row of houses and she watched as he came closer. Now she ran back into the house to check on her mother and collect her things.

"I'm going now," she said, "will you be all right?"

"Of course I will, I'm much better now, but you take care won't you?"

"Yes, I will," she replied lightly, ignoring her mother's look of concern. Htee K'Paw felt her heart overflowing with gratitude once again for what Tim had done for them all just by buying medicines for her mother. It was as if the whole house had been restored to health and was filled with warmth once again. She picked up her bag and stood at the top of the steps already feeling her own heart thumping.

"Ready?" she heard warmth and pleasure in his voice and replied with a smile, then said goodbye to her mother.

"Goodbye, Htee K'Paw, and don't forget to go to uncle's in the Mae Ramoe Road. You can go to church with him."

Trips outside the camp were rare indeed but she had visited her uncle before. She had enough things for the night and knew that she could guide Tim to the place when night fell. Then she was on the back of the bike and Tim was kicking the engine into life. In an instant they were away, moving slowly along the narrow dirt tracks then up the steep rise, out of the gate, and onto the metalled road.

It was cold on the bike. She had put a thin jacket on over her prettiest tee shirt but it was still very early in the day and the warmth of the sun hadn't yet penetrated the cloud layer. She held onto the side of the bike at first, then Tim had suddenly slowed down for a few seconds, taken hold of her arm and placed it around his waist. She clung to him gratefully for the rest of the journey. "I have to make a visit, he had told her. It's on this side of town so we'll go there first." She had nodded, full of excitement at the prospect of her first trip to the town with Tim.

The wind chilled her and she was thankful when they at last reached their first destination. In order to reach it, Tim turned off the main road and onto a side street. After another two minutes he turned again and stopped outside a wooden house, more substantial than the camp ones but still of a fairly basic construction. A woman of about Htee K'Paw's age sat on the wooden bench outside and Tim motioned for her to sit beside her. "Stay here for a while. I won't be long," and shouldering his bag he entered the house.

She was unsure what to do. The woman smiled at her slyly and Htee K'Paw wondered what the smile was hiding. She heard voices above her and instinctively looked up to see a large white man leaning over the balcony and looking at her while Tim stood beside him. She heard the murmur of their conversation and then, as it went quiet, she assumed that they went inside the house again. She didn't know what to say to the woman; she was unsure even what language she spoke although by her appearance Htee K'Paw guessed that she was probably one of her own people. She tidied her hair thinking it would be more sensible to catch it up in a clasp rather than having it blowing all over her face as it had been.

"Very pretty," said the woman and giggled. Htee K'Paw tried to cover her own embarrassment with a smile, which she decided must look equally artificial. She felt like a fish out of water, unused as she was to meeting strangers.

At last Tim reappeared. "All right, good. We can go now. We'll go into town and buy a map and decide what to do from there. I know there are waterfalls and some temples to visit. How does that sound?" Without waiting for an answer he motioned for her to climb back onto the bike and set off once again.

Htee K'Paw was overwhelmed with the thrill of the day. They visited a temple complex set on a hill outside the town. She had never seen such a place and tried to catch some of the wonder of it as she sat barefoot and quiet in front of the gold-leafed Buddha. After the dusty brown and green of the camp her senses feasted on the beauty of the gold and the scent of the incense. Once outside, they sat in the shade of the trees by the side of the cafe to escape the early afternoon heat, and she tasted her first ice cream. Then they returned to the town to wander among the shops and market stalls.

"We should go to my uncle's house," she said. "It will soon be dark. I can show you the way."

"I think we should find a hotel, there are plenty here."

A slight unease drifted into Htee K'Paw's consciousness, like clouds in what had been a perfectly clear sky. "But. . . ."

"Don't worry, Htee K'Paw."

"But, I have no card, I can't stay in town."

"You don't have to worry. My friend Gunter told me about a nice place where they won't ask any questions." And he slid his arm around her waist. "If you're with me there'll be no problem. I'll look after you." The clouds blew away again and she felt herself soften under his touch. "We could go and find a place now. Shall we?" and he leaned across and brushed his lips against hers.

She looked around, imagining that people were looking at her, but nobody appeared to be taking any notice.

"What is it?".

"Oh nothing, I'm just not accustomed to being here like this."

And in response his arm tightened around her and they made their way to the hotel. There she watched apprehensively as he enquired at the desk of the small establishment, which, if she hadn't been so nervous, would have filled her with pleasure. After a minute she relaxed a little and looked through to the back of the bar where tables and chairs were arranged on a small balcony. Beyond was a view of distant mountains, already turning a smoky grey in the gathering dusk. She hardly dared look in Tim's direction but if she had she would have seen him lean across and pass a quantity of money into the hands of the man behind the counter, who quietly pocketed it. "That's done," he was back at her side. "Now lets put our bags into the rooms and you can have a shower if you want, then we can go for dinner. How about that?" And he was cheerful and warm with her, as if nothing unusual had happened.

She stood in the shower room, her feet sliding a little on the unfamiliar smoothness of the tiles on the floor. There were taps and pipes and things to press and turn and she didn't know where to start. She knew she needed to ask Tim for help but didn't want to. Already afraid that he thought of her as just a simple country girl who knew nothing of the world, she didn't want to further reinforce the impression.

"Are you all right in there?" She heard him call out, and then he was there at the door explaining what she had to do.

"The water might be too hot, so if it is, turn this."

"Thank you," she smiled nervously as she tried to remember what he said. She took off her clothes, hung them on the hook at the back of the door and carefully turned the first of the taps. The water came out suddenly in a fine spray from above her head and she jumped in amazement. It was cold but soon grew hotter, almost too hot. She stepped out of the way of it for a few moments until she remembered what Tim had said and turned the other knob. Sure enough, in time the water cooled down and she was able to get under it again. Then, she began to experiment and found that she could turn the knob quite easily and adjust the water temperature. She slid under it and let it run through her hair, luxuriating in the warm smoothness of the water; it was never ending. She took hold of the soap and rubbed it all over herself and watched as the water washed all the suds down into the little drain in the corner, then she did it all over again. She began to sing and stretch her arms up high and let the water course down the whole of her body and still it never stopped flowing. She turned her face up to the ceiling and let the stream come straight onto her face and gasped with the pleasure of it.

"Htee K'Paw?" Tim's voice broke into her reverie. She had forgotten all about him.

"Are you all right?"

"Yes, yes, I shall finish soon," and she turned the water off reluctantly as if she had just made a new friend and was afraid they might not meet again.

"What about strawberry?"

"Strawberry?"

"Yes. Everyone in England loves strawberries. Try it." Htee K'Paw and Tim were studying the menu of the small restaurant closely. They had eaten and she was now having fun choosing her second ice cream of the day.

"Hmm," she laughed freely. And what's this mer. . . .?"

"Meringues. I can't really describe then, they're just very sweet and white. Why don't you just choose that one? Strawberries with meringue and cream; you'll love it."

"Yes please, I will."

"And another beer?"

"No, I don't think so thank you." Htee K'Paw knew she had had far too much to drink. She was used to the rice beer that her mother made for special occasions at home but she had no head for the Chang Beer that was being served in the restaurant and that they had both been drinking throughout the meal.

"Do you like it?" Tim asked as she dug her spoon into the desert with relish.

"Yes I do . . . very much." she replied. In truth she found the desert far too sweet for her taste but she didn't want to hurt his feelings.

"In English we say, 'it's delicious'."

"Delishush," she repeated and, laughing, he made no attempt to correct her.

"You're beautiful, Htee K'Paw," he murmured and leaned across to kiss her. And her mouth, all sticky and strawberry-covered opened in response to his. "What about taking a drink back to the hotel?"

"Coke please. I'll have a coke," she answered. She could feel herself beginning to lose control under the influence of the beer.

"Coke? Good. I'll get us a couple and we can take them back with us." They walked together through the dark streets of the town.

Htee K'Paw opened her eyes carefully. She was unsure of where she was but it gave her the feeling of being strangely confined and closed in. This gave her a stab of alarm as she realised that she was in a place that she didn't know, a room very unlike the bamboo-clad one in her home and, there was broad daylight clearly visible outside. The sound of running water reached her ears, her thoughts slowly cleared and she remembered the restaurant and the hotel, the beautiful dinner, and the ice cream. She was surprised that she had slept the whole night through without any disturbance whatsoever. At home she was nearly always aware of the sounds that surrounded her, be they the noises the family made as they shifted in their sleep or the barking of the dogs in the camp. She had missed, too, the early dawn crowing of the cockerels that always reverberated around the neighbourhood. The bed with its smooth sheets and mattress must have been so comfortable that she had slept more soundly than she had ever done before.

Slowly she became aware of other things. Her mouth was dry, as dry as if it were full of dust, and her eyes lit upon the water bottle that stood on the cupboard across the small room. Seeing the water she began to climb out of the bed and for the first time felt the ache in her head and at the back of her neck and a new sensation in her lower abdomen. Still, it was water she needed, so carefully and slowly she straightened up and made for the cupboard. The room seemed to spin round a little and she had to steady herself against the bed to make sure that she didn't fall over. Recovering, she reached for the bottle and poured some of it into the glass. It surprised her that the glass and the bottle rattled together and she took a deep breath to try to steady herself before pouring the water again. Then she sat down on the side of the bed, took some deep breaths and began to feel better. She was so consumed with the need to drink that she realised only slowly that the sound of running water was coming from the next room and she guessed that Tim was probably having a shower.

She looked around the strange room slowly and carefully and then stopped as her eyes lit on Tim's bag. He had left it in her room. 'He must have forgotten it when he came in to help me with the shower,' she thought and then corrected herself, 'no that wasn't the case either.' She was just beginning to think about why the bag was there when her attention was drawn to something else. Tim's camera was on the top of the bag as it rested against the bed.

Forgetting her slight malaise she reached across for the bag and, overcome with curiosity, took out the camera. She had watched him work it yesterday and listened for the slight click as she turned it on. He had proudly shown her the pictures he had taken of them both and they had laughed together. She wanted to see them again, to remind herself of the thrill of the day and quickly found the button that allowed her to look back through the camera's memory. She saw a picture of herself eating the ice cream, standing beside the enormous reclining Buddha, sitting outside a shop,

121

smiling all the time. She flipped further through the pictures. Here was one of some of the children in the orphanage. The next one was of Mu Ghay looking overjoyed to be in Tim's picture. She felt happy too, happy to see that Tim got on so well with the children. It must do them so much good to have someone like Tim to take an interest in them. She flipped further back. Here was a picture taken by the river; it was of some of the children playing in the shallows

"No."

She had been so absorbed that she jumped. Tim had come into the room with a towel around his waist and his hair wet and tousled from his shower. In an instant he was beside her and had snatched the camera away from her with a shout. She looked up at him in amazement.

"I'm sorry. I have to be very careful with this. It was very expensive."

Htee K'Paw felt her heart beating hard and her head began to ache again. She could see the thinly veiled anger on Tim's forehead.

"Look, I'm sorry I startled you. Shall I get us both some coffee? Do you like coffee?"

"Yes, yes please," she felt curiously deflated.

"You look very pale, Htee K'Paw. Coffee will do you good. And I'll try to get some fruit juice, too," he disappeared into his own room then reappeared dressed in a pair of shorts and a shirt. He hurriedly found some coins from inside his bag and made for the door.

"I won't be long," he said and Htee K'Paw noticed that this time he took everything with him leaving her with a vague uneasiness and her mind filled with confusion.

13

"What about these for your brothers?" Tim was pointing out the toy cars on the market stall.

Htee K'Paw felt a lump rise to her throat. Tim's generosity was overwhelming. He had already bought new sarongs for her mother and herself, shirts and blouses for the whole family and now he wanted to buy things for Ma Nay and Mon Kyaw. In her mind she saw their two happy faces and was filled with simple joy again. "Oh yes, they would love those," and no sooner were the words out than Tim had reached into his pocket for his wallet again.

He smiled at her. "You are the most beautiful girl I've ever known."

"That can't be," she said with a small laugh in her voice. Suddenly, a more present urgency gripped her. "My uncle! We didn't go to see my uncle. Mother will want to know everything, she always does. She'll be full of questions."

Tim turned back to her with mild gentle laughter on his face. "That's no problem. If you can direct me to the place I can take you there. We can finish our shopping this morning and then go and visit your uncle this afternoon before we go back to the camp."

She smiled at him with relief. Once or twice her thoughts had momentarily returned to the confusion of the early morning but she quickly brushed them away, ashamed that she had ever thought that Tim was anything less than good and kind to her. He was exquisitely attentive, just as he had been the previous day, and had duly taken her to visit her uncle so that she was ready to answer all her mother's questions when the time came. The visit to the town lifted her spirits, relieving the monotony and drudgery of life in the camp for just two short days and as Tim turned the motorbike off the road and into the rough wooden gateway near her home, she felt that she could face it once again.

"So what happened? Where did you go?" A chorus of questions greeted Htee K'Paw as she joined her classmates on Monday morning. It was the last thing she wanted, but visiting the town was something of a treat for all of them, and the fact that her visit had been with a foreigner, and a young, eligible man at that, had marked her out and was guaranteed to invite comment.

"Yes, we went to the town."

"And did you go round and look in all the shops?"

"Of course. And he bought things for all the family. He's very kind."

"Did you eat in a big restaurant?"

"No, just a small one, but the food was very good. I had strawberries. Do you know what they are? They are a very famous fruit in England. Very sweet and. . . "

The questions came thick and fast but Htee K'Paw had prepared herself. She filled the air with the practicalities of the visit so that their curiosity was satisfied. She hoped that the excitement would then soon die down. The girls were all desperate for news and information of the world outside. Their lives were all confined to the narrow, dusty brown of the camp and for them the town represented a life of colour and excitement that they could only dream about. Htee K'Paw had risen almost to the point of stardom after her excursion, and her attempts to keep quiet about the whole thing were fruitless. She understood how they felt; hadn't she been just the same until a few short days ago? But still she prayed that they would soon tire of it and allow her to return to normal.

At last the class began and for once she was glad to have something to concentrate on. It was true that she was making very good progress with her English and of course Tim was helping her just by giving her the practice she needed, but she still had to work hard at it.

Today Jonathan was asking for volunteers. He wanted to see the class perform a drama. Htee K'Paw couldn't think how it would work but she strained her ears to listen to what he was asking. "I want you to show me what happens in the villages: when soldiers come." He looked around the class to see if they had understood. "Some of you have told me about the villages. How the people have to leave and the houses get burnt down. Well, I want you to show me; but I want you to do it in English. I want you to perform it for me to help me to see it for myself."

Some of the class were glancing this way and that to catch the eyes of their fellows while some stared straight ahead.

"In English, we call it a play or drama. I want some of you to make up a drama for the rest of us to see. I'll give you a few minutes then I want some of you to volunteer. You can have time to practise and then I want you to show the rest of the class what you have done."

Htee K'Paw wanted to volunteer. She knew she could do it and it would give her something else to think about. Perhaps it would free her mind a little from the strange mixture of disappointment and confusion that she somehow couldn't quite fathom.

"Now, who is going to volunteer?" Jonathan was asking. Everybody sat still, glances passing between them until at last the silence was broken and Po Thaw stood up. "Yes, I'll do it," he was one of the brightest students and a natural leader. Soon two other boys followed him.

"Girls, we need some girls too. Don't be shy," Jonathan was laughing.

Htee K'Paw leaned across to Hser Mu. "Shall we?"

"Yes?" Hser Mu was surprised at her friend's change of heart.

"Yes, I mean it. We can do something. It will be good for us."

"All right then, we'll join the group. If that's what you want."

The two girls stood up, two other boys joined them and the group was complete.

"You can have this class time to prepare your drama. You can practise in your spare time for the next few days, and then you can show the rest of us what you've done. Remember I want you to do it in English. And I want you to show me what happened by actions, not just with words."

The group left the classroom and found a space to prepare in the building that was used as an office and library. Po Thaw took a piece of paper and a pen from his bag and in doing so assumed control of the group. "Now," his authority was quickly established, "we need to write down our story then we have to write down the words. Has anyone got any ideas of what could go in the story?"

"You know what to do, then, Po Thaw?" one of the other boys asked.

"Yes, we did this once before when a visitor came," he replied confidently then placing the pen onto the paper tried to get the group started. "Any ideas? We need something with action in it."

"A fight, we could show how we fight," La Htoo suggested. "My brother once captured a gun. He told me all about it. He said it was very frightening but he got the gun. That was the important thing."

Po Thaw put his pen down. "I don't know. I don't think Jonathan wants to hear about fighting."

"He told us he wanted to hear about how we had to leave our homes. I think he wants us to remember what happened and then show the rest of the class. It must be something that happened to one of us." Hser Mu looked across the group as she spoke, and caught Po Thaw's eye.

"Yes, that's what he wants. We have to think about a story and then show the rest of the class. We must try it a few times so that it looks good. But first we need a story." Po Thaw looked around the group again.

"We all had to leave our homes. We are all the same. We are refugees here," one of the boys remarked.

"Yes, that's true. But perhaps someone has something that they remember," he could see what Jonathan was asking for and wanted to help him.

Htee K'Paw turned to look at her friend and saw Hser Mu's reassuring nod. "Something happened to my family. It's not very much but I remember it so clearly. It was when we left our village. I was just a child then. I was twelve years old."

She saw Hser Mu glance round and then Jonathan quietly approached the group.

"How is it going?" he said as he reached their corner of the room and sat down with them.

"Htee K'Paw was going to tell us a story. We thought it might be something we could use for a drama.

"It is not much, and I was just a child," she wondered how something that happened so long ago could possibly be of interest to Jonathan.

"Yes, that's what I need to hear. That's what I need to see. It would be interesting for the whole group and it would give you ideas for activities for your children when you teach them. It would be good to hear what you have to say."

"It was the first time in my life that something bad happened to me," Htee K'Paw began, "that's why I remember it so clearly. Every day, even when I was very young, I used to go to see the kittens at the corner of the paddy field before school. They were always there. Papa taught me not to touch them but I would

128

watch them. When they were big enough to hold I would take them out and play with them. The mother didn't seem to mind. I think she knew that I wouldn't hurt them. Every day I saw them, it was as if they were my friends. Then one day I went and they weren't there. I was so upset because I knew they were not big enough to leave the nest that the mother had made for them."

"Does Jonathan want to know about kittens? He said he wants action." La Htoo interrupted.

Htee K'Paw looked at the faces around her, uncertain about what to say.

"What is it?" asked Jonathan, sensing unease in the group.

"Htee K'Paw is trying to tell her story but La Htoo says there is not enough action," Hser Mu explained in English.

"What is your story then, Htee K'Paw?" Jonathan said.

"I just began to say what I remembered. This was the first bad thing that happened to me and it started with the kittens. I knew something was wrong when I saw they had disappeared. Then I went home and Papa told me that we had to go away. Now I think that the mother cat knew to run away too."

"And La Htoo says there isn't enough action. Yes, he's right, there isn't much, but Htee K'Paw could make it interesting, she could show how unhappy she is, perhaps she could cry a little."

"But that's just the beginning," Htee K'Paw wanted to continue now she knew that Jonathan was interested. "We left the house with all our things and began to walk along the path into the forest. My father was at the front and my mother at the back but there

129

were other people with us too. I remember my school teacher was there. Then Papa turned back and saw that mother was not with us. He went back to find her and left us there in the forest. My teacher stayed with us but I was very frightened. We heard guns firing and I heard the other people in the groups whispering. I think they were saying things about my mother and that made me very sad.

"Yes? Why do you think they were saying things?" Hser Mu asked.

"Because sometimes mother wouldn't do anything. She stayed in the house on her mat and would not move, she would not speak, she would not see anyone. And she was like that on that day. I had heard my father shouting at her in the night. He must have been preparing for us to leave and wanting her to help him. I didn't know what it meant at the time but now I understand it. She was ill but it was very difficult for my father."

"What happened? Did they come back and find you again?"

"Yes, they did but my teacher wanted us to walk on without my father and mother. I would never disobey my teacher but I did that day. Then we heard some terrible noises in the bushes. My teacher thought the soldiers were coming. She took hold of my arm and made us run. Then we saw that the noise came from the pigs. My father had brought my mother with him and the pigs had followed. The noise was so frightening but it was only the pigs," and Htee K'Paw broke into laughter for a moment.

"Good," Jonathan said, "I think you can make that into a drama. You need to decide who is going to play each part and I want you to think about the feelings that Htee K'Paw had on that day. Can you think what they were?"

"She was afraid," Po Thaw said.

"Yes, she was afraid. But there were other things."

"She was sad," Hser Mu said.

"Yes, she was sad. Also she couldn't understand certain things and she was angry about what the people were saying about her mother. You can show all of those things in your drama by the look on your face. Do you see what I mean?"

Htee K'Paw looked around the group as Jonathan talked. Yes, she wanted to try out some of his ideas. For the first time for several days thoughts of regret about Tim were banished from her mind as she tried to imagine how the group could build their drama.

"So you're telling us some of your story after all," Hser Mu said as they walked towards home in the afternoon.

"Yes, and its good. I can see what Jonathan means. He's a good teacher."

The two walked on in silence, then Hser Mu stopped suddenly and faced her friend. "What really happened when you went to town?"

"I told you. I told everyone. They all asked what I did and I told you all."

"Well, yes, you told us. You told us everything, but really you told us nothing."

Htee K'Paw felt her face becoming hot.

"It's just that you seem different. Since you came back you don't seem so happy. You were happier

131

when we were in the class, I could see that, but now you don't ... "

"There's nothing to tell really. He just took me to town, we did the things I told you and then we came back. There was nothing special, I promise you."

"Well what was he like? Was he kind to you?"

"Yes, of course he was," Htee K'Paw replied but Hser Mu took note of the slight hesitation in her answer.

"And did he kiss you?" She laughed, expecting a laughing reply.

"Yes, he did," but there was no sweet inflection of girlish embarrassment. Instead Htee K'Paw looked at the ground between her feet.

"What is it? What happened Htee K'Paw?"

There was a long pause. "I don't know," she whispered at last.

"What do you mean, you don't know?" Hser Mu could hear the alarm in her own voice.

"He did kiss me, I remember that, of course. But . . . "

"He did more than just kiss you then?"

"Don't keep asking me, Hser Mu. I don't want to talk about it any more."

Hser Mu accepted the rebuke. "I'm sorry, Htee K'Paw, it's just that we always tell each other everything. Now," her voice tailed off as she frowned, suddenly feeling a deep concern for her friend. She couldn't think what to say to make her feel better but she didn't want to leave things as they were. Then to her relief she remembered something that some of the other students had been talking about.

"There's a group going inside at New Year. I thought we could volunteer to go with them."

Htee K'Paw glanced across her shoulder at her friend walking beside her but said nothing.

"They're going to visit some of the villages and take supplies. You know how much they need them."

"But what can we do? We're only students."

"Well I heard that the Education Department want us to help the teachers inside with the new ideas. Now we are doing this training we've got lots to offer." Hser Mu couldn't help being enthusiastic about the venture but she could feel, rather than see, that Htee K'Paw was not responding.

"And it will be like going home again. You know how much you are always thinking about how much you miss home. Now is your chance."

"But it won't be the same," Htee K'Paw spoke at last.

"No, but there may be something we can do for those people inside. They are our people and, well, perhaps some small things will help them."

"But what about Mama? I can't leave her, not now. She needs me and so do the boys and K'Paw Meh. There's so much to do and . . ." her voice tailed off.

Hser Mu was silent for a while as the two of them negotiated the path as it narrowed between the wooden houses close to Htee K'Paw's house. Then she spoke again. "Look, think about it, won't you?"

But she knew in her heart that there was no persuading her friend and she was left with a sense of a growing rift between them.

Thinking about the drama had awakened many memories for Htee K'Paw and in her mind she often recalled even the smallest details of the time that they had abandoned the village of her childhood.

133

They had walked along a wide track for much of the day, but now they had turned up hill into a narrow gorge where the river flowed fast beside them. Sometimes it gushed between rocks and Htee K'Paw could hear nothing but roaring as it poured down and whirled and foamed beside her. She wanted to stop and watch the water for a while; it was so beautiful and yet frightening at the same time, but her father hurried her along. The path was steep in places; sometimes she had to take a very big step onto the rocks that blocked her way. Then she felt her father's strong grip at her elbow as he helped her up.

She walked on in silence, the path now so steep that she could hardly get enough breath to climb up over the rocks. Ahead she could see that one of the villagers had picked up K'Paw Meh and was carrying her on his back. Now she wished she was little like her sister and could be carried on someone else's back. But she walked on uncomplaining.

The path evened out a little and she began to recover her breath. It was hot, and under the basket her back was wet with sweat, so she felt prickly and uncomfortable. She wanted to stop and drink some of the water from the river, but nobody else had stopped. The long line of desperate villagers walked on in grim silence and she knew her father would not let any of them stop, least of all mother, for fear that they might get left behind. He had kept a tight hold on her since her untimely disappearance at the beginning of the journey.

As they walked the roaring that had been in the background grew ever louder and the column of villagers, their friends and neighbours for many years,

134

slowed to almost a stop as they watched the waterfall. Htee K'Paw had never seen anything like this before. The water poured over the edge and fell in a great sheet into the wide pool below. It hit a rock on its way down, so that it gushed out and made a pattern of foaming whiteness. A mist had settled around the falls, and as she watched Htee K'Paw could see a small rainbow. She gasped and felt a strange shiver run through her body; she had never seen anything so lovely to look at. Then her father was beside her; he too looked up and she could see wonder on his face.

"It's beautiful isn't it Htee K'Paw. When we see things like this then we know that we have a good God." Htee K'Paw did indeed find both the waterfall and the rainbow beautiful but she reached out for her father's hand; that was the only secure thing she had to hold onto.

Now it sometimes seemed as if not much had gone right for her for a very long time. But that was true for many of the students. Hser Mu herself had lost her own mother at a very young age and others she knew had no idea of where their parents were or even if they were still alive. There was no place for self pity here in the refugee camp; it was almost an unwritten rule that you had to get on and make the best of things. And now there was a chance for her to do something that was dear to her heart; she often thought about wanting to go home, so why had she told her friend that she didn't want to join in with others and take the first opportunity she had been given to travel across the border?

She didn't want to think about the answer to her unspoken questions. She preferred to be busy, so busy that she had no time to think. And most of the time her life was full, full of the grinding toil of caring for her mother and her young brothers, not to mention her own studies. But there was no escape, in the quiet of her own room at night her mind would churn relentlessly round the thought that the trip with Tim that had begun with such promise on that fine Saturday morning had been tainted and soured in a way that she didn't want to think about.

14

"How is it going?"

Jonathan thought the question sounded as if it came out of politeness rather than real interest but he wanted the company so ignored the inflection that he was certain he could hear in Tim's voice. "Slow, very slow," he wasn't going to pretend otherwise, but he didn't like to admit that he was not gathering material as fast as he would have liked, especially to Tim. "And you? You seemed to have settled in very nicely."

"Yes; I enjoy the teaching more than I thought I would. I don't mind admitting I'm good at it, but then why shouldn't I be? I'm good at what I do at home, so I should be able to turn my hand to teaching English."

"You're an arrogant bastard, too," Jonathan tempered his statement with a light laugh. He found that he possessed an intense jealousy towards Tim but wasn't going to let him see that.

"I get on with what I do," and he shrugged his shoulders. "Anyway, talking of arrogance, isn't there a certain degree of arrogance about wanting to study people? It seems a bit like looking at animals in the zoo."

Jonathan suddenly wanted to defend his position after all. "I'm not studying them. You know it's not like that. I'm trying to understand what has happened to them. I want to make a full political analysis. There's so much misunderstanding of the situation, especially by westerners. I want to try to get to the bottom of it. Ultimately a better understanding of the situation helps those who are trying to find an end to all this conflict."

"So you keep probing them for what they think?"

"I have to, that's the only way for me to find out. And I am making some progress. It's just that most of them are so used to accepting what their elders say that they never think about some of the questions I'm asking. I think it's partly that nobody has ever asked them before."

"And some of them don't want to think about what's happened to them. It's too sad so they don't want to be reminded."

"Yes, I guess that could be true in some cases."

"It is; I know it is."

"You're thinking of Htee K'Paw are you?"

"Yes. You know about that, do you? I thought she deserved a treat, so I took her there for a couple of days. She never gets away from here otherwise. None of them do, poor kids."

"There was a buzz about that afterwards. I don't know much of the language yet, but I caught the drift of it. A lot of them were talking about it. Taking a girl to town for the weekend marked her out a bit. There was bound to be talk."

"I guess so. They must all know everyone else's business. But that's not going to stop me seeing her. Why should it? I've got to know the family too. And I've helped them out quite a bit."

"Oh yes?"

"Yes, that's the sort of thing that doesn't get talked about so much. Her mother is very sick. She has to have medicines for the rest of her life, just so that she can keep going, so I've helped them out by buying what she needs. They could never afford it."

"So you help out one family above all the rest."

"Well you can't help all of then, can you? Anyway, what's the problem?"

"My aunt Sarah, the person who first brought me here, has gone into this sort of thing and she's always very careful to be fair in what she does. She runs a charity but she only gives to projects that help lots of people, like schools or clinics. She doesn't encourage people to give to just one family. It causes jealousy for one thing."

"Look, I saw the family needed help and I helped them out. What else was I supposed to do? The woman might have died, for goodness sake."

"Meanwhile you get that nice warm feeling I suppose. What about when you leave? What happens then?"

"We'll cross that bridge when we get to it. And anyway, what have you really done for anyone here? Answer me that. Going round asking a lot of questions and dragging up the past isn't doing anyone any good as far as I can see."

Jonathan was furious that Tim had taken the moral high ground while his whole purpose of being in the camp seemed to be pulled out from under his feet. He rose to the challenge.

"It's what I came here to do. I didn't set out to help anyone as you think I ought to be doing. I'm not in any position to do that at the moment. Still, there's the teaching. That's doing something."

139

"Hmm, anyone can teach. It's the woolly minded thinking that I object to. The idea that somehow all people can be treated equally. It doesn't work at home, and it won't work here, either. I just do what I can, and I don't like the implied criticism that what I am doing somehow breaks one of your aunt's precious rules."

"I'm sorry; I spoke out of turn," Jonathan attempted to be generous.

"It's just that you sound so bloody sanctimonious."

"I said I'm sorry."

Tim gave a suppressed snort. "Accepted," he said while looking out between the bamboo slats at the river below. "I guess you and I should be better friends. We need each other, don't we, in this place; the only two Englishmen?"

"Hmm," Jonathan nodded in resignation.

"I wish you sounded a bit more enthusiastic. Why do I get the feeling you disapprove of me?"

"No, it's not that. It's just that I need to get close to the people here and . . ."

"And you can see that I'm getting closer to them that you are?"

"Perhaps." Jonathan didn't want to admit to himself that Tim's analysis of the situation was an accurate one.

"Look, I've got some beer back at my place. I'll go over and get some if you like."

Jonathan nodded. He had to admit that Tim was being civil. It spite of the way he felt he decided he would at least try to reciprocate. Tim was soon off down the steps and back with a small collection of beer bottles in a plastic bag. It was very welcome and as they both drank thirstily the gap between them narrowed. "So what's this I hear about you going to the orphanage?"

"Oh, it's nothing much. Htee K'Paw took me there one day a few weeks ago and I just couldn't believe what she achieves with them. She's a very gifted girl. She teaches them music. They sing in harmony, conduct and play guitars. They're all very young but it's amazing what she does with them. I go down there sometimes. Play with them; give the housemother a bit of a break."

"Yes, I went along there too. I saw what she was doing too." Jonathan wanted to change the subject. "Is there anyone at home?" he asked.

"Where? In England do you mean?"

"Yes: girlfriend or whatever?"

"No, nobody."

"And what about your work? You've been here for a couple of months now. Don't you need to get back to it?"

"No, it ticks along quite nicely. I go into town sometimes and check on the website, update it, you know. I can afford to take some time off, I've had a few good years."

"But all the business people I know are always pushing themselves to find new clients and so on. They never seem to take real breaks. I don't think they dare."

"Oh, I have enough clients. I'm not worried on that score at the moment. Look, that's enough about me. What about you? Girlfriend?"

"No. It's a sore point. Natasha and I parted just before I left for here. I was looking forward to her visiting me. We could have travelled around together

141

for a few weeks, seen a bit more of the country. But that wasn't to be."

"Sorry to hear that. A row or something?"

"No. I think it died a natural death, for her anyway. She was very clever, she seemed to have everything sorted out; I don't think there was really room for me. I don't think she really needed me, if you see what I mean." Jonathan tossed the last of the second Chang beer into the back of his throat.

"Have another," Tim reached into the bag. "Well there are plenty of girls here, all hoping for a nice white man like you to take them out of their misery."

"Oh no, not for me, my aunt read me the riot act before I came here. She says they're very strict about that sort of thing and I'm not going to get myself tied into any nasty knots, thank you very much. I don't want any fathers or big brothers after me with their shot guns."

"Seriously?"

"Well it's not like at home. If they're that strict you don't know what might happen."

"Who is this woman that seems to put so many restrictions on you?"

"My aunt you mean? A very strong character and I respect her very much." After a pause he continued. "I was wondering. Where did you go when you took Htee K'Paw to town."

Tim said nothing. He merely tapped the side of his nose by way of an answer.

"I thought they weren't supposed to show their faces anywhere outside the camp."

"Well as far as I can see you can do anything you like in this bloody country as long as you grease a few palms. It was a nice weekend for her."

"Yes."

"She's a very nice girl." Jonathan saw an unpleasant leer pass across Tim's face and he felt his hands clenching into tight fists; there was something about Tim that sickened him and he itched to take a swipe at him.

"What?" said Tim, lifting his hands into the air. "I suppose 'she who must be obeyed' wouldn't approve. Is that it? Are you going to write home to your aunt and tell her I'm taking one of the girls out? Will she come running out here to get me?"

"Don't be ridiculous," Jonathan had to consciously force himself to calm down again, "I just don't like the disrespect. These kids are in my English class. I know the girl you're talking about. I like her. She's one of the brightest and I wouldn't want to be responsible for messing things up for her."

"Hang on there. Aren't you being a bit dramatic? I think I know her well enough by now to know what's good for her."

"So you have her good at heart, do you?"

"Yes I do. Remember it's me that's helping out her family. Without me her mother would probably be dead by now."

Once again Jonathan found himself being defeated by Tim's argument. And once again, Tim was the peacemaker.

"Look, lets just agree to differ; we work in different ways, probably both of them valid."

It was true, Jonathan didn't have any real argument with Tim. He wanted to change the subject to a more neutral one. "Look, I'm going across to the other side for a few days."

"Is this for more research?"

"Yes. There are some villages they want me to visit. Apparently some of the older people have some stories to tell."

"Good luck. From what I hear you'll need it."

Jonathan looked down into his third beer. "Had you thought about what day it is?"

Tim gave a suppressed grunt. "New Year's Eve."

"The Millenium."

"They'll all be partying tonight. There'll be fireworks on the Thames, I hear. I guess the night will pass without too much happening here."

"The students have invited us to a party." Jonathan said.

"A party that has to finish at 9 o'clock because of lights out."

"No, there's no lights out tonight. They'll keep the generators on for a special occasion. I'm going. What about you?"

"What, all that rice beer. No thanks. I'll take the bike into town. I've got some friends there. I'll spend the night with them."

It didn't seem to matter what the circumstances or however much he wanted to get on with him, Jonathan still found his encounters with Tim dissatisfying. It was with relief that he turned towards the dormitories where the party was to be held. During his time in the camp he had gained some insight into what was meant by the expression 'party' and it was a somewhat different concept to that of the parties at

144

home. The students often simply sat down and played guitars and sang together, which is what he hoped they would be doing this evening. During the day he had also been aware of large quantities of fried food being prepared and rice beer being carried in. One of the students had clearly been in possession of the key to the generator so at least there was hope of some light.

He had already heard the electricity being used for another purpose too. Some musicians had set up amplifiers in one of the classrooms and were playing, at quite a passable standard, to a crowd that had gathered. Much as he wanted distraction he soon moved away from the performance. His somewhat fraught conversation with Tim had left him angry and dissatisfied; he needed some gentle conversation, which he knew he would find with some of his own students. Eventually he wandered along to one of the dormitories and joined a group that included Po Thaw and Ko Maung and some of the others he had come to know the best.

Among the girls he saw Hser Mu and Htee K'Paw; he felt glad that she was there enjoying the company of her friends. He remembered Tim's words with a stab of irritation; the sort of male banter that he had uttered was not usually used to describe girls like her. On the contrary, the sweet, gentle smile on her face seemed to him to be disarming and almost guaranteed to bring out the best of male behaviour. Or would it? And didn't they all look like that: inscrutable, difficult to read? What was really behind the smile? There were enough western men looking for women in this part of the world. Perhaps they wanted nothing more than an apparently sweet demeanour, or perhaps they didn't care at all, happy just to have found someone compliant and sufficiently poor to be unable to argue.

He glanced across the group at her. She caught his eye for a moment before looking away. What did he see? Perhaps it was embarrassment. He certainly felt that way for a moment. Or was it anger? There was something, perhaps unease of some sort, or a lack of peace.

The group shifted and reshaped itself. Jonathan understood little of what was being discussed except when the students deliberately included him in their conversation. He didn't mind, he was happy to be with them and glad that they made the effort to speak English for him when they did.

"Hello Jonathan." He turned to see Hser Mu at his elbow with a small package of food wrapped in a banana leaf in one hand and a glass of rice beer in the other. "You must try this. It's sticky rice. We all like it. It's our favourite."

Jonathan smiled gratefully and watched as Hser Mu sat down.

"How are you Jonathan?" she asked.

"I'm fine," he replied. "It's good to be here to see how you celebrate things."

"Well, this is our party. Sometimes the older people want to give speeches. But this is better for us. Tomorrow we have sports and dancing. *Done* dancing: have you seen it?"

"*Done* dancing?"

"Yes, our traditional dances. Like this," and she demonstrated some of the dance with exaggerated movements of her hands.

"Oh, no, I haven't seen it, perhaps I should."

"Yes, you must. But the speeches! You'll find those boring. It's all in Karen, all the older people speaking. We just listen."

"Ah." Jonathan decided he must make the effort to be at the celebrations in the morning even though the speeches sounded as if they were something to be endured rather than enjoyed. It would be one more way of understanding some of the ways of these people.

"What about the drama?" He had originally thought of the idea of a drama not because he was at all skilled at it, but because a previous English teacher had once suggested it, and when he had been casting about for possible ideas that had been one of them. "How have you been getting on with preparing something to show the class?" Htee K'Paw joined them. Jonathan glanced at her and smiled, but her smile was guarded.

Hser Mu glanced at her friend too then spoke for both of them.

"We can work out the words and the action but sometimes we need to have noises, sounds."

"What sort of sounds?"

"Htee K'Paw says that they heard the sound of guns and then the noise of people running through the trees. That's what made them feel so frightened."

"So you want sounds that will make the story seem more dramatic."

"Dramatic?"

"I mean exciting, you were frightened Htee K'Paw and you want the class to feel frightened too. Is that so?"

"Yes, that's right." Hser Mu answered.

Jonathan felt a slight stirring of irritation. As kind and well meaning as she might be, at that moment

147

he wished that Hser Mu would go away and let Htee K'Paw speak for herself.

"What do you think Htee K'Paw? Do you want the class to feel what you felt then?" Jonathan watched as the smile on Htee K'Paw's face opened out and she realised what could be achieved.

"Yes, that would be good. Can we do that?"

"Of course. We call them sound effects. They are very important in drama. It means we have to find something that makes the right noise. Perhaps you can think of something that makes the noise of a gun."

"Firecrackers? We could use some of those; they would sound like guns firing but I don't know about the noises of running."

"Perhaps something that makes a rustling noise."

"We need to think about that a bit," Hser Mu said.

"Paper, paper," Htee K'Paw said," we could use some old paper. It's dry like leaves. Perhaps we could use it to make the right noise."

Jonathan joined in as the two girls laughed together. "You see, you have some good ideas already. I don't think you need my help at all."

"Thank you Jonathan," Htee K'Paw said with a smile, which seemed to reach right down inside him. Suddenly he wanted to touch her lightly, gently, tell her how much he admired her, tell her how much he liked her and wanted to get to know her better. But that would be against the rules; Tim had got there first and at that moment he wished with all his heart that he had never set eyes on Tim.

Then as if to escape from his own embarrassment he turned his attention to the banana leaf package in his hand.

15

For the first time since he had been in the camp Jonathan felt the chill of the night. When he had first arrived in September he had been pleased to see the small gaps between the woven split bamboo of the walls of his bedroom. For one thing he enjoyed watching the view as he woke up each morning. It seemed to him that if he ignored the suffering of the refugees and the political conflict that raged around them he was living in his own little corner of paradise. As he looked out to his left, a sharp steep cliff rose high into the sky. It was partly wooded but above the trees the rock-face rose in lofty grandeur, sheer and white, tinged with a dusky pink at the edges; it was bare of any sort of vegetation. Then, below him and to the right a small tributary of the larger river wound languidly between the small houses. And of course any moving air, of which there was usually precious little, would at least refresh him, because although this was supposed to be the cool season, it could still be oppressively hot in the middle of the day.

But now it was different. He wasn't sure how far the night had progressed but it was still dark so he sat up in bed and reached over to take hold of the spare blanket that he hadn't used for the three months that he had been in the camp and wrapped it around himself. For some strange reason he thought of boarding school and the way he had crept under the blankets for warmth in the cold dormitory. Quickly he drove the thought away by trying to imagine what the day was going to bring. Thaw Reh had spoken about danger. What had he meant? Was he really taking such a risk? Ko Maung had promised to wake him early; he had said that the boat would leave before daybreak. Jonathan was glad, it was good to be going out in the cool of the early morning and getting out of the camp. And he was looking forward to doing more research. He had told Tim when they had last spoken a few days ago, that things were going very slowly but when he thought about it he had made considerable progress since September. It was true he hadn't a great deal written down and the students weren't necessarily saying much yet, but he was getting to know them and they were beginning to trust him. And the ground was being prepared so that some of them understood what he wanted and were prepared to go out of their way to help him. Today's excursion to villages inside Burma proved that. They were beginning to behave as if he belonged with them and Jonathan was looking forward to the trip.

The discussions with Tim that had been conducted in the mellowing haze of several bottles of Chang beer were now, in the cold early morning, beginning to disturb him somewhat.

It had hurt him to hear one of his pupils being referred to in such a way, especially one who was proving to be so good, with apparently so much to offer. He had admired her for being brave enough to try to take part in a drama in a foreign language. He knew how hard many of them found it, especially the girls with their natural shyness, but he had caught a glimpse of real strength and determination behind the seemingly delicate attractiveness. And the drama had turned out better than he had expected. He was finding it difficult to equate what he had seen of her with Tim's attitiude.

He regretted that he had brought Tim to the camp with him, but he pushed that particular thought away with all the others that proved to be uncomfortable. After all, everyone seemed to like Tim well enough, nobody so far had had anything bad to say about him and wasn't he proving helpful at the orphanage too?

Thoughts churned around in Jonathan's head so much that sleep was now almost impossible. It seemed to him that he had just succeeded in dozing off when he was being woken again.

"Time to get up Jonathan. Coffee?" Ko Maung's face was just visible in the gloom.

Jonathan thanked him with little more than a grunt. It was colder than ever and shivering he began to pull on some clothes, zipping his fleece up to his neck. As he hovered at the door of his room he heard the crackle of a fire and the sharp scent of wood smoke pricked at his nostrils. He looked across to the kitchen and saw a small group of people assembled around the fire to warm themselves. They were mostly men, but to his surprise Jonathan saw some female faces, among them Hser Mu's. He quickly scanned the faces again to see if Htee K'Paw was among them too but she wasn't.

A couple of the men moved to welcome him into the circle and immediately he recognised them from his English classes. Hot black coffee was handed round, then the members of the party set to the task of doing up rucksacks, tying on extra blankets, securing straps and so on. He had been told that they would be away for a matter of days but as he looked at the packs that the others were bringing he was suddenly aware of how he had overloaded himself by comparison. He opened the top of his rucksack and quickly began to take out some of the extra clothing but decided to keep the sleeping bag in view of the chill in the air.

Ko Maung disappeared for a few moments then returned with his rifle slung over his shoulder. "We leave now," he said quietly. "Down to the river." And the whole party set off, splashing across the shallow stream and down the well-worn path towards the main river, which was the border with Burma.

It was still dark as they reached the river but Jonathan could just make out some more figures standing on the shore. All of these were dressed in some sort of uniform and sported an assortment of rifles and ammunition belts. Two tiny boats appeared out of the gloom and the party, which now numbered more than a dozen people, began to climb in. Each boat was low in the water even without its load, and by the time two people were aboard they were almost shipping water. The distance across the river was not great but there was a visible current and he could see the first of the boats moving downstream. After an interval of a few minutes, one of the boats reappeared and it was Jonathan's turn to step in. He crouched low, the water perilously close to him. He had enjoyed sailing, and still did so when he was at home on the south coast of England. But here, low down in this tiny boat, he felt more than a little vulnerable. Muddy water sloshed around his feet and the sides of the boat were barely above the water line. Still, as he looked around him he saw that nobody else seemed the slightest bit worried so he decided he must ignore his own disquiet.

Now he was glad he was small and, by western standards, of a relatively light build. That had always been a problem for him at school. He had hated the sense of inferiority that seemed to afflict smaller boys like him. But now he felt happy with his size. Some of the western men he had seen in the town had seemed grossly conspicuous lumbering around with their flabby stomachs hanging over their trouser belts. He had been glad to be small for once and he was now even more so as he jumped out of the boat into the shallows and began the short climb through the trees on the other side of the river. His blond hair was the only thing that marked him out in any way as different to the rest of the party. His skin had become well tanned by the sun so that, except for his blond hair, he looked like the rest of the members of the group. That was how he wanted it. His four months in the camp had showed him that he wanted to belong with these people and he did his best to fit in, at least for the time it took him to complete his research.

And if he had asked his companions they would have told him that they wanted him to be safe and safety meant not being visible, or at least not to the enemy. Jungle warfare meant that you became one with your environment and this was how it was for Jonathan now. The simple diet of little more than rice to eat and few comforts had honed his features and hardened his muscles and it was with a new found confidence that he joined the march through the trees. It was as if he was taking yet another step away from his childhood, from the irritations of Tim, from the life he had always known but found to be unsatisfactory, towards the unknown, the very edge of his understanding, a place where he wanted to be.

The thick forest that lined the river soon gave way to the semblance of a road. Now Jonathan could see more clearly. The sky was lightening, leaving a dense mist that blanketed everything with a damp chill. The soldiers stepped to the front of the column and led the group along the road for a short distance and then they turned off into the trees once again until these also parted to reveal some houses and an old pick-up truck.

"It's the car," called out Po Thaw, "after we have our breakfast we take that."

"Oh," Jonathan replied in surprise. "I thought we walked."

"Car here," said Po Thaw. "Then we walk later. Now you rest in the car."

Jonathan laughed inwardly as he thought that at home such a machine would have been abandoned long ago. The car had once been black but any of the original lustre was long gone. There were patches of rust too numerous to count and the nearside door was completely missing. Still, as soon as they had eaten, two of the soldiers climbed into the front and the rest threw their packs into the back and climbed on. To Jonathan's surprise the engine started first time and with a loud, throaty roar the old truck lurched out of its place under the trees and onto the dirt road. The crowd in the back settled down and Po Thaw laughed ruefully at the discomfort as the relatively smooth dirt track quickly gave way to ruts and potholes. Jonathan tried to keep track of the direction. It seemed to him that the car was travelling parallel to the river at first. Then slowly the track began to climb into the forest and up the side of the valley.

In spite of the discomfort it was good to be out of the camp. It was still cool but the mist had cleared and he knew from experience that by about mid-morning the day would be as hot as it always was. He began to relax and tried to rest his head on his pack. The poor night's sleep was beginning to tell on him and he felt himself nodding with the erratic movements of the vehicle.

Suddenly there was a stomach-churning slide and then the movement stopped. He woke with a start to see his fellow passengers climbing out. The vehicle was stuck, badly so, in a wide patch of thick reddish mud. There was no shortage of willing hands and quickly Jonathan joined the crowd and put his shoulder to the side of the truck and the vehicle was soon moving again. However, it was clear that the track had deteriorated considerably and they were making ever-slower progress. The truck reached the brow of a low hill and partly slid, partly drove down the other side and came to a halt near the bottom, whereupon the whole crowd climbed out again, this time taking their bags too.

"The road has gone," Ko Maung came alongside him. "Now we must walk."

"When did that happen?" Jonathan asked.

"A long time ago. It was last year in the rainy season; there were floods: many roads were washed away."

"And it's too difficult to repair?"

"We don't want to repair it. It makes it harder for the Tatmadaw if the road is broken."

And Jonathan nodded his understanding. He was only slowly beginning to realise how much the conflict dominated almost every aspect of life here.

For a short distance they picked their way around the gash on the hillside that was the result of last year's landslide. Eventually they regained the road but soon left it again for a smaller path that wound steeply uphill. Now the whole group walked on in silence. Sometimes the path was so steep that Jonathan found he had to use his hands to steady himself. He drove himself up the narrow path that was becoming increasingly rocky the higher they went. He had long thrown off his warm clothing but he still sweated and could feel his shirt sticking to his back underneath the pack. The thongs on his feet, worn because that was what nearly everyone else was wearing, were a little large for his feet and were consequently rubbing his skin red and sore. He now wished he had worn the old canvas shoes that he had fortuitously packed in his rucksack and made a mental note to wear them for the next day's walk. From time to time he found his thoughts turning to what he had been told about this trip. He had heard the acronym IDP, short for Internally Displaced People and he wondered just how deep into the jungle they would have to travel to reach any of them with the supplies they had brought.

As the path levelled out again he became aware of the sound of a female voice just behind him and glanced over his shoulder to see Hser Mu there. It seemed to him that no allowance was made for the girls who appeared to have little difficulty keeping up and carried large packs on their backs. He was beginning to see that the western perception of these

156

people as compliant and easily persuaded and of the women as an easy prey for male tourists was somewhat off the mark. They were, many of them, highly intelligent, disciplined and very tough.

"Hello Jonathan," Hser Mu caught her breath again as she drew alongside him. "It's good that you have come with us. You will find out more about our country that way."

"I can see the difference already.

"Its real forest here on this side. There are no big fields of rice, there are too many hills. And in many places the forest is so thick that you can get lost very quickly. There are no paths, just mountains, trees and animals. It's very beautiful, but very frightening too if you don't know the way."

"And do you come from around here?"

"No, our home was further south, but it looks like this. The forest stretches for ever, it seems."

"And your English is very good."

"I want to learn Jonathan. I want to go to study more if I can. One of the universities in Chiang Mai has places for refugees; it's very hard to get one of them but that's what I want to do, that's why I work so hard at my English."

They walked together in silence for a few minutes then Jonathan spoke the words that had been on his mind for much of the morning. "Htee K'Paw hasn't come with you. I thought you were always together?"

"We are nearly always together, yes. We came from different villages but then we met each other when we came to live by the river, on this side. We were at the school and were both asked to work as teachers. Then things became very bad for us and all

157

the people living near the river had to cross over into Thailand. We have been good friends ever since. But now," she stopped as she contemplated what she should say to Jonathan, "I wanted her to come but she said she was too busy. It's true, her mother is very sick and she has to look after the family but there's something else and I don't understand it. We used to talk about everything and have such fun together. But she has changed and I wish I knew why."

Jonathan glanced across at Hser Mu for a moment and her eyes met his.

"You like her, don't you?" she smiled.

He stopped walking for a moment then moved forward again. "Yes, I do, but how do you know?"

"Because you look at her. You look at her more than anyone else."

"You can see that?"

"Yes, of course. And I feel sad for you."

"You feel sad for me," Jonathan repeated. He knew he sounded hopelessly inane but realised that he now had some sort of shared understanding with Hser Mu.

"Because of Tim. You see Tim is very clever. He is helping Htee K'Paw's mother and I think that in some way she believes she has to do what he says. But I don't like him. I don't know why; I just don't."

"The same reason why you could see that I like Htee K'Paw. Women are very good at that." He smiled as he spoke in rueful acknowledgement of his own lack of insight.

"And I feel bad because I encouraged her. I thought he was exciting. And she's so quiet. I thought he would be good for her. But I was wrong. The women's thing didn't work that time."

158

"Intuition. Women's intuition," Jonathan said

"Intuition," Hser Mu repeated and laughed at her own acquisition of a new English word.

"Yes. And I was wrong, too. I brought him into the camp with me. He said he wanted to work as a teacher. But I didn't like him much when I first met him. Perhaps I had more intuition than I thought and should have taken more notice of it." He gave a short laugh at the overuse of the word and Hser Mu joined him. He was beginning to realise that Hser Mu probably had about the most advanced use of English of all the students he had met so far, with the possible exception of Thaw Reh.

"So we both feel bad," Hser Mu brought him back to the subject in hand. "I just wish she was here on this trip. She would have loved it. I'm going to visit some of the village schools; the education department want me to see what's happening now so many of them have had to move because of the fighting. There are books and pencils in some of our packs and then, when we have finished our teacher training they want some of us to help out. I think Htee K'Paw would be so good at it. I really hope she comes on our next visit."

A wide valley had opened in front and to the right of them and a man dressed in a longyi and dirty tee shirt appeared at the side of the path. The group slowed down briefly then moved on with the newcomer at the front.

"There are mines here," Ko Maung said as he joined Jonathan and Hser Mu.

"Mines?" Jonathan tried to disguise his alarm.

"Landmines," Ko Maung repeated. "He's going to show us the way to the village."

"He knows the way across the minefield?"

"Yes, he laid the mines."

Not for the first time Jonathan had the feeling that he knew nothing about life in this place. It was as if he had entered into a whole new dimension. He looked along his shoulder at Ko Maung walking beside him.

"They have to mine the paddy fields. The Tatmadaw soldiers steal the rice. It's the only way to stop them. "

"So do they have accidents?"

"Oh yes," it was Hser Mu who answered. "Sometimes children get hurt; sometimes the person laying the mine is hurt. They lose hands . . . and eyes." She spoke matter of factly, as if this was commonplace, while Jonathan looked ahead in disbelief.

"And they still use mines?"

"They have no choice." Ko Maung spoke again. "Here in these places they would have nothing to eat if they didn't use them."

"Where do they get them?"

"They make them," Ko Maung said flatly.

"Home made mines?"

"Yes, of course." He fell silent while Jonathan walked closely behind those in front of him, not daring to leave the path, and grateful that the village was at last within reach.

16

The sight of long horned water buffalo wandering freely between the rough, straw-thatched houses heralded the group's arrival in the village. They all went straight towards a largish building set at ground level, as opposed to being high up on wooden posts, where a straggling crowd consisting mostly of women and children was waiting. There they immediately opened their rucksacks and began their work of listening to the people and treating the numerous ailments that were presented whenever the travelling medics visited.

Jonathan had hardly noticed the two young men who had come into the clinic. He had imagined that they were patients too, until Po Thaw told him what was happening. "They want us to go to their village. It's another walk, but they want us to hurry."

"What's happened?"

"A landmine accident. And it can't wait. Some of us have to go now. Do you want to come?"

Jonathan instinctively glanced at his watch. He had secretly been looking forward to a rest. It was half past four, the time when he usually began to wind down at the end of school. His stomach had growled more then once, reminding him how hungry he was.

Everything in him was saying no, yet here was a chance to see more and he didn't want to miss it. Also Po Thaw was inviting him, genuinely wanting him to accompany them to the new place. Furthermore he could see Ko Maung making hurried preparations to leave very soon too. "Yes," he said at last, "can I carry something?"

Po Thaw responded with a smile, swung round and quickly gathered up his own rucksack and one of the rifles. "No, you just bring your own things. We'll stay there for perhaps one or two nights. It will be dark by the time we have finished."

Jonathan tried to hold the lamp steady as he watched Po Thaw's hands with grim fascination. Less than an hour ago they had been handling a rifle and hauling the heavy rucksacks that the medics had carried along the jungle paths, but now, washed and encased in pale rubber, they were the hands of a surgeon. He worked methodically and steadily. First, he had tied a band of cloth tightly around the top of the leg, then with one hand he had poured a brown liquid over the wound while he gently washed away the worst of the dirt with the other. Then, tenderly and carefully, he had reached inside the torn flesh searching with his fingers for the pieces of shrapnel that had been embedded there by the blast. Now he had taken a small knife and was painstakingly paring away tiny pieces of flesh that had been damaged beyond repair.

When they had first pulled back the blanket to reveal the leg, bloodied and shattered below the knee, an acute wave of revulsion had washed through Jonathan and he had wanted to run away. He had never had anything to do with medicine of any sort. In that respect he was the total opposite to his sister Claire. She was a doctor now, but in her early days as a medical student she had brought home tales of blood and gore, seemingly just to watch his discomfort. Now, looking at the wound, it was as if the flesh had been simply ripped apart. It glistened in the dim light of the lamp that they had given him to hold, while some of the blood had congealed into a filthy collection of dirt and redness. To him, the worst thing of all was the bone that protruded uselessly from the wound. He took a few deep breaths, determined to remain standing. The last thing he wanted was to appear a wimp in front of the others. After all, he had wanted to come here. Now he had to put up with whatever he saw just like the rest of them.

He looked up for a moment at Ko Maung who was sitting by the man's head watching the rise and fall of his chest. Sometimes he would reach across to press some more of the liquid in the syringe into the cannula in the man's arm, then he would return to his vigil and Po Thaw's hands would be the only things in the room that were still moving.

"*Da K'Paw, Da K'Paw.*"

Jonathan snapped out of his brief reverie. He knew some Karen words and this was one of them. It meant light. He adjusted the beam of the lamp so that it shone more precisely onto the dreadful wound and Po Thaw's gently exploring hands.

Ko Maung reached into his rucksack for his own torch and passed it to Jonathan who turned it on and directed the beam at the leg to provide an extra light.

"*Dablu*," said Po Thaw, glancing up at Jonathan with the briefest of smiles and thanking him in his own language before returning to his work.

He worked deliberately, cutting the bone down to size with a piece of wire rather like a cheese cutter which struck Jonathan as remarkably efficient in its stark simplicity. Then, he reached across to the small array of instruments laid out neatly beside him. Taking one of them in his hand, he used it to grasp a small sewing needle and began to stitch the wound together. His hands circled neatly, first taking up the edges of the flesh, bringing them together precisely, and then deftly circled again to make a tiny knot. Over and over again he sewed until Jonathan could see the amputation taking shape at last. And for Jonathan it was as if the dreadful toll of war was somehow overpowered at that moment: overpowered by the skill of a young medic from his English class. He remembered with some shame that he had once thought of the refugees as simple hill-people; now he knew that he would never think that way again.

Po Thaw reached into his pocket and pulled out a cigarette packet. "American cigarettes," he announced triumphantly as if he had achieved something by obtaining them.

Jonathan took one, accepted a light and leaning back against the bamboo wall looked out at the thick darkness beyond the veranda.

"Where did you learn to do that?"

Po Thaw looked down at the floor between his feet apparently too embarrassed to answer the question.

"Surgery? The amputation? Where did you learn to do it?" Jonathan repeated.

Po Thaw looked at Jonathan and laughed. The surgeon had turned into the shy student once again. "Some doctors came and helped us once and I have seen many," he said with a careless toss of his head towards the house where the patient lay recovering from his ordeal.

"That was the first one he has done on his own."

They both turned to see Ko Maung standing in the doorway to the house.

"He's OK," Ko Maung said in reply to Jonathan's unasked question and sat down with them, but not before giving Po Thaw a playful cuff on the ear.

"He's lucky. It was just one leg, a clean break, and the villagers knew what to do." Jonathan knew better than to ask what happened when the victim wasn't so lucky.

"There is an old man who lives in this village. I think you would like to meet him," Po Thaw spoke after a long silence.

"Yes?"

"He has a very interesting story and he speaks very good English. I can take you to him."

"Do you know this village then?"

"Yes, my mother and father live nearby. We know this place. And it would be good for you to meet this man."

Jonathan felt that he was stepping back in time. The house was dark inside, the gloom only a little relieved by the glow of the fire burning in the wide hearth in the centre of a large room. More eyes than he could count looked at him from the corners of the room, staring at him, the strange *'kolah wah'*. Nearest to the fire he could make out a young woman, naked to the waist, with a small, but apparently healthy baby at her breast. Her skin shone in the firelight and her breasts stood out erect and proud. He found himself staring at her for longer than he had intended, his eyes meeting hers with an intense mutual curiosity that reached across a vast cultural divide, until he pulled them away.

"Peg-gy." The old mans voice was little more than a whisper but his eyes shone with gentle clarity as he spoke the words. Jonathan crouched at the top of the steps, placing himself so that he could watch the man's face, while a cluster of childish faces looked on in curiosity. It was early morning and the strong scent of wood smoke pervaded everything as the other adult members of the household set to work, preparing the first meal of the day. "Peg-gy," the name came again, this time more confidently and loudly as if it hadn't been uttered for a very long time and the old man was getting used to saying it again. Sarah had been right. Some of the older people in the camps did have a very good command of the English language and this man was one of them, a proud remnant of a bygone age.

Jonathan shifted his position slightly and moved closer to the old man. He was having trouble tuning his ear into what he was saying; the perfect English was peppered with coughs and long pauses while the old man recovered his breath again each time.

"My uncle brought her through our valley with her mother. They had to get away you see. The Japanese were coming and there was no other way for them to escape. They couldn't get away to the sea so they came up to here."

"Were they British?"

"Yes, British people. The father was trapped in the city so Peg-gy and her mother had to run away." Jonathan found himself smiling inwardly at the pronunciation of the girl's name. The man would have had no concept of a name with more than one syllable so he had divided it up, making it sound like a Karen name.

"They stayed at our house. They were very tired, so my mother looked after them. She fed them and they slept on our veranda. Then they fell sick with malaria and they were too ill to move so they had to stay where they were. They grew worse and worse. My father bought quinine for them and tried to help them but the mother died. We thought Peg-gy would die too, but my mother took great care of her and although she hardly moved, she kept going. Then slowly she got better. She was very thin because of the fever, but slowly, slowly she took a little food and began to move about the house. She had to stay with us then, we couldn't get her away. The Japanese had taken over every possible escape route, and anyway where could she go? So she became one of us. She was eighteen and I was seventeen and she learnt to do everything that we did. I taught her how to fish from the stream. I remember when she caught her first fish. She laughed then. I remember it because it was the first time she had laughed since she had been ill."

Jonathan watched, as a light seemed to come on behind the old man's eyes.

"They were the last of the happy days." And the light faded again as the rheumy eyes filled with his tears "There were British soldiers hiding in the area. The Japanese knew they were there and they did everything they could to find them. We heard stories of soldiers coming into villages in the valley, taking the men out and shooting them. They thought the people would betray the British but we never did. Then sometimes they sent the Burmese soldiers in, and they did the same. We could never trust them after that."

"You say you can never trust the Burmese?"

"No, never, not after what they did to our people."

"And what about today? Do you still feel the same way?"

"O yes. It's still the same. We shall never trust them." Jonathan looked away for a minute. In that one simple statement the old man had summed up the last fifty years of conflict.

"I'm sorry. Go on," he said at last.

"There were many stories. Many Karen people suffered. One of the British officers, one of those they had all been searching for, gave himself up. He couldn't bear to hear how the people were suffering for him. But they never found Peg-gy." A smile settled itself on the old man's lips. "They never knew she was there, so she was safe with us. I joined the Special Operations and fought with the British, and Peg-gy stayed with our family for many years. Sometimes I came home and she would always be there. She grew more beautiful each time I saw her. She had brown hair, dark brown. I thought she would be here forever; I thought she loved me as much as I loved her.

Then one day, a British company came into the valley. They were Peg-gy's people and there was a lieutenant just like me; his name was Charlie. She left the valley then. She had been with us for over three years and I thought she would stay forever, but they took her away, back to her own people. His name was Charlie. She went with him, and I have never heard from her since that day."

Tears sprang into the old man's eyes. After many minutes Jonathan broke the silence.

"What did you do?"

"They left us then, the British. They let us down. They told us they would look after us but they left us. We didn't want to be a part of Burma but that's what we had to become. So I joined the KNU. I was ready to fight. I wanted to fight for my people's freedom. And I was a good fighter. They had taught us well, the British, and we had many guns then, and many men who wanted to fight. And I was bitter, very bitter. I was ready to die for what I believed. But I didn't die. I got married and had children, and grandchildren. Instead, it was my grandson who died. He died at Manerplaw."

"When was that?"

"Only four years ago; nearly five now. He had his life ahead of him. Most of the young men have lost the stomach for fighting, but he was a good and brave boy. I think about him a lot and I miss him so much. I used to hold him on my knee and tell him some of the old stories. I wish it was me that had died, not him." The old man shook his head. "What have we got now? We've lost almost everything. And now they attack our

169

women and children. It's a dirty war now, a very dirty war."

"What do you want to happen?" Jonathan asked as gently as he could. He had become so absorbed in the old man's story that he had forgotten what he had come to find out.

"Me?" The eyes that had been staring into the distant past returned to the present. "There's nothing I want for myself now. I shall live out my days here but I worry for my children and grandchildren? I want them all to come home, home to their own land."

"Their own land?"

"Yes, back to this side of the river. To our own country to live in peace; that's all I want now."

17

His whole body was running with perspiration. He put his hand to his head and wiped it through his wet hair. He could feel his back hot and uncomfortable and tried to roll onto his side in an attempt to allow some of the sweat to dry, flinging the blanket away from himself at the same time. Only then did he become aware of his surroundings. The whirring sound of the cicadas and the muffled grunting of the animals and the pungent smell of the wood smoke brought him back to the present and he could dimly make out the shapes of the others sleeping on the veranda close to him.

It was a long time since he had had the dream, the dream that he wanted to escape from so desperately. Even now that his mind was full and busy with so many new experiences, it had still come back to haunt him. It didn't seem to matter what he did, and how much time passed, it was still there to surprise him when he was least expecting it. But that had seemed to make it worse somehow; it made him realise that however hard he pushed it to the back of his mind, the memory was still there.

As he began to cool down he again registered the smell of wood smoke. It was all pervading in this jungle fastness. Wherever there were people there was a fire and here in these uplands the fires burnt slowly all night. When they had first arrived in the village around dusk two days ago he had found the heat inside the house stifling, especially after the exertions of the dash through the forest to reach the casualty. He had been glad that Po Thaw had suggested that they all sleep on the veranda.

A sound pierced the darkness, a shout and the cry of a young child. His mind began to clear and he felt for his torch, found the button, pressed it on and directed the beam at his watch: almost 5am. It was still very dark but dawn wasn't far away now and the household would soon begin rousing. He pulled the blanket up to his chin again and settled his head back onto the clothes that served as a pillow in the hope of getting a little more sleep.

The smoke pricked at his nostrils again; this time more pervasive than ever and as his mind slowly turned over it began to register the new circumstance. The smoke was a constant, always there, but always in the background. This smoke was different. It originated from outside the house and the smell was getting stronger by the second. Fully awake now, Jonathan shook Po Thaw to rouse him, then, once he was sure he was awake, he turned his attention to Ko Maung.

As soon as he awoke, Po Thaw was alert to the danger. He got to his feet in the clothes he had been sleeping in and leaned over the far end of the veranda. "No . . ." Jonathan could hear the anguish in his voice. "Wake them up."

And Jonathan peered over to where Po Thaw had been looking and saw for himself. Where houses had been, just 50 meters away, flames were now reaching high into the sky. There was almost no wind, but the intense heat combined with the close proximity of the houses and the fact that they were built almost exclusively of wood meant that they were all in imminent danger.

Hasty, shouted commands reverberated around the house as the members of the household emerged. Jonathan didn't need to understand what they were saying, he could see what was happening as he watched the terrified villagers running along the path that passed below the house.

For a brief moment Jonathan wondered why no attempt was being made to stop the progress of the fire but one look at the growing chaos of people and their bundles of possessions told him that there was simply no time. All their energy was being poured into taking away what they could and saving themselves and their families.

He looked around the veranda for Po Thaw and Ko Maung and felt a small surge of fright when he couldn't see them. Then he remembered the amputee. Jonathan had no idea where they should run to so he watched as they wrapped some of the hand woven cloth around a sturdy pole that looked as if it had been kept for just such an eventuality. Having secured the fabric they helped the patient, who was still unable to walk, into it. Then with the help of a large number of volunteers, the stretcher was lifted down the steps to ground level where the density of smoke and building heat made it clear that the fire was coming dangerously close.

Jonathan quickly hoisted his rucksack onto his back, gathered up the things that Po Thaw and Ko Maung had left behind and hurriedly joined them down the path. Disoriented as he was, he recognised that everyone was moving in the same direction, away from the houses and down the slope towards a stand of low trees and brush which reared up before them in the glow of the firelight. Picking his way carefully behind the stretcher he passed the old man that he recognised from yesterday. He was pleading with the young woman who was holding her baby tightly to her breast, her eyes shining with terror. Jonathan felt a pang of sadness as he thought of the old man's story. He had seen so much, survived so much.

There was a loud hiss and the sky brightened dramatically. The people who had stopped running and were now sheltering in the lee of the hillside all turned to watch as the fire took yet another of the houses. The woman with the baby cried out loud and in answer there began a chorus of distraught sobbing. Jonathan saw Po Thaw looking at him.

"The soldiers," he said, "they started the fire."

"How do you know?" Jonathan asked.

"Old grandfather told me. They said that the soldiers were near. They wanted the people to leave the village, but the villagers wanted to stay. So the soldiers burnt them out."

"The Tatmadaw?" Jonathan asked.

"I didn't want to frighten you."

Jonathan didn't know what to say in reply. "What will happen to them?" he asked helplessly.

"Some will go to the border. They will try to get into the camps if they have family there. But most will stay in this district. There are many people like this. They build their houses again; they try to manage." Po Thaw looked around sadly at the villagers, all of them with faces upturned, unable to look away from the fire which could still be seen from the foot of the hill and now seemed to be burning still more brightly.

"We have to get away from here. We won't be safe until we cross the river. Come on." With a shout he turned and began to make his way down the rest of the slope towards the paddy fields now coming into view in the pre-dawn light. A few yards away Jonathan saw Ko Maung patiently ushering reluctant villagers away from their vigil over their burning homes. Slowly, they all turned away and began to stream across the dry paddy fields. The journey was made difficult, especially for the party carrying the stretcher, by the presence of the levees, which necessitated a small climb every so often. But the river with it's lining of trees was closer now. He could see the trees himself and knew that the river must be just a short distance away. Not much further to go and everyone would be safe. He suddenly became aware of his own heartbeat, just as it was slowing down to it's normal pace. He wanted to get to the trees more than anything else. Just a few more levees to climb over and they would be there.

The boom was so loud it seemed to shake the earth around them. The missile had landed harmlessly out of range but the crowd of villagers surged forward like a wave on the seashore, scrambling in panic over the levees, screaming, panting, pushing. Then the gunfire began. From the corner of his eye Jonathan saw the men running with the stretcher just to his left, Po Thaw with them helping with the load. Then he lost all control over his body. His feet lifted from under him and he flew through the air for what seemed several seconds, but in reality could not have been longer than one, before coming to a halt with a painful slide into blackness on the hard bare earth.

18

Ko Maung's military training meant that he always kept his M16 by his side on any visit that took him back across the border. As the crowd of frightened villagers surged past him towards the river he hurriedly looked around for shelter, soon finding it behind a collection of bushes that grew on one of the levees. Dropping down into the paddy field he wrenched the gun from his back and loaded it carefully. As the dust began to clear he watched for signs of movement in the trees that surrounded the village. He saw none and was consumed with impatience. The villagers were clustered at the edge of the river, some of them, but by no means all, within the shelter of the trees. They were still a potential target for the Tatmadaw. He felt his jaw clench with hatred for their callous shooting at the backs of fleeing villagers and his finger itched on the trigger longing to get some small grain of revenge. He shouldered the machine and looked through the sights at the slope but still saw nothing. The purpose of the gunfire had probably been to frighten the villagers, for no other reason than the perverse enjoyment of the spectacle of them scattering like fleeing ants across the field, rather than to inflict any real injury.

The knot of indignation that had tied itself round his stomach tightened, then slowly released itself; there was no sound from either end of the field. Common sense told him that if he used his machine gun he would only draw more fire from the Burmese and what could he do alone against an unknown number of the enemy? Reluctantly he slowly lowered his gun and carefully glanced around him to see if everyone was now safe in the trees. As he scanned the fields a small movement caught his eye and he carefully lifted his head above the levee to get a better look. He couldn't be sure but it looked as if there were people lying in the next field. Taking a deep breath he began to move slowly towards them, keeping in the shelter of the levee. At some point he had to climb over to the field where they were lying, but he was now close enough to see that there were two of them. He watched them for a while, occasionally glancing towards the river and then back towards the village, but saw no more movement. Had he imagined it? He still couldn't be sure who was still in the field. He felt a chill of fear as his imagination ran riot. He could still hear the sounds of the villagers by the river but there was no movement from the soldiers in the trees by the village. The smoke still hung in the trees and the smell of burning was all pervading, but there were no more flames, and the fire had ceased its fury now it had no more dried wood to consume. He took his jacket off and fixing it onto his gun he lifted it high above the edge of the levee. Nothing. Quickly he climbed over and dropped into the next field where he covered the ground between himself and the two reclining figures in almost no time.

As soon as he saw the torn fabric of Po Thaw's shirt he knew the worst. The blast had opened a deep wound that was visible through the shredded cloth. The vertebrae had been shattered into an unrecognisable collection of bone fragments but the spinal cord that had been ripped apart could be seen clearly from the surface, white and glistening. Ko Maung clutched at his stomach in order to quell the wave of nausea that arose as his eyes took in the pool of blood that had been pouring out of his fellow soldier's mouth, but was now congealing as it spread. It was almost light and although the sun was not up there was no mistaking the damage that the gunshot had caused. He hastily felt the neck for a pulse. The warmth of the body confused him and for a brief moment it filled him with hope. But there was nothing, no sound, no movement and no possibility of life.

So engrossed was he in his own grief that the he was unaware of the approach of someone else. "Look," he heard. "it's the *kolah wah*." Ko Maung dragged his attention away from the body and turned to see one of the village men who had come back to see what had happened. "How is he?" Ko Maung could hardly bear to ask the question as he moved across to where Jonathan lay face down on the earth but clearly alive.

"Jonathan! Jonathan!" He fought to wake himself from the nightmare. There had been a fire and the ensuing chaos of fear and panic. It was one of those dreams where you are running but can never get away; Jonathan had them from time to time. It was with relief that he heard his name being called. As he rolled onto his side he felt pain in his head. His hand lifted instinctively as if to rub it away but stopped as he discovered the sticky, gritty mass that his face had become. Incredulous, he stared for a moment at his bloodied hand then, as reality took hold he felt for his nose, which, to his horror, didn't seem to be there any more.

"Stay there Jon," Now he saw Ko Maung looking down on him. "Are you hurt?"

"Just my head, I think."

"And your face. Anywhere else?"

Jonathan blinked several times and tried once again to understand the circumstances that found him sprawled across the ground in the first light of dawn. "I don't think so," he said at last, and tried to sit up.

"Careful," said Ko Maung. "The soldiers may still be about. We have to get you into the trees and . ."

Jonathan saw the confusion cross Ko Maung's face and glancing around him saw the body just a few feet away.

"Yes, and we have to bury him. We'll have to take him into the trees by the river. We can't leave him here."

The villager who had been hovering beside them spoke for the first time

"He wants to go back to his house to get some spades," said Ko Maung, on seeing Jonathan's quizzical expression.

"What about the soldiers?" Jonathan said. The feeling was coming back into his body, the pain in his head was at least bearable and he was beginning to realise that he had had a lucky escape.

"I don't think that matters to him. He wants to go back there to see what he can salvage. They nearly always do. And they both watched as the man crouched down and began to move along the levee.

By the time Ko Maung judged it safe to cross the field other villagers had joined them and together they carried the body into the trees. "Now we need to clean up your face," he said looking at Jonathan ruefully now that they were safely in the shelter of the trees.

Ko Maung took what was left of the rucksack that, sadly, had offered absolutely no protection to Po Thaw, and found some cotton and a small bottle of liquid. Jonathan sat down and Ko Maung began to wipe the dirt and dust away while the villagers dug the grave.

"What's the damage?" Jonathan hardly dared ask.

"It's not so bad. It just looks a mess; you've lost your pretty face. The girls won't be after you for a few days."

"What?"

"Oh, you know the girls. They all want to find a nice "*kolah wah*" to take them away from here."

"And what do you think about that?" Jonathan winced at the sting of the liquid on the torn skin.

"I don't like it much. You take all the best girls. Then there won't be enough for us," he laughed and Jonathan recognised an attempt to cover up some of the grief. He watched Ko Maung's face as it bent close to his, a broad face set on a strong body, solid and totally dependable. His brow was furrowed with concentration as he worked away. Jonathan guessed that for both of them, this was the one way of avoiding the sight of the sad, broken body that lay close by them, awaiting it's final resting place.

"What was that about? What happened back there?"

Ko Maung was silent for a long time while he tried to extricate a particularly stubborn piece of grit from Jonathan's forehead "They want to frighten the villagers. They don't want us to help them."

"Did they know I was with you?"

"I don't know. Perhaps they did, but then they don't want us to come across the border back inside either. They don't want the villagers to have any help from anyone and a westerner is very bad news for them. They want to cut off all support for the KNU."

"So perhaps I, we, made it worse for the village."

Ko Maung went quiet before speaking again. "You think the villagers are afraid? Well the Tatmadaw are more afraid. That's why they do these things. They don't know any other way."

"And what will happen to them? The villagers who left their homes?"

'They'll go to the next village: where we stayed. It's not too far. Some of them will try to cross the border with us and some of them will go back to their houses and rebuild them."

"Is that safe?"

"There is no safety for these people. And no matter what we do we can never stop the people wanting to go back."

"I can't believe what I saw this morning; I just can't believe it happened."

"Oh, it happens. And you can help us, Jonathan." Ko Maung's eyes bored deeply into his. "When we get back to the camp, and when you go back to England, you must tell them. Tell the people there what happens; tell them everything you saw. People are dying, and nobody knows. We need someone like you to tell them."

19

The journey was a painful one. Every movement jarred Jonathan's head and pulled at the skin of his face; his knee and arm on one side were badly bruised and his whole body ached so that every step hurt. But he wanted no sympathy: he was glad to walk and feel the pain. It proved that he was alive.

They had buried Po Thaw under the trees beside the river with as much dignity as they could muster. Ko Maung had bowed his head and prayed out loud. Jonathan didn't know what he was saying, but he could hear the love between comrades in arms and he understood well enough. He bowed his own head and felt hot tears squeezing their way through his eyelids and adding to the stinging of the skin on his face and the wounds on his head.

The walk back to the camp was a long one. It was made slower because the number of travellers had been increased by some of those made homeless by the fire. They had had enough of trying to rebuild their homes. Plus there were some who needed the care of a hospital, which was simply not available in the jungle. Even the refugee camp had more to offer them.

"I'm sorry Jonathan," Ko Maung had come alongside him as they travelled.

"Sorry? Why?"

"I brought you here and I brought trouble for you. Too much trouble."

"But I wanted to come. Remember?" As he glanced across at Ko Maung he thought he saw a slight smile on the normally inscrutable face, and the silence of shared understanding hung between them.

"OK. So what else do we want to see in our society?" Jonathan, back in his classroom stood with his marker pen in his hand, poised ready to write down some of the answers on the white board.

"We want to be free to live as Karens," ventured one of the boys.

Jonathan nodded and waited for a moment before he responded. "Can you tell me just what you mean by that? What sort of things do you want to do?"

"We have our own language and our stories," another of the students added.

"And we want our own land. We want to farm our land in the old ways."

An audible murmur of dissent rippled around the room.

Ko Maung spoke up then. "Jonathan is trying to teach us about democracy and modern methods. And you want us to go back to that?"

"No," Jonathan interjected. "Let's hear what they have to say."

"Our way of farming, it's what we have always done. It's good for the land."

"It's not good for the land, it destroys the forest and . . . . "

Jonathan stopped the interruption. "Go on, tell us. Tell me how it works. I want to know."

"It's a good method. We cut the trees and burn the scrub. Then, we plant the paddy. After the harvest, we let the forest grow again and we move to a new place. It works for us. But many of our people don't know this way. Now we live here in a camp, they don't learn how to do it. We are forgetting our old ways."

"Swidden farming," Ko Maung's voice had taken on its customary irascible tone. "How can you go back to that? It's no good in the modern world. We have to try to improve things, not go backwards."

Some of the students had begun to stay behind after classes to ask him questions about politics and related subjects so he was now formalising this arrangement into an extra conversation class for them. It was evolving into a time when they tried, under Jonathan's guidance, to discuss between themselves their understanding of society. When it seemed appropriate, he would introduce some political theory and help them to explore how that might have some bearing on the questions that they were answering.

"And women," Ko Maung continued on his diatribe against the 'old ways' that some of the students seemed so determined to defend. "What about the women? They have too many children; they can't care for them all. And then there are the clothes. Some of the things that the women wear are bad for them. What about the spiral?" And he gestured with his fingers to illustrate the golden neck rings that were worn by some of the women of the Karenni, a related tribe.

Jonathan looked across to the other side of the class where a few girls sat quietly together. "What

186

about you girls? What do you think? Do you want the 'old ways' or do you want things to change?"

The girls looked at each other for a few moments. Jonathan had noticed Htee K'Paw among them as soon as she had entered the room. This was the first time she had joined the discussion group but yet it was she who spoke first.

"We can learn from modern ways but we should not forget our past. I think we have to try to keep both. The past and the future." And as his eyes met hers they lingered for just a moment. He was surprised at the frown he saw on her face, and it was that which held his gaze. So far, apart from the women at the burnt village, the only expression he had seen on the women's faces, whatever the hardness of their lives, had been a look of gentle sweetness. The months of having little language in common with most of the people around him had taught him to rely on unspoken communications. He still found this difficult but Htee K'Paw was troubled and it was clear for him to see.

"What about your country Jonathan? Do you have different tribes where you are from?" Ko Maung was speaking, but Jonathan had to drag his eyes away from Htee K'Paw before he could take note of what he was saying.

"Yes. Yes, I suppose we do. We have people in Britain who speak different languages. They have different cultures. And I think they are encouraged to keep up the things that make them different, including language and religion. But they have to speak English too and take part in the life of the country that they are living in now. I think Htee K'Paw is right. We need to try to do both. We want people to be part of the bigger state, while at the same time encouraging variety and some of the 'old customs' that some of you are talking about." He looked around the whole class; he wanted them to think for themselves as much as possible. "So, if you were running a country, how would you keep this balance of encouraging traditional differences and at the same time building a modern state?"

He was glad to be back in the classroom. Some of the boys asked him about his face, but he tried to make light of it. The truth was, he didn't want to talk about what had happened. And the absence of Po Thaw was something of a reproach. He guessed that Ko Maung passed the word around about the attack by the Tatmadaw because the enquiries stopped within the first day or two and as far as Jonathan's work was concerned, things had changed for the better. The students were beginning to open up and talk to him and, as he taught them something of the world he knew, his understanding of their world was growing.

But there were other things that had changed. Where once he had been happy to spend at least some time on his own, reading or writing up his notes and trying to shape them into some sort of theory upon which to formulate his thesis, he now sought the company of the students every evening. He would visit them in their dormitories, sometimes listening to them playing their guitars, sometimes helping with the work that had been set for them. At others he simply sat with them quietly doing nothing in particular but smoking and staring into the dark distance listening to the crackle of radios tuned to distant stations; the young refugees were desperate for the sounds of the outside world.

In recent years he had read enough war books to know that those who had lost fighting comrades often experienced grief that stemmed from a sort of guilt. They couldn't comprehend the strange quirk of fate that had decided that they should survive when others had died. It left them strangely detached from their surroundings, as if they had become invulnerable and somehow untouchable, whatever danger they put themselves in. The question as to why he had been spared when Po Thaw, who had been so near to him in the paddy field, had died so horribly, curled itself round his mind many times every day and he craved company fearing that he might go mad if he didn't have some distraction.

It was a full week since his return, the scabs on his face were loosening now and his skin was returning to normal. Sometimes when he was on his own he imagined he could hear the noise of gunfire and feel again the blast that had thrown him to the ground, but physically he felt better. The scratches had healed and the bruises had mostly disappeared and he woke with a fresh desire to sink any differences he might have had with Tim. He hadn't seen him since his return, but decided he felt recovered enough to seek him out after his classes. Perhaps he would suggest that they travel to town together, find a bar and spend an evening there.

The camp was large and it was a few minutes walk to where Tim was staying. Jonathan had to cross some small streams on the way and he noted they had dried to almost nothing. It hadn't rained for over three months now, and he felt a little disoriented; most of the houses looked the same and it was sometimes difficult to distinguish between them. Then he spotted the motorbike that Tim used and knew he was in the right place. Two small boys sat on the bike. One of them made a low rumbling noise with his mouth, then he shifted the tone of his voice up a note, and then again, mimicking the sound of the bike as it moved up the gears. So absorbed were they in their game that they were oblivious to his approach.

"Tim," he called out as he mounted the steps.

Only then did the boys turn towards him.

"*Thra,*" they called out as they clambered down off the bike and ran towards him.

Jonathan smiled at them but his smile turned to a frown of confusion as he watched them clatter breathlessly up the steps and across the open area in the front of the small house, almost knocking him over in their haste. "*thra . . . thra,*" Jonathan watched them in amazement as they banged on the flimsy door, which appeared to be locked.

He stood for what must have been only a second or two. There was a scuffling noise and then Tim was there, framed in the doorway, naked except for a [14]*longyi* tied untidily around his waist. Jonathan could feel his face set into a frown as, in one stride, he reached the doorway. Tim stood in the way, but Jonathan could see enough. In one glance he took in the contents of the whole room. Two little girls were there with Tim, both of them naked. One was sitting down on the matting that that been spread out on the floor, the other stood in the far corner by a camcorder, which was set up on a tripod. Jonathan's eyes rested on the child on the floor whose glance seemed to shift from him to Tim and back again. He felt as if he had been standing in the same spot for a very long time,

---

[14] Longyi *Sarong-style garment worn by Burmese males*

unable to move. Then it was as if his brain exploded inside his head and he launched himself out of the inertia that had overtaken him and crossed the room towards the camera. "What the hell is going on?" he shouted at the top of his voice.

Tim moved too. He lunged towards Jonathan, and grabbing him by the arm, tried to pull him to the floor. Jonathan would have winced with pain as he felt once again the bruises that were only now beginning to heal, but there was no time. Tim was of a similar build to him, and they were both light on their feet but the anger that was now bursting from the very centre of Jonathan's being gave him new strength. He knew that he had to get hold of the camera and above everything else he had to keep it if these children were ever to know any sort of justice. He stumbled briefly but somehow kept his footing. "You bastard," he shouted again and using all the strength in his body he shoved Tim back against the wall. Tim slumped briefly and then seemed to recover his strength. He kicked his legs wildly and Jonathan had to jump away. Then Jonathan dived forward once again, gasping and fighting for breath. He fell onto Tim and grappled him to the floor. He rested there for a moment, both of them fighting for breath with great gasps. Jonathan moved first and flung his hands onto Tim's throat. He found his Adam's apple with his thumb and began to press down hard on it, all the while trying to avoid the frantic movements that Tim was making. The two were locked together in almost equal combat, Jonathan's only advantage being that he was on top of the struggling Tim. Both of them had forgotten about the children who had quickly found their clothes and retreated from the two grappling men.

With a desperate movement Tim rolled from underneath Jonathan and broke free. The *longyi* that had been tied around his waist slipped away from him and his feet became entangled in it. For a moment he was disabled and Jonathan saw his chance. He jumped onto him once more, this time winding him and leaving him unable to move. Then he quickly scrambled across the floor to the tripod where he tried to release the camera. His fingers fumbled with the mechanism in anxious haste, all the time watching Tim who was recovering from the blow to his chest. Still he couldn't get the catch to work. Then Tim made to move towards him again but before he did so, Jonathan had raised the tripod, complete with the camera, high above his head and brought it crashing down onto Tim. Tim moved to avoid the blow but the winding he had received had slowed him down and the camera glanced down the side of his head, stunning him for a moment and forcing him instinctively to reach up to touch the wound. Jonathan didn't stop. He picked up the tripod and camera together, wrenched the door open, crossed the veranda and leapt down the steps. He ran along the path, panting and holding his arm to his side in an attempt to ease the stitch that he now felt there. He ran straight to the dormitory where he had spent most of the last few evenings. There would be safety in the numbers there. Stumbling sometimes, and gasping for breath, he kept his footing in spite of the gathering dusk. He burst into the student's quarters and saw Ko Maung who was in the kitchen collecting his supper. "Hide me," he panted, gasping for breath. His fingers seemed to be cold as ice, in spite of the warmth of the evening, his hands shook and he could barely keep hold of the camera and it's tripod. "Hide this, please.

Don't let Tim get it. Please," and he held it out in front of him, where it was taken carefully by the students that he had in recent days come to know as brothers. "It's very important. Hide it please," he repeated, suddenly overcome by the difficulty of trying to explain his reasons for the urgency of his request. But he needn't have worried. Ko Maung took his hand.

"Follow me," he said quietly and once again Jonathan knew he could trust this man as he led him into the jungle fastness that started at the edge of the camp and stretched for as far as the mind could reach, and further.

Meanwhile, the students had no trouble secreting the camera and tripod well before Tim came looking for Jonathan, as they knew he would. They dissembled well. Fighting a guerilla war had given them plenty of practice, while Tim found that their command of English was nowhere near as good as he had thought it was when he had taught in their classes. Faced with a wall of blank faces and apparent confusion he soon gave up his search.

20

Once the watching students were sure that Tim had stopped his search they came to bring Jon and Ko Maung back to the dormitory. Jon had already explained to Ko Maung what he believed Tim had been doing. "He's been taking photographs and videos of the children," he had said, trying to make his voice sound as normal as possible. He had watched Ko Maung's face in the gloom of their hiding place among the trees but hadn't seen any real reaction so had continued. "They were naked; they had no clothes on."

Ko Maung's face showed a little surprise, but not much.

"I think he wanted to put the pictures on the web. You see, Tim told me that he had an Internet business that was doing very well, but he never told me exactly what it was. Now I wonder if he was selling the pictures in some way, perhaps to a paedophile ring."

Ko Maung's usually inscrutable face clouded with confusion. Jonathan wondered how he could possibly explain the seamier side of child abuse to a man who knew all about the privations of guerrilla warfare but nothing of the so-called sophisticated world of the Internet. He began again. "OK. There's pornography, you know, pictures," he searched for some further reaction. "People pay to see them on the

194

net, the Internet. That's fine; it's quite legal if the photographs are of adults. But children are different. If Tim is taking pictures of children and using them in the same way, then that definitely isn't legal."

"You are sure about this?"

"Look, I can't be sure about anything, not until I look at the film. But he nearly killed me. The way he fought me, he didn't want me to get that camera for sure. He was doing everything he could to stop me." Jonathan was still shaking inside after the desperate fight with Tim. "That's why I think there was something in that camera that he didn't want me to see."

"We can look at it when we get back later, when it's safe for us."

"And then the question is," Jonathan went on, "what was he doing with the film? You see there are groups of people, paedophiles, who want pictures like these. There's a demand for them. They pay money for them. I don't know if Tim is into that, but he might be. And he wouldn't want me, or anyone else, to find out. That may be why he was so desperate to stop me."

But Ko Maung continued to stare at Jonathan, still apparently as incredulous as ever.

He had been lying half asleep for some time but was sufficiently disturbed to reach out of his mosquito net for his torch in order to be able to see his watch. It read just before 3am. He had tossed and turned for most of the night, but each time he tried to settle down he had woken again, as his body remembered the fall from the rocket blast for the hundredth time.

Before lights out he had plugged the camera into one of the sockets that ran off the generator and viewed the film on his own. The other students had left him in peace and he hadn't invited them to do otherwise. They had offered him food, which he refused. Instead he had withdrawn into one of the corners and cold with fear had switched on the play button. He knew only too well what memories the film would stir in him.

At one point in the night the sound of distant gunfire, or perhaps it had only been something as innocent as firecrackers, had woken him and he had sat up in terror. Lying awake had been no better as he had tried in vain to remove the images of the young child, naked and confused, lying on Tim's floor. He didn't want to wake the students who had elected to sleep in the house with him so he lay still, now wide awake, his thoughts churning relentlessly around his mind, and waited until he heard the cracking of the kindling as the first of the fires was lit.

The voices of the students came closer and louder than usual. Then he heard his own name and quickly roused himself as Ko Maung burst into the room. "Jonathan," he spoke between gasps for breath. "Jonathan."

"Yes?" Jonathan jumped up, his heart already beating fast. He could hear the urgency in Ko Maung's voice.

"It's Tim. He went to the commandant. He's made a complaint about you. He says you stole his camera. The commandant wants to see you."

"How, how do you know?" It was a foolish question. A network of cousins, brothers and all manner of contacts quickly disseminated information about all the dealings of the camp.

"Kler Htoo followed him. He saw him go there last night. Now he wants to see you."

A small group of students had gathered at the bottom of the steps. Jonathan saw them now and his thoughts ran wild as he struggled to understand them. "What are they saying?" he asked Ko Maung in desperation.

After a moment of silence Ko Maung replied. "Some are saying you should go to the commandant. You should take the camera back."

"But what will happen then?"

"We don't know. He might lock you up."

"What, even if I give it back?"

"He might."

"What else are they saying?" He could hear the voices rising. Clearly some sort of argument was underway.

"Someone seems to think he might have told the police too."

"The Thai Police?"

"Yes."

"Oh God. Now what do I do? What do you think Ko Maung?"

"I think you should get out."

"Get out? But . . ." The chill of the early morning seemed to snake it's way through his whole being. His first instinct was to get back inside again for the comfort of his fleece before joining the others outside.

Ko Maung spoke again. "You can go to the Thai police yourself and tell them what's happened. I think that would be better."

"Is that what you all think?" He cast his eyes around the little group of students searching for their responses to his question. Most of the faces stared blankly at him. He looked back at Ko Maung for reassurance but even his face had taken on its customary inscrutability. The thought of being locked up among people who had no experience of the rule of law terrified him. The thought of spending time in a Thai jail was hardly a better prospect.

"Jonathan. Go to the town. You'll be safer there."

"You think so?"

"Yes. You can get a bus out on the road. I'll take you there now and wait with you. And we'll try to talk to the commandant."

Now, standing on the dusty roadside with Ko Maung his mind churned over what he knew and what his imagination only guessed at. Was Tim involved in some child pornography outfit? That might explain why he had spent so much time at the orphanage, where children had no parents to ask awkward questions. Is that why he went into town so regularly on his motorbike? Was he uploading the material for sale on the net? Certainly, if he had been speaking the truth about his business, Tim knew the workings of the Internet better than most. But wasn't it too risky? Wouldn't it be possible for the police to trace any sales back to him? What about a paedophile ring? It could be a hobby that he shared with others like him. But he had been to such extraordinary lengths, half way round the world to this forgotten place. And then Jonathan thought again; there were rich pickings for such an enterprise; lonely, abandoned, parentless children abounded. They were mostly compliant too. They would accept what an adult said where the more

198

sophisticated children of the west had been taught to question. Tim had had little difficulty in persuading them to go along with him, that was clear from the film.

Buffeted from side to side in the back of the bus Jonathan closed his ears to the roar of his own thoughts. He closed his eyes too but then opened them again just as quickly as the face of one of the children rose up before him, just as it had on the film last night. Jonathan knew that look. If he dared enquire inside himself for even a moment he recognised exactly how that child felt. But now, what could he do about it? He tried desperately to think the way an adult should think in such circumstances instead of the way of a child whose cry had never been heard. "Yes," he heard himself whisper. Why hadn't he thought of it before? He would e-mail Sarah. No, he would phone her from town. He had an international card with him. He could contact her, somehow, anyhow. But he would have to be careful; the police might already be looking for him. There was also Tim who might still be around. Still, there was nothing else for it, he would have to take the risk and go to a phone booth. He had to enlist Sarah's help. She would know what to do and would have enough knowledge of the situation to be able to talk to the police about it. For a moment he wondered why he hadn't thought to do that before. The decision to contact his aunt had cleared his mind to some extent and gave him something to focus on.

Opening the notebook in front of him he dialled Sarah's number. It was barely daylight. In his frantic impatience, he had forgotten the time difference. But as his plan, such that it was, had taken shape he had realised that if he phoned early enough in the morning then his aunt might still be up, so he had stopped at the first phone that accepted the international card.

"Hello, Ian Cassidy speaking," Jonathan felt his body flood with relief as he heard his cousin's voice. "Ian, it's Jon. I'm speaking from Thailand."

"Jon! It's good to hear you. It's a bit late isn't it?"

"No, it's first thing in the morning here. I wanted to speak to your Mum. Is she still up?"

"No, she's out. She'll be sorry she's missed you."

"Well, don't worry for now. Look, something has come up. I'm going to e-mail her. Would you ask her to open it first thing in the morning I'm going to go and write it as soon as an Internet Cafe opens."

"OK Jon, no problem. I'll tell her. What's this about?"

"I can't say too much at the moment. But I want to see if she can help. It's quite important. As long as she picks it up first thing in the morning she can deal with it."

"Some sort of trouble then?"

"You could say that. I need her help and I think she'll know what to do. How are you anyway?" Hearing Ian's voice had made him realise how much he was missing home and the cousins shared pleasantries for a few precious minutes before Jonathan rang off. He felt as if he was in deep water that, in his exhausted state, threatened to engulf him; now he stood by the phone booth shaking while he gathered strength for his next task.

There was a market that the locals used, a rabbit warren of narrow lanes lined with stalls and pervaded by the stink of fish. Now he made his way there as quickly as he could. There were clothing stalls and he bought himself a checked shirt, some light coloured trousers and a hat, none of which he had ever worn since his arrival in the country. That done he went in search of a teashop where he could wait until the Internet cafe opened. Once inside and safely settled he went into the toilet to change. His blond hair had been bothering him. It marked him out more clearly than almost anything else and he knew that if he could at least cover it when he was in town he had a better chance of avoiding being spotted by Tim or recognised by the police.

Jonathan feverishly tapped in his account name and password; he could barely control his fingers, so desperate was he for a reply. In his email to Sarah he had written a brief outline of what had happened between him and Tim, then had gone away to sit in a café. There he had bought coffee but could not face eating. He waited for what seemed like an age, wondering if his cousin had detected the urgency in his voice over the phone and had thought it fit to worry his parents on their return home. A shudder of relief rippled through his body as he saw the message and clicked onto it. It was simple and to the point. "Phone me! Any time, night or day. Don't wait, just phone. Sarah."

"Cassidy's, can I help you?" His uncle's voice sounded reassuringly down the phone line.
"Its me, Jonathan,"
"Jon. Thank God. It's good to hear you."

"Is Sarah there?" Jonathan always knew that his aunt was the one who had the clearest grasp of much that went on in the camps of the border.

"No, she's at work now. But look, I saw your email too. Are you all right?"

"I'm OK. Just about . . . Look, I couldn't tell you much in the e-mail. But I managed to get hold of the camera with the film in it. Tim nearly killed me, or it felt that way. That's what made me realise that something pretty nasty was going on."

"Look, Jon, if this guy was that desperate to stop you getting that film he must be up to no good. Sarah has been onto the police about it. They are coming out to interview you."

"Uh,"

"All right, Jon. Are you still there?"

"Mmm. They're taking it that seriously?"

"Yes Jon, they are. Paedophile rings are a big problem on the Internet and the police will take note of every lead. It could be bigger than you think. They'll be out in a couple of days. The question is: how do they make contact with you? Where are you exactly? Are you still in the town?"

"Yes. I'm outside the Sompat Hotel."

"I know it. So at least you can keep in contact with us."

"I can, but there's a complication."

"What's the problem?"

"It's this guy Tim. He told the camp commandant that I attacked him and stole the camera. I think the Thai Police are involved too. So . ." Jonathan's voice tailed off as, for the first time, he realised his utter loneliness.

The line went quiet for a few moments as David pondered the situation. "Look Jon, you're going to have to sit tight for a couple of days. We'll let our police know the situation. They are keeping in contact with us and as soon as we know what's happening then we can let you know. And have you still got the film you took?"

"Yes . . yes, I have."

"And is there somewhere you could put it for safety, just until the police get there? What about a safe deposit box?"

"Yes, I'll do that," he cursed himself for not having thought of that before and then made a mental note to have the film locked away immediately.

"Jon," his uncle's voice came again. "Take care, keep your head down, and phone us, twice a day, morning and evening, so that we know you're all right.

Jonathan put the phone down slowly and carefully. It felt like a rope, the rope that was his link with life itself. It meant home and safety, while letting go of it meant that he had stepped back into the dangerous world outside. He turned round cautiously, his whole body filled with dread at what he might see. Perhaps Tim had been watching him, perhaps there were others, members of the same ring who were all out looking for him, waiting for an opportunity to silence him for good and all.

But there was nothing unusual. Mothers with children around them moved purposefully along the row of shops opposite while a few westerners drifted aimlessly between the racks of clothes hanging on racks outside. Nobody took any notice of him. Nobody even saw him. He glanced around quickly and then putting his head down he walked up the steps and into the hotel.

He saw the brown uniform too late. As he stepped up to the reception of the modest back packer's hotel the policeman stood up from his seat behind the counter and moved towards him. He wanted to turn and run and almost did so. Then from the deep recesses of his mind he remembered that he was the innocent one and, furthermore, the policeman had a gun. For a moment he instinctively began to raise his hands then lowered them. He felt he was losing control of his body and took some deep breaths to try to calm himself down.

The young receptionist spoke first. He had hardly noticed her until that moment. "Mr McCune," she articulated the words carefully and reasonably accurately. "The police want to speak to you. They want to take you to the Police Station." As she spoke his eyes moved from her to the policeman who was now fingering his handcuffs.

"I can explain," he replied. "You see he was taking pictures of children. That's why I took the camera. I'll give it back. I can give it back."

Jonathan knew he was babbling. The receptionist was frowning. Clearly her knowledge of English did not stretch all that far.

"I . . " Jonathan stopped. He tried to work his fingers that seemed to be stiff with cold. Almost certainly there was nothing he could say that would make any difference to the situation and anyway, even if there were he couldn't think what it would be. He wanted to close his eyes and go to sleep in the hope that he would wake up and all would be well again. He wanted to go back to the safety of the camp. No, he wanted to go home. He wanted to get out of the place and put the whole terrible episode behind him. Surely he would forget it all in time. Then he would be able to get a job, the sort of job that his parents had always wanted him to get.

But there was no escape as he stood outwardly silent and unmoving.

Htee K'Paw saw Kler Htoo waiting for her as she walked along the path so she joined him so that they could walk to the orphanage together. Yesterday she had met with Hser Mu for the first time since her friend's return to the camp from the visit across the border. For several days after they had left she had wished she had gone with them. Hser Mu had told her the story of how some of the party, including Jonathan, had gone further inside to another village and had got involved in gunfire that had resulted in the death of Po Thaw. The whole group had come back very subdued but even so Htee K'Paw still had some feelings of regret. She wasn't even quite sure why she had refused to go in the first place. Now the opportunity to do something she really enjoyed had presented itself she decided she must go along and try to lift herself out from under the slight depression that seemed to have afflicted her recently. Going to the orphanage to hear the children sing always cheered her so as she walked with Kler Htoo she could feel some of the old lightness in her step.

They went in through the front of the building. Kler Htoo began to unpack his guitar and the children gradually assembled. Htee K'Paw always let them choose the first song, in order to warm up their voices, so some of the noisier ones were beginning to call out the names of the tunes when Paw Wah came into the room.

"Hello, thramu Paw Wah,"

"Hello, thramu Htee K'Paw," they both exchanged the customary greetings and then Paw Wah spoke again. "Some of the students tell me that Tim has left the camp."

"Oh," said Htee K'Paw, "sometimes he does. He goes to town. He uses a computer there."

"No, Htee K'Paw," the tone of Paw Wah's voice seemed to change very quickly. "He has gone. The other boy Jonathan had a fight with him and now he's gone away."

"But . . ." Htee K'Paw began and then fell silent.

"He was so good to us," Paw Wah went on, her voice rising to a shout. "He did so much for the children and now look what has happened. That Jonathan had a fight with him. He stole his camera, and now he's gone."

At first Htee K'Paw was only half listening to Paw Wah but now the words bored into her consciousness. As the children clustered round the room thinking only of their songs she felt some stirring in the back of her mind. It was full of questions that had no answers and she could not make sense of any of it. She wanted to get out of the room to be on her own where she could think clearly.

"You look after the children please," she said to Kler Htoo quietly. She knew he was quite capable of doing some of what she usually did with them. "I have to go to see Hser Mu."

206

"Wait, " he was saying to her while she made her way to the front of the house and down the steps hastily pushing her feet into her sandals as she did so. "Wait Htee K'Paw, I must speak to you."

"Yes, what is it?" She said impatiently. She just wanted to get away.

"I know what's happened," he said and something in the quietness of his voice made her stop in her tracks and listen to him. "Jonathan found Tim taking photographs of children. He got very angry with him and they had a fight. Jonathan stole the camera and," Kler Htoo faltered for a moment, took a deep breath and resumed the story. "Tim went to the commandant and told him that Jonathan was a thief. And we think he went to the Thai police too. Now the commandant wants to question Jonathan and perhaps the police do too. And both Jonathan and Tim have disappeared" He ended his summary with a helpless gesture of his arms as he watched Htee K'Paw's mouth open and her face turn pale.

"I must go," she said, "I must go. I'll find Hser Mu," and she stumbled down the path leaving Kler Htoo frowning at the strangeness of it all. He shook his head and in an attempt to ignore Paw Wah's unprecedented angry outburst he picked up his guitar and turned his attention to the children.

Htee K'Paw slowed her pace again. The path was rough and steep in places and she forced herself to walk carefully. At the foot of the hill she turned along the wider pathway and then up the narrow approach to where Hser Mu lived.

Her friend was poring over a notebook on the veranda when Htee K'Paw ran up the steps, kicking her sandals off as she went. Hser Mu opened her

207

mouth to speak but Htee K'Paw got in first. "Jonathan," she began breathlessly, "have you heard what's happened to him?"

Hser Mu had no chance to speak before her friend began again. "Jonathan had a fight with Tim and stole his camera and now the commandant wants him and I think I know why." She stopped to catch her breath again.

"Htee K'Paw! What? Sit down and tell me slowly."

"I'm sorry," Htee K'Paw began again. " You remember my visit to the town? When I was there I looked at Tim's camera and there were lots of pictures on it. Some of them were of the children with no clothes on. I didn't think too much about it but when he saw me with the camera he was very angry. He shouted and frightened me. And there's something else. I know Tim isn't a good man. I can't explain why, but I think Jonathan is right. I think he stole the camera to stop Tim taking more pictures and," she faltered for a moment, "we must tell the commandant. I don't want Jonathan to be in trouble."

Hser Mu stared at her friend. "What makes you think Tim is so wrong?"

"I can't explain but he took me to a house and I didn't like it. Then he took me to a hotel when I wanted to go to my uncle's and," she broke off. "Please don't ask me anymore. I know he is not a good man. Will you come to the commandant with me?"

"Yes. I will do that. I was just trying to think up some ideas of how we can get the children to write their stories but I can do that anytime. Do you think we should speak to the boys first? Jonathan spends a lot of time with them, and they know him better than we do.

And the commandant is Kler Htoo's uncle, so I think we should ask him to come with us too. That will help."

"I know where Kler Htoo is now. He's at the orphanage with the children." Htee K'Paw felt herself brightening as she uttered the words.

"Lets go then," said Hser Mu as she tidied away her notes.

21

The noise bothered him; the chanting and occasional shouts regularly woke him from the drowsiness that he wished would overcome him more completely in the afternoon heat. The Mae Rama Detention Centre was a relatively small establishment, in keeping with the size of the rest of the town. The walls were made of breezeblocks and old wrought iron gates slid open along rollers to admit more prisoners from time to time. The room in which Jonathan had been locked was close to the other rooms, which were larger and more crowded, but he drew some comfort from the fact that he could see other people around him. Through the long row of bars he could even see the street outside where passers by sometimes peered in with curiosity and then went on their way.

The place was a holding centre for those who had crossed the border illegally, for foreigners who had allowed their visas to lapse, and the police lock-up all in one. Every so often the rooms would be partially cleared of the inmates and they would be sent back across the border. Jonathan had heard the stories and guessed that most of them would probably be back on Thai soil again very soon. There was a sort of camaraderie between the prisoners, which he tried to appreciate in spite of the incessant noise; at least, he told himself, it was better than a completely solitary cell, which he had feared might be the lot of a westerner. He felt that the humanity that surrounded him in the place would somehow act as a sort of buffer should Tim come to find him which, he decided, was always a possibility. Still, he tried not to think about it; instead he concentrated on David's words. 'The British police would be out in a couple of days.' Was that true? Would that really happen? Did they think what had happened to him was so important that they would travel that far to find someone who had now apparently disappeared? And would they believe him when he told them what had happened? And what about the film? The Thai police had stripped him of all his possessions including the film, before locking him up. Had they realised how important it was to him? It was the only concrete piece of evidence; but would they realise that and did they even care?

John Pasco had never gone back to his native land, or at least never for more than a few weeks at a time and then he always hankered to be back here, in the place he now called home. At the end of the Vietnam War in the 1970's the American forces had slowly trickled home, many of them taking their newly acquired wives and children with them but John had stayed behind. He took his bar to the Cambodian border where he fed and watered the Peace Corps Volunteers and aid workers who had flocked there. He did a brisk trade for several years until they too went home and John moved to the small town of Mae Rama, close to the Burmese border.

Now there was a new sort of clientele. Tourists were coming in ever-increasing numbers, eager to find new destinations and hungry for what they imagined to be adventure. Now he was to be found dapper, neatly dressed as ever, hair flecked with grey but otherwise carrying his more than fifty years lightly and with no hint of what he had seen in the war years. He knew what they all wanted and was able to give them the answers to all their questions. He was regularly to be found sitting at the front of the bar that was open to the street, smiling and chatting to any westerner who happened to be passing.

He went behind the bar at around sunset, as he did every day, and made sure everything was neat and tidy. He took it upon himself to check all the glasses, taking down each one to polish it. Then he would straighten the ashtrays and menu cards and check the bottles in the fridge to make sure there were enough for the evening ahead. There was to be nothing to disturb the smooth running of his carefully built up establishment.

Over the years John had gained another vitally important skill to add to that of catering to the needs of the tourists; he was fluent in the language that most of them made no real attempt to learn. This meant that he was regularly called upon to assist when westerners found themselves in any sort of trouble, including falling foul of the law, which seemed to happen all too often. So, he was neither surprised nor dismayed when the shadow of a local policeman fell across the open doorway What slightly surprised him was that this time the policeman was not alone; he had three westerners in tow, a middle-aged man and a younger man and woman. He greeted them cheerfully and having exchanged the necessary pleasantries, left the bar in the capable hands of his small staff.

Jonathan watched as the policeman accompanied by a neatly dressed westerner came towards the cell and unlocked the door. He felt his spirits lift as the man came closer and he saw his features, clean, and open: surely someone who would help him. He did his best to contain his excitement as the key turned in the lock and the heavy handle twisted in the policeman's hand. With his whole being he wanted to cry out and protest his innocence, but common sense told him that here was his first chance to explain himself to someone who would certainly understand and he shouldn't blow it with some crazy outburst that would destroy his credibility. Instead he fought to slow himself down, took some deep breaths to maintain control and followed the policeman and the stranger down the corridor to an office at the back of the building.

His uncle stood up to greet him, and Jonathan, losing any semblance of the control that he had fought to maintain in the prison, felt his eyes fill with tears.

"OK, Jon," David told him. "This is Martin, and this is Donna. They are from the Paedophile Unit based in Scotland Yard."

"Hello Jon," Donna spoke with the utmost softness. Black curly hair framed her face; she could not have been much older than he was but she seemed almost maternal towards him. His lungs emptied in a rush as the tension washed out of him.

"So you," he began before his voice tailed off.

"Yes," Donna seemed to know what was on his mind. "We're taking this very seriously. We've been trying to get leads into a paedophile outfit working here for months now so we came as soon as we could."

"And you, David?" Jonathan still could not believe his good fortune. The person whom he trusted almost more than anyone else was here too.

"Oh, business is quiet at the moment. And I've taken on a junior. He can take care of things for the time being. I thought you sounded as if you needed a friend, so here I am."

"And? I recognise you from the bar. I'm afraid I don't know your name."

"It's John, John Pascoe. The police often call on me to interpret for them. It happens all the time, to tell the truth."

"But as far as the police know, I'm the one in the wrong. You see, I attacked Tim and stole the camcorder. And Tim went to the camp commandant to complain and to the local police as far as I can see. I guess that's why they arrested me."

Martin spoke for the first time. "We hope that's all been sorted out now. You see, one of the girls in the camp found out what had happened and she verified your story."

"You mean . . .?"

"It seems that she knew what had been going on and persuaded the commandant that you had the interests of the children at heart and had done nothing wrong."

"One of the girls? Do you know her name?"

"Tea something." Martin struggled to articulate the unfamiliar sounding syllables.

"Htee K'Paw," the American interjected. "It seems that she had seen some of the photographs that this Tim took and was upset by them, but she didn't know what to do about it. Once she found out what had happened to you she realised the importance of what she had seen and came forward."

Jonathan felt his eyes begin to fill with tears again as relief surged through him and then, remembering his situation, he motioned to the handcuffs still attached to his wrists.

"You're free to go," said Donna. "You are on the right side of the law now. We just need to get you out of here then we'll go back to the hotel for the night. We have some work to do in the morning."

"The film," said Jonathan, "I intended to put it into the safety deposit box but I never got that far."

"It's all right," John Pascoe said as the policeman opened the cuffs with a key tied to his belt and brought a small package. "It should all be there."

Jonathan snatched up the package and reached inside for the one piece of evidence that he needed.

"OK," he said quietly as he felt another wave of relief.

Jonathan settled into his evening meal with the others; for the first time in weeks he had an appetite, coinciding with the availability of something reasonably palatable to eat.

"We want to begin to work on Jon's story a little, but we're not going to talk business here," Martin said. "We have a room in the Sompat. We can talk there later." And he reinforced his reassuring tone with a wide smile.

After they had eaten the little party wandered slowly along the street towards the hotel. Jonathan was filled with impatience. The fear that he might meet Tim was still with him and he wanted to get off the street as quickly as possible but Donna stopped regularly to finger clothes and peer into the stalls that were ranged along the route.

"Hmm," Martin laughed quietly. "Don't tell me. It's a bargain," rolling his eyes in the manner of a man faced with a woman intent on shopping.

Jonathan warmed to Martin's gentle Welsh accent and wanted to join in with the reproach but his face wouldn't smile. In spite of the presence of the others he was still stiff with tension. He watched as Martin waved a small bundle of notes across a stall and purchased a lighter, then felt a small nudge as he spoke to him again.

"What are you going to buy? Do you want a lighter or something else? Here, what about one of these?" And he gestured casually at the wallets.

If Jonathan hadn't been so distracted, he would have admired their acting. They were a couple of tourists out for the night, wandering the town, and a casual observer would never have guessed their true intentions.

The four of them settled down in the room and Jonathan told his story. Martin and Donna occasionally added the odd encouraging nod or question but apart from that they listened without interrupting. Afterwards they all fell silent until Martin spoke at last.

"So Jonathan, did Tim ever tell you what sort of Internet business he had?"

"No, he didn't."

"Did you ever think to ask him? Were you curious?"

"No. Strangely, I wasn't. I guess I was so busy thinking about what I was doing. And I think . . ," Jonathan stopped.

"Yes? You think?" Martin probed gently after a brief period of silence.

"Perhaps I was a little in awe of him, or of people who can make money like that. My parents," he looked across at his uncle for a moment and was rewarded with a reassuring smile. "Well, some of their friends seem to make money out of nothing, and I don't really like it when they go on about it too much. It seems arrogant. You know?"

"Is that how you felt about Tim?"

"Hmmm. There was something I didn't like about him at first. I guess that's why I didn't ask him about his business. But he seemed all over me, wanting me to take him into the camp. He told me he wanted to help the kids; do some teaching. Then I felt bad that I hadn't liked him, so I took him in with me. I thought he must be all right if he wanted to help them, and that it was me being oversensitive."

"So, he persuaded you that he was a real good guy?"

"Oh yes. And every time I came across him he seemed to be doing yet another good deed and was getting on so well with them all. They loved him, it seems. While I was struggling with my research, he seemed to be getting on fine. Look, is this really the sort of stuff you want to hear?"

"Yes. Yes it is. We've been monitoring some of the material that comes out on the websites. Some of it is obviously from Southeast Asia but it's almost impossible to track down a precise location without knowing where the material is being uploaded. But there are several things we need to know. Firstly, was he taking pictures with the intention of loading them onto a website? With his knowledge of e-commerce that would seem likely, but it's not necessarily the case."

"Oh come on Martin. Don't pussyfoot around. It's all there, the worming his way into the place, the grooming of the young kids; he was up to no good, that's a certainty. And Jon here says he didn't like him from the beginning. That's another pointer."

"Ah, but now you're into the realms of intuition, flower. Let's keep to the facts."

Donna looked as if she was going to fly at Martin for a moment and then seemed to think better of it.

"But the facts are there. He was grooming them."

"He was spending time with the children and giving them presents. That's as far as Jonathan knew at the time."

"Then we get onto the video. That's when it begins to look nasty."

"I grant you that. But lets go back a bit. Is there anything more you can tell us about Tim? Was there anything he did that you noticed? Even if it's just a small thing it could be important. We want to build up a picture of him."

"Well, he taught classes, English classes. That's what they want the most here. He was good at it too, or that's what he told me. And he got hold of a motorbike. Yes, he rode to and fro on the motorbike quite a bit now I come to think of it. Yes, I don't exactly know where he went, but he went out of the camp quite a lot. Much more than I did, anyway."

"That could be the uploading," Donna interjected.

"OK. You could be right. That could be him uploading. Once he had established his software into a computer then he would be away. I don't think he would use an Internet Cafe. That would be far too dangerous. He would have to have a private computer with a large memory, perhaps one in place for the purpose. And what about friends? Did he spend time with some people more than others? Did he make what you might call close friends?"

"Yes, he did. He seemed to get on better than I did at first. Then he was always visiting the orphanage and he got very friendly with one of the girls. It was Htee K'Paw, the girl who told the commandant about the pictures. She was one of my students, but he seemed to single her out. I guess she must have seen something too, enough to make her realise that he was up to no good perhaps. I don't know. He spent a lot of time with her family too. I remember I told him I didn't like it because he was favouring one family above the others. He put me in my place pretty quickly. Made me feel like some sanctimonious idiot."

"Uh?"

"Well, I'm afraid he often made me feel like that. That's why I didn't spend too much time with him."

"So he made friends with one of the girls?" Martin pulled the conversation back to where it had been.

"Yes, yes." Jonathon could feel his thoughts slowly coming into some sort of order. "And he took her out of the camp. He took her out for the weekend. The refugees aren't allowed into the town. They risk getting picked up by the police. But I guess if she was with him she was in less danger. But I remember thinking how it marked her out somehow. Perhaps the others talked about her a bit after that, but I'm not sure. It's difficult to get to know them, really get to know them, I mean."

"But he seems to have tried."

"Yes, maybe. But I didn't trust him from the beginning. It's all right when you have money, and he seems to have had plenty of that, buying things right, left and centre, of course they liked him. I was different, I was only working as a teacher, and I didn't have anything else to give them. I just had to get to know them the best I could." He saw Donna nodding at him as if he should continue. "I went inside for a few days."

"Inside?"

"I mean I crossed over the border. Some of the students took me. I had a nasty experience there. I saw a guy shot dead, in the back. We were running away and the Burmese soldiers shot him dead! I shall never forget that. But it brought me closer to them. I'm doing research for a PhD and after that I was more determined than ever to try to understand what's going on here. But then this happened and . . "

Nobody spoke for a long time until Martin eventually broke the silence. "I think we need to speak to the girl you mentioned?"

"Htee K'Paw."

"Yes, she may know something. She must have got to know him better than anyone." As he began to feel better, Jonathan's mind had started to work on the practicalities. "There's the problem of access to the camps."

"Don't worry. The local police have given us permission," said Martin. "They've given us the authority that we need. I'll get onto them now. And we need a search warrant and John to interpret for us."

22

"Jon?"

Jonathan glanced across at his uncle. They had come out to the street once again and now sat outside one of the bars. Neither said anything for several minutes then David spoke again. "I was watching your face. The film . . . "

Jonathan pushed his chair backwards so that the legs scraped against the wooden decking and sat staring at the ground. Confusion had rendered him speechless.

David picked up his glass and took a long mouthful of his beer.

Jonathan echoed the movement himself, staring out across the top of the glass at something far away. David watched him and waited; he could see that his nephew was thinking something through.

"All the things that have happened: they've really knocked me. I saw this guy Po Thaw blown up right beside me. I shall never forget that, never. I remember at school we read those war poems. You know, Wilfred Owen and the others? And I've just seen one person killed, just one. But that's enough. I think it gives you some insight. What must it be like to lose all your friends? I never thought I would see anything like that in my whole life," Jonathan paused, then after a few moments he continued, "but I coped with it all right, or at least that's how it seemed at the time. The other students treated me like one of them, which I was by then I suppose. I'd had my baptism by fire. My face was a mess and I was covered in bruises but basically there was no lasting damage. I even did some teaching. Now I look back at it, I was nearer to the answers to some of my questions than I had been before."

"The students saw you as one of them?"

"Yes, I think they did. It was what I had been hoping for months."

"So, at that point, everything was OK? I mean, you'd seen some pretty nasty things but you were coping?"

"Yes, I was." Jonathan picked up his glass again and drank some more. "It was seeing Tim with those girls. I didn't know I could be so angry." He looked across at David who was watching him quietly from the other side of the table.

Suddenly David spoke, "did Tim remind you of anyone?"

Jonathan nodded.

"In your childhood?"

Jonathan stared distractedly across the crowded street. He had never spoken about it before and couldn't think how to begin. At last he opened his mouth. "It reminded me of something that happened to me. I thought I'd forgotten it. I had forgotten it. But it all came back to me. I saw what Tim was doing and I went mad. It came out of nowhere. I didn't think I was very strong but I was then. When I saw him I just wanted to kill him for what he was doing."

A slight frown had appeared on David's attentive face but otherwise he was still.

"It happened at school; one of the masters. His name was Mr Dixon. I don't know what happened to him. He must have left the school soon afterwards. Perhaps someone else said something, I don't know, but I didn't see him after that. Perhaps he went away and so I forgot it. I probably would have remembered it if he had stayed in the school."

David waited until he stopped speaking before asking quietly."Did you ever tell anyone what he did?"

"No, I didn't. I didn't realise what was happening at first. I thought he was playing with me. I didn't understand."

"Did you try to tell anyone?"

"Not in so many words. I remember telling Mum and Dad that I didn't want to stay at the school anymore. That was all. I said I wanted to go to a school near home so that I didn't have to board but I couldn't explain why. Now I understand what he had done. He had persuaded me that there was nothing wrong with what he did. In fact I thought he was good to me. I was a bit studious at school. That doesn't always go down too well with other people and he seemed to be protecting me. He gave me some attention. He helped me. I remember I wanted to understand something and he helped me. Then . . ."

Jonathan saw David nodding his head slowly.

"He wanted me to . . . He undid his trousers, and I didn't understand. I didn't know. I didn't know what I was doing."

David looked at him intently. He didn't move until at last he spoke. "And seeing Tim brought it all back to you."

"Yes. I'd forgotten all about Mr Dixon. I must have been quite young because I was still in the first year. He made me believe he was being kind." Jonathan began to repeat himself. "He was at first, he was helping me, that's why I couldn't say no. And Tim was just like that. He had everyone thinking he was the good guy. He brought presents for the children and the housemother in the orphanage worshipped the ground he walked on."

"That's the problem. These people are very charming. They have to be, or the children wouldn't go to them so readily. It would be easy to recognise them if they grew horns but they don't."

Jonathan continued. Now he had begun to talk the words seemed to flow from him like water from a bottle. "That's why I fell apart. After the fight with Tim I didn't know what to do. For the first night I was scared that he would come and look for me. I thought he might find me but the students I had been working with looked after me. I don't think they really understood what had happened but they could see that I needed help. Then in the early morning they found out that Tim had reported it all to the camp commandant. That's when I came to my senses and decided to get out. I came to town on the bus and phoned you. You know the rest; the police arrested me. Tim must have reported the theft to them as well." Jonathan felt the hand that held his glass shaking uncontrollably so he placed it carefully on the table.

"That's what I can't understand. Tim had the audacity to report you to the police when, if the video is anything to go by, he was doing something so wrong himself."

"I guess he wanted the film back more than anything."

"But when the Thai police took your possessions away they could have done anything with it, thrown it away, watched it, even given it back to Tim . . "

"But they didn't. That's because Tim reported the camera missing, not the film. So they didn't think about it either."

"OK, Jon, so something has gone right; try to hold onto that. And what about you? What about another beer?"

"Yes please, I'll have another Chang," and while his uncle busied himself attracting the attention of one of the waiters Jonathan stared out at the street where tourists thronged the narrow roadways. He scanned the faces for a glimpse of Tim but saw nobody that he recognised. Would it always be like this from now on? Would he always be looking over his shoulder or studying the faces in a crowd? The police had come from Scotland Yard to talk to him but there seemed to be little chance of them ever doing that, or that was how it felt.

"Well, how are you feeling now?" His uncle's word brought him back to the present as two fresh bottles of beer landed on the table between them.

"I don't know. A failure? I don't know; I just don't know. It's been good to talk about it though. It's the first time I've ever talked with anyone about Mr Dixon. I've never breathed a word of it to anyone before. Please don't . . . ," it occurred to him that David might tell someone else, perhaps even his parents.

"Don't worry. I'll keep it all strictly confidential. I promise."

Jonathan gave him a weak smile.

"And we'll go back to the camp with Donna and Martin tomorrow. They want to interview this girl."

"Htee K'Paw."

"Yes. And I'll stay with you as long as you want me to."

Jonathan luxuriated in his first hot shower in months. Once he had finished washing his hair he turned his attention to his feet, which in spite of regular washing were covered in ground-in dust. Martin had booked Jon and David into the hotel with them. In spite of appearances to the contrary, he and Donna weren't a couple. They were just very good actors.

He tried to sleep, but it proved more difficult than he had imagined. The noises of the camp and then the detention centre had been incessant, but they were now replaced by the more intrusive clatter of the air conditioning. He also felt strangely enclosed, almost claustrophobic. He had come to enjoy the experience of sleeping on a bamboo floor where he had been able to watch the dawn lighten over the stream as it curled close to the small house that he had come to call home. Now, sleeping within bricks and mortar seemed unnecessary and he craved the fresh air that he had breathed though the woven lattice of his bedroom in the camp.

Martin's gentle irony and the reassuring presence of his uncle made him realise how lonely he had been. Now, more than ever, he wanted to go home to get away from the terrible mess that his life had become.

But he felt safe in the hotel room with his uncle and the police close by. And they seemed to have everything in hand too. They had viewed the videotape late into the night and Martin and Donna had been easily satisfied of the seriousness of the case. Now if they could just find evidence of the uploading. 'If', it all hinged on that 'if'. Whatever they did it seemed to him to be an almost impossible task. But that wasn't his problem, he tried to tell himself, as he tossed and turned through the night.

The journey to the camp was easy in the air-conditioned car that they had hired for the purpose. It was a different world to the rickety bus or motorbike that had been his usual form of transport in recent weeks. The commandant welcomed them into his office near the entrance to the camp with a smile, and mugs of coffee and water were passed around the group. Jonathan's place in the camp, as a member of the teacher training team had always been quite legitimate. It had been Tim who had slipped like an eel through any hole that he could find in the security system. Until he had reported the attack and the loss of his camcorder he had been a non-person as far as the camp was concerned, never wanting to bother with formalities. Jonathan now understood why he had wanted it that way.

23

Hser Mu walked quickly along the path beside the primary school classrooms. Like many of the teachers she found it easier to mark books in the quiet of the early morning before the children arrived. Out of habit, more than for any other reason, she glanced into Htee K'Paw's room to see her friend's head bent over a pile of exercise books. The teacher training had stopped for the time being and the school classes, which had had to be temporarily combined, had been divided up again so that the essential winding-up process of the school year could be carried out.

Having slowed her pace for a moment she would have passed on with little more than a cheerful greeting had it not been for her seeing the vicious jab with which her friend stabbed her pen at one of the books. Htee K'Paw's name meant 'clear water' and her personality matched the name that her parents had given her. Everywhere she went she carried an aura of clarity with her, a clear, cool beauty, just like the water of her name. But, it seemed to Hser Mu that the water had become muddied of late. She had been watching her friend and had found the change difficult to comprehend. Htee K'Paw's natural integrity had become clouded with deceit. Hser Mu could see she was hiding something; the conversation of two days ago before their visit to the commandant had confirmed that. In spite of the upturn in the family's fortunes, and the improvements in her mother's health, Htee K'Paw was deeply unhappy and this was made all too obvious by her demeanour. Hser Mu turned into the classroom and called out.

"Hello," Htee K'Paw replied, sounding cheerful enough.

"How's the marking going?"

"It's too much. I've got too many to do, I don't know how I'm going to get through them all."

The two girls exchanged a look of sympathy. The training that they had been given had born fruit, there was no doubt of that. They now expected higher standards from themselves and their classes. But, of course that meant there was more work to do.

Then Hser Mu, filled with impatience, could bear it no longer. "What is it? What's wrong, Htee K'Paw? I can't bear to see you like this. You don't seem yourself," she paused to look for some reaction from her friend, some clue, some softening of her face. When there was none she continued, "you seem so unhappy, and I don't want to see you like this. Please tell me what's wrong." She watched as Htee K'Paw's mouth stretched into a hard line across her face, then as she waited she saw a tear drop heavily onto the book that lay spread out in front of her.

"It's mother," Htee K'Paw gasped through her tears.

"But isn't she better now?"

"No. She will never be well. He, Tim gave us some medicines for her, but it won't be enough. She has to have them. If she doesn't, she'll die. We have no money for medicines. We can never buy enough to keep her well, they cost too much. And now he's gone."

230

Hser Mu had no idea what to say to her friend. Overcome with frustration she broke the silence. "You can take the day off, *Thramu Silvie* will understand. I can tell her you are sick and you can go home. Then you can take care of your mother."

"No, I don't want to. If I go home I will think too much. If I stay with the class then perhaps they will help me to forget."

"I don't know." The usually talkative Hser Mu knew that the conversation was going nowhere.

"I'm going to stay. I don't know what else to do," and Htee K'Paw turned back to the books while Hser Mu looked on in frustration and then turned away herself.

It was true. By concentrating on the children, Htee K'Paw was able to quell the storm of emotions that had been so disturbing her recently. First she gave out the books that she hadn't finished marking with an apology to the children. They cared little, for them it only put off the moment of reckoning that loomed so large for them. Htee K'Paw found the space to try something that her and Hser Mu had wanted to do ever since she had started the teacher training; she was going to try to get them all to write their own stories. Sometimes she wondered if the *kolah wahs* realised how hard it was to encourage the children to write. Many of their parents had never been to school and were unable to read or write. As for her own education, she had been brought up to repeat what the teacher said and it had taken a huge leap to discover the thoughts and ideas that lay buried deep inside her. She knew that in each one of the children there lay a story, perhaps of a home hurriedly abandoned, or of parents

231

or brothers lost forever, the story of a lonely, frightened child. As she looked around the children in her care she felt a sudden rush of emotion, maybe it was anger, anger that someone had possibly taken even more from some of them than had already been callously snatched from their young lives. She knew then that she had to stand tall, in spite of the shame that bowed her down so much. She had to somehow recover what she could of her dignity and surely the best way that she could do that was to help these children to be stronger: stronger than she had been.

"Now, children, we are going to try something new today. I want you to write something for me. You are to think of your own words. I will help you if you want me to, but I want you to use your own ideas. I want you to think about 'going on a journey' and I want you to write it down in your books. It can be any journey, perhaps your journey to school each day. It could be about a time when you went on a car or in a bus or on an elephant, or it could be . . . "

The light coming in through the doorway was suddenly blocked out. Htee K'Paw looked up at the intrusion. "Htee K'Paw," she heard Hser Mu's voice softly calling to her.

"Yes?"

"The commandant wants to see you in his office. I'll come with you."

"The children?"

"*Thramu Silvie* said she will come in to look after them."

And quietly Htee K'Paw put down her book and followed her friend.

As they reached the commandant's office Htee K'Paw hung back and let Hser Mu go in first. As she

232

stood waiting near the doorway of the large room with its liberal scattering of dusty files and papers she saw Jonathan in the gloomy far corner of the room. He too seemed to be hanging back but her eyes met his for a brief moment while a current of understanding seemed to flow between them.

Htee K'Paw had seen many westerners before. Several had come to the camp in the four years since she had lived there and she had been one of those lucky enough to have benefited from their input. Gradually, Htee K'Paw and the others had got used to their ways. The visitors were usually bigger and louder than Karen people and much happier - or that was how it had seemed to Htee K'Paw. But in that momentary glance at Jonathan she saw something quite different. She knew she was angry, confused, hurt and other things she couldn't understand, but what was happening to him? There was none of the cheerful bluster that she had come to associate with people of his colour; instead she saw a slightly hunched figure who seemed to be almost trying to hide away in the corner of the room, while his eyes were those of a frightened animal.

Hser Mu had gone into the next room and had spoken briefly to the commandant before speaking in English to the visitors.

"She won't speak with a man."

"A white man?" Martin interjected.

"Any man."

"Donna is here," Martin volunteered and he watched Hser Mu's inscrutable face for a moment before she answered.

233

"Yes," she replied, "And I will stay with her." It was stated as a fact.

Martin was not used to having the control taken from him but he could see no other way to proceed. He glanced at Donna and saw her nod briefly.

"Yes, all right," he conceded.

"And we must be alone."

"Of course."

"Perhaps she will not talk to anyone."

Donna nodded.

Donna regarded the head bent over the young body on the chair before her. The girl had whispered something to her, but so far she had been unable to hear anything coherent. That did not worry her, she was used to it. There were many girls who were afraid to talk at first. She didn't mind that, she would wait. It was the only way to proceed. In many ways this situation was no different to some she had met at home. The other girl, Hser Mu, sat straight-backed beside her friend, also looking as enduringly patient as she had learnt to be in these cases. "What was he like, this Tim? What was he like to you?"

"He was very good to her at first," Hser Mu spoke for her friend.

"Htee K'Paw," Donna said the unfamiliar syllables slowly and deliberate.

"Htee K'Paw," she repeated with more conviction. "Is that right? Was he good to you?"

"Yes," the girl spoke clearly at last. "Yes, he brought things for my brothers and medicines for my mother; she is very ill. Tim helped us a lot."

"Is that why you liked him so much?"

"He was very kind to me too. He talked to me, helped me with my English. He was good to everyone. We all liked him."

Donna saw Hser Mu quietly nodding her assent. "All right Htee K'Paw, that's good. Now I want you to tell me if there was anything that was a bit different about Tim, anything that you didn't like. Was there anything that made you a little bit unhappy, even just a small thing. It may be important for us."

Htee K'Paw's face creased into a small frown. "It's just a small thing. It was when he took me to the town. I looked at his camera. I know I should not have done it, but he was so angry, very angry. There were pictures on it. Some were of me and of other things, but I saw some of the children when they were in the river. He stopped me looking at them. But he was so angry that I think he did not want me to see them."

"So you think he might have had pictures in the camera that he didn't want you to see?"

"Yes, maybe he did. It's just that he was so angry. I can remember that very clearly, because before that he was always very kind."

"So it seemed unusual to you?"

"Yes"

Htee K'Paw watched as Donna wrote in a small book then looked up and smiled at her. "And he took you to town you say?"

"Yes, but only once. He took me for the weekend."

"And where did you go in the town?" Donna watched as the girl drew herself up in the chair.

"He took me to a guest house. My mother wanted me to visit my uncle, but he wanted me to go to the guest house with him."

"So he took you somewhere you didn't really want to go?"

"Yes, but I didn't mind too much because I was with him."

"You see, we shouldn't go into the town," Hser Mu interrupted by way of an explanation.

"But because you were with him you thought you would be safe, is that it?"

The girl nodded.

"Did he take you anywhere else?"

"Yes. We went to a pagoda - a temple and a restaurant and to the market. And to my uncle's house, the next day."

"Anywhere else? Anywhere else at all? Did you go to an Internet Cafe or computer shop? Think about it Htee K'Paw."

"He had to go to see someone. We went to someone's house. But I didn't go inside. I stayed downstairs, outside. And he went inside, upstairs."

"So he went inside and left you outside?"

"Yes."

"Did he tell you anything about what he was doing there?"

"No, he didn't."

Donna tried to disguise her excitement. The last thing she wanted was to upset the girl's hard-won flow of words

"And can you remember where it was?"

A frown crossed Htee K'Paw's face again before she shook her head.

"All right. So he took you to this place, but you can't remember exactly where it was. Was it near here, or near the town, or on the main road?"

"It was off the main road, I do remember that. And I think it was quite near the town but . . . "

"All right Htee K'Paw." She already had it in mind that they would take the girl along the route to find the house. Perhaps they could jog her memory in some way.

"Is there anything more you can tell us about him? Did he ever talk about other people outside the camp? Did he ever tell you anyone's name?"

Htee K'Paw slowly shook her head.

Donna waited. She knew from the past how slowly the truth comes out. How important it was to wait, when every pore in her body was driving her to probe. She saw a glance pass between the girls and sat up alert and ready for the next revelation. But no, nothing came. The girl seemed to sink down again in the chair with her shoulders slumped forward. It was as if a door had shut on whatever it was that had passed silently between the two girls. She decided to probe gently again into what she already knew.

"All right, Htee K'Paw, the house that he took you to, the one outside the town. Could you take us?"

The girl shook her head. "I didn't think about it, he just took me there, I didn't look where it was."

"But if we took you in the car, back to the town. Perhaps you could remember."

Again, there was the anxious shaking of the head.

Donna wanted to put her arms around the girl who sat in front of her. She decided she needed to change tack. "Do you know what the Internet is?"

Both girls nodded. "We have a computer here in the camp," Hser Mu explained.

"Do you have access to the Internet?" Donna's hopes rose for a moment. Perhaps the pictures were being uploaded right here in the camp.

"No, people go into town for that."

Donna smiled at her. It had been too much to hope that the answer would be that simple. She continued with her explanation.

"There are people who take photos of children and put them on the Internet. There are people who want to look at pictures like the ones that Tim had on his camera."

Htee K'Paw had broken into sobs in front of her.

"And we think that Tim may have been taking photos and films for that reason. And we need your help to stop it, Htee K'Paw. If we can find the people Tim was working with, if we can find the computer that he used, then perhaps we can break into the ring. That's what we call it in England, a paedophile ring. We want to stop these people if we possibly can. That's why it's so important. And that's why I want you to try to remember everything you can possibly think of. Will you try?"

Htee K'Paw nodded.

The pick-up truck was luxurious by local standards but the party had grown larger. Htee K'Paw sat in the front with Donna so that she had the best view of the road while Martin and Hser Mu sat in the seats behind. The Thai Police escort followed behind with John Pascoe, the interpreter, in their car. Donna wanted to watch Htee K'Paw's face as they drove towards the town but it was almost impossible. Still, the girl seemed willing to do what she could to help although Donna remained convinced that there was more to the story; the glance that had passed between the two girls seemed to confirm that.

Htee K'Paw suddenly spoke. "I remember this, the road got wider. I remember."

"Was it past here?"

"Yes, but not too far."

Martin asked the driver to slow down.

"What side of the road, can you remember?"

"Yes, this side," the girl indicated with her left hand.

"And was it on the road, or down a side road?"

"A side road, we turned down a side road."

Htee K'Paw sat upright in her seat, seemingly awakened at last to the importance of the task. "Here, I think it was here."

The driver braked sharply and turned into the road on the left and drove slowly as Htee K'Paw directed.

"Here," she indicated with her left hand again and the driver continued slowly onwards while she watched each house that they passed, until, turning back to Donna she shook her head. "I can't remember. They all look the same."

"All right," Donna tried not to sound disappointed. "Don't worry. We can try other roads. Can you remember what colour the house was? Was it large or small, was it made of wood or brick? Was it old or new?"

"I think it was quite an old house, made of wood, and quite big."

"And the other houses around about. What were they like?"

The words needle and haystack went through Martin's mind and he had to cling to what had brought him to this job in the first place. It had been his attention to detail, his ability to hold onto every shred of evidence that had put him head and shoulders above most of the other applicants for the job. But here it was Donna who had taken the reins of the investigation. He hadn't worked with this young girl at all; as far as he was concerned she was a closed book and they seemed to be getting nowhere. The thought of visiting every road and byway in the increasing tropical heat filled him with dread.

The driver turned the car and with infinite patience drove back to the highway, continued on the main road, then turned down the next side road. In the cramped confines of the back of the cab Martin's head began to loll sideways and eventually found a resting place against the window. Woken by Htee K'Paw's triumphant cry he sat up confused and thick headed.

"This house!"

Donna wanted to hug her. The lines of the girl's anxious frown had eased away and the three women sat quietly in the air-conditioned vehicle while the police entered the house.

Martin brushed past the woman who was loitering in the front of the house. He found her stupid smile unnerving in the extreme and wondered if she was mentally deficient. It occurred to him that if anyone wanted to do anything underhand they could get away with it here. The woman looked too pathetic to ask an intelligent question.

Already, the Thai Police were searching the property when Martin stepped back towards the car and wrenched open the door. "All right," he said then hesitated.

"Htee K'Paw," volunteered Donna.

"Yes," said Martin. "What did you see when you came to this house? Try to tell me exactly what you saw."

"Steady on, Martin, don't go at her like a bull in a china shop."

"I'm sorry. Look we have to find out. I'll start again."

"What did you see when you came here?" he asked again, this time more gently.

"I saw the woman, the same woman. And I sat on the bench with her. Tim told me to sit there," she pointed.

"All right now. Could you get out of the car and go and sit there, please?" He glanced at Donna who was nodding her approval. "Now, what did you see?"

Htee K'Paw looked upwards. "Tim, and the other man. They were up there. They looked over the side and down at me."

"What was he like, this man? Was he a white man? Was he Thai?"

"A white man. He was a white man."

"And did you hear anything?"

"I heard them talking, but I couldn't understand what they were saying."

"What language were they speaking? Could you hear that?"

"Oh, Martin."

Martin ignored her. "Could you hear them?"

"Yes."

"Could you understand them?"

241

"No."

"Could that have been because it was a language that you don't know?"

The girl slowly nodded her head.

"And you know English quite well?"

Again she nodded.

"So, they were speaking in a language other than English. And what did he look like, this man? Could you see him?"

"I could see his head and the top part of his body."

"Anything you can remember about him? Was he smaller than Tim, or bigger? Brown hair, light hair, younger, older?"

"He was bigger, much bigger. Fat around here," she indicating her own waist." And older, I.think."

"Anything else about him? Can you remember anything else?"

She saw Donna watching her as she tried to recall the man's head.

"His hair. His hair, he didn't have any hair. Just a little, here," and she reached around to the back of her own head.

Donna broke into the conversation, "Htee K'Paw, can you remember what you felt when you came to this house?"

Htee K'Paw did remember quite clearly. "I didn't like it. But I didn't think about it much. I just wanted to go to town. I wanted to forget it."

"If there's anything it's up there, in the room above this seat, behind the balcony. Look here," Martin, in spite of the heat had bounded up the stairs, working out the geography of the place as he did so.

242

"Here," he said.

"Nothing," John Pascoe met him on the stairs, "there's nothing here."

"Do they know what they're looking for? It'll be computers, or anything to do with them. Look in here. Anything, anything to do with a computer," he repeated himself as the two policemen came in and together they began to check every inch of the room again. There was a desk to one side and Martin crouched down to look underneath it, his trouser belt straining as he did so. He had never really thought of his weight as a problem, but here where everyone seemed so lean and small he realised how big he was. He struggled to look into the corners of the room under the desk, puffing a little as he did so, but it was worth it.

"OK, that's what we've been looking for." He stood upright triumphantly and called out to Donna, who was now standing outside the room.

"It's not much, but there's a phone connection here, now unused, which could mean that it was used for the Internet."

"Yes,"

"And there are several electrical points down there. And the dust has been disturbed very recently. I reckon they moved everything out as soon as Jonathan got hold of the camcorder. She's not a very efficient cleaner, this woman, whoever she is. Lets get the camera and photograph it all."

24

The air hung hot and still as Jonathan and David made their way to the tiny house by the river. Martin and Donna had decided that their going in the car to try to locate the house that Htee K'Paw had described could serve no useful purpose. Jonathan had been glad that they had gone without him; they would meet again tomorrow. He could not decide whether or not he wanted to be alone. There were points in the day when he felt such acute loneliness that it was almost painful and he craved company; then there were times when he wanted to be alone to try to sort out the tangle of wires that his mind had become. There had been days when he had felt lonely before of course. By any stretch of the imagination life in the refugee camp was strange for a westerner, but he had enjoyed that. It had all been part of what he had wanted to do and he had seen it as part of the challenge along with getting used to the food and coping with the rudimentary sanitary arrangements. He had a sort of pride in the fact that he had fully embraced the life of the people that he had been living with for the last six months. But this loneliness was more like a deep hole inside him that he did not understand and didn't know what to do with.

He had looked briefly at the film, enough to satisfy himself that he had been right to snatch the camera from Tim. But Martin and Donna had rented a video player from the hotel and Martin had gone out to buy the necessary leads so they could watch it on the television. Then they had gone over every sickening detail, pausing and replaying until they were fully satisfied. They had enough of a picture of Tim, they said, to be able to recognise him on sight in the future. As far as they were concerned it had been a good evening's work.

As he and David walked past the women washing in the river against a background of children chanting in the primary school classroom Jonathan became aware of what he could only describe as panic rising inside him, panic suffused with lethargy. It was as if his brain, which had been running wild for days, had begun to slow down and was now shutting down with exhaustion.

"I'm going to lie down," Jonathan said as they reached the house.

"That's fine by me. I think I'll do the same," said David and he watched as Jonathan stumbled through to his bedroom. There he flung himself on top of his blanket, lay with his head close to one of the spaces between the bamboo uprights so that the cooling air wafted over his face and begged for sleep.

David slept too; the heat and the jet lag together meant that he was able to ignore the hardness of the bamboo floor. It was almost dark by the time he woke to the sound of masculine voices and laughter.

"Jon," he heard his nephew's name and drifted up into the next layer of consciousness. He looked up to see a stranger standing over him and shook his head to try to overcome the stupor. Jonathan, his eyes equally heavy with drowsiness appeared in the doorway of his bedroom.

"You sleep well, Jon," Ko Maung said and as he did so Jonathan saw the glow of the reddening sky through the spaces between the bamboo uprights and realised just how long he had been asleep.

"Yes. The first time for days, many days," he said rubbing his eyes. Then realising his uncle had no idea who the fierce-looking young man was, he introduced them.

"How are you?" Ko Maung asked David, emphasising the words into the western greeting he had been practising.

"Very well," David answered with a smile but Jonathan decided it was time to be honest and resist the trite answer.

"Not so good," he said as he dropped his head into his hands and rubbed his face as though trying to massage some life into his brain. "I was arrested. It seems that Tim reported me to the police in town and they put me in the detention centre for a couple of nights. Then the British Police came and got me out."

"The British Police?"

"Yes," replied David as he saw the confusion on Ko Maung's face. "It's very serious. What Tim was doing is against the law. And the police want to stop it."

"Taking films of children?"

"Yes. It's not just the pictures. They think that he was putting them on the Internet."

"And they want to stop it."

"Yes. Sometimes it seems almost impossible to do anything about it but they have to try. They'll do everything they can."

"Have they found Tim?"

"We don't think so," Jonathan answered. "But perhaps they will one day, I don't know." The weight of it depressed him, but he did not want to ignore Ko Maung's questions.

Just then a roar of laughter was heard from the nearby dormitory. It gave Jonathan a much-needed chance to change the subject. "I wish I knew what they were laughing about? You've all made me very welcome but it's hard when you're all together, and I feel that I can never really belong. Do you understand what I mean?"

"Yes I do. I don't know what they are laughing about either."

"No?"

"No, I'm Burmese. I can speak some Karen but I still don't understand all of it. And I still don't get all the jokes."

"You, you're Burmese? I didn't know."

"Yes, I'm Burmese. You can tell by my name."

"I didn't think about that. I thought you were in the KNU."

"I am now, but I wasn't always."

"So what happened?" Jonathan felt his mind clearing at last. He glanced across at his uncle."

"I was a soldier. I was in the Burmese Army. Then I left."

"You deserted?"

"Yes, I deserted."

"Isn't that dangerous? What if they catch you?"

"I make sure they don't." Ko Maung smiled.

"So . . . tell me."

"It was the uprising. Do you know about that?"

"Yes, in 1988, we've heard all about it." Jonathan spoke for David too.

"I was a soldier in Rangoon. And I saw what they did. They shot people in the street; some of them were only schoolchildren. And then they killed nurses and doctors at the hospital. It made me sick. I hated it."

Once again Jonathan saw how Ko Maung's rather gruff, solid exterior belied his inner nature.

"Then one day some students talked to me. They wanted me to join them. I didn't want to at first. I couldn't see how I could do that and not get found out. And I didn't want to leave my family. Then it became more dangerous for the students; the police were arresting them, thousands of them, so some of them arranged to escape from the city. That's when I saw my chance and I asked if I could travel with them. I couldn't stand what I was doing any more so I came out here."

"And now you're a Karen soldier."

"Yes," Ko Maung laughed quietly.

"And a good one."

"They trained us. Life was very different out here, for me, for all of us. We knew nothing of the forest before that. And Malaria, lots fell ill with Malaria; some died."

"And I thought you had always been here. In the forest."

"No, not me, I'm a city boy. We were taught that these people were all savages, wild people who were causing trouble to our country. Now we know what they are really like we can understand."

"So you are saying that you knew nothing about what happened in Karen State before you came here?"

"No, nobody in the cities knew. Until they come here they don't know. That's what the government is like, they tell us a lie. They don't want us to know the truth."

"Propaganda," said David.

"What?"

"Propaganda," David repeated. "That's what it's called when the government doesn't want you to know the truth so it tells you a lie. It happens in lots of places, not just in Burma."

Ko Maung reached into his trouser pocket, pulled out a packet of cigarettes and offered one to each of them. Jonathan took one gratefully. "That's why we need you Jonathan. We need you to teach us. The schools inside aren't allowed to teach anything except what the government want. Then sometimes they're closed. Maybe they open for a day and then they are closed for a week. Even here in the camps you've seen what they do. The students have no chance to think for themselves, they just have to accept what the teacher says. And the teachers don't know much either."

Jonathan felt himself warmed by Ko Maung's words. "So you really think I should carry on?"

"Yes. I do. You could do more of your classes, and you're writing. You said that you wanted to hear our stories, our problems."

"I don't know. I seem to have got stuck. Now I feel as if I am getting nowhere."

"Jonathan, what you are doing is good. You should put your work together then you can make the people in the world outside understand. Then you will really help us."

Jonathan watched for a while as Ko Maung drew slowly on his cigarette. He was unsure what to say. All three slumped wearily on the bamboo floor.

Then a question occurred to him. He sat up so quickly that David almost jumped.

"Htee K'Paw. They told me she went to the commandant and spoke to him."

"Yes. First she came and talked to us. She told us that she had seen photos taken by Tim. She said he was not a good man. Then some of the students went with her to the commandant."

"And then what happened?"

"I don't know, but we were all surprised. We thought she loved him, but then she said she thought he was a bad man."

"So she changed her mind about him?"

"Yes."

Jonathan stared at the glowing end of his cigarette. "So . . . "

"Does that make you feel better?" asked David at last.

"Yes, it does. It means that someone else knows what I am talking about."

"And that means that if he comes back they will be more determined to catch him."

"Do you think that will ever happen?"

"Don't go down that road Jon. You'll only depress yourself again." David said and they both watched as Ko Maung climbed down the steps, stubbed out his cigarette in the dust outside and went to find some food for supper.

"Well, you heard what the man said Jon,"

They both sat on the veranda after supper. His uncle had elected to stay the night with him, for which Jonathan was quietly grateful. The air was substantially cooler than it had been under the hot daytime sun and it was pleasant to sit outside in the evening warmth.

"What?" For a moment Jonathan couldn't think what his uncle was talking about.

"The lectures, the classes, he obviously appreciates what you do, so perhaps you should teach some more. If Martin and Donna don't need to see you for long tomorrow you'd be free by the afternoon.

"Do you think so?"

"Of course. And putting your mind to teaching could provide you with a distraction. It looks like you could do with that at the moment."

"I guess you're right," Jonathan spoke without conviction. As far as he could see, any confidence that he had once had had drained away in the last few days.

"And you've been with them for some time now. You know what they want, and it looks like they want to hear what you have to say. You know your stuff, Jon. How about it?" David looked across at his nephew.

"All right, I've got some lesson plans. I suppose I could use those."

"And I could come along too. That is if you want me to. I might learn something, and it would be interesting to see what you do."

"Communism," Jonathan looked around at the expectant faces of the students in the small bamboo classroom. "There was a massive spread of communism in South East Asia after the second-world-war and on into the 60's. The West was very afraid of this; they saw it as a serious threat. So I think we need to look at some of the issues and try to understand them."

He turned round and wrote the names 'Marx' and 'Engels' on the white board. As he did so he heard mutterings from some of the students behind him. He turned round wanting to bring some of the talk out into the open. "OK, then, one at a time," and he pointed across the room to where the most strident of the voices had spoken.

"My father hated the communists," said the student.

"But why? They fought against the Burmese so they were on our side. They helped us."

"They didn't help my family. They wanted to take our land. They tried to steal it from us, so my father hated them for that."

"I think the communists want everything to be fair, that's why they took land from wealthy people like . . ."

"But my family is not wealthy."

Jonathan held up his hand. He decided he had to interrupt the argument if the class was going to proceed at all. "Before we look at how communism affected ordinary people I want us to consider the background. We are going to look at the theories of Marx and Engels, see why communism grew, and then we'll look at how it worked out and why it declined."

He turned round to look at the white board to remind himself of what he had written there before looking back at the class. He couldn't remember his lesson plan so he opened his notebook. After a few turns of the pages he found the correct one and quickly looked at the lesson outline. The words 'The conditions which led to the growth of communism' were written clearly on the page. He looked around the class again where every eye was on him, waiting expectantly for the lesson to continue. Then he looked again at the page, shaking his head as he did so in an attempt to remember his lesson plan.

He had forgotten everything.

25

"God what a mess," Jonathan spat the words out as he stared gloomily across the veranda rail at the stream wending its way towards the border. Everything was grey confusion; he couldn't imagine how he had ever thought himself capable of doing research, writing a thesis, much less a book.

"Jon?" David stood beside him.

"I was doing something so elementary with them. How could I forget that? I know my stuff. And now look at me. I can't even think what I'm doing."

David stared across the thatched roofs of the nearby houses before he spoke. "I know this isn't really my territory, but perhaps your mind shut down because of everything that's happened."

"Huh! I don't know," Jonathan heard the bitterness in his own voice, "and I wonder what they all thought. What sort of teacher stands up in front of the class and then forgets everything?"

"I doubt if they think any the worse of you. I thought they all seemed pretty sympathetic. And that Thaw Reh guy stepped in and took the class over. I think they'll have forgotten it in no time."

Jonathan stared straight ahead. "I'm a bloody failure. It's the one thing I've always been good at. Now I can't even do that right."

David turned away from his nephew. In the tiny room that served as a study, pens, blankets and notebooks lay where they had dropped. He busied himself for a few minutes picking up, folding and piling the clothes in an attempt to restore some order to both the little house and his own mind. His thoughts went back to his years as a young teenager in Northern Ireland as he remembered the fear that he had felt every time his father went to work.

Satisfied once again with the appearance of the room he turned back to Jonathan. "I think I can imagine some of what's happening to you," he began carefully. Jonathan looked up from his brooding for a moment and then looked away again. David continued. "When I was young, maybe fourteen or so, my father owned the same shop that he still has. It was in the seventies, and there were pictures of bombs every night on the television. They were often in shops, just like ours, or cars or in the street. Every morning when he went out of the door we never knew if we would see him alive again. Sometimes he would have to go out at night too; they would call him if they were suspicious of something. But nobody ever talked about it. It was like a conspiracy of silence, a part of life; we just got on with it. Now I think back to those times I realise I was terrified. But I never told a soul. Just like you. I didn't think that what I was feeling was that important."

He stopped for a moment and caught Jonathan looking at him. His eyes looked flat, almost expressionless. David felt a stab of fear for his nephew.

Was he out of his depth? Perhaps the psychological effect of what had happened to Jonathan was way beyond his own understanding. He decided to press on with his own story. "Anyway, I thought I'd put it all behind me. I had, but it was all buried deep down inside. Like your Mr Dixon." He glanced across at Jonathan again, this time there was a flicker of recognition.

"But I hadn't forgotten it. It was there all the time. And it all came out one day when we had to take Ian to the hospital. He was about fifteen months old. He had a convulsion and stopped breathing. Sarah took hold of him and breathed into his mouth and I just drove. I took them to the hospital, Sarah holding little Ian in her arms. I thought I was fine. The crisis was over almost in no time. By the time we got there he was breathing again. They took him in and hooked him up to wires and you name it. And suddenly I just fell apart. I was like you: I couldn't think, my mind went blank. I was completely incapable of driving after that. When I began to feel better the doctor said the lid had blown off. And it was like that; what happened to Ian made everything come back to me. That's when I felt the effect of everything that had happened to me as a teenager." He stopped for a few moments. "And slowly I came to terms with it all, and in time I felt better. And, well, I just wonder if it's a bit like what's happened to you, the lid blowing off," David looked up for a moment as the strip-light flickered then lit up the room. He knew that would happen; the parts of the camp that were lucky enough to have a generator were able to use electric light every evening for a few hours. Then he waited in the silence.

256

At last Jonathan spoke, "You could be right," he paused, then repeated: "You could be right," and his voice tailed off. "What happened? I mean, were you ill? Did you have to have time off work? How did it affect you?"

"Well, the doctor said it was depression. I didn't know anything about illness before; that had always been Sarah's line. And yes, I took some time off, took the tablets, and gradually life went back to normal. But I had to face it all fair and square. I had to go through it all in my mind before I could lay it to rest. I cut it down to size, you might say." He glanced at Jonathan again. "Why don't you come home for a while?"

"I don't know. Did you ever tell your parents about what happened to you?" Jonathan was curious to know more of his uncle's story.

"No, I'm afraid I wasn't sure how they would take it. Perhaps I should have done, but I didn't."

"You see I'm not sure what mine would think. They were never very happy about me doing this. They wanted me to take the Law Conversion course after I graduated. They don't seem able to understand any sort of uncertainty. And now this mess, what would they make of all this? What would they tell them at the Golf Club? Their son's a failure. It wouldn't go down too well would it?"

"But everyone needs a break sometimes. And you don't have to tell them everything. You could think of it as a retreat. That's what armies do. They regroup and start afresh. Talking of understanding Burma, isn't that what happened here in 1942? The longest retreat they called it. It was the longest retreat in British military history. And the allies came back stronger and better than ever before and won all that territory back."

257

"You know your history then."

"Yes, coming here every year has made me interested in what happened in the Second World War especially. But I'm interested in you Jon. What about it? You could come home. I'll sort a ticket out for you in town. You could be back here again in a couple of months. How about it?"

Jonathan's face broke into the faintest of smiles. "Maybe you're right. I'll give it some thought. But . . "

"But what?"

"I don't want my parents to know. You won't tell them, will you?"

"No. You can trust me. But can I tell Sarah? I think she would know what to do. She might have some ideas about how to proceed."

"Yes, yes of course," Jonathan uttered distractedly. He knew he could trust both his uncle and aunt.

"And there's another thing. We don't have to think about this immediately but sometime you have to consider the question of this Mr Dixon." David waited before continuing. "There may have been other people that he abused. He may still be out there."

"Oh God, I wish I had never met that bastard Tim. If it hadn't been for him I would have forgotten all that."

"But it would have come back to you some time Jon. Perhaps when you least expected it and in ways that you don't realise."

Jonathan looked up with a frown on his face.

"Oh, relationships can be affected by that sort of experience. Or you could get bad dreams; suddenly you're in the middle of a nightmare and you don't know where it's come from." And then he saw that that was indeed true for his nephew. "It's best brought out in the open, then your mind can begin to deal with it."

"To be honest with you. I didn't hold out much hope," said Martin as he and Donna sipped their beer on the terrace of the Sompat. "Well done for getting her to remember what the guy in the house looked like."

"Ah, but the best of it is, I think I know who she was describing. Or at least I've got a good idea."

"OK. You're dying to tell me."

"Well, I can't be sure, but it could be Gunter."

"Gunter Groschiede?"

"Could be. She described him pretty well. Overweight, bald, with a bit of hair at the back. Older than Tim, although I grant you we don't know exactly how old he is."

"The general understanding seems to be that he is around late twenties."

"Yes, I guess that's right. The kids like him, think he's one of them. He's a bit of a whiz kid with the Internet. It all fits with that sort of age."

"Interesting. So Tim could be part of Gunter's outfit."

"Could be," he repeated." It's all a lot of 'ifs'. But it looked sure as hell to me that there was once a computer there, which had been moved in a hurry. There were all the signs."

"So we've got another piece of the jigsaw."

"Yeah, and I guess they'll lie low for a while. Jonathan must have given them a bit of a fright."

"I think there's more to it."

"How do you mean?"

"There's something she's not telling us."

"Who? The girl?"

"Yes. She was very slow to come out with what she did say. And I grant you she was very helpful. More helpful than I thought she'd be, to be honest. But there's still something she's not saying."

"Well, we're back there tomorrow. You can try again."

Donna appeared not to hear him.

"You see, there's something about her. What do you see when you look at her?"

"I see a pretty girl. Quite serious. Nice, helpful. What else were you thinking?"

"How old would you say she was?"

"Seventeen, eighteen perhaps. I don't know."

"She's twenty three."

"Well, she doesn't look it."

"Precisely. And I think that's what he thought too. Perhaps he almost thought of her as one of the children. He picked on her because she looked so young."

"Maybe."

"Almost certainly I would say. And I think he might have abused her in some way but she's too ashamed to say."

"But she went with him willingly."

"Yes, she did. But if you lived in one of these camps and a nice young westerner offered to take you out for the day, wouldn't you go? Especially as she told me that he had been giving her medicines for her mother. It's all there: the charming young man, the grooming of the young children. And she did let out that he took her to a hotel, or guesthouse where she didn't want to go. She wanted to visit her uncle. But he

260

had her where he wanted her. Once they're in the town they risk being arrested. Did you know that? She could hardly get away from him under those conditions. She had to stick with him. She had to do what he said."

"So that's your assessment of the situation. Have you got any facts?"

"Martin, don't start that again. All I'm saying is that I'm sure there's more."

"Well, we're going out there again tomorrow so you can talk with her again."

"And then I have to face the worst thing of all . . . I've got to somehow get to talk to those children on the film. God, if there's one thing I really don't want to do, it's that."

"Jonathan,"

"Hi there," Jonathan replied, pleased to see the solid, reassuring face of Martin once again. "How did it go yesterday?"

"We found out quite a lot."

"Did you find what you were looking for?"

"What, a computer all in place? No. They, whoever they are, were gone. That's not surprising really. But the girl. . ."

"Htee K'Paw."

"Yes. She was very helpful. We took her to the place and she was able to describe another guy pretty well. From her description we think he may be someone we've come across before."

"But nothing more than that?"

"That's how it is in this business, but everything we find out helps. And you never know what new facts you may find out."

"And now what?"

261

"Oh, Donna's here to speak to the girl again. Thinks there's more that she hasn't told us yet."

"Could be. She's pretty quiet. It takes a while to get to know these people."

"And you, how are you? You looked pretty rough yesterday, if you don't mind me saying."

"You're right. I wasn't feeling too good."

"This business got to you has it?"

"Yes, it has, but it's not just that. Some of the guys took me inside as they call it."

"You mean across the border?"

"Yes. They take medicines and so on. At least the people here have got most things that they really need. Inside many of them don't have much. Soldiers burn down the villages, there are land mines . . . the things you hear about. Well they're all here."

"Soldiers? Which soldiers do you mean?"

"Burmese soldiers. There's civil war going on here. Has been for years, decades. These people have been fighting the Burmese Army. Anyway, we were staying in one of the villages when they set light to it. It was first thing in the morning, not even daylight. We had to run, all of us, across some fields. Then they started shooting. The guy next to me was killed. I was thrown to the ground but I was fine except for a few cuts and bruises. But seeing him dead was the worst. He was shot in the back; his name was Po Thaw. He was a great guy, too, always friendly and very clever. I watched him do an operation on a man's leg, there in one of the little houses in the jungle. He just got on and did it. Then the next day he was dead."

Martin licked his lips and reached into the bag that he had brought with him. "Here. Have one of these," and he handed Jonathan a can of beer.

"Thanks. Yes, I will."

"You hear about that sort of thing happening. But you never think it's going to happen to you."

Jonathan shook his head distractedly. "My uncle wants me to go home for a while, but then that seems like running away and I don't want to do that. After all, these kids can never go home. But at the moment I can't see how I can carry on."

"Tell me a bit about what you're doing here Jon. I know you're doing a doctorate, but what's it all about?'

"Well, I'm not just doing the doctorate. I work as an English teacher. That's the only way I can get into the camp legally. Everyone wants to learn English. And it helps me to get to know them all and learn about what's going on here. I'm studying the politics."

"Sounds like clever stuff."

"Not really. I'm trying to understand the situation, get to the bottom of it as much as I can. It's very complicated."

"How's it going?"

"It was slow at first, very slow. Then things started picking up and I was getting some good material together. I think it took some time for them to trust me. But now, this has happened and it's put me off my stroke a bit. I don't know if anything I do will make the slightest bit of difference."

"That's how I feel sometimes. This job. It's a thankless task. You make a tiny bit of progress but it makes no difference to the bastards. But we have to keep going. We can't just let them get away with it. We have to do what we can. Every little bit helps. That's what my grandmother was always saying."

"Are you from Wales?"

"Yes, but I work in London now. And you?"

"My parents live by the sea, down in Dorset. It's good sailing country, I go whenever I can. At the moment I'd give anything to be skimming across the waves in Poole Harbour."

"Well there's no harm in taking a break, is there? You can always come back when you feel better."

"Maybe."

"What about money? Have you got enough for a ticket?"

"Oh, that's no problem, I've got some in the bank, and I've spent almost nothing since being here."

"Well think about it. It'll do no harm, surely."

"Yes, I will, thanks." Jonathan tipped his head back to empty the beer can and then watched Martin walk across to stare out across the veranda.

"It's beautiful here isn't it? Or at least it would be. Look at that cliff. That's an incredible sight."

"Oh yes. It is, very. Down by the river and across the other side, it's pure jungle, thick forest. And the people, they're amazing too. I just don't how they keep going when you hear what some of them have been through. And none of them show a shred of self-pity. That's why I feel as if I'm letting them down if I leave."

"You are a mixed up kid, Jon. Go home for a while. And then come back and finish whatever it is you're doing. And when the book comes out, make sure I get a copy, understand."

Htee K'Paw watched Donna press the button on the small tape recorder and quietly say some words into the microphone. She licked her lips and looked down into her lap where her hands were tightly clasped together. She realised that in her nervousness she had been working her fingers into such a tight knot that they hurt. As she stopped the movement she became aware of another pain; this time in the upper part of her stomach. She had felt it several times recently but had been so busy that she was mostly able to ignore it, but now, in the quietness of the commandant's office it was there again, and she sat up straight so that she could more easily press her fingers into her flesh in order to rub it away. She felt the firm touch of Hser Mu's hand on hers.

"The children in the orphanage," Donna began and Htee K'Paw was almost overcome by the wave of nausea that seemed to wash though her. She looked down at Hser Mu's hand still resting where it had alighted a few seconds before. Donna was still talking and Htee K'Paw tried to block out the sound but she couldn't.

"We know what he was doing because it was on the film." Donna continued. "And it's important to get them to talk about it, to tell someone what happened. You see if they don't tell anyone then they will think that nobody cares. It will make things hard for them as they grow older." She spoke steadily and gently, her voice never wavering.

Htee K'Paw felt hot tears fill her eyes and then she began to sob. It was as if one of the heavy, drenching storms of the monsoon had suddenly broken inside her. She shook, she cried, and she clung desperately to Hser Mu. "It was my fault! I took him to the orphanage. If I hadn't done that, it wouldn't have happened," she wailed.

"I don't understand," Donna said quietly to Hser Mu who translated for her.

"She says . . " Htee K'Paw heard Hser Mu beginning to speak for her but Donna quickly interrupted her. "It's better if you tell me yourself, Htee K'Paw, I know it's hard but I want you to try."

Htee K'Paw fought to control her shaking. "It was me who took Tim to the orphanage. But now I see what has happened I feel so bad, and it's all my fault."

"So do you think that if you hadn't taken him there this would not have happened to the children?"

Htee K'Paw nodded silently.

"You can't know that, Htee K'Paw. He could have asked any number of people to take him to see the children. I'm sure he would have found a way."

Htee K'Paw still said nothing.

"So now you feel that you can't forgive yourself, is that it?" Donna asked.

Htee K'Paw nodded. It was true. Donna had said exactly the right thing. She lifted her face to look across at her and saw the policewoman's face break into a smile before glancing again at the tape recorder. She began to feel that she quite liked Donna. With her round face surrounded by short black curls she was both pleasant to look at and to be with. Htee K'Paw had always thought that the police were to be feared, whereas this woman seemed almost motherly. Donna gave the impression that she knew her job very well, indeed it would be difficult to hide anything from her but Htee K'Paw had the growing feeling that she could trust her.

"Htee K'Paw, I don't want you worry about the children. It was not your fault; you must believe that. And I've spoken with the Women's Welfare Group.

266

They are going to find the right person to talk with them. They have been very good to us and they want to help. So we are going to leave that in their hands. Martin and I don't think the children will talk with us, even with an interpreter. It would frighten them too much."

"Yes," Htee K'Paw answered. "Yes," she said again, unable to think how else to answer.

Meanwhile Donna was contemplating the tape recorder again. She wanted to reach out and turn it off for a few seconds so that she could ask the question she wanted to ask so badly but knew she shouldn't. Jonathan's aunt Sarah had told her about the culture when they had interviewed her. She had prepared them for the fact that these people, especially the women, would be very reticent. But she had to somehow try to find out just what was making this girl feel so bad. Donna's best guess was that she still felt very guilty about something. After an interval of what could not have been more than a few seconds she sat up straight and took a deep breath. The tape recorder would just have to record it. She began again. "When he took you away to town, how did he make you feel? Did he hurt you at all? Did he threaten you?"

Htee K'Paw found it difficult to think back to the time before Tim had taken her to town but, after a few moments thought, she was able to answer. "No, he didn't hurt me, but when I was in the town I felt a little afraid of him."

"Afraid of him?"

"Because he took me to the hotel instead of my uncle's house and because he was so angry about the camera. I didn't want him to be angry because I wanted him to keep buying the medicines for mother.

And I didn't know what he might do to me. I thought that he wouldn't take me home again. And I was afraid because I was in the town."

"But you weren't afraid of him before that?"

"No, no, he made me very happy. He was so kind. But, I don't remember, I can't remember." The truth was that she didn't want to remember, she didn't want to think what lay behind the confusion that had clouded her mind on that strange morning in the hotel. She composed herself and began again. "I felt strange in the morning. I never felt like that before."

"Strange?"

"Very sleepy, and there was a pain. No, it was a strange feeling in here," Htee K'Paw poked her hand into the soft flesh of her lower abdomen.

Donna was suddenly aware of her own flesh. A chill had made the fine hairs on her arms stand upright.

"Did he give you anything to drink?"

"Yes. Beer, and coke." Now Htee K'Paw remembered how Tim had ordered several bottles of beer between them and she had drunk thirstily after her long day out.

"Was there any strange taste to the drinks?"

"No." She shook her head wondering why Donna should ask such a question.

"And yet you woke up feeling very strange. Can you tell me what that feeling was like?'

"Very tired. My head felt, " she stopped and lifted her hand to her forehead.

She glanced at Hser Mu and said something quietly.

"Dizzy?" suggested Hser Mu.

"Dizzy," repeated Htee K'Paw nodding as she did so.

"And had you slept well?"

"Yes, I slept very well, but I woke up so tired."

"Do you think that something happened to you while you were asleep?"

Htee K'Paw felt the almost involuntary nodding of her own head. Donna was exactly right. Something had happened to her while she had been asleep, but why hadn't she woken? This was the truth that she had wanted to hide even from herself so how did Donna know? She felt her mouth dry as she looked across at the policewoman.

"Can I ask something?" her own voice sounded strange to her, quiet and far away. Again she fought to control the feeling of nausea.

"Of course," Donna said.

"Why don't I remember? Why didn't I wake up? What?" Her voice tailed off.

"Can you think why?" Htee K'Paw was surprised at the kindly tone of Donna's voice.

Htee K'Paw did know. It was almost the most uncomfortable fact of all. She had never stepped outside of her self-imposed boundaries before, but the first westerner who had ever given her attention had somehow persuaded her to behave in a way that was, for her, completely out of character. With a flash of insight she remembered that she had always reserved a certain nervousness for anything that was outside her experience, so what had Tim done to make her change her ways so completely? Now she was overcome with the shame of her own stupidity.

"Htee K'Paw?" Donna was saying again. "Can you think?"

She nodded her head. "It was the drink. It must have been. I have never tried beer before but . . .?"

"And he might have put something into the drink too, a sort of medicine, something to make you forget. But it was not your fault Htee K'Paw. You must remember that. None of it was your fault."

Hser Mu looked across at Donna from her place by Htee K'Paw's side, her face pale with shock and anger. "So, you made her remember. She had forgotten, but you made her remember. Now you . . . "

"No, Hser Mu," Htee K'Paw could sense the rising anger in her friend. "I did remember. At least, I half remembered, and that's worse. I felt strange because I was . . ."

"Confused?" Donna volunteered.

"Yes, confused," she gripped Hser Mu's hand. "But perhaps it's for the best. Now I know what happened when I went to town with him, "she stopped, feeling the cold on her arms. "Now I know what he was really like. And now I know why I was so sure that Jonathan did the right thing."

"Can we go now?" Hser Mu whispered.

"Yes, and thank you for telling me, Htee K'Paw. And it will help you. It's good to talk about it, better than keeping it all inside you." Then she reached into her bag and pulled out a card. "Take this," she said as she reached out to her again, "If you think of anything more. Anything. If you want to talk to me about something then you can let me know. You can write, or someone can arrange for you to email us. It's all there on the card. And thank you," Donna smiled as brightly as she could. Then she watched as Htee K'Paw rose to her feet and was ushered out by her friend without a backward glance.

Donna hated her job then. She hated what she had had to do. What good could it really have done to

270

make her remember what that man had done to her? He had hurt her in every way it was possible for a man to hurt a woman and now she felt that she had added to the pain. It was as well that she didn't see Htee K'Paw tear up her card with a vehemence that she would not have thought possible.

26

Htee K'Paw stared gloomily over the edge of the veranda and out across the roofs of the houses below. The hot, steamy air was all-pervading, but that was only a small contributing factor to her acute exhaustion. She was grateful that it was still the holidays; she hardly knew what she would do when the school started again next week.

In the morning it had been K'Paw Meh who had been the cause of all the trouble.

"Don't just go off with your friends today, the way you always do. I need you to help me," she had said to her sister. She remembered clearly that her request had seemed quite reasonable at the time.

"I don't always go off."

"Yes, you do. You're never here when I need you," Htee K'Paw had felt her voice rising in pitch but she had continued, blinded by anger and frustration. "Look at all this," she had yelled, gesturing at the pile of wet clothes that had accumulated over the last day and night, while feeling herself drowning in a sea of helplessness. "I have to do everything and you never help me."

"You're always shouting that's why. You're so miserable all the time. I hate it!"

"What about mother?" She had lowered her voice then, remembering that her mother was at last sleeping after a disturbed night.

"You're always there whenever I go to her," K'Paw Meh protested at the injustice of her sister's accusation. "Anyway, I take care of the boys, and help with the cooking. You can't say I never do anything."

"Sometimes, maybe," and for a moment she had realised how she must sound and was sorely disappointed by her own bad temper. Then she had thought again of the muddy clothes that she had taken off the boys yesterday and felt herself sinking into despair.

It was too late; the raised voices had disturbed their mother and she had begun to cough uncontrollably. Htee K'Paw had rushed into the bedroom and pulled her up to a sitting position. There she had held a rag to wipe away all the frothy mucus that she was permanently spitting out whenever she was awake and cursed herself for allowing her own voice to get so loud. Slowly, the coughing fit had subsided and Daw Nee Meh had sunk back exhausted, but not before soaking another sarong with urine.

And K'Paw Meh had helped. Htee K'Paw could see the clean clothes hanging over the side of the house baking in the hot air. She knew she needed to keep an eye on them; there was almost certain to be rain soon, but she could hardly raise the energy to move herself, let alone go collecting washing.

K'Paw Meh hadn't just helped with the washing; she knew that, at that very moment, her sister lay beside their mother, sleeping in the early afternoon heat. When she had first made that discovery Htee K'Paw had been filled with jealousy. That was the

273

place that she reserved for herself, so that, however busy she had been, she could give herself to her mother's comfort when she needed it. Even now, the nausea of envy was in her stomach with it's accompanying pain, sharp and strong that sometimes, as now, made her bend forward and for a few moments forget everything and think only of her own agony. Then it passed and she straightened out again, perspiring and chilled. Eventually she too gave in to weariness and lay down to rest.

The sound of her mother's voice penetrated the heavy afternoon drowsiness and she sat up with the realisation that the air was already clearer. It was raining heavily. The fact that she had not heard the clatter and roar of the rain on the leaf thatched roof surprised her and she got up quickly and peered out and along the side of the house. Someone had obviously had the forethought to bring the clothes in. As she stood up she rubbed at her stomach, feeling again the spot from which the pain had emanated; then she stretched out her *sarong* and tied it round her waist, choosing to ignore the inescapable fact that she was having to pull tighter than ever before to be sure that the garment stayed in place.

She swept round the front of the house and then went round to the little kitchen at the side where she put a few lumps of fresh charcoal onto the small stove and set a pot of water in place to boil. Her mother liked to drink *la pa htee,* an infusion of black leaf tea that many refugees enjoyed so much. Her father had bought a small packet of tablets from the pharmacy in town so she reached up to their hiding place on a high shelf, took one out and counted them quickly as she did so.

At the rate of one a day, they would only last one more week, and still Daw Nee Meh seemed to be gaining very little benefit from them. She placed the tablet carefully onto a dish then taking the jug she threw some of the crude tea-leaves into it. As she waited for the water to come to the boil she stared gloomily at the stream of water that poured through the place where the thatch had come away. It was like a reproach, reminding her that it had been far too long since they had replaced the leaves. That was another task that needed to be done, but it was now too late for this season. They would just have to patch up where they could and endure it.

The water came to the boil. She filled the jug in order to make the reviving concoction her mother enjoyed so much, took a small tray and found three of the best glasses. Having done all to her satisfaction she once again took hold of the fabric of her *sarong*, ran her hand across her stomach where the pain bit so hard sometimes, paused for a moment to take note of the bones of her pelvis that she could feel so sharply and drew the garment tightly round her. She took up the tray and, moving carefully, entered the bedroom. At the threshold she stopped for a moment at the sight of her mother. Her body had become almost unrecognisably bloated with excess fluid. K'Paw Meh was bending close to the sick woman in order to try to make out what she was saying; each syllable being separated by a gasp for air. "*T . . . Tee . . . T . . "*

"What is it?" Htee K'Paw asked as she set the tray down carefully to one side before moving closer herself and straining to understand.

"She's talking about home. She wants to go home. She says it over and over again," her sister said, while Htee K'Paw took note of the obvious distress in her voice.

Htee K'Paw looked across at her sister in the gloom of the bamboo hut and thought of her own desire to see once more the forests, valleys and rivers of home. Of course she wanted to go back, they all did. What was there here for them in this place that was either dry with dust or slimy with mud? They had done everything they could to make it homely. Their tiny patch of ground boasted a small vegetable patch and a few trees of banana and papaya. Indeed, the younger boys had never known anywhere else; this had always been their home. For K'Paw Meh and herself there was always the optimism of youth, and father at least had the opportunity to go and work somewhere else, although for what pittance, Htee K'Paw had little idea. But mother had never settled here properly. That had been clear from the beginning and nothing had ever changed for her.

She poured some of the tea into the glasses and waited until it cooled to a reasonable temperature. "I've got some *la pa htee* for you here mother. You know how you like it and here's one of your tablets. They will help you to feel better," she said brightly in spite of herself. "Here," and she placed the tablet carefully in her mother's open mouth, "and have some of your drink. It will be good for you." And reaching behind her mother she pulled her to a sitting position, more roughly than she meant to.

Her mother spat the tablet out. "No, here, take it," Htee K'Paw struggled to keep her mother in position by placing her own shoulder behind her, gathered up the tablet and put it in her mouth again. "You must take it, it's important for you," she could

276

hear her own impatience as she placed the glass of tea on her mother's lips and tipped it carefully upwards. Her mother accepted the drink, gasping between each tiny mouthful and Htee K'Paw began to relax again. Then, to her dismay, the tablet reappeared. This time it was no longer in one piece, but broken into tiny grains and mixed with the dribble that slowly trickled from the corner of Daw Nee Meh's mouth.

Htee K'Paw let her mothers body sink back onto the pillow that had been supporting her and dropped her own head onto her chest. She wanted to cry, no, to cry out with anger and frustration. "*Moe,* you must have the tablet. Now I'll have to get another one," and quickly climbing to her feet again she hurried outside.

"No, don't," she heard K'Paw Meh's voice behind her.

"K'Paw Meh, what are you saying?"

"I'm saying she doesn't want them. She doesn't want to take the tablets any more. They're not doing much good anyway are they? Look at her."

"And how do you know she doesn't want to take them any more?"

"I found one. Yesterday. She had spat it out. Just like now. She doesn't want them. If she did she would take them."

"We can't just leave her," Htee K'Paw's voice fell to a whisper. "She'll just go on getting worse."

"She's doing that anyway."

"But it's no wonder if she hasn't been taking the tablets. You should have made her take it. You have to watch that she swallows them properly."

"You can't always tell. Like just then."

"But we have to, she's our mother. We have to help her."

"There you go again. You want to control everything. You want everyone to do exactly what you say. She doesn't want them."

Htee K'Paw took a step backwards and held onto the post for support. Her mouth began to form words but no sound came out.

K'Paw Meh paused for a moment then dropped her voice to little more than a whisper. "She doesn't want to get better. Can't you see that?"

Htee K'Paw was silent. There was no sound except for the clatter of the rain on the roof and the dripping of water through the hole in the thatch, now slowing down as the rain abated. The two girls looked at each other and Htee K'Paw knew that her sister was right. Her hand went again to her stomach and she pressed it again. Then she looked around her at the things in the little kitchen, moving them, rearranging, silently sorting, as if to organise her own thoughts while her sister watched her.

At last she spoke. "We must tell father."

Hser Mu looked for every opportunity to further her chances in the world. She was serious. She had heard it said of her that she knew what she wanted and would move the earth to get it.

Many foreigners came into the camp, some of them just for a few days, but most of them to teach something to people who were simply desperate for contact with the outside world. Whenever Hser Mu heard about them, she would go to find out what they had to say and try to talk to them. She liked westerners. Most of all she admired the way they thought, moving

278

step by step through a problem until they found the answer. They didn't seem to start from the point that their elders knew everything and you only had to listen to them and you would learn the important things of life. No, they asked questions, not just of their students, but also of themselves. Some of them, and these were the ones she liked best, were prepared to stand in front of a class and admit they didn't know something. Then they would ask the class to try to find the answer themselves, as if they thought themselves no better than anyone else. Together, the class would have to think about the problem and find the answer.

Jonathan had been like that. He had asked them to help him, as if he really needed them. And he had allowed himself to become like them in his quest to find out more. The more she knew of Jonathan, the more she had liked him and it was with deep sadness that she contemplated the suddenness of his departure. She wanted to see him again, to talk with him and tell him how much she appreciated him.

If she had a regret in her recent life it was that she had been so flippant in encouraging Htee K'Paw to accept Tim's advances so readily. Many times she had tried to understand her reasons for doing that. First she had checked to see if she had in fact been projecting her own desire for Tim onto her friend, but that particular search had born no fruit whatsoever. Perhaps she had been trying to encourage Htee K'Paw to spread her wings a little after the death of Hsa Mya, from which event she seemed to have never really recovered? Htee K'Paw had seemed to prefer the ways of the past to anything that the westerners brought to the camp. So why had she fallen for Tim so completely and unquestioningly, apparently throwing off all her customary modesty and quiet disposition?

It was partly to try to answer these questions that Hser Mu had joined this class. 'Women for Women,' it had announced itself, and a tall, pleasant looking Englishwoman named Esther was teaching them. Hser Mu had invited her friend to join her, imagining that Htee K'Paw would benefit from whatever it was that the woman had to say. "No! I don't want to." Her friend's reply to the invitation had been overloud and uttered with almost the force of a bullet and Hser Mu had recoiled in surprise at her tone.

"No," Htee K'Paw had corrected herself, once she realised how harsh her response had been. "No, I can't, I can't. You know how sick mother is. We can't leave her, not for a moment. We have to help her with everything. She can hardly breathe."

Hser Mu accepted the refusal. She had to. She knew well enough how sick Daw Nee Meh was and how worried Htee K'Paw and the rest of the family were. But it seemed to Hser Mu that this was also an excuse, that Htee K'Paw would have refused the invitation anyway, even if she had had the time to attend. Hser Mu could see her friend retreating into herself and knew instinctively that some of her angry response was because Esther was a foreigner, but she also knew that there was nothing she could say or do to change things.

Now she sat on the classroom floor with a reasonable selection of the camp women. There were young women like herself, some even younger girls, and the usual smattering of older women. "This course is about listening," Esther began. She waited for her interpreter before she continued. Hser Mu could understand her quite well, she had always enjoyed listening to the English language being spoken, but there would be many present who would need the interpreter. She felt a pang of disappointment at the simplicity of Esther's opening words. 'Anyone can listen, surely. We listen all the time, don't we?' she thought to herself.

"Of course, we all think listening is easy, we do it all the time don't we?" Esther was saying. Hser Mu smiled to herself, "but real listening is a skill. Many of us don't realise how difficult it is. And we can help our friends so much, especially other women, if we really learn to listen properly."

She continued with her introduction. Hser Mu liked Esther. She was tall and dark haired. She spoke with confidence, as if she really knew what she was talking about, "now I want us all to do something," Esther was saying. "I want you all to listen now. I want you to close your eyes and listen to the sounds around you. They will be sounds that you hear all the time, but I want you to really listen and pick them out, one by one."

The whole room obeyed her. Hser Mu watched for a moment then closed her eyes and listened. It was true; there were sounds that were there all the time. Sounds that she never even thought about: the child crying, the water splashing, the heavy axe being used to chop the firewood, the local open-sided bus noisily announcing itself on the road outside. There were sounds in the distance, the rippling of the stream and sounds close by, the gentle, almost silent rustle of the leaves in the breeze, and her own breathing, steady and deep.

"Good," Esther broke into the quietness. "Now I want to know what you heard," and each woman told the sounds that she had noted.

"How did that make you feel?' Esther was asking and Hser Mu looked around the room. The women were not used to being asked this question and an embarrassed silence hung over them.

Esther tried again. "Did you like that? Did you discover something new?"

And slowly they responded. "Yes, I heard things I never think about."

"I heard the river for the first time."

"You wouldn't know there were so many sounds." And the group slowly relaxed and a restrained laughter of shared experience rippled around the room.

Hser Mu was laughing quietly to herself; she glanced round and saw some of the other women felt the same way. They hadn't realised they could laugh and learn at the same time.

Now Esther and the interpreter were doing a role-play, as Hser Mu had heard it called in the teacher-training course. The interpreter, who happened to be one of the leaders of the women's association, was telling her story. Meanwhile Esther was not listening; instead she gave a display of interrupting and turning away from the speaker.

"Do you see what I am doing?" she asked the class through the interpreter after a number of minutes.

The class remained quiet.

"Am I a good listener?" she asked again. This time some of the women were shaking their heads. At last, they could see what Esther meant. Hser Mu had seen immediately and had also recognised her own tendency to talk too much and fail to listen. She was becoming more convinced of the necessity of listening carefully and attentively when someone was talking but, as far as she could see, that was not the problem with Htee K'Paw. The most difficult task seemed to be to persuade her to talk at all. She winced at the memory of the earlier encounter with her dearest friend when she had invited her to come to Esther's classes. Hser Mu had wanted to plead with her. She had wanted to try to reason with her. "I know you have been wronged, but not all westerners are like Tim. You know that," was what she had wanted to say. But she knew the words would sound as hollow as a drum and anyway, Htee K'Paw was in no mood to be persuaded.

Wasn't that just what Esther was talking about? You weren't supposed to argue, just listen. Wasn't that what she was saying?"

But that was no help if the person wasn't saying anything. What could you do about that? She decided that it was time to ask Esther's opinion and find out what she would do in such a case.

The opportunity came quickly, that lunchtime in fact, and Esther welcomed Hser Mu to her side.

"I've been watching you," Esther said to Hser Mu's surprise. "You're the most attentive person here. It's always good to see that people are really paying attention to what you're saying."

"I want to talk to you about my friend."

Esther smiled warmly and Hser Mu began.

"You see, she's my closest friend.'

"Is she here with you today?"

"No. She couldn't come. Her mother has been very sick. I think she may die soon."

"I'm sorry to hear that."

"You talk to us about listening, and it's very good, and helpful. I can see how important it is. But what do you do when a person won't talk? I want to listen to her; I want to help her; I know that she's very unhappy but she just won't talk about it."

"Have you tried to suggest it to her?"

"Yes, I have. She did once; she had to. The police came and she had to talk to them but it seemed to make things worse. It made her think about something bad that had happened to her. Now she feels worse than ever and she won't talk to anyone about anything. "

"I won't ask you any of the details as that would break a confidence. Do you remember me telling you how important it is not to do that?" Hser Mu nodded. "But we don't really ever forget things completely. They are stored up inside our memory and I would guess that what she said to the police has brought the problem to the surface, where before it had been pushed down inside her." Hser Mu nodded again. That certainly made sense. "And now, she's so busy thinking about her mother dying that she can't even think about dealing with anything else at the moment. But she needs to know that you are there. You need to be ready when she's ready. Does that make sense?"

"Yes, it does."

"But you may have to wait some time. And she needs you now. She really needs you to be there. She needs you now more than ever."

"I know she does, but . . . ." And Hser Mu turned away as the tears began to sting her eyes. 'Oh God help us, please help us,' she prayed silently.

27

Htee K'Paw wiped the perspiration away from her mother's face. Daw Nee Meh sat propped up on all the pillows that the family possessed plus more borrowed from neighbours. But for several days she had shifted and struggled and, in the effort to breathe, would regularly slip down again. Htee K'Paw would then have to sit her up, replace the pillows and force them down behind her to make her sit again. One of the nurses had come in from the clinic and had shown her how to turn her mother onto her side sometimes, so that she would have a change of position, but each time she would roll onto her back again and Htee K'Paw would have to try to make her mother comfortable once more

Father had come home yesterday. He told the family that he would stay with them for a while. Htee K'Paw didn't want to ask how he had managed it, or what was going to happen now he was no longer working. Her only thought was that at last she felt some relief from the burden. Together they cared for Daw Nee Meh and between them the family was somehow fed and kept clean. The boys helped with the hauling of water and wood and together the family did all they could. The days stretched into nights so that it seemed that there was no difference between them.

Htee K'Paw had grown used to the rhythm of her mother's breathing, it had become the stuff of her own waking and sleeping, the background noise to everything that happened in the little house so when the sound changed she knew immediately. What had been heavy, uncomfortable gasping now became a quiet grunt. The breathing was shallower and less of a struggle and Htee K'Paw was quietly grateful for the fact that her mother, after many days of misery, began to be more comfortable once again. She carefully turned her onto her side, using the pillows to prop her up and then quietly tip-toed from the room.

Her father was in the kitchen, patiently chopping the vegetables he had brought from town. "*Po quow mu,* " he looked up and smiled at her as she approached.

"She's quieter now. More comfortable, I think," Htee K'Paw said.

"That's good," he replied, continuing with his chopping.

Neither spoke for some moments.

"Htee K'Paw," her father broke the silence. "I have something to discuss with you."

"Yes?" Htee K'Paw had always been glad to hear him speak that way. She knew he looked to her as one he could trust. It had been that way since her childhood, but then she had not understood why, of course. Now she realised that he had always needed her support. She watched him swallow nervously, gathering his courage before he spoke.

"I have a chance to do something new. But I need your help."

286

"Yes?" Htee K'Paw wondered what the new thing could possibly be.

"You know old *Pu Mucah*?"

"Yes, of course." Everyone knew the man who kept one of the most popular market stalls in the camp. He sold the cotton sarongs, fabrics and coloured threads for weaving.

"He wants to sell up and move away."

"Yes?" Htee K'Paw couldn't think what the relevance was of this particular piece of intelligence.

"And he has offered the business to me, and well, I would like to take it on if I can."

"Papa?"

"It would mean that I could stay here. I wouldn't have to go away all the time. I would be able to see my family grow up and I could take care of you all"

"Papa, that's wonderful news."

"But it won't be easy. He has a good business and he will want a good price."

Htee K'Paw nodded slowly.

"I have some money; I have saved a little but I need more."

Now Htee K'Paw knew what was coming.

Her father saw her expression change. "You have been working as a teacher, *po quow mu,* and I'm sure you have been saving a little, too. I want you to help me to buy the business. It will help our family. Think of it. It's a real chance for us."

Htee K'Paw shook her head slowly. "But what about mother? We have to use our money for her medicines."

"So you have no money to help me?"

287

"Perhaps, but we can't use it while mother is so ill. She needs the medicines."

"Htee K'Paw, this is our future. It's for you and for the boys and K'Paw Meh. If I can do this it will be for you, and that is what mother would want."

"But while she is so sick, she needs those tablets. She's been very sick for a few days but she's a little better now. She's quieter and her breathing is easier. She will recover and then. . . "

"*Poquowmu,*" Htee K'Paw heard the tenderness in her father's voice as he reached out to take her hand. She felt his grip and was suddenly afraid.

"Papa? What is it?"

But all he did was shake his head as he went back to the chopping and preparation of the meal.

"Papa? Tell me. What is it?"

"We must do everything we can for her. You are right. We must make her comfortable and help her to get better."

After the family had taken their meal, while his daughter was busy with the dishes, Saw Ker Reh went into his wife and wiped away the dribbled tea that had escaped from her mouth, together with the crushed remains of the last tablet that his daughter had given her. And he gave thanks for her, the mother of his children and spoke quietly. "You will soon see our home, with its mountains and valleys and rivers and forests. It will be there waiting for you." And then he prayed the blessing of *Ywa*[15] on her.

The family had been in the camp for a sufficiently long period to enable them to divide the

---

[15] *Ywa* Karen name for God

sleeping area into two. So now that her father was home Htee K'Paw no longer needed to sleep beside her mother. However, before the family retired for the night, together she and her father turned her mother, washed her face and put a fresh cloth underneath her. Htee K'Paw fetched some cool water and using a spoon, placed a little on her mother's tongue. Then she watched and listened. The breathing had become even shallower, little more than a whisper, but still she did not understand. She was just grateful that her mother was now at rest after so many days of struggle. And she herself needed to sleep after so many disturbed nights so it was with gratitude that she lay down to rest in the room with her brothers and sister.

The butterflies danced among the trees, big, with yellow and black stripes. And there were others too, brown and orange, just like those at home, in the place on the other side of the river. She wanted to watch the butterflies, especially the yellow and black one, so she followed them, through the trees and bushes. She wanted to look more closely so she began to run, faster and faster until she was flying herself. She was up in the air now, it was as if she had become one of them and could look down, down at the bushes and trees. There were houses there too, houses just like the ones of her childhood. And there was her mother, smiling and well, standing outside the house with a child in her arms. The child was happy and laughing and she saw, to her surprise that it was her, Htee K'Paw. She was looking at herself in her mother's arms and she knew she wanted to stay there forever. Then she saw a baby. Now her mother was holding the baby and the older child had to stand on her own. She watched the expression on the child's face change from one of sweet contentment to one of fear and anxiety. There was something else, too. Now, as she looked closely at herself, she could see it was pure anger, anger that the new baby was now the one that was the object of her mother's love, anger that was almost hatred for the child that had taken her place.

A cock crowed and Htee K'Paw stirred on her mat. Feeling a slight chill in the air, she pulled her blanket up around her shoulders and then was awake enough to know that she been dreaming. The vividness of the dream surprised her and for a moment she imagined she could return to it. She wanted to see the child's face, wanted to go back to that time; she wanted to see her mother again as she had known her so many years ago. As she tried to return to sleep she became aware of the noises of the night, the constant, almost musical, whirring of the cicadas and. . . .

But one sound was missing. There was only the thinnest bamboo partition between the room that she shared with her brothers and sister and the room where her parents slept and the fact that she could no longer hear her mother's laboured breathing roused her completely. Now she was wide-awake and sitting bolt upright in her bed.

The little house was crowded, full to its very margins with family and neighbours. Those who couldn't fit inside or on the little apron at the front were standing around the outside, some clinging to the posts, others uncomfortably perched where they could to avoid sliding in the inevitable mud of the monsoon. The choir were singing. Htee K'Paw would have been with them were it not for the fact that they were singing for her mother, and so she listened instead, hardly able to contain the pain that had settled inside her chest. This was another pain, not the one that bored its way into her stomach at some stage almost every day now, but a pain of anguish from which she could not free herself. There was no rubbing away such a pain. It had to be endured as she knew from bitter experience.

She looked across at her father although she could hardly bear to do so, and as he glanced back at her there was some comfort in their shared grief. They had bought a simple coffin and K'Paw Meh had gone around the camp looking for flowers. She had come home with an armful of hibiscus, bougainvillea and bright greenery with which to garland it. She had found some frangipani and this had filled the house with its heady scent so that Htee K'Paw felt almost drunk with the grief and beauty. Ma Nay stood still and upright, a boy wanting to be a man, his face grey and quiet. Only Mon Kyaw spoke, enquiring quietly about his mother.

"Mother has gone home, Mon Kyaw. She has gone to a better place," she whispered to him, only then remembering that he had never seen the mountains, valleys, rivers and forests of home. This place of dust and mud was the only home he had ever known. She began to cry.

28

Saw Ker Reh drew on the first cigar of the day as he abstractedly watched his daughter prepare the breakfast, the muscles of her thin arms rhythmically tensing and relaxing as she pounded the chillies. She stared into the bowl with intense concentration, grinding the contents more finely that she needed to, or so he thought, but he said nothing. Then, at last satisfied, she turned her attention to the vegetables, cleaning and chopping and cleaning again, and chopping.

If it had not been for the terrible tragic death of his wife, he would have everything to be pleased about. Pu Mucah had been very happy with his bid for the fabric business, even going so far as being willing to wait for some of the payment. Now he was in the process of taking over the work. There was a great deal to be learnt, but Saw Ker Reh was happy to do that. He had spent enough of his life working for low wages in uncertain conditions to appreciate that here was a chance for him to better himself and his children by his own efforts. He was happy, almost excited, about the future. Who would have imagined that such a good opportunity would come his way? But it had and he was grateful. But he could hear, by the very tone of the pounding and chopping that his daughter was far from sharing his contentment.

"Where is K'Paw Meh?" he asked her. Perhaps he could ask his younger daughter to help her sister. Surely that would make Htee K'Paw feel better. He couldn't help feeing worried for her.

"She's not here," she replied shortly.

"So, where . . ?"

"I expect she's with Mu Aye; sometimes she stays there. She's always away with her friends. She's never here when I want her to be." Htee K'Paw knew her bitterness could be heard in her voice but made no attempt to disguise it. There was so much to do. She had to prepare the first meal of the day for the family and then there was the washing to do: that would have to wait for now. There was no time to do it all before the school day began.

"What about Ma Nay? He can help you."

"Yes, and he does." It was true, her brother was usually ready to carry water for her and keep the woodpile tidy and well stocked.

"And he's old enough to do his own washing now. But I will speak to K'Paw Meh about it. She should be helping you."

It was true enough, but Htee K'Paw could hardly bear the arguments that she had with her sister whenever the subject of work around the house came up so she let it go. Also, at the back of her mind were the more pressing concerns of the day. School had started again and there were lots of new ideas to try out with the children so Htee K'Paw knew she should be looking forward to being with them again, but she could hardly raise the necessary enthusiasm for the day ahead. Still, with the meal ready at last, she called the boys who prepared the low table and together the family sat down to eat.

As she sat down Htee K'Paw knew she didn't want to eat. Sometimes the pain made eating difficult, but this time there was a vague feeling of nausea that meant she didn't want food at all. She spooned some rice onto her dish, took a small amount of the vegetables and helped herself to a larger portion of the chillies; they always made the food taste more palatable. She then mixed the food with her fingers and began to eat.

There was no such loss of appetite with the boys and almost as soon as they had begun they were finished and ready for school. Both of them helped to clear the table and then they left with their father, the boys to their school and he to his new business venture.

Htee K'Paw moved carefully. The pain had returned but in an attempt to ignore it she went slowly around the house cursorily tidying and collecting her school things together at the same time. She stepped out into the kitchen for one last time to check that everything was tidy and covered against flies when the pain that had been gathering itself just below her ribcage hit her like a knife. She bent herself in two; there was nothing else to be done. The pain was so severe that she could not even move. A cold nausea spread through her body and she could feel perspiration soaking her. Unable to stand she sank helplessly to the floor and felt the familiar rush of burning liquid up into her mouth. She hated it when her whole stomach seemed to rise up into her chest. It had happened many times but this was different, she had never felt this bad before. She coughed and spat out the dreadful stuff that had filled her mouth. Then she saw it, bright red and trickling onto the bare earth of the kitchen.

By the time Hser Mu had started teaching her class she knew something was very wrong. She could hear the children in Htee K'Paw's class chatting restlessly among themselves without the authoritative voice of their teacher to control them. Picking out the most gifted of her class she set her the task of continuing with the reciting of the letters and went quickly to the headmaster's office to seek his permission to leave for a short while. From there she very quickly reached Htee K'Paw's home and began to call out her friend's name. There was no sound. She climbed the steps at the front of the house and saw Htee K'Paw's bag full of books and papers ready for the day at school. She quickly glanced into the two small bedrooms feeling a rising panic as she saw no other evidence of her friend's presence. She called again; there was still no sound. For a moment she wondered if Tim had come back and taken her away, and a picture of a terrified Htee K'Paw, pleading with him to leave her alone, flashed through her mind.

To the side of the bedrooms was a small area where the family kept their possessions and now she ran quickly around there to the back of the house. It was as she reached the couple of steps that led down into the kitchen that she saw her friend at last. She was flooded with relief that quickly turned to horror. Htee K'Paw lay sprawled on the floor, her head under the little table where the family prepared the food for cooking, her legs perilously close to the still-warm charcoal stove. For the briefest of moments Hser Mu wondered if she was dead but a small movement reassured her otherwise. Calling her friend's name she quickly knelt down beside her. Then she saw the blood, oozing, trickling from Htee K'Paw's mouth, already congealing on the earth and acting as a magnet to the flies. Htee K'Paw responded to her voice and opened her eyes.

"Don't move, Htee K'Paw," Hser Mu's voice trembled. "I'll get someone to come and see you."

"But I have to," Htee K'Paw tried to sit up, wiping her face with her hand as she did so. Seeing the blood on it she began to cry with pain and fright.

"No, you must stay still." So saying she reached across to move the stove away and then went to collect some blankets from her friend's room.

If Htee K'Paw was aware of what was happening to her she didn't show it. Two orderlies came from the clinic with a bamboo pole and between the two of them they lifted her carefully into a hammock and carried her back there. As if from far away she heard comments and anxious whispers. One of them remarked that she was so light that he could have carried her on his own. Then came another voice, that of a foreign women, gentle and authoritative. "It looks like a bleeding gastric ulcer, we need to put a tube down into her stomach."

"Swallow, swallow," the command was firm, almost harsh. She felt something in her mouth. Someone was trying to push a tube down her throat. "Swallow," the voice came again and she resigned herself to obey it. She had no strength to do otherwise.

Then another sharp pain pierced her, this time in her arm. Opening her eyes she saw one of the nurses fixing a drip to it. She turned towards the wall and as she did so felt the discomfort of the tube that had passed through her throat and was still in place. Meanwhile there were more voices, then the distant noise of hammering; turning her face to see what was happening she watched as the medic fixed a long plastic funnel to the end of the tube and began to push crushed ice down it. Her mind worked slowly to connect the events, but now she understood what the hammering had been. They had been crushing the ice.

The strange voices had been those of the visiting French doctors. It was they who had recommended the treatment of ice in the stomach tube. They had told the local medics that if that was not enough to stop the bleeding in her stomach then she would have had to be taken to hospital for surgery

Then there were the voices of her father, and Hser Mu. Sometimes she was aware of them; at others not, but hearing them was enough; it meant that she was still alive, but she knew little more than that.

The day became night and night became day again. She lay hardly knowing what was happening around her. She felt the band on her arm that was left there in order to measure her blood pressure. At first she woke a little every time the nurses came to measure it and check her pulse, but soon she did not even respond to them. Sometimes she would open her eyes and Hser Mu would be sitting beside her; at other times it would be her father. He even brought the boys with him for short periods and she felt her heart quicken as if just the sight of them was enough to give her new life, then just as quickly she sank back into stupor. They brought one of the pillows from home and made her more comfortable; the bleeding stopped, the pain in her stomach slowly eased but still she lay quiet and inert on the bamboo bed.

Saw Ker Reh grew anxious for his elder daughter. And he had other worries that he dare not concern her with. On the second evening after Htee K'Paw's collapse his second daughter had not returned home. He had quickly instigated a search for her assuming that it would be a simple matter of visiting some of the young people that he knew to be her friends. At the home of Mu Aye he met with some news, but it was of little comfort to him. Mu Aye was also missing. It didn't take him long to move on to the many boarding houses of the camp. There, children who had lost contact with their parents or who had been sent to the comparative safety of the camp lived together. He imagined that perhaps his errant second daughter had chosen to spend time with her friends instead of her family. His anxiety mixed with anger with himself as he thought of how he had neglected his children while trying to help them by earning some money. At the same time he could hardly believe that the girl had become so wayward that she had just gone away without telling anyone. In desperation he had gone to visit the commandant who had promised to look for her, but was less than reassuring. Although he said nothing to Saw Ker Reh, he himself was acutely aware of how many of the refugees disappeared from the camp every week, some of them returning a few weeks later, some of them never seen again.

So it was with a heavy heart that he sat with Htee K'Paw. It seemed that the simple happiness that he and Daw Nee Meh and their young children had once known was gone forever. Now even the tiny thread of contentment that he had tried to weave into the family life had snapped and he couldn't see how it could ever be repaired. He would not have ever wanted it to be said that he loved his elder daughter more than his other children; however there had always been a special bond between them. His wife had never enjoyed the best of health so he had always relied on the eldest of his children, perhaps more than he should have done. Now his mind played with the thought that Htee K'Paw had somehow become a copy of her mother. The girl who had once been so strong and so full of hope for the future was now rigid, fearful and anxious and that, of all things, made his heart want to break with sadness.

29

Three days had passed since Htee K'Paw had been found cold and bleeding on the earth floor of her kitchen. During that time she had scarcely been aware of their passing. Instead, she had been immersed in a sea of pain and misery. Small periods of consciousness had been interspersed with lapses about which she had no memory.

As she lay drifting between sleep and wakefulness she wished with all her heart that she had died and gone to be with Hsa Mya all those years ago. In the height of fever, with the sad realisation that life held nothing for her, she had wrenched the drip, with its life saving contents, from her arm and had then lain still, allowing the spreading pool of blood and water to chill her body until one of the nurses had found her. After that she had lain inert and exhausted and had allowed them to place a new needle in her arm. She hardly had the strength to resist. The desire to end her own life had given way to a dull despair with no strength for any sort of resistance.

They had to run away. Everyone was talking about it and Htee K'Paw could feel the danger. It was everywhere, in the air she breathed and in the sounds of the night. They left their home and ran into the jungle, anywhere to get away from the soldiers. But still they were in danger. It didn't seem to matter how far they went they couldn't escape from the fear of being caught, perhaps even killed. Then Hsa Mya was beside her and she knew that he would take care of her. He knew the paths through the mountains and forests and they travelled together, just the two of them. There seemed to be nobody else with them. Sometimes they had to run and in her fear she could feel the beating of her own heart. She felt as if she couldn't run fast enough but he was there beside her and calmed her fears. He took her hand and together they looked for a place where they could rest.

He found strong branches and the broad leaves of the forest and wove them together so that they could hide and nobody would find them. As they lay down to sleep he wrapped his arms round her. As long as he was with her she would be safe. That was all she wanted, to be safe in his arms.

"I love you," she heard him whisper. As she lay in the darkness she lifted her hand to feel the contours of his face. To her faint surprise there was nobody there.

The quiet voice came again. "I love you." She could make out no form yet the arms were still around her. No, they no longer felt like arms, but there was someone with her still. Or was there?

Yes there was, and he was looking at her, not just at her face but reaching deep down inside her. She knew no fear, the presence and the voice only filled her with warmth and love. He seemed to know everything about her yet she knew nothing but peace. In that

301

moment she saw all the shame and bitterness and anger that had gripped her for so long, but then it all seemed to melt away in an instant. It had no power over her any more.

After her school day was finished and all was quiet, Hser Mu came into the clinic. As she hurried towards the bamboo platform that served as a bed she looked anxiously for the signs of improvement in her friend's condition. It was time, she had decided, that something had to be done. Htee K'Paw had to be lifted out of the inertia that she had lain in for too many days now. "Let her talk," Esther had said, but Htee K'Paw hadn't been at all inclined to do so.

She stopped by the bed, not knowing what to say. She had been looking forward to seeing her friend most of the day but at the same time dreading the encounter knowing, in her heart, that there was little likelihood of any change.

"Hello, Hser Mu," Htee K'Paw sat propped up against the split bamboo wall behind her bed.

"You're better," was all Hser Mu could say.

"Well, not completely better. Not yet. The bleeding has stopped now but I have to take medicine," and with her eyes, Htee K'Paw indicated the drip that was once again feeding the necessary drugs into her arm.

"But you seem a lot . . . " Hser Mu decided it would be best not to talk about the sad and lonely vigil she had kept by her friend's bedside with Htee K'Paw lying miserably beside her, her face turned to the wall in stony silence more often than not.

302

"I had a dream," Htee K'Paw began. "Well I'm not sure if it was a dream or not but it made me realise how angry I am."

"Angry?" exclaimed Hser Mu, "but you're not angry. You're one of the sweetest, kindest people I know. I just wish I was more like you sometimes."

"I am angry, Hser Mu. I know I am."

"But what are you angry about? Is it Tim? Is that what has upset you so much?"

"Maybe, but the anger goes much deeper than that, I know. I just know it does."

"What sort of dream was this, then?" Hser Mu began to feel as if she didn't understand what was happening at all, yet there was no mistaking her own eyes. Htee K'Paw was much better. It was almost as if she was a different person.

"Its hard to describe," Htee K'Paw dropped her voice almost to a whisper. "It was . . . it was as if God came to help me. At first I was dreaming, but then I woke up and I could feel someone with me. And I know he loved me so much. I just can't describe it. And for the first time I felt that Jesus was real. And I still feel him with me."

"What? So . . ."

"And I saw myself. I saw myself as I really am, and I'm not as sweet and kind as I look. Maybe I am on the surface. But deep down I'm so angry, or at least I was." She paused to look at Hser Mu, who nodded slightly as if to tell her to go on. "I'm angry because we had to leave our home, I'm angry because Hsa Mya died and because mother died, and because we have to live here and . . . "

"But we all feel like that sometimes. It's . . "

Htee K'Paw ignored the interruption. "And it goes back further than that. I was angry when K'Paw Meh was born. I was jealous of her. It's strange, but it goes back that far."

"And you think that God showed you all this?"

Htee K'Paw nodded her head. "But he didn't show me to make me feel bad, just the opposite. He showed me that he loves me. He loves me whatever I'm like."

Htee K'Paw's eyes ranged around the clinic then looked back to her friend. "You know, for years I sang songs in the choir and we believed we were singing for God. We go to church and teach the children, but I had never known anything like this. He was so close to me. I shall never forget that feeling. And now . . ."

"Now you feel better."

"Yes, I do. I feel as if I can make a fresh start, except for," Htee K'Paw's voice tailed off.

"Except for?"

"Except I feel so ashamed about what happened with Tim. I was so stupid to go with him."

Hser Mu watched her friend's distraught face. "But it wasn't your fault. You couldn't help what . . ." She stopped herself as she remembered Esther's words. 'Listen, don't talk so much; just listen.' "I'm sorry," she said. "What is it you wanted to say?" And she looked on for a few anxious moments fearful that she might have done the wrong thing.

"I should have realised," Htee K'Paw began again. "He gave me beer to drink and I should have known. I never had that sort of drink before. And then he took me to the hotel. I could have asked him to take me to my uncle's house. He said he would do that but he didn't and I forgot all about it." And she turned herself over on the little wooden platform that served as a bed as if to face the bamboo wall again.

"No, please, don't turn away. I don't think you were stupid but," she put out her hand to try to persuade Htee K'Paw to face her again, "do you believe that God can forgive us whatever we do?"

"Yes, yes," she answered slowly.

"Then he can forgive you for any stupid thing you might have done. You made a mistake, Htee K'Paw. God can forgive you for that. I know he can." She watched as Htee K'Paw stared ahead with a frown on her face as if she were turning the words around in her mind.

"Perhaps the thing that you need to do is forgive yourself," and Hser Mu knew she was right when she saw her dearest friend slowly nod her head.

30

"Why didn't you tell me?" Htee K'Paw's voice rang out as a cry of anguish.

It was the first time that her father had spoken of K'Paw Meh's disappearance with his elder daughter. "How could we? You were so ill. I didn't want to do anything to make you feel worse. I was so worried for you."

Htee K'Paw, in her recovered state, could see the sense in what her father was saying.

"When did she go?" She asked more quietly.

"The same day you fell ill. I was so busy thinking about you that I didn't miss her until the evening. Then I imagined she was at the school. It was only after lights out that I went to look for her and discovered that nobody knew where she was. She and Mu Aye had both disappeared."

Htee K'Paw turned her troubled face to make a slow survey of the lonely house where there had been so much sadness of late.

Saw Ker Reh sat in the shade of his shop on the main thoroughfare of the camp. He had been over that scene every day; many times every day. His older daughter had only mirrored his own distress at the disappearance of her sister, and neither of them had spoken about it, hiding their anxiety deep inside themselves. They were so alike, father and daughter, and the slightest glance across the kitchen or backyard spoke many words that were never uttered.

He had seen the sort of shops that there were in town. They were neat establishments with tiled floors that could easily be swept clean every day if one wished. Many had glass cabinets where the fabrics could be stored and displayed. A customer could see clearly what she (and it usually was a she) wanted and could ask for it knowing that it would not be covered in dust and in need of washing before it was made into a garment.

Here there were no such niceties but there was a regular trade. There was no doubt that he had bought into a business with a great deal of good will and as long as he maintained this he knew he could build up a very promising future for himself. There were no problems there, just a matter of learning as much about the business as he could as he went along, and he was quite capable of that.

No, his problem lay in his having to maintain an exterior demeanour that told his customers that all was well with the world, while at the same time trying to cope with an anxiety for his family that sometimes almost overwhelmed him so that he could hardly hold up his head and greet a valued customer.

He had imagined that once he found a good business, which allowed him to stay with his family in the camp then all would be well. Instead it seemed to him that his whole world had fallen apart almost the moment his new life had started. As soon as he had found the opportunity to look forward to a life of greater safety and stability disaster had struck, and continued to strike repeatedly, until he felt he could take no more. It was only the daily necessity of caring for the two young boys that had kept him going in what had been his darkest hours.

Now Htee K'Paw was home and gaining strength it seemed as if a small light had been lit in his life and he had begun to smile again, but there was no mistaking the gaping sore that K'Paw Meh's absence had left in their family life.

Htee K'Paw ladled some hot water out of the large pot that had been set to the side of the fire and began to tidy up the kitchen after supper. She felt glad to be well enough to undertake domestic chores once again and she was back at her work teaching the children she loved so much. Now in the quiet of the evening she felt content. The dream or vision (she didn't really know what to call it) had clearly been the catalyst that had lifted her out of her illness and its impact had never left her. Rather, she hid it within the deepest recesses of her being so that she could lift it up to her consciousness whenever she needed. It had been a vision of pure love that reached both deeper and higher than anything human possibly could and she knew with certainty that it was from God. There was still grief, of course. Her mother had died and there was no escaping the deep sadness that pervaded the whole family. Furthermore she had to live with the fact that her sister had run away from the camp, an action possibly precipitated by her own anger and self-pity, which she now realized had spoilt almost everything that she touched.

The shame was still there too, shame at her own stupidity and culpability in bringing Tim into the orphanage. Now both Tim and Jonathan had left the camp there were no extra classes for teachers and therefore fewer opportunities for socializing, for which she was glad. She couldn't bear to imagine what the other students and teachers thought of her and had already decided that she would avoid mixing with them if at all possible.

Ma Nay came out to the small lean-to that served as a kitchen with a small pile of dishes balanced between his hands.

"Papa says I am to help you."

"That's good," she smiled at her brother, "you can wash these things and I shall tidy up a bit." She began to move around the kitchen, covering up the rice bucket and collecting the scraps together for the chickens to peck at. "How was school today?" She asked her brother distractedly as she did so.

"I got into trouble with *tharamu*."

"Oh, what sort of trouble?"

"It wasn't fair," Ma Nay pulled a face.

"What wasn't fair?"

"We were playing football and Ko Klaw pushed me over and I slipped in the mud."

"Ko Klaw? I don't know him."

"He's a new boy. He's rough and he cheats."

"So, how did you get into trouble?"

"I hit him. *Tharamu* didn't see him push me but she saw me hit him so she pulled me out of the game and hit my hand with the stick."

"Oh, I see, that doesn't seem fair. But she is right, too. You shouldn't hit people, even if they have hurt you first."

Ma Nay did not seem inclined to listen to his sister so went on with his tale. "*Tharamu* said that I was to say sorry to Ko Klaw."

"Yes, and . . " already Htee K'paw could feel her attention wandering aware from the perennial issue of fairness that she knew was always occupying the minds of the children in her own class too.

"She said that sometimes you have to forgive someone or say sorry even if you don't feel like it. You just have to do it."

Htee K'Paw looked up from her tidying and across at her brother who was slowly rubbing at a plate. "What did you say? Say that again?"

"*Tharamu* said that we must do the right thing even when we don't feel like it. Sometimes we have to say sorry even when we don't want to. We just have to do it."

Htee K'Paw felt a slight shiver shake her body. "Yes, Ma Nay, that's true. We sometimes have to do things because they are right. And what happened? Did you say sorry?"

"Yes, I did."

"And then?"

"Ko Klaw said he was sorry too and he wants to be my friend."

"And do you forgive him?"

Ma Nay nodded, a little bewildered that his sister was being so persistent.

"So it was the right thing to do, wasn't it?"

"Yes."

'Yes,' Htee K'Paw said to herself. She stared out of the lean-to and across the yard. Hser Mu had told her what she needed to do and now her little brother was telling her exactly the same thing. It was

310

so simple, so why had she not done it? 'I have to forgive myself, I just have to do it and then believe it's done.' She took hold of her brother's shoulders and hugged him. "Thank you for helping me," she said to him as he shrugged off his sister's embrace in youthful embarrassment, not realizing what he had said.

"When I've finished these can I go out to play before bed time?"

"Yes, Ma Nay, and thank you for telling me your story," and Htee K'Paw wasted no more time. Hser Mu had told her and she knew it was true: God forgives us but we have to forgive ourselves too.

She was going to forgive herself and she was going to forgive Tim. What ever he had done she was going to forgive him and put it behind her. She knew that only then would she be free of him.

31

Jonathan heaved the package full of books onto the rough wooden desk at the front of the classroom. They were part of a collection that friends in England had made for him. He had only had to say the words books and library in the small community where his parents lived and people's generosity had surprised him, so much so, that he had had to make some extra shipping arrangements in order to get them to the camp. But these particular books were for his class and he began to carefully untie the string that was tied tightly round the brown paper.

It had been almost two months since he had left the camp with such a sense of failure and defeat. He had gone home to England but had found no peace there. At first, being inside a house with doors and windows had made him feel closed in so that he would wake up in the small hours fearing that he was suffocating. He would jump out of bed gasping for air and rush to open the window. There, he would look down at the moonlit garden until his body returned to normal.

During his stay at home two events occurred that he knew he would never forget. The first of these had been the most terrifying that he had ever witnessed but its aftermath turned out to be one of the best.

"Jane McCune speaking," Jonathan's mother answered the phone in her usual breezy manner.

"Hello," the voice came at the other end of the line. "This is James. I'm a friend of Jon's . . . from university. I've heard that Jon is arriving home from Thailand soon. I wonder if you know exactly when he'll be home?"

"Yes, yes, of course. It's the day after tomorrow: Wednesday. The flight gets in at 6am. His cousin Ian is going to collect him from the Airport. He should be here soon after nine."

"Thanks. That's 6 o'clock Wednesday."

"Yes. Er . . James. I don't recall Jon speaking about a James at university."

"Its James, James Marshall. We were friends at Oxford. We did Politics together."

"PPE?"

"Yes, that's right. It will be good to catch up with him again. Thanks again for letting me know."

"Is that all?"

"Yes, that's all. Bye."

Jane put the phone down and thought no more about the call; her mind was too full of the concerns of welcoming her son back home again.

On Wednesday morning Jonathan's cousin Ian and his girlfriend Laura were up very early to make their way to the airport to collect him and David from the 6 o'clock flight. Jonathan was immensely grateful for his cousin's company on the journey home. It meant the beginning of a return to normality for him.

The weather forecast for the next few days was good and as they drew close to Poole Harbour they talked about the possibility of sailing together. By 9 o'clock they were home. After a quick cup of coffee Ian left Jonathan and Laura at home; he was soon back on the road again in order to take his father home before returning to spend a few days with Jonathan. As he drove away along the lane his mind was so full of the anticipation of a few days with his cousin that he took no notice of the dark coloured car that he saw parked about a hundred yards away from the house. Jonathan's parents had seen it too but they thought nothing of it. It was a little unusual to see a car parked there so early in the morning but many tourists visited the area in summer so they too were unperturbed.

Tim, who had been sitting in the car watching as the two cars left, waited for several minutes then, satisfied that Jonathan was now alone in the house, climbed out of the front seat and made his way quietly to the house.

"We've finished the coffee," Laura said as she gathered up the cups that the others had left.

"Do you want me to make some more? It's no trouble."

"Yes please, I always need a lot of coffee to get me going in the morning and we were up so early. How long do you think it will be before Ian gets back?"

"Maybe a couple of hours. That gives me time to do a bit of unpacking."

"Don't you want to go to bed after such a long flight?"

"No, I don't think so; I slept a bit on the plane."

314

"You're lucky. I can never get to sleep when I travel." Laura looked around the perfectly appointed kitchen. "This place is amazing,"

"Its my Mum. She has to have the best of everything. She'd have a fit if she saw where I'd been living in the refugee camp."

"What was that like then?"

"Well, I had my own house. It was very small but I liked it. It was just made of bamboo and I could look through the spaces in the wall to the river below. Quite picturesque really, but not my Mum's cup of tea."

"What are you doing there?"

"You really want to know?"

"Yes, of course."

"Well, I've been living there for about six months so far. I've been teaching English so that I could have a good reason for being there. They brought a whole lot of people together, mostly about the same age as me, I guess, and set up a teacher training course for them. It was my job to give them English lessons. That way they can get access to more books, because there's not much in their own language. Anyway, I hoped that once I taught them they would be able to tell me about themselves in return. That way I hoped to get together the material for my thesis."

"And have you got what you needed?"

"Yes, I've made a start, but it's taking a long time. The trouble is that a lot of what we believe about these people seems to come from over-simplified assumptions. There's the whole issue of separatism and ethnicity. You think it's going to be a straightforward question of a minority group fighting for independence or separate identity or something like that; then you find that the whole thing's much more complicated. For one thing, it seems that by no means all the members of the ethnic group are fighting. Some of them are hardly aware of what is going on and seem to have no part in it. Then there are some who are fighting with the other side; they're fighting with the Burmese. And then to cap it all, you've got some who are Burmese but are fighting with the Karen."

"The Karen?"

"Yes, that's the group that I'm trying to understand. Then there are landmines. Some students took me over the border into the land that they're fighting over. We came to a village and had to have a guide because of the mines. I thought, quite naively I suppose, that the enemy soldiers, laid the mines. But that's not always the case. Sometimes it's the ordinary people who put them down to keep the enemy out of the villages and to stop them stealing things like food and animals, and so on. The kids I had been teaching knew all about landmines. They lay them sometimes, it seems. They see them as a good thing. So much for trying to rid the world of them! There doesn't seem to be much chance of that. People lose legs and eyes but that doesn't seem to stop them. Sorry, I'm going on too much."

"That's no problem. I'm really interested." Laura saw his surprise at her remark. "Really. We're doing international law. That sort of thing comes into it. Landmines. War Crimes."

"And there's plenty of those going on too. It's unbelievable, but when you meet some of the people and hear the things that have happened to them it's hard to take in."

A short snatch of melody rang through the ground floor of the house.

"What was that?" Laura laughed.

"Oh, the doorbell. It's my mother's idea. It's embarrassing, isn't it? I'll be back in a moment. Just pour the water onto the cafetiere when the kettle boils," and somewhat chagrined, he made his way to the front door. He might not be feeling too tired but he didn't want to deal with callers. Whoever it was at the door at this time of day would have to be dispensed with pretty quickly.

"Hello Jonathan," Tim greeted him cheerfully, all smoothness and charm.

Jonathan's mouth dried; in an instant he could feel himself shaking inside. "Tim," he managed to whisper and then, regaining some presence of mind, he began to push the door shut again. But Tim was too quick for him. Already his foot was between the door and the frame and it was too late. He could no longer shut him out. In a moment Tim had pushed himself through the gap and into the house.

"You have something of mine if I remember rightly," there was a cold edge to Tim's voice, terrifying in its intensity. "I've come to collect it."

"How did you know where I was? How did you find me?"

"It wasn't difficult. In fact it was surprisingly easy. McCune: there aren't too many McCune's in this part of the world."

"But . . . "

"You told me where you lived. Remember? You told me you went sailing in Poole Harbour. And you'd let slip the name of this cosy little enclave. And

317

when you want something as badly as I do, you don't stop until you find it. I spent months preparing, working, getting to know those kids, but you had to go and ruin it all. Everything I worked so hard for. You took it all away." Tim's voice had risen in volume. Then it suddenly went quiet again. "And now I've come to get it back. The film, where is it?"

Jonathan, who had been backing away from Tim, stopped himself in an attempt to regain some control over the situation. He saw that, without realising, he had backed himself into the lounge to one side of the hall inside the front door. Now he stood his ground.

"I haven't got it," he said slowly, and as steadily as his fast beating heart would allow. "I destroyed it."

For the first time Jonathan noticed a sort of madness in Tim's eyes, a terrifying anger that would never be satisfied. "You what? You're lying."

Jonathan said nothing. There was nothing he could say. He watched as Tim quickly turned his head to sniff at the air but if he had wanted to catch him off guard there was no chance. In an instant he had turned his head back to face him again. "What's that? You making coffee?"

"Yes . . . Yes, I'm making . . . Do you want? " In his panic he had forgotten about Laura in the kitchen. Jonathan stopped. In the moment of distraction when his attention had been on the coffee, Tim had reached into the inside of his jacket and brought out a knife. Jonathan recognised it immediately. He had seen that sort of knife being wielded regularly in the camp. Everyone had one, sharp and heavy, it was used for all the tasks that work in the forest required. The dull metal of the blade belied its power as an implement, and as a weapon, for surely Tim was here for one reason only. Jonathan watched dry-mouthed, as he carefully fingered the blade.

It is an interesting fact that the human eye can see things even if it does not appear to be looking straight at them. And so it was now. Tim had followed Jonathan into the lounge but Jonathan was facing the open doorway. At the edge of his field of vision he caught a slight movement, a small flash of a pale yellow. It was Laura just outside the door. He felt a flush of warmth in his face. Then forced every muscle of his body to freeze. He thought about his face. What must it look like? A mask contorted with terror? Had there been an unconscious flick of his eyes when he had first caught sight of Laura? He had to do everything to make sure his face gave nothing away. He dare not let Tim know that there was anyone else in the house, that he had any cause for hope. He prayed, a desperate, urgent prayer. "God, help me. Please. Help."

His aunt Sarah talked about prayer, as if it was something that she did every day but surely she never had to deal with anything like this. He concentrated on the knife, on the contours of his own face. He licked his lips to moisten his mouth and tried to speak.

"Where did you get that, Tim? How did you get that past the customs?" He spoke slowly and carefully, desperate to retain some sort of control. But he hardly recognised his voice, shaky and broken as it was.

"When I want something I do everything to get it. Something you know nothing about. Focus. I focus on what I want. It's not difficult; the bumbling idiots in customs are easily fooled. Where is it?"

"I told you, I haven't got it." Jonathan, frightened as he was, knew that Tim wasn't seriously looking for the film. He had come for revenge.

"Your suitcase, where is it?"

"Its upstairs. I haven't unpacked yet."

"Well, you're going to take me upstairs and you're going to unpack it. If you've got it I'll find it if I have to rip everything to pieces."

"But I . . ," Jonathan's voice had been reduced to little more than a whimper.

"Upstairs, in front of me, go on."

Jonathan thought of Laura. By a miracle it seemed that Tim still had no idea that anyone else was in the house with him. Now he had to cross the hallway in order to climb the stairs and he had to hope that Laura was out of sight when he did so. For a moment he wondered if he could distract Tim so that he did not see her but in his weakened state his mind refused to work properly.

"Go on, upstairs," Tim raised his voice again and Jonathan walked past him carefully and came out into the hall. He glanced sideways toward the kitchen but there was no sight of Laura so he climbed the stairs quickly, hoping that Tim would do the same and not start to explore the rest of the house. Once upstairs he went into his bedroom with Tim close behind him, all the time conscious of the heavy knife that he imagined was poised ready to come down on him at any moment.

"Open the case, go on, you know what to do," Tim's voice was sharp with anger. Jonathan obeyed and began to tip out the contents of the case. Unwashed tee shirts, underwear, books all spilled out onto the bed.

Tim had followed him into the bedroom so ruling out any possibility of escape. For a few moments he vented his fury on the suitcase, slashing at the material with the machete, then he stopped and stared at Jonathan with a terrifying intensity. The suitcase was forgotten and Jonathan began to inch backwards out of the range of the blade. He tried to remember if there was anything behind him that he could use as a weapon, but panic took over; his mind and limbs had descended into a useless, shaking chaos.

There was no sound of any movement in the entire house. 'What was Laura doing? Where was she?' The flicker of hope that Jonathan had registered when he had first seen her downstairs in the doorway of the lounge had disappeared. "Tim, please, put the knife down. I won't tell anyone you've been here. Just go away and leave me. Please."

"After what you did to me? You have to be joking." Tim casually swapped the knife into his left hand, then to his right. Jonathan watched his hand tighten around the handle.

And there she was at the doorway of the bedroom and clearly within his field of vision. Keep him talking. Distract him. Don't give him any reason to turn round. Jonathan shifted his gaze from Tim's face to the knife and back again and from the edge of his vision watched in amazement as Laura silently crept closer to Tim's back, her movements purposeful and deliberate.

"It was what you were doing to those children. I couldn't bear to see that."

Silently Laura inched forward, her hands formed into fists and raised before her face, her whole body taut like a coiled spring.

"I gave them what they wanted. Don't you realise they loved me for it? They loved me. They would do anything for me. And I loved them, all of them. You have no idea what it is to love children the way I do. And you took it all away. Everything I had worked so hard for."

Jonathan watched as Tim's eyes widened with anger and his voice rose to a shout.

Laura was behind Tim and he was apparently still unaware of her presence in the bedroom. What was she doing? Jonathan wanted to cheer for her audacity, so much so that he had to fight to keep still. He could feel the air rushing into his lungs and out again as he concentrated on his breathing, the movements of his face, his hands, anything except Laura.

Then he knew what to do. As Tim's arm rose for the first thrust of the knife Jonathan stepped backwards quickly, distracting Tim for no more than a second. But it was enough. Laura moved so fast that even Jon who was facing her had difficulty understanding what was happening. In a flash her feet were in the air. The first blow to the middle of Tim's back winded him and caused him to stagger forward, his feet clumsy beneath him. Quick as a flash came the second, which sent him to the floor, the knife flying from his grasp as he did so. But Laura wasted no time congratulating herself on her triumph. She landed a third blow to the top of Tim's back and then jumped on him, making it impossible for him to move.

Jonathan reached for the knife, which had slid harmlessly across the bedroom floor and stepped quickly across to land with all his force on Tim's legs.

"I phoned the police," Laura said quietly to Jonathan as she regained her breath.

For several nights he had thought about almost nothing else but what had happened that day. Ian and Laura had talked about it with him and they had laughed and cried with him. "My God, where did you learn to do that?" had been Jonathan's first words once the police had gone.

"Kick boxing classes," she had said simply before tears filled her eyes and she could say nothing more.

Then David had suggested that he accompany him to Somerset in order to visit the police in the area of the school where he had been a pupil. Jonathan had then been faced with an array of emotions but the episode with Tim had, for some reason that he could not fathom, galvanised him into the realisation that he could do something that would make him feel better. He had finally consented to the venture and the day of the visit went better than either he or David had imagined it would.

There had been many times when he had been unsure about what he had experienced at the school, he often wondered if he had imagined it, but the police took him very seriously. Mr Dixon had indeed been abusing young pupils, not just at Jonathan's school but also at another one, a year or two later. One of the boys in the second school had been brave enough to speak out; Mr Dixon had been convicted and would never be allowed to work with children again. That had been something of a turning point for Jonathan. Slowly he let the facts settle in his mind and began to regard the events of his time in Thailand in a new light.

But then other thoughts had begun to fill his mind. He saw again the faces of the students in the camp and knew that this was where he belonged. And Ian and Laura had promised to come to visit him. Indeed, he had been so pleased with their plans that he had gone to the travel agent with them to make sure they really did buy their tickets. There would be a trial, the police had assured him of that and he and Laura would have to be there, of course, but in the meantime, he had decided he would travel out to Thailand to continue his research. And now he sat in the classroom while the students slowly joined him as they were released from their own duties of the day.

32

Htee K'Paw looked up to see Hser Mu's face at the doorway of her classroom. "Come in," she called out. "I'm just finished."

"Are you ready?"

"Yes," Htee K'Paw rushed around the classroom while her friend watched her. Yes, she was ready and as the afternoon of trying to encourage the children in her class had worn on her anticipation had intensified.

In spite of the sadness in her own family she could see such a difference in herself now and she realised how self-indulgent she had been, wishing for things that could never be, wanting to go back to their homeland and hopelessly imagining that Hsa Mya was still alive. Outwardly there had been no great improvement to her life but she knew now that her feet were firmly planted back on the ground and that from now on she would keep looking forward. "Do you know what we are going to do today?" she asked excitedly as at last she swept out of the classroom and along the path towards the High School.

Jonathan had been back in the camp for more than a week now. Foolishly she had not gone to the first of his classes and she wanted to put that right today.

"Last Friday we did something Jonathan called 'problem solving'. It was very interesting. I think we'll do more of that today. I hope so."

"What was that? What happened?"

"Well, he talked about how we should try to look at things in new ways, not in the old way we have always done. Then he put us into groups and gave us a problem to solve, and at the end of the class he asked us all to tell him the answer."

"What sort of problems?"

"He said that we had to pretend that we had been given some money and had to spend it in a way that would help the most people in our village."

"That's not really a problem is it?"

"Yes it was, because we couldn't agree on the best way of spending the money. Then he told us that we should think about it a bit more and come back today with more ideas and also tell him why we have those ideas."

"So, what ideas did the groups have?"

"Oh, lots wanted to build a new school, but Jonathan didn't seem to think that was good enough. Our group thought we should build a bridge over the river, but then we didn't all agree on that either."

"I can see why he called it problem solving."

"Yes, and I can see what he's doing. He's making us think about the future, really think about what we want."

'Yes,' Htee K'Paw thought as they rounded the last corner of the High School buildings and went into the classroom. One glance at her friend's face told her how much Hser Mu relished the activities that

Jonathan devised for them. Hser Mu's confidence only seemed to highlight her own feelings of inadequacy. But she had decided she would come and put all her energy into this class. She had gone so far as to prepare the evening meal and leave it carefully covered against the flies in the deep shade of the lean-to kitchen so she would not have to worry about rushing home to cook. Now, she decided, if thinking is what Jonathan wanted, then she would think as hard as ever she could.

"We need a school. That's the most important thing. We need education more than anything. That's why we need a school." The group of four girl students all nodded in quiet agreement. Htee K'Paw nodded too. She knew that was the right answer. Of course it was.

"But *thra* wants us to think about some other things," Paw Ni interposed quietly. Htee K'Paw glanced across at Hser Mu's group. She could hear them talking more about the bridge that they wanted to spend their money on. The words 'road' and 'business' came into the discussion and drifted across the simple classroom.

"Look, we have to think of something more than that. Education doesn't have to mean a building. We can learn anywhere, can't we? I think that what we need is someone to come to the village and show us how to be better teachers. Then everyone will get a better education, not just a building." Htee K'Paw suggested.

"What about using the money to pay a trainer to come to show us other things, too? What about learning more about farming? Or running a business?" Paw Ni's voice was becoming louder with growing confidence. The other two girls in the group looked at each other, then one of them spoke up. "In our village lots of babies die. Here in the camp it's better but we need someone to show us how to have healthy babies."

Htee K'Paw found herself staring intently at the speaker, a girl she only knew as Muh Ghay. She had never even heard her speak out before. She was amazed, not just at the ideas that were coming forward but at the fact that they were coming from the girls who had never even spoken in the classes before. Htee K'Paw could not believe how quickly the time passed. Soon it was time to settle on one idea and prepare a proposal that could be shown to the rest of the class.

The group decided on a plan to employ a teacher to train the village birth attendants. This would lead to improved health for mothers and babies and therefore, ultimately, the whole community. Then came the difficult part; the reporting back to the rest of the class had to be in English. Because Htee K'Paw spoke the best English in their group they chose her to be their spokesperson.

When her turn came she carefully picked up her notes and walked to the front of the class then pausing for a moment to quieten her nervousness, she began. "In some of the villages there are many babies who die when they are very young." As she read out the group's ideas she thought again of her own little brother who had died after such a short life. At the time her mind had been full of her own troubles, the endless walking, the fear of soldiers not far away, of hunger and sheer exhaustion with nowhere to rest; now she understood that her mother had simply been too weak to care for him or even feed him properly. And he had not been the only one; she knew there were many like him.

"So we want to spend our money to pay someone to come to teach the women of the village to care for their babies." She looked up from her notes to judge the effect her words were having on the class. Glancing across at Jonathan she saw him nod at her and then smile briefly. Looking back at her notes; she realised she had lost her place and forgotten what to say next. Jonathan's look of approval had startled her; she so much wanted to do the right thing. Now, since that briefest of glances between them she knew she wanted to please him above everything else. She shook her head briefly to try to clear the confusion, found her place and began again.

"We would like our trainer to be a nurse who knows about how babies are born and the best way to feed them."

"A midwife, perhaps?" Jonathan suggested.

"Yes, a midwife. We think she would need to teach the women who help at the births. And she would need to show the mothers how to eat good food so that they can make good milk. Then the mothers need to know what to do for the baby when it becomes sick. She would need to show these women how to pass their knowledge onto other women, so she must be good at teaching too. Our money would pay for the trainer for three months and for her food and transport and a place to live."

As she drew her short presentation to its close a ripple of applause went round the room and Jonathan came towards her. "Thank you, Htee K'Paw, thank you. That's an excellent plan but there are some questions I want us all to think about. Do you think anyone would oppose your plan to teach the women?"

329

Htee K'Paw hadn't expected the question and she couldn't think what to say. "I don't know," she replied as she felt her face growing hot with embarrassment. She didn't like being the centre of attention.

"Perhaps others in the class would like to think about that too. Does anyone else have any ideas? Who might not like this plan?"

Hser Mu stood up in her place. "Some men might not like it. They might think it is a waste of money."

"Yes, that's possible. Anyone else?" Jonathan asked.

Htee K'Paw suddenly had an idea. "The birth attendants themselves might not like it. They might think they are already good enough at the job."

"Yes," said Jonathan. "It is always difficult to persuade people to accept new ideas. Can anyone else think of who might oppose such a plan?"

There was a pause and then one of the boys stood up. "The older people. They always believe their ways were best. They might not like it."

"Yes," interrupted Hser Mu. "Even when babies are dying, and mothers too, they still don't like change."

There was a moment of silence as the class heard the vehemence in Hser Mu's voice. Htee K'Paw met her eyes for a moment and an understanding that hadn't been there before sprang up between them. It had seemed such a small thing to come to a class like this but, as if from nowhere, had come a new sense of purpose.

"I think this group's idea is a brilliant one. Well done," Jonathan broke the silence as he smiled again at

Htee K'Paw who returned to her place with the rest of the girls relieved to be away from the front of the class once again. "So I'd like us all to think a bit more about it. You see an important part of the plan has to be to help people to accept the changes. So how do you think we can do that?"

All too quickly the class came to an end and now the students hung back wanting to discuss their ideas further. From the corner of her eye Htee K'Paw saw Jonathan beginning to tear at the paper wrappings that were around a large paper parcel on the front desk. "I brought these for the library," he announced as a group of students with hungry eyes quickly gathered around him. "They are books that you can make use of when you teach your own classes." Htee K'Paw wanted to join them so she quickly moved to the front and reached for one of the books. She picked it up and moved towards the doorway to have more light with which to look at it.

"Pictures of the National Gallery," Jonathan's voice startled her; he was looking at the book over her shoulder. "That's an amazing place in London. I thought that perhaps some of the children would like to see the pictures."

"Yes, they're beautiful." She slowly turned the pages, still aware of him following her eyes as she did so, until one of the pictures caught her eye.

"Oh, that one's not so good," Jonathan was saying. "But there are others, lots of them. Look," and he reached his arm across her to find some of the more famous pictures.

Htee K'Paw watched as he did so, the light hairs on his arms shone clear against his pale skin. He

331

had never been so close to her before, but it wasn't just a physical closeness that she was thinking about at that moment. As they stood together and looked at the pictures it occurred to her that the awe that she had always felt in the presence of westerners had been quite misplaced. In that moment she knew herself to be Jonathan's equal. It was only the poverty and remoteness of her people that had separated them, nothing more than that. As far as intelligence and appreciation of the world were concerned there was nothing between them. The same was true of the capacity for suffering.

"This is by a Dutch painter named Vermeer. Look at all the detail." Jonathan looked away for a moment to see the rest of the class still busy sharing the books around. Htee K'Paw chose the moment when he let go of the book to flick through the pages in an attempt to find the painting that had caught her attention a few minutes ago.

The painting was of a room that was almost completely in darkness. Light was coming through just one window and shining on a seated figure. As she looked more closely it became obvious that there was a great deal more beauty in the picture than was at first apparent; the fine tracery of the window lights became clearer and the details of the dark recesses of the room could be seen. Htee K'Paw had found it impossible to put her recent experience into words but the longer she looked at the picture that slowly seemed to fill with light she saw that it spoke for her. The rest of the students were still busy talking about the books but she hardly knew they were there. Only slowly did she become aware of Jonathan again when he spoke to her.

"You like this picture?"

"Yes, I do. The others are beautiful, but I like this one the best."

"Why?"

"It was like that for me. My life was very dark. Everything seemed to be wrong, but then everything changed. It was just like this picture. When I opened the page, I saw that it was me there in the picture."

"So." Jonathan couldn't think what to say. For a moment he felt embarrassed by her honesty; but she exhibited no such embarrassment, instead her clear, steady gaze seemed to give him new strength, as if he were on the verge of some new discovery.

Htee K'Paw looked at the picture again as if gathering her courage, then spoke, "Are you a Christian, Jonathan?"

The question took him by surprise. He had never thought of himself in those terms. Without waiting for an answer, and emboldened by her new-found confidence she continued. "We are Christians here; many people in this camp are. Our family always went to church and worshipped with everyone else. But a few weeks ago I was very ill; I had to stay in the clinic. One day while I was there I felt God speak to me in a dream and then all the bad things in my life seemed to melt away. After a time I realised I had to forgive all those who had hurt me in any way. And I could, I had the strength to forgive them all. It was as if my life started again and everything was new"

She watched as Jonathan's gaze shifted from the book that rested flat on the desk before them to her face and back again.

"So?" He tried again.

"Jonathan, I think that what you are doing is right. You are making us think about things. It's very important for us. We have to think about the future; we have to stop hating and start to forgive, that's the only way forward for us."

"You say you should forgive?"

"Yes," she answered simply.

"And what about Tim?" He was tentative, not sure he should ask her this, "Can you forgive him too?"

"Yes. I can," her voice fell to a whisper, but the words were as clear as anything she had already said.

"But he hasn't said sorry."

"But I can still forgive. Its the only thing I can do."

"But,"

His mouth dried and the words that he might have said had disappeared

As he walked through the camp Jonathan reflected on how its entire appearance had been radically changed since he had left it in such a hurry several weeks ago. Where the heat had been intense, sometimes even overpowering, and the leaves had hung dead and brown from the trees, the vegetation was now an intense luminous green. The rains had come and great banana leaves swung like flags at every corner. It was good. Everyone seemed to be happier now they were no longer harried by shortages of water and food. Tiny gardens flourished and children splashed happily in the streams that were now full of water - even though that water could not be called clean.

Jonathan could feel the difference; he had felt it in the welcome that the students had given him on his return to the camp. The young teachers that had been part of his classes had returned to their work but some of them were enthusiastic enough to want to learn more from him. But it had been Htee K'Paw who had surprised him the most. She wanted him to go on with his classes. That was fine, he could do that any time; he would enjoy it. It was the rest of his conversation with her that had troubled him. He had felt like a child before her. All his intelligence, his academic prowess, the one strength he had had when almost everything had been stripped away, seemed to count for nothing. He wondered how someone apparently so frail could have found such certainty, such strength. But she had.

He wanted to get back to his house by the winding stream so that he could think about it. He needed to be alone. Or did he? Didn't he want someone to talk to, someone who could tell him how he could get rid of the ghosts that still haunted him? He had recovered a great deal, he reasoned to himself, he had managed to cut the demons down to size. However they were still there, ready to erupt and take him by surprise at moments of weakness, and who knew when they were going to happen? But who could he talk to here? He began to recite some of the names of the students he had grown to like, but he knew he could not really bare his soul to any of them.

That was what Htee K'Paw had done though, hadn't she? She had told him, with the utmost honesty, what had happened to her. She had told him of her own recovery: no it had been more than that. It was as though her whole life had been changed, radically, deeply and yet so simply. Could it really be that easy?

Just hearing her story had left him feeling hollow and empty. She had defeated the things that had afflicted her for so long. It was as if she knew that the things that had made her so sad and angry were almost the same as those that had held him in their thrall? But how could she? No, she had given him no indication that she knew. Yet, that they were very similar was obvious and she had seemingly walked free. It was as if she had experienced a miracle.

Perhaps that sort of thing happened here? After all, people obviously had less to rely on in the material sense and even in everyday conversations there were regular references to prayers and to God that were never heard at home. He couldn't imagine anything like that ever happening to him.

He had almost reached the stream and was about to step over the tiny wooden bridge when he stopped.

But it had. He had laughed about it, so had Laura. Once the experience of that awful morning had passed it had been a way of releasing the tension that they had both felt. Now, as he thought about it again, he could see that it had been the nearest thing to a miracle that he was ever likely to experience.

He stepped across the bridge and walked on to the house. He found a small bottle of beer and the bottle opener and poured it into a glass trying all the time to recall what he knew of the Christian faith. There was the Christmas story of course, but that was about as far as his knowledge went.

Unlike his aunt, his father had apparently rejected any sort of religion and had never encouraged any such inclinations in either of his children. For the first time, Jonathan wished things had been different. He had nothing to go on, no point upon which to fix his thoughts. He was curious. No, it was more than that. He needed to know what it was that had caused such an obvious transformation in Htee K'Paw's life. True, in some ways he felt better than he had for many months, but he was still a victim, helpless to do anything about the uncertainties that swirled about him.

He didn't know how long he had been staring through the bamboo slats to the side of his bedroom. The sight of the water in the stream flowing round at the bottom of the slight slope below the house was almost mesmerizing. Often it was a comfort to him and he found himself watching it for long stretches at the end of the day with a beer in his hand.

A sharp rap on the post of the house startled him out of his thoughts and carefully setting down his glass, he hurried to go through to the tiny veranda.

"Thaw Reh," he exclaimed, "And, I can't remember your wife's name."

"Suu Meh."

"Suu Meh," he repeated and the young woman who had hovered behind Thaw Reh looked up for a brief moment before returning her attention to the small child who clung to her hand while looking up in alarm at the white face at the top of the steps. "Come in, please," he felt a glow of pleasure at the sight of these gentle people.

"We are going home," Thaw Reh told him as the little family climbed the steps and came to join Jonathan. "I have to go back to the Karenni camp. They want me to work in the school there."

"Oh." Jonathan couldn't think what else to say. Thaw Reh had been in most of his classes and had always impressed him with his good sense and a mature grasp of concepts that had been beyond that of most of the other students. He would miss him.

"I have permission to travel tomorrow morning so we will go. I want to thank you. You are a very good teacher. I have learnt a lot from you."

"Really?"

"Yes," Thaw Reh extended his hand to him.

But Jonathan didn't want to say goodbye just yet. "And I from you, from your story, thank you for telling me. It's a real help, all your stories are. You see, I find it hard to know how you cope with what happened to you and to your wife." He watched as a small frown of misunderstanding passed across Thaw Reh's face. "I mean I don't know how you live with what happened, with what happened to you both."

Jonathan glanced across at Suu Meh who was busy talking to the young child.

"She can't understand us. She doesn't know any English."

Jonathan watched as Thaw Reh became very still. Then he pulled himself to his full height.

"It was hard, very hard. I hated them. I hated them for killing my father, I hated them for what they did to her." His voice fell to a whisper, "I hated her too, for a while but I couldn't live like that. I couldn't live with all that hate in me. I went to see the catechist and he told me I had to forgive, And God helped me to see what I had to do. Now I have put it all behind me. I still feel angry sometimes but it's better now."

Jonathan stared at Thaw Reh. The only sound was that of Suu Meh singing quietly to the child. "Someone else said almost the same thing to me earlier today. They told me that they could forgive. Forgive the soldiers, forgive everything, and they . . . Well, it was as if they could start life again."

"Yes, it is like starting again. Sometimes I want things to be as they were when we lived in our village, when everyone was happy. It's not going to be like that, but life can be good and we have to do what we can."

"That's what I need. I need to forgive too. I need to know that I can go on, whatever happens." Jonathan's voice was little more than a whisper.

"But you, you don't have our problems. You are from England, a peaceful country."

"That doesn't mean everything is good for us. Things can still be very difficult, believe me. And I need to know what you do, really I do."

Thaw Reh glanced across at his wife then back to Jonathan again. "The soldiers, the *Tatmadaw,* took everything away from me. I was brought up as a Catholic and they took that away too. I couldn't believe in God after they killed my father. How could God let that happen? That's why I became a soldier; I wanted to get revenge. Then I was ill; I had malaria. That gave me time to think and I knew I couldn't live like that for ever."

"So did you find your faith again?"

"Yes, I did, and it was because I learnt to forgive. That was the most important thing for me. I wanted her," he looked at his wife again, "and I knew that's what I had to do."

"So you forgave, just like that. Was it that simple?"

"Yes, it was for me."

"So I . . . " Jonathan's voice tailed off. When he began speaking again his voice was steady. "Yes, that's what I need to do."

"Then I think God will help you."

"Yes, I think so too."

The two men sat in silence again.

"Thaw Reh, thank you for everything."

"I should thank you. And I want you to come and visit us. We're in Camp Tewa. You can ask at the school, Kaw La Htoo will know where I am."

"I will, I promise. I know where Tewa is, I was there a couple of years ago."

Thaw Reh extended his hand once again. "Brother! You are my brother now."

And as the little family made their way down the steps Jonathan knew that the light that he had been so desperate for had at last begun to inch its way into his life.

33

At the end of the afternoon's teaching Htee K'Paw went into one of the senior classrooms and sat down with a girl that she had been working with during the class a few days earlier. From her place she watched Jonathan as he taught. She was interested to see how little actual talking he did himself. Rather, he made the students do the talking, all the time encouraging them to think about things for themselves. Following his usual pattern, once he was satisfied that the class had assembled he began his lesson.

"I've heard lots of your stories. They are all about what has happened to you. Some of them go back a very long way but they are all about the past. Everything I have been told is about the past, about your history. Now I want us to think about the future. What do you want for yourselves? For your country?" He turned round to write a word on the white board.

'Federalism'

"Do any of you know what federalism is?" He asked as he turned back to them.

Ko Maung responded first. "The country is broken up into parts. Each part has its own government."

"Yes, that's right. There is a central government. In the case of Burma it would be governed from Rangoon, but each region has its own separate government, too. Many people think this is the best way for your country to proceed." He took a marker pen and began to write the words 'Army' and 'Foreign Relations' on the board. "These are things that affect the whole nation and then, the local government controls, say, things like education, police, and so on. Different countries work out different systems that suit them. The United States is probably the best example of federalism. But there are many others."

Ko Maung was slowly shaking his head.

"What are you thinking, Ko Maung?"

"It wouldn't work for us. It would mean the country is too broken up, too weak. The government has to be strong."

Htee K'Paw could feel herself bristling at Ko Maung's words. She looked around at the rest of the class.

"What do the rest of you think?" Jonathan was asking, his eyes sweeping around the room.

Hser Mu stood up. Htee K'Paw was glad she did so. She had no stomach for a real confrontation with anyone in the class, especially the fearsome-looking Ko Maung.

"The Burmese government is so strong now that they don't allow us to do anything. They close the schools, they attack the villages," Htee K'Paw could hear the emotion in her friend's voice.

A tall girl, someone that Htee K'Paw had never got to know, stood up suddenly. "We can't trust them. We cannot forget what they did to us," she sounded belligerent.

Htee K'Paw glanced around at the members of the group and saw small nods of assent.

"Tell me about it will you. Tell us what you cannot forget," Jonathan suggested.

"My grandfather told me," the tall girl continued, "he told me that they killed our people, many of them."

"When? I'm sorry, I don't know your name."

"It's Nyi Nyi."

"Nyi Nyi, When was this?"

"In the war."

"The war? You mean when the soldiers came to your village?"

"No, the war with the Japanese."

"You mean the second-world-war. Go on,"

Nyi Nyi looked around the class before she continued. "The Japanese hated us because we helped the British soldiers. So they killed our people."

"But that was the Japanese. They are long gone, surely?" Jonathan was confused.

"It was the Burmese, too. The Burmese helped the Japanese, and we can never forget. We can never forget what they did."

Jonathan looked around the class. "Do you all feel like this? Do you all feel the same way? You can't forget?" Htee K'Paw saw his face cloud over with dismay as nods of assent passed around the class. It was as if all the years of war and unhappiness sat like a heavy weight on them, locking them into an impasse from which there was no moving forward.

It was a moment of the sharpest clarity for Htee K'Paw. Suddenly she knew she had something to say.

Until a few days ago she had rarely spoken out loud in the class, but before she had time to think she was on her feet. "We can't go on like this," her voice was shaking. "We have to put that all behind us. We have to begin to trust each other, begin to move forward."

The whole class looked at her. It seemed that they were willing to listen to her simply because she was usually so quiet. Her voice steadied and became clearer as her confidence rose.

"I always thought that we should fight. I hated the soldiers who came to our village and made us leave. I hated so much that in the end it made me ill. Like everyone else I saw many of our people killed. And it was for nothing. Look at us here now. We have no country. There has been so much killing, so much waste. I think that one day we will get the chance to go back. One day our country will be a democracy and then we have to try to work together. I think Federalism is the only way forward for us, I really think that." She sat down suddenly. She had said all she needed to say.

The whole group of students stared at her in amazement. She heard a small hand clap which was repeated quietly until the applause had rippled right round the classroom.

Hser Mu stood up again. "There must be some way for us to keep our language and our customs without the Burmese being afraid that their country is being broken up."

Again there were small nods of agreement.

"Look," Jonathan said, "it won't be easy. It's sometimes hard for people to work together. There will be a lot of problems. But the most important thing is that people should really want to do it. If you really

344

want things to work, then they will. And it can begin here, with us, with you. Remember, you are the leaders of the future." It was a dream, for this class it was a dream that might never come true in their lifetimes, young as they were.

"But what can we do? They attack us; they kill us. We have to defend ourselves. We can't just let them take everything from us and do nothing." Nyi Nyi was speaking again.

"I know. I know that's true. But you can prepare yourselves for the future. And most of you teach younger children. You can pass on some of the things that we have been talking about in these classes. Do you think you could do that?"

"What about more classes like the one last week?" one of the boys asked.

"Yes, the problem solving, that would help us," said another.

Htee K'Paw saw Jonathan smile again.

As they dispersed Jonathan watched Htee K'Paw moving towards the door. He wanted her to linger, he wanted to thank her for what she had said so bravely in front of everyone else, for her willingness to swim against the tide and speak out. At the same time he didn't want to single her out in any way. She turned towards him, her eyes caught his for just a moment and he felt his pulse quicken. He willed her to stop long enough for her to lag behind the rest of the group. Then he couldn't bear it any longer. "Thank you, Htee K'Paw," he called out to her as loudly as he dared.

She turned back to him. Jonathan smiled with relief as she moved closer to him. "Do you have to hurry home? Or can you stay for a few minutes? There's something I want to talk to you about."

"I can stay for a little. What is it?"

"I want to thank you. You spoke so well that you made everyone think again."

"I really believe it," she said turning to face him fully. "Once it would have been hard for me to speak like that, but now I can do it. And I remember that once you wanted to hear our stories."

"Yes. Yes I did, I do."

"Is it too late? Do you still want to hear them?"

"No. I mean yes. It isn't too late; I want to hear. It all helps with the research that I'm doing." He motioned her to sit down on the front bench in the classroom and sat down opposite her. "I remember you saying that you found it too difficult, that it was too painful to talk about. Do you feel better now? I don't want to press you if it will make you sad again."

"No, I feel quite different now."

Jonathan inclined his head in a silent questioning gesture and with the faintest nod indicated to her that he was listening and she could begin her tale.

And so she did. She told him everything, slowly and carefully, beginning with the time when they first had to leave their village and find a new home by the river. She told him about her school and how she had met Hsa Mya and went on to explain how they had finally had to cross the river itself and begin their lives as refugees in a strange land.

Jonathan listened in silence. He knew the story, he had heard it, or others very similar to it, many times now. He had even experienced some of it himself when he had witnessed the burning of the houses.

346

"And you can tell me this without the hurt that you used to feel?"

"No, I still feel the pain, but I can forgive them."

"How? That can't be easy for you."

"Easy? No, but I can do it. I realise that I must, we must, it's the only way for us." Htee K'Paw paused.

Jonathan watched her as she looked around the bamboo classroom with its simple desks and bare earth floor. He felt himself shaking slightly and wondered if she noticed. "I want to ask you about something."

He saw her gently nod her head.

"Remember you told me about what had happened to you when you were ill?"

"Yes."

"It's difficult for me to explain, but I wasn't brought up to believe anything. My family thought that money and possessions were the most important things. There was no place for religion in our house. Now I wish there was. And you seem so certain."

"It's what I was taught. But that wasn't enough, I had to come to know it for myself." She touched her chest in a small guesture. "I found Jesus for myself when I was ill. No, he came to me. It was as if he came to me. And I shall always remember that moment. It changed my life."

"I can see that and I wish I could find that certainty." He watched her face as if he could find the answer to his questions right there before him. As they sat facing each other across the rough wooden desk he reached out his hand to place it on hers. He felt it stiffen under his for a moment before she pulled it away. Then she seemed to hesitate and placed hers on top of his. Her touch sent a pulse of electricity though him.

"You are troubled Jonathan."

"Yes I am, I have been. I've had so many shocks this year, and . . . " He couldn't find the words to explain. "And I need to know what you know. This Jesus you talk about. That's what I need." He watched her nod her head again as if thinking very hard.

"You can find him Jonathan. If you ask him to come to you then he will."

The noise of footsteps outside the classroom came closer. They sprang apart and the moment passed as Hser Mu bounded into the room.

"Post," she called out triumphantly. "Letters for you Jonathan, two of them. Look."

34

Saw Ker Reh lifted up the sheet of plastic so that the woman could look at the sarong fabric underneath. This simple action always led to the same train of thought; his younger daughter was missing and he had no notion of where she might be. As his latest customer bent her head to look at the choice of fabrics that he had on offer he knew that he could do better. Old Pu Mucah had been supplying the women of the camp for many years. He had known what all his customers wanted but Saw Ker Reh could see the inadequacy of his stock. It was clear to him that most of his customers were middle aged or mothers of young children, but there was a part of the market that he was hardly touching. Where were the younger women of the camp, the ones who were now working as teachers or nurses or in sundry other occupations? They weren't well off, but they could afford occasional new clothes. Where were they taking their custom, he often wondered, and how could he persuade them to spend their money at his stall? There was only one answer to his unspoken thoughts. He needed his younger daughter, K'Paw Meh. She had a flair for clothes and colour, and, as much as her older sister might disdain it, she was in touch with the very people he needed to attract to his business. Quickly brushing his chronic anxiety for his family out of his mind he looked up again to meet the eyes of his customer smiling as warmly as he could.

Mornings were the busiest time for him. Once the work of cleaning the stall and ordering and arranging the stock was finished, he took advantage of the customary lull and rested. By the afternoons there was only the occasional customer demanding his attention. The time would wear on, his spirits lifted by the anticipation of his children returning from school. First the two boys joined him behind the stall and then later Htee K'Paw, who had taken to returning later than ever, would come and take the two boys home. He would join them there after he had closed up the business. They had slipped into this routine and it suited him but even when he was busy the aching gaps remained. His wife had never been well, and the strain of caring for her had sometimes felt almost too much to bear. But her loss to him had been worse. He wished with all his heart that he could see her face again; sad and bloated it might have been but it was dear to him and he had never once been tempted to look for satisfaction elsewhere. Now his mind was suffused with a mixture of grief and anger as he contemplated again the disappearance of K'Paw Meh.

There was a sudden movement as Mon Kyaw shot out from the stall and into the main street. He had seen his oldest sister's approach and went out noisily to greet her.

"[16]*Dablu* Papa, *Dablu*" there was a brightness to her tone that he had not heard before, or at least not for a very long time.

---

[16]*Dablu :* A Karen greeting meaning 'Hello' as well as Thank You

"Daughter," he replied, already warmed by the sound of her voice, "and how was your day today?"

"It was good, very good. After school *thra* Jonathan took a class for us."

"Oh? I thought you finished the teacher training."

"Yes, we did, but this is an extra class he does for us. Politics: it's very good, everyone finds it very helpful."

"Politics? What good can that do for us here?"

"It can Papa, Jonathan's helping us a lot. He makes us think about what we can do in the future."

"But how can he know, daughter? How can he understand our situation?"

"He studies it. He's trying to find out as much as he can about our history. He's very clever, but kind too. He wants to help us."

"Daughter, daughter." Saw Ker Reh had caught a glimpse of the light in Htee K'Paw's eyes. "What is it about these *kolah wahs?* Aren't our own boys good enough for you that you have to go running after foreigners? First it was Tim, now it's this Jonathan."

Htee K'Paw felt a stab of embarrassment mixed with anger. "Papa, it's not like that. Jonathan isn't like Tim."

"I don't want to hear it! I have already lost one of my daughters to God knows where."

"But Papa . . ."

"No, daughter," He sounded angry but felt a stab of regret as he watched the sparkle fade from his daughter's eyes. "Help me." He knew he had spoken more harshly than he had intended. "Help me to lock up, then we can go home." He began to tidy away the

351

fabrics, threads and clothing that had become his livelihood.

Saw Ker Reh knew he had hurt her when he had spoken to her in the shop. Theirs had always been a close relationship and, later, as he watched her, crushed and miserable, clearing up after the family meal, he could hardly bear the sadness he felt.

"You know why I don't want you to see this Jo Na Than, don't you?" He blurted out awkwardly as she moved about the little house, clearing and making tidy as she went. "It's because I don't want you to be hurt, and I don't want to lose you. I don't trust them. I can't trust them, not after what Tim did."

"What?" Htee K'Paw exclaimed quickly. She could feel her heart thumping.

"The way he left you so suddenly. And I thought he liked you so much and you liked him too didn't you daughter?"

Htee K'Paw felt a momentary check in her breathing at her father's words. She fought to retain a calm exterior. Had her father noticed her disquiet? He had no idea of the real truth of what Tim did. That was one thing that she hoped always to keep to herself.

"But they aren't all like that," she cried. "Of course they aren't. That's something that we have been thinking about with Jonathan. We always judge people by the colour of their skin or the language they speak. Then we end up hating people just because they are different from us. He made us see that we don't have to be like that. He says that we need to be prepared to work with all people. That's the only way for us in the future. We can't say that we won't trust someone just

352

because they are Burmese or foreign. We can't go on like that."

Saw Ker Reh stared into the distance. His daughter had spoken more wisdom in those few words than he had heard from his peers in all the years of fighting. What good had all that done them? Where were they now? They had lost more territory than they had any hope of gaining and there was little hope for the future. It was his children that worried him most. What was to happen to them? How could they be expected to live out their lives in this narrow strip of dust? The disappearance of K'Paw Meh had rendered him almost paralysed with fear for her, although he could understand her wanting to get away from the place, assuming she had gone willingly. Now he could say the same for Htee K'Paw. He could hardly blame her for wanting to make friends with people who could help her get away and find a new life. As she had spoken about this young *'kolah wah'* he had seen her eyes light up in a way that he had not seen for a long time. It had made him both glad and afraid at the same time and he had responded more harshly than he had intended.

"Daughter," he spoke more gently this time, " I don't want you to be hurt. I see these white men in the towns. They want a woman, any woman. It makes them feel important. I don't want you to be one of them, you must know that."

Htee K'Paw felt her face growing hot. Without her realising it, Tim had made her into just such a woman. She had hung innocently on his arm trusting him and he had abused that trust. She wouldn't make the same mistake again, but how could she reassure her father. "I thought Tim was a good man when he helped

353

us with Mama's medicines but I don't think he really cared much. He just wanted things for himself. But Jonathan is a really good teacher. He doesn't have money, so he can't give it to us. Instead he gives himself. He tries to understand us and he wants to find ways that will help us in the future."

"But, still, you can't know what he is really like, Daughter. I don't want you to be hurt and I don't want to lose you."

"Yes father." Htee K'Paw stopped. Her mind filled with what Jonathan had told her in the afternoon. "He's very worried about something. I know that, and I want to . ."

"No, daughter," Saw Ker Reh interrupted, "stay away, I beg you. What can you do to help him anyway? And it may be a trick."

For an instant, thoughts of Tim flashed through Htee K'Paw's mind again as she remembered how he had used trickery to persuade her to go away with him. Perhaps her father was right. Perhaps all white men wanted to deceive and dominate. Perhaps they were here in the camp ostensibly helping the refugees, while at the same time believing them to be simple and easily taken advantage of. She felt a small stab of anger at the memory of her own stupidity.

But no, Jonathan was quite different, she was certain of that. He had held her hand that afternoon and she had immediately felt the integrity of his touch. Now she remembered with a little shame that she had pulled her hand away but then had known instinctively that it had not been necessary to do that. It had been Jonathan who had needed her, her reassurance, her new-found strength. How strange it had seemed to her, indeed it still seemed so, but the truth was unmistakable. He hadn't said anything, but the yearning in his eyes had been plain enough. She had instinctively reached out to touch him herself and knew that in that simple action she wanted him to find happiness.

"Papa, Jonathan, he's . . ."

"No, Htee K'Paw, I will hear no more of it."

"Yes," she answered sadly and made her way to her room.

Jonathan waited while the class assembled. He was looking forward to teaching them today; he wanted them to consider the Swiss model of federalism.

He had received two letters with yesterday's post. The handwriting on the first had been unmistakable. It was from Sarah with news of home. The second, with its official looking postmark, had perturbed him. It was inevitable that it would arrive sooner or later but that hadn't stopped him shaking as he opened it. And now, just as he was settling in to his research, he had to return home to face the ordeal of Tim's trial. To counteract his distress he had forced himself to look through his material and had spent a profitable morning analyzing and writing on his laptop. The heat of the early afternoon had forced him to sleep for a while, but now, fully awake, he was looking forward to the class. Here was an opportunity to forget everything else but what the students talked about for the next hour and a half.

He waited. Slowly, released from their own duties, the students drifted in. He saw Hser Mu and his spirits lifted; that meant Htee K'Paw wasn't far behind. The two of them usually arrived at almost the same time. A noisy banter rippled around the bamboo classroom. He knew almost nothing of what was being said, but that didn't matter. They would often include him in their conversations and that gave him all the satisfaction he wanted.

He looked again at Hser Mu and she in turn returned his glance. She looked away and then her eyes returned to meet his. Did she see his unspoken question? Where was Htee K'Paw? Since yesterday he had thought of little else. The letter from the Dorset County Court had disturbed him at first but he had quickly turned his thoughts back to his encounter with her and found all the comfort he needed. But now he could feel his anxiety rising. He looked up again. "Where is she?" he addressed Hser Mu across the room.

"She. Her . . " Hser Mu hesitated and then got up from her seat and moved forward to talk quietly to him. "Htee K'Paw can't come today. She's busy. She has to," the girl looked away for a moment. "She has to help her father." Hser Mu turned back to him once again. "She has to help her father," she repeated. Jonathan's mind flashed back to something he had once been told but had immediately dismissed as being unimportant. 'They will tell you what they think you want to hear.' He had treated the comment with the sort of contempt that he always reserved for such over-simplifications. But it came back to him, and in an instant he knew that Hser Mu was lying. She was lying because she wanted to protect him from the truth.

"Oh," Jonathan knew his disappointment and annoyance must show. He licked his lips. The one person he really wanted to be in the class, the person who had come to be his greatest support, wasn't going to be there and he didn't know why. Now he had to carry on without her. He moved his head briefly as if to shake away the cloud that seemed to have interfered with his thinking. "OK, that's a shame," he spoke as evenly as he could and Hser Mu returned to her seat. He watched until the rest of the class were reasonably well seated then told them, "I have to go home again, back to England. I don't know how long I shall be away."

"Why?" Ko Maung called out. "You have only come back to us for a short time. Why do you have to go again?"

"Because . .," Jonathan hesitated. He had debated with himself the question of whether he should talk to the students about the trial. They had no experience of any legal processes and he wondered whether they would understand what he was talking about. But now one of them had come right out and asked him so he decided he would go ahead and explain as far as he could. He started again. "I have to go to a court of law. When I was back home in England Tim found me. He threatened me with a knife; I think he would have attacked me. The police took it very seriously so they arrested him."

"How did the police catch him? Did you have a fight with him again?" Ko Maung asked.

"No. There was no fight but someone helped me. We stopped him. And it was the film that the police were most interested in. They wanted to stop Tim making any more films. That was why they arrested him."

The room was quiet for a minute and then one of the most serious boys of the class spoke up. " A Trial? Tell us about that. What does it mean?"

Jonathan had guessed that might happen and he turned his attention to explain and discuss what he knew of the judicial system. It took his mind off the issue that had seemed more pressing at the beginning of the class, his sudden instinctive feeling that Hser Mu was hiding something. It was only at the end of the class that he thought again of what she had said and he determined to face her once more. He went across to her as she packed her bag ready for the walk home.

"Will you tell Htee K'Paw for me? Tell her I have to go home again?" He watched as Hser Mu gave a tight little nod.

"What is it?" He asked her. "Please tell me. Why didn't she come today?"

"I told you, she has to help her father."

"That's not all, I can see there's something else. Tell me. Please, you must tell me."

He watched as the girl looked down at her own feet and then lifted her head to face him again.

"It's her father. He doesn't want her to come to the classes. You see, he's quite old fashioned, and he doesn't want her to learn things like this, and . . " her voice tailed off.

"And she does what he says?"

"Yes, of course she does. We all obey our parents, our elders, and I'm sorry Jonathan."

"Yes?"

"Her father doesn't want her to meet with you because you're a foreigner. He doesn't trust foreigners." She spoke the words in a rush, as if she were relieved to be rid of them.

Jonathan felt cold. "He doesn't trust me because I'm a foreigner?" He repeated slowly as if trying to gain some sort of control over his emotions.

"I'm sorry, Jonathan," she said again.

"It seems so unfair."

"I know. That's why I didn't want to tell you."

"But . . . " he began. He couldn't think what else to say.

"Her father, Saw Ker Reh, used to work in the town. He saw lots of foreigners. He saw them with girls. It means he doesn't trust them, any of them. He thinks you are the same." She paused as she saw the disappointment register on Jonathan's face. "He can see she likes you. He's afraid for her."

"She likes me? Does she?"

"Yes, she does. I know she does. Don't you know?"

"I didn't want to hope, but, yes. And now I have to go away again, so I can't do anything."

"He might change. Perhaps when he feels better himself then he will let her go. But just now, well, its difficult for him. You see, Htee K'Paw's sister has disappeared and he's very afraid for his family."

"I guess it must be hard for them." The words sounded so hollow and he was sickened by the pathetic sound of his own voice.

"Don't give up, Jon. Don't give up. And please come back to us."

She looked at him intently for several seconds then swung her bag onto her shoulder and left the classroom.

35

"Jon," the sound reached him across the bar. The intrusion was welcome. He hadn't seen anyone he knew since being back in Thailand. Turning round in his seat he saw Phil, an Australian doctor working with Medicins Sans Frontiers, smiling at him from the table on the other side of the small room.

"Why don't you join us?"

Jonathan picked up his drink and made his way towards the table where several westerners sat.

"I haven't seen you for some time. Where have you been hiding yourself?" Asked Phil.

"I had to go home and I've only just come back. I go out to the camp tomorrow."

"Went home for a holiday, then?"

"Kind of," Jonathan didn't want to talk about the trial although in the end the outcome had been as much as he could have hoped for. At first he had imagined that it would be simple. Tim had threatened his life, after all. But the defence had worked hard and there was the question of Laura's attack on Tim. The jury had been asked to consider the question of what was 'reasonable force' and how it was used to defend the person. Since that time Jonathan had often reflected on the good fortune that the one who had fought Tim off had been female. She had the sympathy of the jury which might not have been the case had she been male. While it was true that the police had, as yet, insufficient evidence to gain a conviction as far as the Internet was concerned, they still had the video as proof that Tim had been involved in child pornography. All the evidence was weighted against Tim.

"I had to go home to sort out something."

Phil looked at him. He suddenly asked the question that had been on his mind for a minute or two. "Wasn't there some trouble with the police in that camp a few months ago?"

"Yes. That was it. The British police came out to deal with their side of things."

"So you were involved with that?"

"I knew about it, but . . ," and he shrugged his shoulders as if it all meant very little to him. He looked around the rest of the faces around the table. He didn't know any of them except Phil's and he felt uneasy about trying to explain the whole story to them. As far as he knew any of them might be involved in a ring similar to Tim's, possibly even the same one. He had had his fingers so badly burnt with Tim that he had become very wary. He wanted to change the subject. "Look, how about a drink? What does everyone want?"

Phil spoke for the rest of the group.

"We thought we might move on to another bar. Why don't you come with us?

"OK. That sounds good. I'll join you." A vague smile of acceptance rippled round the small group. They seemed to have enough drink on board to care little about what he, the newcomer, said. In a minute or two they had all drained what was left of their drinks and had slowly and moved noisily out into the open. Phil joined Jonathan at the back of the group and the two of them followed the small crowd. Turning right out of the bar they walked down the street, still crowded with local stalls serving food and tourists thronging around them. At the next junction they turned right past the tuk-tuk drivers park, then crossed the road that they met almost immediately. From there they took off down one of the alleys that ran between shops. At this point they were in territory hitherto unknown to Jonathan. The alley quickly deteriorated into an unmade-up path that crossed a small stream. Small, ragged children looked out at them from one of the doorways. The houses were now not much more than shacks and there was very little light to see the way. The group turned down some more side alleys one of which then broadened out to a slightly better road.

"Where are we going?" Jonathan asked quietly. He didn't want to sound nervous, but he had no idea where he was.

"Oh, some place that Dave knows," Phil indicated his slightly overweight compatriate leading the party.

"Do you know these guys?"

"I know Rob there. He works on our research programme. He's here for six months. The rest of them are his friends. They've come to visit him and look around the place."

The party came to an untidy halt and then Dave dipped his head low and led the way through a doorway that opened into a largish room that was clearly another bar.

"OK, drinks all round. They're on me this time" called out Dave, the self-styled leader of the group. "You too. What's your name?"

"Jon."

"OK Jon, what'll you have?"

Jonathan joined Phil at one of the tables ranged around the bar and began to drink his second beer of the evening. He was still thirsty. "What is this place?" he asked as they began to relax over their drinks.

"One of the more seedy bars as far as I can see. I wouldn't be surprised from what I've seen of Dave already. All he seems to talk about is women."

"Yes?"

"Look at him with that girl behind the bar. He's already telling her he's going to show her the world. Does he think he's the first white man she's ever met or something?"

Jonathan's face creased into a sort of half smile and he and Phil exchanged a glance of common understanding. Others joined them at the table, Rob produced a pack of cards from his pocket and they settled down for a quiet game while Dave and the others attempted to work their charm on the girls in attendance.

Jonathan enjoyed a game of cards; he had a sharp intellect and a very good memory. The laughter from the other end of the bar grew louder as the drink flowed. One of the girls that he had seen behind the bar came to clear the table and take another order from them. He glanced at her as she did so. Then he looked again as she caught his eye. He had had a few beers but was by no means intoxicated. He knew this girl. He had seen her before, and her eyes had lingered on him as well. Did she recognize him too? As he looked again he felt himself frowning in concentration. How did he know her?

"Jon, what do you want to drink?" Phil was asking him.

"Oh, another beer. The same as before."

"You feeling OK?"

"Yes, no problem."

"You sure?"

"Yes. But I know that girl, I'm certain."

Phil laughed.

"I've seen her somewhere."

"There must be hundreds of them looking like that. She could be anyone."

"But she recognised me too, I know she did."

"Maybe she fancies you."

Jonathan laughed. "Maybe. But I know her from somewhere. I'm sure. Wait a minute."

"Hey, you two," Rob's voice broke into their conversation. "Are you playing with us or not?"

"OK, sorry. We're playing." Jonathan pushed thoughts of the girl to the back of his mind. The combination of the beer and jet lag was making it harder to think."

The evening passed amiably enough. The same girl came back with the drinks but this time he didn't look her way.

"Where are you staying?" Phil asked him as they began to tire of the card game.

"The Sompat. I always stay there."

"Me too. Shall we get off home now? I've got to get back to work in the morning. Not like this crowd of lazy gits."

Jonathan laughed and then watched as Phil got to his feet. He then edged round the table himself and stood up. For a moment he felt the floor move beneath him, then it righted itself again.

"OK. Let's go." The two of them made for the door. "Do you know the way?" Jonathan added as an afterthought.

"I think so," and they picked their way along the almost pitch-dark street towards the better-lit centre of town.

Jonathan woke with an awareness of increasing cold. The fan was still working. He remembered that he had switched it on last night after he had come into the room and the stifling heat had struck him, thick and uncomfortable. Now it irritated him so he leaned over to switch it off and lay back on the pillow. This always happened when he first arrived in Thailand. Still jetlagged, he would wake very early and find it impossible to go back to sleep. In spite of his wakefulness he could still feel the effects of the beer on both his mind and body, and the last evening's activities floated round his brain. The face of the girl in the bar came to the surface of his mind and for a moment he tried to remember where he had seen her. The effort of thinking made his head hurt so he pushed thoughts of her aside and rolled over. Perhaps he would try to sleep again. Sometime he would have to think about his plans for going back to the camp, he then had to prepare some classes. In truth he was looking forward to it. Some of the students were his friends now, especially Ko Maung, Hser Mu and of course Htee K'Paw; she had never been far from his thoughts. Htee K'Paw! That was it. The girl looked like Htee K'Paw, but it wasn't her. He turned over again in the hard bed.

Of course, that was it! He had taught that girl in the early days of his time in the camp last year. She had been learning English. She wasn't Htee K'Paw, she was her sister, and hadn't Hser Mu told him that she had gone missing? Of course the girl would remember him. He had been one of her teachers for weeks.

He sat up now, certain of who the girl was. His headache, accompanied by nausea, intensified so he lay down again. OK, he had found Htee K'Paw's sister, or was almost certain he had. Now what could he do? Was she working in the bar willingly or not? If not, then would she be allowed to leave just like that, or was she bonded in some subtle way? Did she want to go back to her family? Perhaps she was making enough money to make the risks that she took, working in such a place, insignificant. In spite of the seedy nature of the place, the bar girls had looked cheerful enough and surprisingly in control. They certainly didn't appear to be victims.

His thoughts spun round his head now. He couldn't think what he could do, or if he should do anything at all. Why hadn't she made herself known to him? Perhaps that was easy to answer. She didn't know anything about him, he was just another punter as far as she was concerned. Was it his business anyway? Yes, he decided, it was.

There was one thing certain, which he did remember. At the end of his last visit the family didn't know she was here in the town. They had no idea whether she was even alive or dead. Perhaps they still knew nothing. If so, he could do at least one thing. Or perhaps he could go and ask the girl? No, that wasn't going to be easy. He had no idea where the bar was. He had had several drinks and the maze of alleys and dirty streets had been impossible to take in. He could feel himself sweating with discomfort again. He reached over and turned the fan on again. Oh God, what a mess.

36

"You look rough," Phil said as Jonathan stared into his first cup of coffee of the morning.

"I shall be OK soon. I was awake half the night, thinking about that girl, strangely enough. I remember where I have seen her before. She was in one of the classes that I taught."

"So what's she doing here?"

"Well you know how it is. A lot of them want to get out. There's not much for them in the camp, not when they get to her age. But I've met the family, and I know for a fact that they're worried about her. It's no surprise. They haven't heard from her - at least that was the case when I came away last time."

"And so you want to stick your oar in?"

"Well I was going to ask you what you thought."

Phil looked at Jonathan and laughed mildly at his deathly white face. "You had better sober up. Have some more coffee. And what about some breakfast? Look, here," he said, reaching for the menu, "Eggs, sunny side up," he read with a smile on his lips.

Two cups of coffee later Jonathan felt well enough to think straight. "What do you think we ought to do about her? I don't want to make any big mistakes. After all, she may be quite happy where she is. She may not want to go back home."

"Well, I guess we have to talk to her before we do anything. At least we can put it to her that her father needs to have some news of her, if nothing else."

"I can't even remember where the place is."

"I could take you there."

"You go there often do you?"

Phil laughed again. "No, but it's near the Epidemic Study Centre. I know that part of town. We'll have to go quite early. I have to pick up some stuff and then get back to the camp for midday."

"Saturday?"

"Yes, I have to supervise an afternoon ante-natal clinic there once a month." Phil stopped for a moment. "I wonder if it would be better if we took a woman with us to the bar? Two guys together might scare her a bit."

"That's a good idea. Have you any thoughts about who we could ask?"

"I was thinking about that. What about Katie? She runs our health education programme. Do you know her?"

"Katie. I remember meeting a Katie a couple of years ago. English girl. She worked in the Karenni camps."

"Yes, that's her. She's in town at the moment. We could see if she's free this morning then we could walk out to the place and talk to the girl, see what she wants to do. And what about cash? Perhaps we need to

369

have a bit with us. You never know, we might have to buy off the owner of the bar."

"Do you know who I am?" Jonathan asked carefully and slowly.

"Yes, answered the girl. You're *thra* . . . " her brow creased into a slight frown. She obviously had difficulty with western names.

"Jonathan," he smiled at her as reassuringly as he could. "And, I'm sorry, I've forgotten your name, but I remember you from my English classes.

"K'Paw Meh," the girl replied as she looked warily at the three white faces watching her in the otherwise-empty bar.

'Of course,' he remembered; part of her name was the same as her sister's.

"Yes, K'Paw Meh," he repeated the name in order to better imprint it on his memory.

"We want to talk to you." Jonathan didn't really know how to begin. He didn't want to alarm the girl and he needed to persuade her that they had her best interests at heart. "Your family are worried about you. They are worried because they don't know where you are."

The girl said nothing. Perhaps she didn't understand them.

"Are you happy here?" Katie tried a different tack. She spoke slowly and clearly. "Are they kind to you? Do you like the work?"

The girl looked carefully around the bar. "We have to stay here. We can't go out. We can't go. The police will find us. Then . . . ."

'So that was it,' thought Jonathan. She was afraid to go anywhere for fear of being arrested.

"It's true," said Katie, "they could be picked up anytime. It's a real danger and they never know when they could be deported back over the border."

"But what do you want?" Jonathan tried again. "Do you want to go back to your family or do you want us to take a message to them to tell them that you are safe?"

K'Paw Meh looked round again. "I want to go back, but I can't. He won't let us. He tells us it's too dangerous." Her eyes widened in fear.

"So you want to leave here, but you can't because you are afraid." Katie spoke again. "Is it a bad place, this bar?"

K'Paw Meh shrugged her shoulders listlessly. Whatever she thought, she wasn't telling them.

"So why do you want to go back?" Katie persisted.

"Because I miss my family."

"Is that the most important reason?"

The girl nodded her head.

"Do you think he will let you go?"

"No. It's too dangerous."

"We can take you. You can come in the clinic car. You will be safe with us if you want to go."

For the first time K'Paw Meh's face brightened.

"And Mu Aye, she wants to go home too."

"Now hold on," Phil interrupted, "how many of you are there?"

"Just me and Mu Aye"

"Ok," he breathed again. They all smiled with relief.

By midday they were on their way, the two girls seated in the centre of the van where they would attract little attention. Phil was grateful that he hadn't brought an open truck. It would have been much harder to slip through the checkpoints that way. As it was he was stretching a point. There was no real guarantee that they wouldn't be noticed, it was just less likely this way.

The plan was to drop Jonathan and the two girls and then take the van further north to where Katie and Phil worked. They had tried to elicit information as to the true nature of the bar where K'Paw Meh had been working, but since she was completely unforthcoming they had had to let the matter rest. In the end it seemed enough to them that she and Mu Aye were safe. They had come to no real harm and had both clearly wanted to go home. And the bar owner had been happy to let them go after a suitable payment for his inconvenience. It seemed as if there were plenty more girls where they had come from. Jonathan realised once again that there were many things that he could not fully understand and so had to leave them to rest.

It was in the full heat of the early afternoon that the three of them stepped out of the van onto the roadside. There the dust and the chaos of the camp lay before them. He looked at the two girls with their small bags of belongings and saw the anxiety fall away from them. He knew for certain then that he had done the right thing. He shouldered his rucksack, but before he could pick up his two bags the girls had reached down to help him. They laughed with him. It was as if they had reverted to the teenagers they actually were instead of the surly, waitresses that he had seen in the bar.

Htee K'Paw began to unpack the handcart, which was full of fabric for the stall. They had had a delivery earlier that morning and she was anxious to get the goods stowed away in a dry place before it rained again.

"I thought we could use this rail," her father said as they worked. "What do you think, Htee K'Paw? Shall we hang some of these up here, then people can see them more clearly?"

"Yes," she agreed rather listlessly, "that's a good idea." In truth she wasn't sure of the best way to display goods. They both knew that K'Paw Meh would know exactly the best way to arrange the stall, and the fact that she was still missing hung between them at times like this. Most of the time Htee K'Paw was distracted by other things. Ma Nay had gone up to the playground for a football match. She had promised to go and watch him later and now she hoped that the game wouldn't be over before she finished her work. Meanwhile little Mon Kyaw ran between their stall and the next with the neighbour's children, occasionally coming to entertain them with his fantasies. She had prepared some food, which they had carried down with them from home, so that they could all eat together at lunchtime, but her mind was always full of what needed to be done next.

The heat was becoming oppressive and flies buzzed around their heads as they worked. Htee K'Paw wiped her brow with the back of her hand and paused to look up the hill as she did so. She vaguely noted a small group of people picking their way carefully down the muddy slope before returning her attention to the materials once again. As she did so she registered the fact that there was something familiar about the approaching group and looked up again to watch them more closely.

"Papa!" she called, as curiosity became certainty.

Her father's response was muffled and somewhat impatient; he was intent on sorting the fabrics.

But any further explanation was rendered superfluous as soon as Mon Kyaw saw his sister. Htee K'Paw watched him as he stopped his game for an instant and then, with a whoop of excitement, ran up the side of the muddy path to greet K'Paw Meh.

On hearing the noise Saw Ker Reh emerged from the stall and joined his children as they embraced each other. There was no need for words.

As Htee K'Paw looked up from her sister's arms she saw Jonathan looking down at her with wonder. He smiled briefly and then turned away to begin the steady climb up the slope again. He had a large rucksack on his back and a bag in each hand and as he stepped she saw the heaviness of his burden weighing him down.

"Papa!" she cried, "Jonathan helped us. Now, look, he's going away again. We must speak to him. Papa!"

"Yes, daughter, tell him, ask him to come back."

Htee K'Paw turned back to where she could see Jonathan carefully negotiating the patches of slippery mud. "Jonathan," she called to him as loudly as she dared. "Jonathan, Jonathan!"

He turned round and she, in turn began to walk towards him. "Jonathan, come back, my father wants to talk to you." She watched as his load seemed to lighten before her eyes.

"Come and rest with us," she said in English then translated for her father as the whole family gathered in the space behind the stall while Saw Ker Reh sought out a chair for the visitor and sent Mon Kyaw to purchase some coke and sweet biscuits from a neighbouring shop.

"Please sit down Jonathan," Htee K'Paw said, and turned her attention to her father who was already speaking again, while the whole group settled themselves down as best they could within the confines of the tiny space.

"He wants to thank you," Htee K'Paw translated as Saw Ker Reh transferred his gaze from her and back to Jonathan again. "But he doesn't know how to say it in English."

Jonathan looked at Saw Ker Reh and returned his smile.

"He says you brought back his daughter. He wants to know how he can thank you? "

"I was glad to help you sir, "Jonathan replied and waited awkwardly for the translation.

"My father says that he didn't want to trust you, he thought that all foreigners were bad people. Now he is sorry that he had that thought. He knows he was wrong."

Jonathan watched as the older man looked down at the dusty ground then lifting his head, looked steadily into his eyes and spoke again. Jonathan waited.

"I want to do something to thank you," Htee K'Paw spoke for him.

The words were out before Jonathan had a chance to measure them in any way. "Sir, I only want one thing. Will you let me meet with your daughter Htee K'Paw? I would like to get to know her better."

As he spoke Htee K'Paw felt her whole being flood with happiness. She quickly translated for him.

Then Saw Ker Reh extended his hand to Jonathan "Welcome son, welcome," he said using his halting English for the first time. He turned to hand round the coke and biscuits, the simple tokens of celebration.

Suddenly, Htee K'Paw stood up. "Ma Nay," she exclaimed, "I said I would go and watch him playing football. He will be so disappointed if I don't go."

"Where is the game?" Jonathan asked her.

"In the school playground. It will be starting soon."

"Well, I can walk with you. We can go together. That is, if your father is happy for me to join you," and he glanced quickly in the direction of Saw Ker Reh.

"Papa?" Htee K'Paw looked across at her father smiling contentedly at his reunited family.

"Yes, Htee K'Paw, you go."

.

37

June 2003

Hser Mu hurried down the hill. She kept putting her hand into her bag to check that the letter was still there. In fact there were two letters, both of them handed to her after the school classes. One was from Htee K'Paw, bearing the unmistakeable postmark and stamp from England. She had ripped it open immediately and had read with growing pleasure of the new life that her dear friend had found there with Jonathan and his family.

The other had remained in its envelope for some time, she hardly dared open it for fear of what it might contain. Then curiosity had overcome her and she had read it. The contents caused her to quicken her pace as she reached the main street and the market stall that K'Paw Meh managed with her father.

Well stocked with the items that all the young women wanted, it was now one of the most frequented shops in the camp. As Hser Mu approached she saw the array of colourful clothes and, to one side, the display of cosmetics and creams that K'Paw Meh now managed with skill and flair. K'Paw Meh herself greeted Hser Mu with a wide smile. Her hair was swept up on her head and secured with a clasp that complemented her features beautifully while her clothes made her the perfect advertisement for the items on sale.

"I've got a letter from Htee K'Paw," she began breathlessly. "Do you want to read it?"

"Yes, but we have one too. We received it today. She says she can come back to us in a few months now. Jonathan has a study grant from the Open Politics Society so that means he can work here for as long as he likes. They'll always be near us. Father is so happy."

"And do you want to hear my news?"

"Yes, tell me. What is it?"

"I've got a place at University. I can go to Chiang Mai to study. I've waited so long that I didn't believe it would ever happen. But it has! There's a scholarship and I've won it. I can't believe it."

"I'm glad, Hser Mu. You deserve it, you really do. Come and tell father. He'll want to hear your news too."

Jonathan held the car door open as Htee K'Paw pulled the zip of her fleece jacket up to the very top and put her gloves on. It was early June but here in the mountains of the Lake District the air was fresh, cooled by the wind that sent the clouds scudding across the sky. He smiled at her as together they started along the stony path. It was narrow, and steep in places, so he took her hand to help her over some of the rocks. They could hear the sound of the water far below them, so far down that it was impossible to see because of the density of the trees in the valley.

They walked for almost half an hour but she didn't mind how far it was as long as he was there. She knew that he would never take her anywhere that she didn't want to go. It was that understanding between them that had made her happy to come half way round the world to be with him.

The way levelled out a little and the path became easier to walk on. They had come so far down that they were now right beside the water. Then the path turned left away from the river and ran in a wide curve, steepening again into a deep gorge. Again they were close to the water. The path narrowed until they had to step onto rocks that were actually in the water. He took her hand again and the sound of their laughter echoed around the narrow gorge as they tried to avoid slipping on the rocks. The sound of the water grew ever louder. Then they both stopped and looked upwards. The water fell in a single sheet from high above them into the pool at the foot of the gorge. At a point to the far side it fell onto a ledge that jutted out so that the water sprayed wide across the pool. As they watched, a shaft of sunlight pierced the canopy of trees and shone down onto the spray, lighting the waterfall with a small rainbow.

Jonathan heard a small gasp. "What is it?"

"I was thinking of home, that's all."

"Tell me."

"It makes me think of when we first left our village. I was just a child then but I remember it so clearly. That's what we saw, my father and I. We saw a rainbow on the water, just like that. My father told me that it's a sign of God's promise, but I didn't think that at the time. I was so unhappy and afraid. I didn't know what was going to happen to us."

"And now?"

"Now? Now I think that it is true. He's been with me all the time. I just didn't know it."

Acknowledgements

I would like to thank all those who have helped and encouraged me in the writing of this story.

Jenny Kyriacou's help and support has been invaluable. She has spent many hours editing and checking for grammar and content; I would not have managed without her.

I would also like to thank the lecturers at the School of Oriental and African Studies, London University for their teaching. I especially want to thank Professor John Sidel, now of the London School of Economics, for increasing my understanding of South East Asian Politics.

The support of my family has been very helpful. I really appreciate Lucy, my daughter in law, for her suggestions; the same goes for my husband David whose patience has been boundless; he now adds editing and proof reading to his many skills.

Most importantly, I want to thank the many Karen friends and acquaintances I have come to know over the years. I am especially grateful to the Karen Youth Organisation and the students of the Karen North Further Education Project who let me work with them for a number of months. From them I have gained just a little insight into what it means to be a displaced person, a refugee, one who has to keep going and remain hopeful in spite of all the privations that life throws at them.

Bibliography

Brown, David. The State and Ethnic Politics in South East Asia Routledge London and New York 1994

BURMA: The Voices of Women in the Struggle ALTSEAN   Bangkok 1998
In particular the story entitled Living Apart from my Family by Naw Der Lweh Htoo.

Dudley, Sandra. Displacement and Identity: Karenni Refugees in Thailand D Phil Thesis Oxford 2001

Smith, Anthony D. Ethnic Nationalism and the Plight of Minorities   Journal of Refugee Studies   Vol 7 No 2/3 1994

Smith, Martin. Burma: Insurgency and the Politics of Ethnicity Zed Books London and New York 1999
A highly informative and scholarly analysis of the history and situation in Burma until about 1991.

About the author

Mary Bolster works in the Operating Department of a North London hospital. **'To dwell in safety'** is her second novel. Like her first, 'in a strange land', it looks at some of the issues surrounding ethnic conflict and the displacement of people.

She first went to the Thai-Burmese border in 1993 and since then has visited the area many times.

There are currently around 150,000 refugees from Burma living in Thailand, largely forgotten by the rest of the world.

Mary is a trustee of Karenaid, a charity that supports Eye Care and other projects on that border.

She enjoys being in the great outdoors, on a boat, among mountains or simply with the family.

www.marybolsterbooks.co.uk

'in a strange land'

A Novel set in the conflict zone of the Thai Burma Border

by Mary Bolster

'Anyone who reads this book must feel profoundly moved. There is a saying: "Pity weeps and turns away; compassion weeps - and puts out a hand to help".' **Baroness Caroline Cox of Queensbury**

'. . deserves a wide readership' **Association of Christian Writers**

'This book was touching emotionally, and proactive in the fight against the Burmese totalitarianism. I recommend it whole-heartedly!' **Amazon reviewer**

'. . . appeals emotionally to a wide general readership with a gripping story of Karenni people caught up in the conflict.' **British Burma Society Review**